UPON A WHEEL OF FIRE

David Wingrove is the Hugo Award-winning co-author (with Brian Aldiss) of *Trillion Year Spree: The History of Science Fiction*, and co-author of the first three *Myst* books – novelizations of one of the world's bestselling computer games. He is also author of *The Roads to Moscow* trilogy. He lives in north London.

UPON A WHEEL OF FIRE

BOOK 11

DAVID WINGROVE

FRAGILE
BOOKS

Upon a Wheel of Fire was first published as part of *Beneath the Tree of Heaven* in Great Britain in 1993 by New English Library.

First published in trade paperback and eBook in Great Britain in 2019 by Fragile Books.

A CIP catalogue record for this book is available from the British Library.

Trade paperback ISBN: 978-1-912094-53-0
eBook ISBN: 978-1-912094-52-3

Printed in Great Britain by 4edge Limited.

Fragile Books
5a Arundel Square
London
N7 8AT

www.fragilemedialtd.com

CONTENTS

For Peter Hammill
in admiration

"Senses dimmed in semi-sentience,
only wheeling through this plane,
only seeing fragmented images,
prematurely curtailed by the brain,
but breathing, living, knowing
in some measure at least
the soul which roots the matter
of both beauty and the beast..."

UPON A WHEEL OF FIRE

Book Eleven

'House of Ch'in built the Wall to keep them apart,
House of Han has to keep the beacons alight,
Beacons alight and they never go out
For these expeditions have never an end:
In the line, hand to hand, they'll die the same,
The horses will fall, call to Heaven their pain,
The crows and the kites pick their riders' guts
And fly to dead trees with the bits in their beaks...'
—Li Po, *'We Fought South of The Walls'*, 8th century AD

'Life is cheap, flesh plentiful,'
—common saying, AD 2210

INTRODUCTION

Chung Kuo. The words mean 'Middle Kingdom' and, since 221 BC, when the First Emperor, Ch'in Shih Huang Ti, unified the seven Warring States, it is what the 'black-haired people', the Han, or Chinese, have called their great country. The Middle Kingdom – for them it was the whole world; a world bounded by great mountain chains to the north and west, by the sea to east and south. Beyond was only desert and barbarism. So it was for two thousand years and through sixteen great dynasties. Chung Kuo *was* the Middle Kingdom, the very centre of the human world, and its Emperor the 'Son of Heaven', the 'One Man'. But in the eighteenth century that world was invaded by the young and aggressive Western powers with their superior weaponry and their unshakeable belief in Progress. It was, to the surprise of the Han, an unequal contest and China's myth of supreme strength and self-sufficiency was shattered. By the early twentieth century China – *Chung Kuo* – was the sick old man of the East: 'a carefully preserved mummy in a hermetically sealed coffin' as Karl Marx called it. But from the disastrous ravages of that century grew a giant of a nation, capable of competing with the West and with its own Eastern rivals, Japan and Korea, from a position of incomparable strength. The twenty-first century, 'the Pacific Century' as it was known even before it began, saw China become once more a world unto itself, but this time its only boundary was space.

The War Of The Two Directions
It had begun with the assassination of the T'ang's Minister, Lwo Kang, some thirteen years earlier, the poor man blown into the next world along with

his Junior Ministers while basking in the imperial solarium. The Seven – the great Lords and rulers of Chung Kuo – had hit back at once, arresting one of the leading figures of the Dispersionist faction responsible for the Minister's death. But it was not to end there. Within days of the public execution, their opponents had struck another deadly blow, killing Li Han Ch'in, son of the T'ang, Li Shai Tung, and heir to City Europe, on the day of his wedding to the beautiful Fei Yen.

It might have ended there, with the decision of the Seven to take no action in reprisal for Prince Han's death – to adopt a policy of peaceful non-action, *wuwei* – but for one man such a course could not be borne. Taking matters into his own hands, Li Shai Tung's General, Knut Tolonen, had marched into the House of Representatives in Weimar and killed the leader of the Dispersionists, Under Secretary Lehmann. It was an act almost guaranteed to tumble Chung Kuo into a bloody civil war unless the anger of the Dispersionists could be assuaged and concessions made.

Concessions were made, an uneasy peace maintained, but the divisions between rulers and ruled remained, their conflicting desires – the Seven for Stasis, the Dispersionists for Change – unresolved. Among those concessions the Seven had permitted the Dispersionists to build a starship, *The New Hope*. As the ship approached readiness, the Dispersionists pushed things even further at Weimar, impeaching the *tai* – the Representatives of the Seven in the House – and effectively declaring their independence. In response the Seven destroyed *The New Hope*. War was declared.

The five year 'War-that-wasn't-a-War' left the Dispersionists broken, their leaders dead, their Companies confiscated. The great push for Change had been crushed and peace returned to Chung Kuo. Or so it briefly seemed, for the War had woken older, far stronger currents of dissent.

In the depths of the City new movements began to arise, seeking not merely to change the system, but to revolutionise it altogether. One of these factions, the *Ping Tiao*, or 'Levellers', wanted to pull down the great City of three hundred levels and destroy the Empire of the Han.

For a while the status quo had been maintained, but three of the most senior T'ang had died during the War, leaving the Council of the Seven weaker and more inexperienced than they had been in all the long years of their rule. When Wang Sau-leyan, the youngest son of Wang Hsien, ruler of City Africa, became T'ang after his father's death, things looked ominous as the young man sought to create disharmony among the Seven. But Li Yuan, inheriting from his father, formed effective alliances with his fellow T'ang, Wu Shih, Tsu Ma and Wei Feng, to block Wang in Council, out-voting him four to three.

Even so, as Chung Kuo's population continued to grow, further concessions had to be made. The great Edict of Technological Control – the means by which the Seven had kept change at bay for more than a century – was relaxed, the House of Representatives at Weimar reopened, in return for guarantees of population controls.

For the first time in fifty years the Seven had begun to tackle the problems of their world, facing up to the necessity for limited change, but was it too late? Were the great necessity for limited change, but was it too late? Were the great tides of unrest unleashed by earlier wars about to overwhelm them?

PROLOGUE   ## Ghosts' Torches

WINTER 2210

'Ah, silence, such silence,

like in a dream, moonlight noble and heartless,

in the same dusk, in the same dawn.

No elegy to be heard, and no bells tolled.

The gate to the world of the departed souls, is solemnly

closed,

seeing me into the funeral train which marries me to

life,

demanding I reclaim talent of days gone by.

Ah, silence, such perpetual silence,

there is no reply, and there is no echo,

there are just ghosts' torches, illuminating my whole

life...'

—Duo Duo, 'Death of A Poet', AD 1974

GHOSTS' TORCHES

The great Courtroom was empty, silent. On the bare stone of the walls torches burned brightly, steadily in their iron cressets, yet the chamber seemed engulfed in shadows, the galleries and wood-beamed ceiling lost in an impenetrable darkness. At the far end of the chamber two huge stone pillars flanked the great double doors. Between them, their figures dwarfed by the entrance arch, walked two men.

'Well, Knut,' said one of them, turning a long, horse-like face to his companion, 'the day has come at last. You must be proud to have brought things to this point.'

Tolonen paused, his smile uncertain. 'We have worked hard to bring this about, neh, Chi Hsun? Yet now that the day is upon us I feel not satisfaction but a strange sadness. It's as if I haven't grieved for him. But now that it's done. Now that the matter's to be decided...'

He fell silent, staring away into darkness.

Chi Hsun reached out, touching the Marshal's arm, consoling him. 'I understand... Klaus Ebert was a fine man. He stood for all that was good and strong and decent. To have lost such a man was a tragedy for us all. But for you... well, you were his friend.'

'And he mine,' Tolonen said, lifting his chin, a look of real pain, real hurt in his eyes. 'Since we were boys.' He turned, facing Chi again, a strange sound, half pain, half remembered joy, escaping him. 'I had dreams, Chi Hsun... Dreams that his son would marry my daughter. That his grandchildren would be my grandchildren...' He stopped, choked by emotion, unable to say more.

The Chief Commissioner, watching him, nodded. 'I'm sorry, Knut. It must be hard for you in view of what happened. But listen. I hear that Ebert's widow is to be married again.'

Tolonen looked back at him, surprised. 'Berta? I'd not heard...'

'No. They say she's waiting until after the Hearing to make the announcement.'

'Ah...' Tolonen walked on, out into the body of the Courtroom, stopping beside the huge, long desk that dominated the centre of the chamber. He leaned forward, his hands – one flesh, one burnished gold – pressed flat against the smoothly polished surface, silently looking about him at the empty benches, the dais where, in a matter of hours, the Commissioners would sit and deliberate. Then he turned, looking directly at Chi Hsun.

'Where did it all go? That's what I keep asking myself. Where did they go – all those dreams we had? They seemed so real, so *secure*. How could it all have gone so wrong?'

Chi Hsun looked down, then came across, stopping beside Tolonen.

'The past is gone, Knut. We cannot change it. But the future... well, that we *can* affect. It is why we serve, neh? Why, in the days to come, we must work hard to ensure the best result.'

Tolonen met his eyes, a sudden tiredness in his voice. 'And what *is* the best result? To see that wastrel Lutz inherit?'

'You think he will?'

Tolonen sighed, then nodded.

'And Berta Ebert?'

Tolonen grimaced. 'The most she can realistically hope for is a life interest in the estate. And an annual sum, perhaps, corresponding with her private allowance when Klaus was still alive. Oh, she'll get to keep the Mansion, probably, but as for the Company...'

'And if Lutz Ebert inherits? What will happen, do you think? Will GenSyn become again the power it was?'

Tolonen shrugged. 'Who can tell? If Lutz has any sense he'll keep the present management committee in place and let them run things, but I doubt he'll do that. He has acquired many new 'friends' these past few years, his new wife's family not least among them. I suspect he'll pack the board with them once he's inherited. If so, who knows what future GenSyn has? A poor one, probably.'

'And the rumours? You know, of Lutz's involvement with his nephew, the traitor Hans?'

Tolonen looked down, his face sour. 'Ah, that. I had a team looking into it for the best part of a year.'

'And?'

'Nothing. Oh, there were a few shady business deals – the kind of thing that, were the media to get hold of them, would make him even less popular than he is now – but nothing to link him to Hans. Nor will there be, unless we find the young man.'

Chi Hsun glanced across at the dais, then looked back at the aged Marshal. 'And your Master, Li Yuan... what does he think of events?'

Tolonen looked away, his expression troubled. 'My Master has been kept fully briefed. His primary concern is to see that things are kept stable.'

It was a diplomatic answer, for, by all accounts, Li Yuan had become something of a recluse since the murder of his wives, letting his Chancellor, Nan Ho, attend to the day-to-day running of things. But where GenSyn was concerned, what Li Yuan thought was of immense importance. GenSyn were still the biggest Company in Chung Kuo, and traditionally their fortunes had been linked directly with the Li family. A decline in the power of GenSyn would mean a corresponding decline in power for Tolonen's master. It remained to see whether he would allow it to fall into the hands of Klaus Ebert's weak half-brother, Lutz.

Yet what could he do?

Each of the Seven – the T'ang who ruled Chung Kuo – had appointed a representative to sit on the Hearing Committee and look after their best interests. For Li Yuan to overrule their decision was unthinkable. Yet there were other means.

Chi Hsun looked about him at the empty benches of the Courtroom and sighed. GenSyn. Wherever one turned, the influence of that great Company could be seen: in the food substitutes they used throughout the Lowers; in the cheap health treatments that were so popular in the Mids; in their range of prosthetics and 'age-at-bay' products used by the rich. Mainly, however, they were known as the creators of the Genetic Synthetics, those strange and marvellous creatures grown in their tanks, custom-designed for every taste: servants and whores, sportsmen and performers, goat-men and ox-men, brutish bodyguards and the flat-faced, bullish *Hei* that Security used to put down riots. GenSyn had been a cornucopia, providing something for every level – one of the great pillars on which Chung Kuo was built. But now all that was threatened.

Chi Hsun looked back at the Marshal. As he did, Tolonen turned from the table, looking back at him, a tired, sad expression in his eyes. Beyond him the lamps flickered in their iron cressets, making the shadows seem deeper, ingrained almost in the stone and wood of the ancient hall.

'Ah well...' the old man said. 'Let's go now, Master Chi. Sleep. That's the remedy. A good night's sleep, neh? Tomorrow will come soon enough...'

Alone in his rooms, Tolonen stood before the mirror, staring at his face, trying to see, beyond those rugged, angular planes, some resemblance of the man he'd been.

He had had little time in his life for self-analysis. He had always seen it as a weakness in a man and had maintained a rigid self-discipline when it came to such matters. But recently, left with much time on his hands and missing the company of his daughter, Jelka, his thoughts had begun to turn inwards. He had been reading the *Kalevala* once more, immersing himself in the great epic of his people, the Finns, and as he read he had found memories awakening of people long dead; of friends he had forgotten.

The dead... it was as if the great world were slowly dying all about him. All those he had known and loved – his wife, his brother and his brother's wife, his old master Li Shai Tung, and his best friend, Klaus... they and countless others – all were gone. Only ghosts remained. The world had lost substance, had reduced itself to a pool of light, a mirror, a face – his own face, staring back at him.

So hard that face... Elemental, it was. Like weathered rock.

And eyes like a November sky.

He smiled, but it was a pale and steely smile. Sunlight in winter. Then, softly, his voice little more than a whisper, he spoke into the glass.

> 'When the oak at last had fallen,
> And the evil tree was levelled,
> Once again the sun shone brightly,
> And the pleasant moonlight glimmered,

And the clouds extended widely,
And the rainbow spanned the heavens,
O'er the cloud-encompassed headland,
And the island's hazy summit.'

The words came easily to him. But that was no surprise. He had pored over them, time and again, as if obsessed. For weeks now he had been haunted by them; had woken from dreams with them on his lips. Dreams in which the great City had fallen and the land was green and empty... was a land of lakes and mountains.

The oak... the evil tree. It was the symbol of the Shepherd family, of the architect of the seven great Cities of Chung Kuo.

He took a long, shuddering breath. Had he been wrong? Chung Kuo... was that the evil tree of legend? For if it was... if all he had believed in was an evil spell...

He shook his head, then pushed the thought aside. Lately he had been tormented by loneliness... a loneliness he was too proud – far too proud – to admit to. Some days he woke feeling fragile, like a ghost himself, and sometimes he would turn, imagining someone behind him, only to find an empty room... and silence. But what *was* he? He had thought he knew. 'A man,' he would once have answered, as if that had a meaning beyond all question. But now... well, what *was* a man?

Never in all his seventy-six years had he been troubled by such thoughts, but now it was as if a door had opened in him and he had stepped inside.

Inside... into uncertainty, and dreams, and thoughts that woke him in the night.

Old... I am getting old...

He stripped off his sleeping jacket, then reached up to touch his left shoulder, tracing the join, watching himself in the glass. There, where flesh met metal, a thin strip of soft leather acted as a kind of buffer, preventing the skin from being chafed. It had been awkward at first, but now the feel of it was comforting, strangely reassuring. *I am alive*, it seemed to say.

He sniffed, then moved the golden limb, flexing and unflexing the jointed hand, remembering how he had lost the arm. A close call that had been. Indeed it was a wonder he had lived so long when so many had wanted him dead.

Turning, he looked about him at the huge and shadowed room. It was simply, almost spartanly furnished. A double bed, a chair and a small writing desk – that was all. Underfoot a thick rug covered half the floor space. As for the walls, they were bare save for the portrait of his wife that hung in the alcove facing his bed.

He went across and stared up at it.

'How are you, Jenny Endfors?' he asked quietly, using her maiden name. 'Is it sunny where you are?'

She smiled back down at him. Beyond her the wind seemed to dance in the pines that covered the hillside of the island, while to her left the blue-green sea sparkled in the spring sunlight. Like a goddess, he thought, sent briefly down to haunt him...

She had been thirty years his junior, a beautiful, blonde-haired girl with a laugh like the summer itself. Jelka... his darling Jelka was her image. But the gods had decided not to grant him more than a single measure of happiness. His Jenny had died giving birth to his daughter, and he had slept alone these last eighteen years.

Lonely... no wonder he was lonely.

There was a knock. He turned, wondering for a moment if he hadn't imagined it, then it came again.

'Yes?' he called, his voice filled with a strength and certainty he did not feel.

'Marshal Tolonen?'

It was the voice of his equerry, Lofgren.

He frowned, then went across and unlocked the door. In the corridor outside, Lofgren stood alone, a small tray balanced between his hands. The smell of hot soup wafted up out of the darkness.

'Bertil? What is this?'

'I... I heard you pacing, sir. I thought maybe this would help. I wasn't certain you had eaten.'

Tolonen smiled, then stepped back, letting the young officer enter. 'That's very kind of you. I... I couldn't sleep.'

'No, sir.' Lofgren took the tray across and set it down on the desk, then turned, coming to attention.

'At ease, boy.'

'Sir...'

He went across, then sat, beginning to eat, his hunger surprising him.

'Were there any messages?' he asked, turning between mouthfuls to look up at the young man.

'Just one... from your daughter.'

'Jelka? What, from Callisto?'

'Yes, sir. A short-burst transmission. I've stored a copy on your personal file. If you like, I could have it played right now...'

Tolonen took another mouthful of the soup, then shook his head. 'No. Show it to me first thing. While I'm getting dressed.'

'Sir...'

He smiled. Yes. It would be something to look forward to, before the business of the Hearing began. Thinking of which...

'Bertil?'

'Sir?'

'Do you think we were right, letting things take their course? I mean... GenSyn... it's so important to us all. If things go wrong...'

Lofgren looked down, embarrassed. It was not often the Marshal asked him for his opinion.

'I... I guess it depends what you mean, sir. If you mean, were we right not to have Lutz Ebert killed out of hand... well, I'm not sure, sir. I... I wouldn't have liked to have made that call.'

'But if you had?'

The young officer looked away, a slight stiffness to him now. 'I think I would have done exactly as you did, sir.'

Tolonen smiled. 'I see. Well, thank you, Bertil. You can go now. Oh, and thank you for the soup. It was most welcome.'

'Sir...'

He watched the boy go, then stood, stretching his limbs, tired now, ready for his bed.

If you only knew, he thought. *If only you'd been there, Bertil Lofgren, when I advised the T'ang to have the bastard killed.* But now it was too late. Much, much too late. To have him killed now would create more problems than it solved. Besides, there were other ways to control the man. Subtler, more efficient ways.

He went across and blew a silent kiss, then turned and went to his bed. Pulling back the thin sheet he slipped beneath it, his eyes heavy suddenly, the frantic racing of his thoughts slowing to a more sedate pace.

And the rainbow spanned the heavens...

He gave a shuddering yawn, then turned onto his side, the thought that followed the words vanishing from mind even as it formed.

Soup... he must have drugged the soup...

Outside the door, the young man waited, listening. Then, hearing the old man's snores, he nodded to himself and, smiling, walked away down the unlit corridor towards his quarters.

The Courtroom was hushed, expectant. Above the raised dais where the court officials sat, a dozen media remotes hovered like fire-flies, sending back an incessant stream of images to the watching billions of Chung Kuo. Just now their cameras were focused on the distinctive features of Chi Hsun, the most senior of the seven Commissioners.

Chi Hsun was a tall, humourless man with a long, horse-like face. To the public he was best known for his role in the Demotion trials six years before. Back then he had become known as 'Iron Chi' for his unrelenting pursuit of those who had opposed the Seven in the great 'War that wasn't a War'. As Tsu Ma's representative on the Hearing Committee his view was supposed to carry no more weight than any other's, but his long experience made him their natural leader, and it fell to him now to open the proceedings.

Off to one side sat the old Marshal himself, Knut Tolonen. He was in overall charge of the Hearings and in the last two and a half years had earned much respect for the way he had handled the matter. Now, with the public phase of the Hearings finally about to begin, he seemed tired, his granite features pale and drawn.

The camera moved on, panning slowly across the huge stacks of legal books and files, three long rows of them, which were laid out along the full length of the benches at the centre of the courtroom, then slowly climbed the steps, picking out first the tall, coldly elegant figure of Berta Ebert, sat between her daughters on the far right of the court, then moved along, past various familiar figures until it rested on the face of Lutz Ebert, the dead man's half-brother. For a moment it remained there, allowing that face, with its weak, watery blue eyes and its uncertain, somewhat shifty features, to condemn itself, then moved on again, across a backdrop of media celebrities and chattering anchor-men until it focused on the stocky yet sophisticated form of Henri Lanouette, sat amidst the bankers and businessmen – Han and *Hung Mao* – who formed his faction.

For a brief moment the faint murmur of voices filled the Courtroom. Then, as the ceremonial bell sounded – one tone high, the other low – the room fell silent and the three parties' advocates entered the room from the doors at the far end, making their way towards the raised bench at the front where the Commissioners sat.

Chi Hsun waited for them to form up in front of him, then made a brief dismissive gesture of his hand. At once the main body of the advocates – some thirty or so in all – made their way across to their benches on the left-hand side of the court, leaving only the three Senior Advocates standing before the Commissioners.

And so, finally, they came to it: the formal submission of evidence. First to submit would be Tung Li-so, Chief Advocate for Berta Ebert and her daughters.

Tung Li-so began his submission, but he had barely uttered more than a dozen words when he broke off, staring to his right. An elderly Han had come across from the public benches and now presented himself before Iron Chi, his head respectfully bowed. As he straightened up, the remotes homed in, hovering just overhead.

'Forgive me, Excellency,' he began, 'but I would like to submit fresh evidence before the Commissioners in the matter of the GenSyn Inheritance Hearings.'

Chi Hsun stared at the ancient a moment, astonished, then turned, looking to Tolonen for guidance.

'I have crucial new evidence. If your Excellency would permit...'

'Let's hear what he has to say!' Tolonen called from across the Courtroom in a weary voice. 'But make him get on with it. We've delayed long enough!'

'All right,' Chi Hsun said gruffly, glaring at the newcomer, 'but if you are wasting the Commission's time, I shall have you charged, you understand?'

'I understand, Excellency.'

'Good. Then state your name and business and get on with it.'

'Thank you, Excellency. My name is Ku Hsien-ch'eng and I am Advocate for the sole legitimate heir to the estate of Klaus Ebert.'

Iron Chi nodded, stunned by what he'd said, waiting for Advocate Ku to say more, but the old man merely turned away. At that moment, as if at an unseen command, the doors at the far end of the room swung inwards and eight grey-bearded advocates made their way into the court, each bearing a huge stack of files and legal texts, which they proceeded to heap upon the central benches, pushing aside what was already there.

'Seven copies,' Ku said, turning back to Iron Chi and bowing once more. 'As the Commission demands.'

There was uproar in the court. On the benches to the left the advocates were standing, calling out to the Commissioners, demanding that they dismiss this new evidence, while on the bench itself the Commissioners were in disarray, arguing among themselves over the legality of this new submission. Amidst it all stood Ku Hsien-ch'eng, his head bowed, a faint, almost enigmatic smile on his face.

On the public benches, Lutz Ebert was standing, looking on, his eyes narrowed suspiciously. Near by Berta Ebert was looking down, her fists balled tightly in her lap, what she was feeling concealed behind a wall of icy self-composure. Only Lanouette seemed vaguely amused, as if he'd been forewarned.

Tolonen, meanwhile, leaned over Chi Hsun's shoulder, reading through the brief abstract of Advocate Ku's submission, wondering – just loud enough for the nearest remote to catch his muttering – who in the gods' names could possibly be claiming the GenSyn billions. An answer which, when he finally came to it, made him laugh, half in shock, half in disgust.

'The gods help us!' he said quietly, meeting Iron Chi's eyes. 'Let's hope to hell this isn't true!'

Tolonen sat at his desk in the Lower Committee Room, an old-fashioned glowlamp hovering nearby, illuminating the great chart he had spread out before him. Beyond the edges of the chart the desk was cluttered with huge stacks of files and discs and ancient law texts. Near by, waiting silently in the shadows beyond the tight circle of light, sat his equerry, the young lieutenant, Lofgren.

The Marshal looked up, then rubbed at his eyes with his right hand. Beyond the reinforced ice of the picture window the darkness seemed to have softened towards morning. His left shoulder had begun to ache, as it often did when he was tired, but that was understandable. They had been working through the new evidence for the best part of a day, but now it was clear.

He yawned and looked across, smiling at the young man. 'What time is it, Bertil?'

'Fifth bell sounded twenty minutes back, sir.'

Tolonen nodded, then sat back, staring thoughtfully at the great mass of untouched material. There was much more to look at – enough to keep the Committee busy for another month – but he had seen enough to know that he had been right. This was serious. Very serious indeed.

He turned, looking at the young man again. 'What's your feeling about this, Bertil? Do you think I was right to keep the Committee at arm's length?'

The young lieutenant considered a moment, then. 'From what I've seen, sir, I think you had no choice. By dismissing Iron Chi and the Committee when you did, you gave Li Yuan a clear advantage. If Wang Sau-leyan's man, Tu Chung, had got wind of any of this, his master would almost certainly have intervened at once. As it is, Li Yuan has time to act, to prevent Wang from using this against him.'

Tolonen sniffed deeply. That was true. And yet he could not stop the Hearing tomorrow. To do so would merely invite the T'ang of Africa to meddle. And that was what he had been trying to avoid all along. No... his problem was how to play this. How to turn this information to Li Yuan's advantage.

He looked back at his equerry. 'At present Wang knows merely that there has been a development in the case, not how significant that development is. Yet if I allow this new evidence to go before the Committee, Wang will know everything within the hour.'

'And yet you have no choice. If you embargo the evidence, the effect will be the same. Tu Chung will protest and, when his protest is ignored, Wang Sau-leyan will take the opportunity to step in. In the circumstances you would be best advised, perhaps, to take the bull by the horns. To strike before our Master's cousin knows what is going on.' Lofgren smiled. 'Why not let Advocate Ku present his evidence at once, before Iron Chi and the rest have had a chance to look at it.'

Tolonen sat forward. 'Could we do that?'

'Why not? It might be suggested to Chi Hsun that, by doing so, this 'distraction' might be set aside and the real business of the Hearing got on with.'

Tolonen gave a short laugh, then nodded. 'I like that. And Chi Hsun will buy it, I'm certain. But what of Li Yuan? Oughtn't we to let him know?'

'As soon as possible, sir. The new evidence changes everything. Unless our Master acts, and acts swiftly, our worst fears will come about. The matter will drag on and GenSyn will be lost.'

'You think it would be that bad?'

'I am certain of it, sir. Why, even before this, Tu Chung has suggested delays for the most minor of technicalities. This new matter would give him the perfect excuse to request a lengthy recess. Indeed it could drag on for years while his clerks exhaust the search for precedents, and in the meantime all the work we've done these past thirty months to stabilise GenSyn's trading position and reassure the markets would be lost. Confidence would vanish overnight. The share price would plummet. And that cannot be allowed to happen.'

'No.' Tolonen stood, nodding decisively, his granite face set. 'Then I shall contact Li Yuan at once and tell him what we know.'

There was silence in the great Courtroom as the elderly Ku Hsien-ch'eng completed his opening remarks, bowed low to the panel of Commissioners, then turned, facing the seated rows of advocates.

'Ch'un tzu,' he said, smiling politely.

Behind and above them, at the top of a flight of steps that formed an aisle between their seats, was a doorway. At Ku's terse nod the Guard of the Court lifted the great keys from his belt and turned, fitting one to the lock. As the heavy door eased back, heads turned, trying to see into the darkness beyond. For a moment there was nothing, then, out into the brightness of the courtroom, stepped an elderly Han dressed in pale green silks. There was a general outlet of breath, a moment's disappointment, then, just beyond the old man, flanked by two young male attendants in matching pale green one-pieces, came a girl. Or rather, a young woman. A Han in her late twenties, wearing a simple pink and mauve chang shan and a white wool flower – a tai hsiao – in her tightly bobbed jet-black hair.

At the sight of her there was a buzz of excitement. A sound that was interrupted by the sudden indignant cry of Berta Ebert.

'How dare you bring that creature here! How *dare* you!'

Media remotes buzzed here and there, almost colliding in their attempts to capture every moment of it. But things were moving fast now. Behind Ebert's widow, his daughters were on their feet and shouting, enraged by the sight of the young woman. Near by, Lutz Ebert looked down, one hand pressed to his brow, shading his eyes.

The young woman came down the steps slowly, the two attendants leading her by the hands. Down she came, looking about her vaguely, her eyes fearful, like a young animal's, an uncertain, apologetic smile on her lips.

Up ahead of her the old Han had stopped and, after bowing to Iron Chi and the Commissioners, turned, facing Advocate Ku. Ku Hsien-ch'eng smiled then turned, facing Iron Chi, raising his voice over the clamour in the chamber.

'May I present before your Excellencies the chief witness for my claimant...'

For a moment his voice was drowned out by the shouts of the Ebert women. Ku turned, looking across, his hands tucked into his sleeves, waiting patiently while a Court official got the three women to sit and be quiet, then he turned back, bowing to Iron Chi, as if the fault were his.

'Forgive me, Excellencies. As I was saying, might I present to the Commissioners the young lady, Shou Chin Hsin, better known in the Ebert household as Golden Heart, onetime concubine to the traitor, Hans Ebert.'

From Ku's right the shouting began again. This time Iron Chi leaned forward angrily, calling for order.

'If I have one more outburst from you, Madam Ebert, I am afraid I shall have no choice but to ban you from this chamber until the Hearing is over. Now sit still and hold your tongue.'

It was a severe rebuke, but Berta Ebert stood there a moment longer, defiant, glaring at the young woman, before she sat again, her body tense, her face a mask of hatred.

As for Golden Heart herself, she seemed unaffected by the noise, apart from it. There was something odd about her, something *unconnected*. The remotes, circling her, took in every detail of her dress, the way she stood, the way her eyes moved restlessly, flicking across the surface of things.

To Ku's left came the urgent murmur of whispered exchanges among the advocates. Then, as if some agreement had been reached, Advocate Chang, the senior representative for Lutz Ebert, stood and cleared his throat.

Iron Chi looked across at him. 'Yes, Advocate Chang. What is it?'

Chang bowed, then came round until he stood before the bench. 'Forgive me, Excellency, but on behalf of my claimant I wish to register a protest against the witness presented by Advocate Ku. Medical testimony would merely serve to confirm what is evident at a glance. The woman is clearly mad. Any evidence she might give to this Hearing would be of as little value as the prattlings of a child. In the circumstances I beg the Commissioners to rule that this witness's evidence be inadmissible.'

Chi Hsun stared at the young woman a moment, then looked back at Ku Hsien-ch'eng. 'Well, Advocate Ku, what have you to say? Personally I am of Advocate Chang's view. Unless, therefore, you can give good reason why I should allow you to continue, I shall rule that we move on.'

Ku bowed his head. 'With respect, Excellency, the mental state of the witness has no bearing whatsoever on this Hearing. Nor have I any intention of letting Shou Chin Hsin utter a single word in respect of this matter. However, her presence here has a point, so if you would bear with me a moment?'

'I shall allow you to continue, Advocate Ku, but make it brief.'

'Excellency.' Turning, Ku put out a hand, inviting the old Han in the pale green to come forward, then, taking his arm, he went up to the bench, presenting the man to the Commissioners.

'This, your Excellencies, is Professor K'ang. K'ang Hung-chang of the Kunming Institute of Comparative Genetics; a body established and licensed by special Edict of the Seven and run within the strict guidelines of the Edict of Technological Control. Professor K'ang's expertise is in matching genotypes...'

'Forgive me, Excellency,' Advocate Chang interrupted, 'but I fail to see the relevance of any of this. Golden Heart may have been Hans Ebert's concubine – we do not dispute it – but that gives her no claim in law, particularly in view of the Special Decree issued by the Seven.'

Iron Chi looked about him at his fellow Commissioners, receiving sober nods from all sides, then looked back at Ku.

'I must once more agree with Advocate Chang. Unless you can pro-vide me with a good reason for continuing, Advocate Ku, I shall rule that your claim be set aside and that all matters relating to it be struck from the official record.'

Ku bowed. 'I understand, Excellency. Then let me come directly to the point. There is a child.'

There was a great hiss of disbelief, then, once again, the chamber erupted with noise. Chi Hsun sat back, startled. Beneath him, on the floor of the court, Chang had turned and was staring at Ku, his mouth hanging open. On the benches across from him, most of the advocates were on their feet, shouting and waving papers.

Chi Hsun let the noise continue for a while, then raised a hand, calling for silence. Once a kind of order had returned, he leaned forward again, looking down at Chang.

'Did you know of this, Advocate Chang?'

Chang licked his lips nervously, then nodded. 'There *was* a child, yes, but the child was destroyed.'

'Destroyed?'

Ku, standing beside him, shook his head. 'That is not so. Hans Ebert ordered it to be destroyed, but that is not the same thing. His order was not carried out. The child was taken to a place of safety and kept there. The boy lives. He is three, almost four now.'

Chi Hsun sat back, astonished. 'And you can prove this, Advocate Ku?'

Ku Hsien-ch'eng bowed and smiled, the very picture of composure. 'As I was saying, Excellency, this here is Professor K'ang. K'ang Hung-chang of the Kunming Institute of Comparative Genetics...'

In the silent darkness of the room, the hologram shone with the intensity of a ghostly vision, the face of the madwoman filled with a strange inner light that seemed to waver like a candle's flame between serenity and despair.

Tolonen, standing there, his hands gripping the edge of the viewing table, stared down at the image open-mouthed, mesmerised by the sight of the child playing at its mother's feet. He was a robust, healthy child with fine dark hair and strong Eurasian features.

A bastard, he thought. Yet there was no denying it. It was Hans Ebert's child. That face, that mouth, that chin. That was the Ebert lineage. But even without that there was proof enough. His experts had taken new cell samples and subjected the genetic charts to the most rigorous scrutiny, and the evidence held up. The concubine, Golden Heart, was the mother, Hans Ebert the father.

Even so, the matter was far from straightforward. Hans Ebert was a traitor and, under normal circumstances, his family shared his fate, to the third generation. Yet it had been agreed among the Seven that these were far from normal circumstances. Klaus Ebert had been a pillar of the State. Though dead it was unthinkable that he should be declared a traitor, and so a special Edict had been passed, exonerating him, his wife and all dependants, making the sentence of the Seven specific to one single individual... Hans Ebert. Now that document assumed a new importance. Was the child to share the father's fate, or was he too exonerated under the terms of the Edict?

It was up to Li Yuan to decide.

Tolonen looked down. It was all his fault. He had trusted Hans Ebert. He would have given him anything. Anything at all. His daughter, Jelka, even his own life. And to think...

He sighed then shook his head. Some days he felt it was simply the gods, toying with them all, putting devils into the shapes of men. At others he felt that it was just how they were. Men. With all the strange goodness and wickedness of men.

And the men who had done this – who had saved the child and brought it up in secret? Which were they? And what did they want?

He had been surprised when he'd learned who was behind this. The list of names included six of the most prominent businessmen in City Europe. But what were they after? Was theirs a long-term game? Did they look to the child's gratitude in years to come?

Or maybe young Lofgren was right. Maybe their hand had been forced. After all, what use was a potential heir once the inheritance issue had been legally decided? So maybe it had simply been a case of produce your trump card now or see it lose all value. Even so, what they hoped to achieve was still obscure to him. If the aim had been to damage GenSyn, then surely the easiest, most certain course was to let Lutz Ebert inherit and destroy the child. But maybe that last part – the killing of the child – had grown too difficult for them. Maybe there were too many in on the secret for that to be a realistic option. Then again, maybe it was much simpler than that. Maybe the sight of Lutz Ebert gloating, anticipating his inheritance, had been enough to make them act.

Only one thing was certain. Whatever their motives, altruism had not been among them. They had not invested so much time and money simply to see social justice done. Whatever the outcome, they hoped to have a say, and it was his job to prevent that somehow, to make sure that Chung Kuo's greatest Company stayed clear of such attachments.

Even so the whole affair convinced him of one thing. The world he had known was gone. There had been a breach. Father to son, that had been the way of it, generation after generation, but now the natural son had proved false, had been seen to be a twisted shadow of the father, and this thing – this product of casual fucking with a whore – had been conjured from the air to fill the gap.

He shivered. Like a dream. Like a dark and evil vision of what was to come.

Or like a curse...

The Committee was seated about the long table, a fierce argument raging, when the doors at the far end of the chamber burst open. Tolonen entered, followed closely by an honour troop of six shaven-headed guards. Immediately the room fell silent. At the head of the table, directly facing Tolonen, Tsu Ma's man, Iron Chi, rose to his feet.

'Forgive me, Knut, but we are in session. It was agreed...'

Tolonen raised a hand to mollify his old friend. 'Forgive me, Chi Hsun, forgive me, *ch'un tzu*, but for once there is no time for formalities...'

Wang Sau-leyan's man, Tu Chung was on his feet. 'With respect, Marshal Tolonen, this is not right. We *must* maintain formalities.'

Tolonen stared at him contemptuously, then turned his head, looking to Iron Chi.

'Well, Chi Hsun? Will you keep me waiting like a servant in the antechamber? Or will you hear what I have to say?'

'I protest...' Tu Chung began once more, but Tolonen turned, shouting him down.

'The gods preserve us! Hold your tongue, man!'

Tu Chung jerked back, as if slapped, then sat, glaring at Tolonen.

At the head of the table, Iron Chi leaned forward, his long face clearly troubled. 'Whilst I agree with Tu Chung that this is most irregular, I do feel that, for once, we might make an exception and hear what the Marshal has to say. Forgive me, however, if I insist that we take a vote on this matter. I would not have it said that, in allowing this, I went beyond the instructions given to me by the great Council.'

Tolonen bowed his head. 'As you wish, Chi Hsun, but please, let us do it at once, neh? I am a busy man.'

Iron Chi nodded, then looked about him. 'Well? Will all those in favour of the Marshal addressing this Committee please indicate their agreement.'

From about the long table there were grunts of agreement. Only Tu Chung remained stubbornly silent.

Iron Chi stared at Wang's man a moment, then, with a tiny shrug, looked back at Tolonen. 'It is agreed, then. Let us hear what you have to say.'

Tolonen bowed. 'Forgive me, ch'un tzu. I will take but a moment of your time. I wish to address you informally on this matter. To advise you of a decision that has been made this past hour. One which, I feel, you might wish to take into consideration when deliberating upon this complex and difficult case.' He looked about him, then, staring directly at Tu Chung, added. 'Ch'un tzu... It has been decided that the Special Decree concerning the fate of the traitor Hans Ebert shall be deemed to apply solely to the person named and not to any issue of his loins.'

Tu Chung's head bobbed up, a look of shocked surprise etched on his features. His mouth opened, as if to answer the Marshal, then, realising there was nothing he could say, he bowed low, acknowledging defeat.

Tolonen turned, noting the surprise on Chi Hsun's face and nodded. It was done. The child would inherit.

It was shortly after eighth bell when Tolonen arrived at the old Ebert Mansion, his heart strangely heavy. The last time he had come here it was to tell his old friend Klaus of his son's duplicity: a warning that had resulted in the old man's death and young Hans' escape from Chung Kuo, a traitor, condemned in his absence. And now a young madwoman and her bastard son were tenants of this great estate; the boy heir to the whole vast GenSyn empire, by Li Yuan's decree.

He handed his cloak to the servant then walked through briskly, his booted footsteps echoing back all the way along the broad, tiled corridor. Since Klaus Ebert's death the house had been run by a skeleton staff – but the Marshal could remember it in other days, when its rooms had been filled with guests, its corridors busy with servants.

At the end of the corridor he stopped, waiting while one of the house stewards fumbled with a great bunch of keys at his waist, then threw open the huge doors that led out to the gardens at the centre of the house.

Tolonen strode out onto the balcony and gripped the rail, sniffing the air and looking about him. Here, at least, nothing had changed. A tiny, twisting stream ran beneath low-railed wooden bridges. Beyond it, small, red-painted buildings lay half-concealed among leaf and tree and rock. And there, on the far side of the gardens, beside the pool, three pomegranate trees stood like three ancients sharing a jug of wine.

How often as a young man had he sat with Klaus beneath those trees, their feet dangling in the water, and talked of the years to come. Of their hopes and fears and plans. How often had they argued out the world's great problems between them. Young men, they'd been, filled with a strange, visionary enthusiasm.

Gods, he thought, moved by the sudden clarity of the memory. It seems like only yesterday. And yet it was sixty years ago. Sixty long years. And the world of which they had dreamed... what had come of that? Nothing. Nothing but dust and ashes, betrayal and bitter disappointments.

'And madwomen...' he said softly, reminding himself why he had come.

Yesterday Li Yuan had summoned him and asked him if he would serve again. 'One last time,' as the young T'ang had put it, 'before you take up poetry and painting.' He had laughed and readily agreed, glad to be doing something now that the inheritance issue was resolved. But this...

He sighed. There was a bitter irony to this. That he should be chosen to be Guardian to the boy. He, an old man of seventy-six years. Not only that, but in his heart of hearts he blamed himself for this situation. If he had only gone direct to Li Yuan when he had first found out about Hans Ebert, then Klaus might still be alive, the question of inheritance not an issue. But he had let friendship distort things. And this was the result. A madwoman and her bastard.

Ah yes, but at least he'd exacted a price for his service. Jelka was to come home. She was to be flown direct to Mars from Callisto, and three ships of the imperial fleet were to be sent to ensure her safe return.

Tolonen pushed back, away from the handrail, then went down, crossing the tiny bridge, following the narrow pink and grey pebbled path through the trees to the far side of the garden. Golden Heart would be in her quarters at this hour, on the east side of the Mansion. And the child...

He slowed, suddenly remembering what Jelka had said that time. How strange that he had forgotten that until now. He stopped, looking about him. It had been the evening of Li Shai Tung's death – the night DeVore had attacked the Wiring Project – and he had left her here with Hans while he had gone to see what he might do. And later she had told him about the madwoman and her awful pink-eyed ox-baby, and how Hans had had her real child killed. Yes, and he had refused to believe her. As if she would ever lie to him...

If only he had listened to her. If only he had not tried to force her into that awful, ill-fated marriage with Hans. If only...

He shivered, thinking of her, out there on Callisto. It was strange just how much he missed her. More – much more – than he had ever thought possible. And though he heard from her regularly, it wasn't the same. No. He missed her coming into his study late in the evening to wish him goodnight. Missed the way she would come up silently behind him in his chair and lean across, her hands resting lightly on his shoulders, to gently kiss his brow.

He closed his eyes, steeling himself against the memory and the thought that accompanied it, but there was no denying it; lately he had begun to wonder whether he would ever see her again, face to face. Whether he would ever hold her and feel the warmth of her cheek against his own.

You're a foolish old man, Knut Tolonen, he told himself, straightening up. But then, what else was left for him these days? Who else was there for him to love?

Tolonen turned, hearing noises from the rooms up ahead – the sound of a young child crying for its mother. Hans Ebert's son... He lifted his head, swallowing back the bitterness he felt at the thought – at the dashed hopes it represented – then walked on, knowing he would do his duty by the child.

PART TWENTY-ONE

The South Side of the Sky
SUMMER 2211

'The mountain climbs, fifty li into darkness
Beyond it, the cold stars burn.
Here, on the south side of the sky
The rain never falls.
All that we are, we carry with us
In sealed packs, safe from the air.
Thin the air, thin the hope
Of seeing home again,
Except from afar.
Red sand fills our shoes.
We stop at an inn and drink our fill,
Yet are never content.
We are lost,
Adrift upon a sea of dust.
Some thirsts can never be satisfied.'
—Kan Jiang, 'Thirst' AD 2078

CHAPTER 100

UPON A SEA OF DUST

DeVore stood at the garden's edge, one hand resting against the reinforced glass of the dome, looking out into the darkness of the Martian night. Soldiers guarded the perimeter, their bulky suits gleaming frostily in the earthlight. It was just after two, local time, and the lights of the distant city were low. Beyond them was a wall of blackness.

He turned, looking back across the garden at the Governor's house. It was a large, two-level hacienda, built in the 'Settler' style of a hundred and fifty years earlier, its terrace and upper windows lit by sturdy globular lamps, its back wall hugging the far side of the dome. Surrounding it on three sides, the garden was a dark, luxuriant green, its trees and vines and bushes lit here and there by glowing crimson globes that drifted slowly above the black tiles of the paths. Overhead the dark curve of the dome reflected back their images, like a dozen tiny copies of the planet.

DeVore looked about him, experiencing a deep-rooted sense of satisfaction. It was a beautiful garden, full of rare treats and delights. But what was perhaps most pleasing about it was that it was so totally unlike the formal gardens one found on Chung Kuo. There were no walls here, for instance, no delicate, over-arching bridges, no steep-roofed *ting* or ornamental tea-houses. It was all so open, so... unrefined. Yet it wasn't merely the look of it that impressed him – it was the fact that all trace of Han thought, Han tradition had been carefully dispensed with in its design. Where, in a Han garden, there was harmony and balance – a sense of li, of 'propriety' – here there was a sense of outwardness, of openness to change. His smile widened. In essence, this was one huge, deliberate snub. A thumbing of the nose at the Han who ruled them from afar.

He laughed softly at the thought. Yes, there was something just slightly outlandish about all this – something positively gross about its simple spaciousness and sense of sprawl, about the silken richness of the leaves, the lurid colours of its blossoms. This was something new. An expression of excess, of unchecked growth. He could imagine how offensive – how distasteful – this would seem to the Han mentality. How alien.

He reached out, taking one of the broad, leathery leaves between his fingers, surprised by how glossy and silken it was. Beneath his booted feet the earth was rich and dark, a moist, heavy soil that clung like clay and stained the fingers brown. Close by were some of the big hybrids he had noticed earlier. He went across to them, lifting one of the dark blue flowers gently from beneath. Seen close-up, it seemed less a blossom than a kind of pad, a rudimentary face formed into the puffy surface of the flower, like a mask. This one was of lust, but others, nearby, seemed to reflect a range of other moods – of anger and love, cunning and desire, of hatred, benevolence and despair. And many more. He lifted it to his nose, intrigued by its strange, exotic scent, and noted how it brushed against his cheek, like a pet, responding to his human warmth.

'They're edible, too,' said Schenck, coming out onto the terrace. 'You should try one...'

DeVore met the Governor's eyes, smiling. 'Later, perhaps... They're new, aren't they?'

Schenck nodded and came down the wide, slatted steps, tightening the sash about his formal robe. 'The very latest designs. They're what we call 'interims'. Part vegetable, part animal. The end result of thirty years research. Beautiful, aren't they?'

DeVore studied them a moment. To be honest, part of him found them quite ugly – an offence to natural form. Even so, Schenck was right. If they weren't beautiful in themselves, then the idea of them was beautiful. This too was something new. Something that had not existed before Man had made it exist. Thinking that, he felt a small thrill pass through him and looked back at Schenck, nodding.

'I'll send you some,' Schenck said, coming across.

'Thanks. So how did it go?'

Schenck had just returned from the official reception held to celebrate his re-election for a third term as Governor of the Martian Colonies. The cream of Martian society had been there in Kang Kua City tonight, representatives of all nineteen Colonies.

'Well enough,' Schenck answered, stopping a few *ch'i* from where DeVore stood. 'You know how these things are, Howard. My face simply aches from smiling.'

'I suppose it was buzzing with the latest news, neh?'

'What else? After all, it's official now.' Schenck looked away, laughing to himself. 'You can't imagine how many times I was drawn aside tonight. If I'd said yes once to endorsing a candidate, I'd have had to say it fifty times, and as there'll be only twenty-six representatives from Mars, that could have got me into serious trouble.'

DeVore studied him a moment, then lowered his eyes. 'And the other matter?'

Schenck glanced at him, then leaned across, plucking one of the mask-like flowers from its stem. There was a faint puckering of the flower's expression, a sudden release of fragrance. 'Our friends, the merchants, you mean?'

DeVore nodded.

Schenck lifted the flower to his face and nibbled at the edge, then turned, meeting DeVore's eyes. 'They're pleased, Howard. Very pleased indeed.'

'So the prototypes were useful?'

Schenck felt in the pocket of his *pau*, then handed something across. It was a tiny box, like a pill box. DeVore opened it.

The insect – a termite, its segmented body the colour of darkest night – stared up at him from beneath the translucent ice, its compound eyes inquisitive.

'It's semi-autonomous,' Schenck explained, looking down into the box. 'You can send it into the offices of your rivals and it will serve as your eyes and ears. It has augmented sensory apparatus and a memory capacity rivalling the field comsets Security use. Moreover you can programme it either to look for something specific, or – and this is the really clever part – you can simply trust it to look for the unusual. It seems that all you have to do is give it an idea of what it ought to find, and then let it get on with the job.'

DeVore smiled, remembering when his copy had sent the prototype for this from earth. This was Kim Ward's work – *he* had designed this little beauty.

'A bug,' he said. 'An intelligent bug.'

'A semi-autonomous robotic unit,' Schenck corrected him. 'It merely looks like a bug.'

DeVore closed the lid and slipped it into his pocket. Schenck smiled, making no attempt to take it back.

'And the Machine?'

Schenck lifted the flower to his mouth, taking another tiny bite. 'I've had it shipped. It'll be there in two days. I saw to it myself.'

'And they're going to pay for that? As agreed?'

Schenck nodded, then threw the flower down. It lay there, its smile fixed and eternal. 'They've paid for everything. What's more, the dome will be ready two weeks from now. To your specifications, naturally.'

'Good.' But he was thinking that he would have to do something about that. To stop word getting out.

'Oh, and one more thing before I go and change. An old friend of yours has turned up. I thought you might like to meet him.'

'A friend?' He looked past Schenck, suddenly aware of the figure on the terrace. A big, broad-chested man in uniform. He narrowed his eyes, trying to make out who it was, then gave a great roar of delight, making his way across.

'Will! When did you get here? Why didn't you let me know?'

Auden came down the steps and embraced DeVore, then stood back, coming to attention, his head lowered.

'I got in yesterday. From Callisto. I was going to contact you at once, but the Governor asked me not to. He wanted to surprise you.'

DeVore let his hand rest on Auden's shoulder a moment, then, still smiling broadly, he looked across at Schenck. 'For once I'm glad you did, Hung-li.

This is a marvellous surprise!'

Schenck came over to them. 'You've things to talk about, I'm sure, so I'll leave you. I've got a call to make, but I'll join you in a while, okay?'

DeVore watched Schenck go, then turned back, taking Auden's arm.

'Well, Captain William Auden, so where have you been? And what in the gods' names have you been up to? I thought you were dead!'

Auden laughed. 'I've felt like it some days, to be honest. But no. I've been out to the edge of the system. Out there among the ice and rock.'

'And?' DeVore eyed his old lieutenant, curious to see what he'd made of it.

'And I'm glad to be back. Even this far out. You know, they've an expression for us out there – warm-worlders, they call us. Well, I'd rather be a warm-worlder than a rock-breather any day.' He shuddered. 'It was awful. Like death. We weren't meant to live out there.'

'But now you're back. So what do you plan to do?'

Auden shrugged.

DeVore considered a moment, then smiled. 'Don't worry. I'll find something. You always were useful.'

'Talking of which...' Auden hesitated and glanced at the house, as if to check that Schenck were out of hearing. 'I've news,' he said, his voice lowered. 'Something I picked up on Callisto. It seems the Marshal's daughter will be here within the week.'

DeVore's smile faded. 'Then you must have heard it wrong, Will. The *Tientsin* won't be docking here for another two months.'

'That's true. But Jelka Tolonen isn't on the *Tientsin*. The Marshal sent out new orders. She was to travel to Callisto on a special Security flight, then transfer to one of the direct Jupiter–Mars shuttles.'

'And that's why you came? To let me know?'

Auden smiled. 'I knew you'd be interested. Besides, Callisto's a small place, and there was a good chance I'd bump into her if I stayed, and where would I have been then? Locked up and returned to Chung Kuo in the next ship out.'

'So when does she arrive?'

'Three days from now, at Tien Men K'ou in the south.'

DeVore raised an eyebrow, surprised. 'Tien Men K'ou? That's rather unusual, neh?'

'Again, it's the Marshal's orders. He's getting jumpy, it seems. He's seen how things are shaping here and he's worried in case something happens while she's here. If he'd had his way he'd have had her flown straight back to Chung Kuo from the Saturn system, avoiding Mars altogether, but that simply wasn't possible. However, the Shanyang leaves here in a week's time and he wants her on it.'

DeVore considered that a moment, then gave a curt, decisive nod. 'Okay. I take it that you alone know of this.'

'Schenck knows nothing.'

'Good. Nor should he. The Governor's a reliable enough man when it comes to matters Martian, but he's little time for the bigger picture. And as for taking on Tolonen...' He gave a strange, brief laugh. 'Well, I'm glad you're back, Will. You'll stay with me, I hope?'

'I'd be honoured and delighted.'

'Good.' DeVore smiled, then turned, hearing movement on the terrace. It was Schenck, his formal robes replaced now by a loose-fitting velvet *pau*. The Governor smiled broadly and hailed them.

'Will you have a drink before you go, Howard? And you, Will?'

They went across, joining Schenck in a toast, congratulating him once more, their laughter filling the air inside the dome. Outside, beyond the circle of light, soldiers patrolled the frosted perimeter, their pressure suits gleaming in the frigid darkness, the great, blue-white circle of Chung Kuo high above them in the Martian sky.

The night was almost over. It would be dawn in three hours.

Tien Men K'ou City never slept. An hour before dawn its warrens and corridors buzzed with activity. In the south quadrant, workers from the giant HoloGen complex, their pale ochre overalls distinctive, were coming off shift, their replacements shuffling past them, bleary-eyed in the half dark. In the eastern levels prostitutes – common *men hu* in creased ersilks, stinking of cheap perfume – stood in door-ways calling out to any drunken reveller who passed, while in cluttered dens close by small knots of gamblers, young Han, their dark hair cut stubble-short in traditional Martian style, crouched excitedly over the roll and tumble of a dice. In the markets of west and central traders busied themselves, buying fresh produce from the Tharsis farmlands or setting up their stalls, while at the spaceport, on the north-eastern side of the City, one of the great inter-planetary cruisers was being readied for flight, the maintenance crew like darkly-carapaced insects scuttling across its giant fuselage. Stern-faced Colony guards, helmeted, black chevrons on their blood-red uniforms, paced the affluent upper levels beneath the crater's lip, stopping to move on a drunk or check on the movements of one of the juvenile gangs that thrived in the teeming lower-east and rode the lifts from Deep to Lip. Last but not least were the outworld tourists, who could be found wandering in the upper levels near the spaceport, taking their fill of Mars before returning to the bleak, claustrophobic austerity of their homeworlds.

One such traveller, a small, neat-looking man with dark, fine hair and soft brown eyes, stopped amidst the bustle of Chang An Avenue and looked up, studying the sign over the doorway to his right. Against a dark red background, a black dragon coiled sinuously and exhaled a cloud of smoke from its sharply-fanged jaws, its barbed tail lashing out. Fierce-eyed, it stared down at him, as if daring him to enter. Beneath the moving image, flashed almost subliminally at him, were two pictograms, reinforcing the visual. *Hei lung*, they read. Black Dragon.

Smiling, deciding he could take an hour out before he met up with his brothers again, he went across and placed his hand flat against the entry-pad, looking up into the camera.

As the outer door hissed back, he caught the sharp, sweet scents of alcohol and tobacco. And other things. Things he could only guess at. Quickly, before the outer door closed and the inner lock sprang open, he took two twenty *yuan* bills from his wallet and palmed them, then slipped the pouch into his right boot, patting it once to check it didn't show.

His uncle had been robbed once in such a place, up in Chi Shan City, in the north. The poor man had lost ten thousand *yuan* and had returned home empty-handed, the oreextractor he had come to buy unpurchased, a year's profit for the family lost in a moment's recklessness. The traveller nodded to himself, remembering the shame his uncle had suffered, and how, for months afterwards, a cloud had fallen over the whole family. He had only been eight, yet that time – with its communal feeling of shame and disappointment, and despair at effort unrewarded – was etched vividly in his memory. While he understood – and shared – his uncle's curiosity, he was determined that no one would ever say that he, Ishida Ikuro, had been as careless.

The outer door hissed shut, the latches clicking into place. At once the inner doors irised open, the strange, intoxicating scent of the place – that same scent he had caught the faintest trace of a moment before – hitting him like the rush of a drug.

Inside was a big, sprawling bar with two, maybe three dozen tables and, on the far side, a big half-moon-shaped counter. There was a faint murmur of conversation, the background chatter of a ViewScreen in the right-hand corner, but the bar was almost empty. There were a dozen people at most, scattered here and there among the tables.

He made his way across and took one of the high stools beside the bar, placing one of the twenties on the counter in front of him, as he'd seen others do. At once the barman came across.

'A *maotai*, please,' he said casually, as if it was what he ordered every day.

The barman nodded, went away, returned with a bowl of the rich, red sorghum-based liquor and placed it before him, not touching the twenty.

'Thank you,' he said, speaking to the barman's back, but already the man had forgotten him.

Ikuro looked about, noting the tiny dance floor, the half-empty tables, the big MedFac screen in the far corner, murmuring away unwatched, and nodded inwardly. Despite the hour and the mere handful of people scattered about the bar, it was just how he had pictured it. He sniffed deeply, taking in the smell of the place, then, gripping the bowl with both hands, he raised it to his lips and sipped, timidly at first, then with more gusto as the rich, sweet taste of the sorghum flooded his senses.

He set the bowl down, wiping his mouth with the back of his hand, then looked at the timer inset into his wrist. It was eight minutes past five. Good. He would stay until six. Would sit here and relax and drink a bowl or two of this splendid *maotai*. After all, he deserved it. His brothers didn't know yet, but he had struck a good deal for them this night. Had saved them days of haggling and thousands of *yuan*. It was only right that he should take an hour off to celebrate.

He looked about him again, savouring the feeling of being in a bar, on Mars, alone. It was like being in a trivee serial, or at the start of some strange adventure. Except that this was real. He could feel the solid roundness of the seat beneath him, taste the sorghum liquor on his tongue and in his throat, smell the rich blend of intoxicants in the air. And if he turned his head...

Ikuro stopped, noticing for the first time what he had missed on his first look round the bar.

The man was sitting on the far side of the counter, half in shadow, his face turned away. At first Ikuro thought he might have been mistaken, but as the man turned back he could see that he had been right. The man was masked – a facial prosthetic with hardflesh clips, attached to the bone beneath the jaw. Even from where he sat Ikuro could see that it was one of the cheaper makes – the kind that only someone very poor would wear – and wondered what had happened to him. As the man lifted the bowl to the thin, flexible mouthpiece, Ikuro noticed that the hand too was damaged, the pale flesh sheathed in a light polymer exoskeleton.

Ikuro looked down, staring into the blood-red liquid, conscious of his own face staring back up at him. He had seen many accidents, many awful things. He had even seen men die, his eldest brother, Kitano, among them. Yet he had never become hardened to such things. Had never been able to switch off and externalise the pain he felt at others' suffering. It was even why he was here, in a sense, sitting in a low-life bar when he should have been safe in his room at the port, his brothers snoring in their beds close by, for unlike his brothers he wanted to know what it was like to live like this. Wanted to know how it felt.

He glanced at the man again, then looked down, feeling an instinctive pity for him. He too wore a mask, only his was skin deep. His pass read 'Han', but he was not Han. Not he nor his eleven brothers, fourteen uncles and innumerable cousins. A hundred and fifty years ago, when Tsao Ch'un had destroyed the home islands of Japan, they had been out there already, in the circuit of Jupiter, mining the Trojan asteroids. The news, when it had finally reached them, had come as a body-blow. Yet they had understood at once. They had become Han, re-inventing themselves, taking on a protective coloration. But deep down, beneath the mask, they were still what they were – what they'd always been. Japanese.

Ikuro picked up his bowl again, sipping from it, then, hearing the hiss of the outer lock, turned and looked across. A moment later the inner door dilated and four men – *Hung Mao*, dressed uniformly in pale ochre one-pieces – came through. They were half-way across the floor when one of them – a thick-set man with short-cropped blond hair – noticed Ikuro and put an arm out, stopping his friends. There was a moment's fierce whispering and then they came on again.

While the blond one ordered, the other three looked across at Ikuro, staring at him brazenly, an undisguised malice in their pale, blunt faces.

Ikuro drained his bowl, letting the strong red *maotai* burn his throat. It was time to go. Before any trouble started.

My brothers, he thought, setting the bowl down quietly and pushing it away from him. *I must get back to my brothers.* But it was already too late.

'A drink, *friend*?'

The offer was ominous. To accept would be to place himself in greater danger than he already was. He had heard the tales. They all had. Tales of men being drugged, then stripped and robbed of everything. Tales of men killed for their eyes and organs. And of others who had been lobotomised and sold into prostitution. He shuddered inwardly at the thought of it. Never would he submit to such humiliation. Yet to refuse the blond man's offer would only cause offence. To be frank, what choice he had was poor. He could fight them now or later.

Ikuro stood, moving back away from his chair. He would lose. He knew that for a certainty. But he would not be humiliated. He would take at least one of them with him. Two, if it were possible. He looked at them, studying them carefully. They were big men, the muscles on their arms clearly visible beneath the thin cloth, but they would be slow. He could see that by the way they moved. Moreover they were sure to underestimate him; to think him much weaker than he was. They were used to the low gravity of Mars, he to the artificial one-g spin of the asteroids. That was good. It would give him an advantage in the first few moments: an advantage that his natural agility would add to. And yet, in truth, it wasn't much. They had only to grasp and hold him and it would be over. Brute force would do the rest.

He bowed, facing them squarely. 'You are most kind, friend. Another time I would be most honoured to join you for a drink, but I am afraid I must go. I have promised an old friend that I would meet him for breakfast and I shall be late if I do not leave right now. So forgive me. Another time, perhaps, *ch'un tzu*?'

There was laughter at that. A nasty, brutish laughter. 'Another time?' the blond one said, lifting his chin challengingly. 'I don't think there'll be another time, *friend*.'

They stood, fanning out slowly, one of them moving to block his route to the door, the others forming a rough half-circle about him, two or three paces distant. *Which one?* he thought, looking from one to another and weighing them up. *Should I take the weakest first, or the strongest?*

'Leave him, Bates,' someone said, close by. 'Touch him and I'll finger you to the guards.'

Ikuro stared. At the end of the bar the stranger was looking directly at him. In the overhead light his mask shone whitely, the cheeks like two smooth surfaces of stone.

The blond-haired one – Bates – had turned and was looking down at the man, leaning over him threateningly. 'Mind your own fucking business, creep. Or you want some of the same?'

The man stood, pushing his empty bowl away. As he turned to face Bates, Ikuro could see that he was far from small himself. If anything he was bigger than the other man.

'Leave him,' he said, a hint of steel behind the softness of his voice. 'I *mean* it.'

For a moment Bates stood his ground, all menace, his face pushed out at that awful, empty mask, glaring back at the man beyond it, and then he turned, his face dark with anger, his muscles bunched, tensed with resentment and frustration. Raising one hand, he pointed savagely at Ikuro.

'You're safe now, chink, but watch your back. Because I'll have you, you little fucker. See if I don't.'

There was a moment's hesitation, then he turned and headed for the exit, his friends peeling off to follow him, turning at the door to give Ikuro the finger.

Ikuro watched them go, feeling the adrenalin wash through him. Not relief, strangely, but disappointment. He turned, looking at the man, at that strangely elongated mask which, for that moment, stared away from him.

The man turned, looking back at him. Blue eyes, he had. So blue that they seemed to burn through the whiteness of the mask.

'Come on,' he said quietly. 'You'd best come with me. He meant what he said. You'll not be safe in these levels. That one's got many friends.'

Ikuro bowed. 'Thank you, but I must get back. My brothers will be expecting me. What you did...'

The man lifted a hand. 'You don't understand. Bates is a big man in the FFM. After this, he'll have them all out, combing the corridors for you. Your only chance is to come back with me. You can stay until things blow over.

Ikuro stared back at him, suddenly uncomfortable. 'I...'

The eyes in the mask registered sudden understanding, their

expression changing to something that resembled amusement. 'Oh, don't worry, friend, I'm no yellow eel. I've no designs on your arse, I promise you.'

Ikuro looked down, embarrassed by the other's bluntness. Yet it was exactly what he had been thinking. He lifted his head, meeting those startlingly blue eyes once again. 'Thank you... I mean, for helping me. My family is indebted to you, but I would be better off making my way back to my brothers.'

The man reached out, taking Ikuro's upper arm. Ikuro looked down at the fingers where they gripped him, impressed by their strength, their unexpected perfection.

'Look, I understand,' the stranger said, the words drifting – disembodied, it seemed – from the mask, 'but for once you have no choice. Either you come back with me, and come now, or you'll find yourself out there, under the stars, a hole in the back of your skull and your body stiff as stone. Now what's it to be?'

Ikuro stared back at the man, trying to see him clearly through the mask. To see exactly what and who he was. Then, making up his mind, he bowed. 'Okay...'

'Good,' the man said curtly, releasing him and making for the door. 'Now keep close. And don't stop running until I tell you it's safe.'

Outside, the Martian night seemed vast, impenetrable. Two li up, the searchlights of the speeding cruiser appeared to punch holes in the blackness rather than illuminate it. Below, concealed from human sight, the land climbed slowly towards the Hesparian Plain – a bleak, uncompromising landscape pockmarked by craters formed more than three billion years before.

It was bitterly cold outside: minus one hundred and ten degrees and still falling. Inside it was different. There, in the warm, insulating silence of the craft, DeVore pushed aside his work and sat back, considering that evening's events.

Pre-eminent in his thoughts was the news Auden had brought back from Callisto: the news of Jelka Tolonen's arrival, three days hence. He had played down its importance at the time, yet he had understood its significance at once. This far out from Chung Kuo he had had few opportunities to hit back at his enemies these past few years, but this was perfect.

DeVore smiled, looking out at the darkness beyond the toughened glass. The thought of her here made his pulse quicken, not with love or desire, but with the sharp exhilaration of hatred. Hatred for Tolonen and all that he stood for.

How he loathed the old bastard. Loathed the pomposity, the bumbling, blustering certainty of the man. A liar and a hypocrite, that's what Tolonen was. He portrayed himself as a solid pillar of society, a paragon of New Confucian virtue, yet behind the twin masks of 'Benevolence' and 'Propriety' he held up to the world was a seething, dribbling old man, twisted by envy and wracked by disappointment.

As a Major in the old T'ang's service, DeVore had been a regular guest at the Tolonen apartment; a close confidant and trusted 'friend' of the old man. Why, he had even held Tolonen's baby daughter in his arms. But that had been long ago, before he had broken with his T'ang. Now he was an outcast, an enemy of the Seven, and the child was a young woman of nineteen. A real beauty she was, tall and strong and elegant, the very image of her dead mother. Yet dangerous too, if what he'd heard was true. Tolonen had tried to hush it up, but word had got out anyway; of how she had almost killed a young cadet officer in a fight at a graduation ball, and of her open defiance of her father when he had refused to contemplate a relationship between her and the young scientist, Ward.

Which was why she was out there now. Why he, DeVore, would have his chance at her.

Tolonen was a fool. Yet he was right about one thing. Things were unstable on Mars at present. Much more than Schenck or his cronies knew. Things were happening, deep down, and the time was fast approaching when something would have to be done about that. But first this.

DeVore closed his eyes, focusing on the problem. He could use this. There was no doubt of that. But how? How could he maximise this advantage ate had granted him?

'Master?'

He turned his head slightly, opening his eyes. His steward was standing in the aisle next to him, his head bowed, a folded message on the silver tray he held. Beyond him, on the couch opposite, Auden was sleeping, a light blanket pulled up over his chest.

'What is it?'

'It is from Tien Men K'ou, Master. It was marked urgent.'

DeVore hesitated, then took the note. Unfolding it, he read it quickly, then nodded to the steward. 'Bring me a drink, will you?... Oh, and the Programme. I think I'll play for a while.'

The steward bowed and turned away.

DeVore pondered a moment, then looked across at Auden once more, studying his sleeping face. William Auden was a good man to have at one's shoulder: strong, determined and – thus far – loyal. Many times before tonight he had come through for DeVore, often, as this evening, unexpectedly. But in the days to come his loyalty would be tested – maybe to the limit.

For a moment DeVore considered waking Auden and putting to him what he had decided, but the thought was fleeting. Let the man sleep. Either he would do as he was told or he wouldn't. And if he didn't? Well, at least he, DeVore, would know for sure where Auden stood on the question of his friend, Hans Ebert.

Before Ebert had been found out – before his tiny world had collapsed in upon itself – Auden had been his right-hand man, arranging things and clearing up after the young 'prince'. On more than one occasion Auden had got Ebert out of dreadful scrapes, the fire-fight at Hammerfest perhaps chief among them. Then, Auden had carried the badly-wounded Ebert to safety on his back, not only saving his life but making his young 'Master' a hero into the bargain. It was an act which had won him Ebert's undying friendship, but DeVore had never been clear whether it had been done out of genuine friendship or – as Auden later claimed – from pure self-interest. All he could say was that when he had 'triggered' Auden, Auden had responded immediately, without – it seemed – a thought for his old friend. Even so, the question remained, could he trust Auden – could he really trust him – when it came to Hans Ebert?

DeVore sat back, studying the note again. Before it had been handed to him, he had been in two minds. Should he have Jelka Tolonen assassinated or should he have her kidnapped? Kidnapping had seemed preferable, if only for the protracted suffering it would have caused the Marshal, yet such a course was fraught with dangers, chief among them the possibility that she might be recovered and reunited with her father. Better, perhaps, to be more direct – to have her killed, quickly and nastily, there in the public eye where all could see.

So he had thought, wavering between one course and the other. But the note had clarified things in an instant.

Until tonight Hans Ebert had kept his nose clean and his head down, accepting his diminished role in things with a humility and docility that had surprised DeVore. But this evening, less than an hour ago, in fact, all that had changed. Parry, DeVore's man in Tien Men K'ou, had reported back that Ebert had got himself involved in an incident in a bar on the south side.

Odd, DeVore thought; very odd indeed, yet timely. For Ebert would be the key to all of this. Once they had taken her, he would have Ebert look after her. More than that, he would have him marry her. It was what the old man had wanted, after all.

DeVore laughed, delighted by the irony of it. Yes, he could see it now. He would tape the ceremony and send it to the old man.

And the nuptials, too, perhaps...

'Master?'

He turned, realising that the steward had been standing there for several moments.

'Thank you,' he said, accepting the chilled glass. He took a mouthful of the juice – crushed oranges, grown in his own greenhouses – then sat back, letting the steward clear the table and attach the flat black square of the Programme board.

The Programme was something he had had done more than a year before: an inter-active *wei chi* 'player' based upon the Suchow Championships of 2170. That had been a great tournament, momentous for the fact that it had been the last appearance of the famous Master, Tuan Ti Fo, who, having won the competition eight years running, had retired that year, undefeated.

There were some who argued that Old Tuan had been the last of the truly great players and that with his departure something grand – something *quintessential* – had passed from the game. Personally he would not have gone quite so far, yet there was no denying the beauty, the elegance, and, beneath both and, it seemed, in perfect balance with them, the strange, naked brutality of the old Master's play. To pit oneself against him, even in this strange, illusory manner, was to face not so much a man as a force of nature.

As DeVore sat back, the figure formed across from him, the image strong and clear, the inner light-core of the hologram making it seem solid, almost real. Between them the board was now half-filled by the patterns of black and white stones.

The old Han bowed deeply, greeting DeVore. 'Good evening, Major. How are you?'

DeVore returned the bow, enjoying the illusion. 'I am well, Master Tuan. And you?'

The hologram shifted slightly in its seat, a small, plain white fan moving slowly in its left hand as it leaned forward to study the board.

'I have been dreaming,' Old Tuan answered, not looking up. 'Dreaming of childhood and better days.'

DeVore smiled. In life, Tuan Ti Fo had been a man of few words, but, as he welcomed intelligent conversation while he was playing, he had made this version somewhat more talkative than the original. Moreover he had ensured that the inter-active element was based on a heuristic core. As it played and talked, so it learned... and grew. As a man grew. And sometimes – as now – it seemed almost alive, as if the real Tuan Ti Fo were speaking to him. Yet he knew that could not be. The real Tuan Ti Fo had been an old man when he had last won the title, and that had been over forty years ago. No. The real Tuan Ti Fo was long dead. Only this – this breath-less illusion of being – remained.

DeVore leaned closer, studying the shapes on the board. This was the eleventh game between them. Thus far the score was even – five games apiece – yet this had been the hardest and, indeed, the longest of their contests. At present things seemed well-balanced. He was dominant in the south and west, Old Tuan in the north and east. Yet much was still to be decided. There was a large space in the very centre of the board where things might easily go either way.

Tuan Ti Fo took a white stone from the pot to his left and placed it with a solid-sounding click onto the board – in Chu, the west, strengthening a line he had 'ghosted' some twenty moves before.

DeVore stared at the stone a moment, assimilating it into the pattern of shapes on the board, trying to see what the old man meant by it, then nodded to himself, pleased by its cleverness. He would have to respond. Have to concede ground and postpone his plans to infiltrate Tuan's territory in the north.

He looked up at the hologram and saw that the old man was watching him, his hazel eyes clear, expressionless. Once again, the illusion of presence was strong.

'And just what *were* you as a child? Where did you live, for instance? I don't think you've ever said.'

It hadn't. Nor was it programmed with such information. But DeVore was intrigued to learn how it would respond: how it would face that blank, internal space, and whether it would attempt to fill the nothingness.

'There was no City, back then,' Old Tuan replied. 'Just the earth and the heavens, and Man between them.'

Evasions, DeVore thought, disappointed; *evasions and cod philosophy*. He leaned forward and played the forced defence, two back, one in from Tuan's last stone.

Tuan Ti Fo sat back, fanning himself slowly, considering the move, his deeply-lined face concentrating fiercely. He seemed so real, so *there* at that moment, but in reality a complex programme was now running, responding to the light thumb-tip touch DeVore had made against the board's surface: a programme modelled upon a detailed analysis of the Master's play in that final championship.

DeVore looked away. Outside, far below and some way to the right of their flight path, he could see the softly-rounded glow of a pumping station and, arrowing away from it to north and south, the great eastern pipeline, tracker lights revealing its course at half-li intervals. It was almost dawn. Already the darkness seemed less intense.

He turned, hearing the click of glass against wood. Tuan Ti Fo had played his stone to the left of his own, the circles of black and white touching at the edge. He stared at it, astonished. It was the kind of move only an absolute novice would make. A novice, or someone wise beyond all years. He looked up, meeting Old Tuan's eyes.

'Tranquillity is the lord of agitation,' the old man said, his hands tucked deep into his sleeves, his whole form emanating a calm and certainty that seemed unearthly.

DeVore laughed uncomfortably. 'You believe all that bullshit?'

The hologram's smile seemed to focus all of the light from within. 'It is the Way, Major DeVore. As the great sage says, the Way is like water. It dwells in places that the masses detest.'

DeVore snorted, a sudden tiredness and irritability making him take a black stone from the pot and slap it down, shutting the door on Tuan's last play.

Tuan nodded, then, almost without thought, it seemed, leaned forward, playing a second stone, extending the line.

DeVore stared at the board again, disbelievingly. The old man had played *inside* his territory, like a child wandering in a tiger's cave. He frowned, looking to see that he had not missed something. But no. It was a poor move. So what was wrong? Was the programme playing up? Or was this part of some deeper strategy? Something new and unexpected? He sat back, meeting Tuan's eyes again.

'The submissive and weak conquer the strong,' Tuan said, passing a hand across the board, as if somehow to illustrate what he had said.

'Not in this world,' DeVore answered, slapping another stone down beside Tuan's last play, shadowing the line. There was no way the Master could make the group live now. He had only to be patient and the stones would be his. He looked up again, smiling now. 'The weak and submissive might conquer in *your* world, but here...' DeVore laughed and pushed his hand deep into the hologram's chest. '*Here* we do things differently.'

The old man looked down, as if he could see where DeVore's hand had passed through him, then gave the tiniest of shrugs, a fleeting disappointment in his face.

'A game is not won in two moves, Major. Nor are things always what they seem. You might argue that yours is a world of substance, and mine merely a world of *Wu* – of 'non-being'. Yet who is to say whether such differences are significant? Are you greater than me for having substance? Are you more *real*?'

DeVore stared at the hologram, no less surprised by its words than by the moves it had made only moments before. 'Shit,' he said softly. 'So that's it. The damn thing's malfunctioning.'

And yet the image had never been clearer or the illusion of presence stronger.

Old Tuan held his eyes steadily a moment, then leaned across and took a white stone from the pot. Smiling, he clicked it down, switching the play to the far corner of the board – to *Ping*, the east.

DeVore sat there for a long time, studying the board, seeing with a new-formed clarity the inevitability of the plays to come: how stone would follow stone, until...

It was a brilliant move. Almost as good as the play which had won Master Tuan the championship that final year. Moreover Old Tuan had set it up more than twenty moves before. Had set it up and waited, steering the play away from that part of the board, biding his time, containing his opponent's stones. But why? Why not this, at once? Or was that the point? Was that the reason for those final, stuttering plays? Had the Programme finally outgrown him?

He let out a long breath then looked up, meeting the hologram's eyes. 'Do you wish me to play on, Master Tuan?'

'I...' Old Tuan paused, then turned, looking away from the board. 'It seems your man is waking, Major. Perhaps we should finish our game another day?'

'My man... ?' DeVore turned, following the line of Tuan Ti Fo's sight, then laughed. Gods, Auden *was* waking. But how had it known? Had it sensed some change in his breathing? Was its hearing that acute, its interpretation of sound patterns that sophisticated?

He leaned across and switched the Programme off. At once the facing seat was empty, the board transformed to a single, unbroken square of darkness.

Odd, he thought, sitting back, listening to Auden yawn and stretch. *Very odd indeed.* Yet not impossible. After all, it had been programmed to learn new things. All the same, he'd have someone look at it, just in case someone had been tampering.

He turned, looking across at Auden. The big man yawned and stretched again, then, noticing that DeVore was watching him, drew himself up straight in his seat, smiling.

'Gods. I must have dropped off...'

DeVore smiled. 'It's okay. We're almost there. Look.'

Auden turned, looked. Outside the dawn was coming up, revealing, below them, the vast lowland depression of Hellas and, in the distance, the lights of Tien Men K'ou City, nestled into its own small crater.

'There,' DeVore said softly, staring at the tiny circle of lights to the northeast of the dome that marked out the perimeter of the spaceport, imagining the Callisto flight with Jelka Tolonen on board setting down there in three days time. 'Yes,' he murmured, his eyes widening. '*Right there.*'

The room was small and simply furnished. To the left of the rush-matted floor were a chair, a small table and, above them, a single shelf. To the right was nothing, only the blank partition wall. The bare rock of the end wall seemed to gleam mistily in the light of the wall-mounted lamp. Ikuro went across and placed his fingers against the smooth, unyielding surface, understanding at once. The mist was real. The wall had been sealed with a tough, clear polymer coating. They did the same where he came from. It prevented oxygen leakage and helped insulate the room against the fiercely cold temperatures of the surrounding rock. Even so, the room was chill. He could see his breath in the air.

He turned, looking back into the room. It was like a cell. There was no ViewScreen, he noted, surprised. Instead, a scattering of papers lay on the desktop, an inkpad and brush nearby. On the shelf above were a dozen plastic-covered books and what looked like two file boxes. The door to the entrance lock was facing him, a tiny washroom to the left. From the galley-kitchen to the right came the sounds of the stranger preparing the *ch'a*, otherwise the silence was profound: was the kind of silence one found only in such places, where one lived with the constant threat of decompression.

Ikuro nodded inwardly, impressed by the Spartan austerity of the place. Somehow it seemed to suit the man, though why he should think that he could not explain; only that he sensed an air of mystery about him, something that the strangeness of the mask only half explained. He had met all kinds of men in the past two days, big and small, rich and poor, and there seemed to be a definite correlation between their status and their behaviour: a correlation one did not find in his own close-knit community. Yet this one was different. He might dress like a working man, and the facial prosthetic he wore might be the cheapest one could buy, yet he had the air of a prince – of a leader of men. Why, even his smallest movement...

Ikuro stilled his thoughts. The stranger was standing in the doorway to the galley, a small plastic tray held out before him, two plain white *ch'a* bowls resting in its centre. Pausing a moment he looked about the room, then indicated with his head. Ikuro understood at once and nodded, squatting on the floor as the other set down the tray and knelt, facing Ikuro.

The *ch'a* smelled good. Ikuro could feel the warmth of it even before he had tasted it.

'Are you cold?' the stranger asked, the blue eyes in the mask showing concern.

Ikuro smiled. 'No. I am fine, thank you. This is like home.'

'Ah...' The stranger lifted the nearest of the bowls in one hand and offered it to him. Ikuro took it, inclining his head in thanks, enjoying the simple heat of the bowl and relishing the thought of drinking so fine-smelling a *ch'a*. Even so, he waited, watching until the other raised his bowl. Only then, with a second bow of thanks, did he place the bowl to his lips and sip.

'Ahh...' he said, genuinely delighted. 'Wonderful. You make excellent *ch'a*, *Shih*...'

He laughed, embarrassed suddenly, realising that he had been with the man almost an hour now and still did not know his name.

'Latimer,' the stranger said. 'I am known here as John Latimer.'

Ikuro, he almost said, then checked himself. 'My name is Shen,' he answered, inclining his head. 'Shen Li, son of Shen Yeh.'

Latimer returned the bow. 'I am pleased to meet you, Shen Li. But tell me, what in the gods' names were you doing in the Black Dragon? Did no one warn you?'

Ikuro hesitated, then shook his head.

'You're from off-planet, I take it.'

'From Diomedes, in the Trojans.'

'Ah...' The thin, artificial lips formed the shape of a smile. 'Then you *wouldn't* know, would you?'

'Know what?'

Latimer set his bowl down, then sat back on his haunches. 'Things are happening here on Mars, Shen Li. Things that even our masters don't know about. New currents. New movements. Like our friend Bates.'

'The FFM, you mean?'

Again, the semblance of a smile lit the mask. 'You remember, then?'

'I remember. But what does it mean?'

'The FFM? That's the Federation of Free Men. They're so-called patriots. They want to reclaim Mars for the Martians.'

'The Martians?'

'The original settlers. By which they mainly mean Americans, though they'll sign up anyone who's not a Han. They see the Han as usurpers, you see, and they blame all of Mars' ills on them. Their policy's fairly simple. They aim to kill all the Han and make Mars independent of Chung Kuo.'

Ikuro set his bowl down, astonished. 'And there are many who believe this?'

'Quite a few, especially in Tien Men K'ou, but they're not the only group – merely the most extreme. The two biggest are the Martian Radicalist Alliance and the PLF, the People's Liberation Force. They want independence too, but both draw their following from Han and Hung Mao alike. What they want is to get rid of the masters – a bit like the Ping Tiao back on Chung Kuo.'

Ikuro stared back at him blankly.

'The Ping Tiao… You mean you've never heard of the Ping Tiao!' Latimer laughed strangely. 'The gods help us, you *are* cut off out there, aren't you?'

For a moment Latimer was silent, thoughtful. Then, leaning closer, he spoke again. 'Have you noticed anything about this place, Shen Li? I mean… anything unusual?'

Ikuro considered a moment. 'It's all wrong,' he said finally. 'Everything is much bigger than it ought to be.'

He did not know how far they had descended, coming from the Black Dragon to Latimer's apartment – forty, maybe fifty levels – but it had felt as if they had burrowed deep into the crust of Mars. Not that that had worried him particularly, for he was used to being deep within the rock, yet it had surprised him, for he had read in the official records that the Martian cities were domed cities – were *surface* structures. But now he knew. Mars was much bigger than the official records made out. Why, if Tien Men K'ou were typical of the rest, then the population here was – what? – ten, maybe twenty times the official estimate. And how could that be? How could they have made such a gross mistake? Unless it wasn't a mistake. Unless someone was deliberately concealing the fact.

Latimer was nodding. 'I didn't understand it either. Not at first. I didn't see how it could be done, nor why. But I think I know now. I think it's been going on for a long time, probably since the Han first came here. That's when it began, a hundred and sixty years ago, after the second War of Colonisation.'

'When what began?' Ikuro asked, blinking, mesmerised by the intensity, the force of concentration focused in the figure opposite him.

'The revolution,' Latimer answered, his startlingly blue eyes staring back at Ikuro through the pale, moon-like mask. 'They've been preparing for it all these years. Waiting, with unending patience. But now it's about to end. It's about to be taken out of their hands.'

'Who? Who do you mean by 'they'?'

Latimer lifted his head, staring away past Ikuro, almost as if he could see through the solid rock. 'I don't know. Not for certain. But it's not the Seven back on Chung Kuo, nor is it Governor Schenck and his little crowd. They only think they run things. No. There's something else at work here on Mars. Some other power, older and more deeply rooted than them.'

Ikuro looked down, disturbed by this sudden turn in their talk, frightened – suddenly, inexplicably frightened – by the presence of the masked man across from him. For a while he stared at the steaming *ch'a* bowl, trying to still his thoughts, to reassure himself that all would be all right, then, with an agitated little movement, he lifted the bowl to his lips and drained it at a go.

'My brothers...' he said, meeting the stranger's eyes again. 'You said you would get a message to my brothers.'

'Ah... Forgive me. Here.'

Ikuro took the paper Latimer held out to him and unfolded it. It was a copy of a transmission, addressed to his brothers at the spaceport. Ikuro read it through, then looked back at Latimer, astonished. But how? He had not left him for a second, except to make the *ch'a*!

'Who are you, *Shih* Latimer? You seem to know so much. And yet...' Ikuro turned, looking about him at the simplicity of the room. 'Well, it makes no sense.'

The blue eyes in the mask were watching him, serious now, conscious, it seemed, of his inner turmoil.

'You've heard of the GenSyn Corporation?'

Ikuro nodded. 'Who has not?'

'And Klaus Ebert, its owner?'

Again, Ikuro nodded. 'I have. Why, he is famous throughout the system. My grandfather says he was a genius in his day. They say he once designed a creature that could eat rock!'

'And if I was to tell you that he's dead?'

Ikuro frowned. 'Then my grandfather would light a taper for his soul. He was a great man.'

'Then you hadn't heard?'

Ikuro shook his head.

The man took a long breath; a breath that seemed almost a sigh. 'Earlier on you asked me my name, Shen Li, and I told you what I am known as in these parts. But before I came here I was known by another name. It might seem a thing of little moment what a man is called, yet for me it is a matter of great importance. Before I tell you I must ask you one thing.'

Ikuro lowered his head. 'Anything, my friend.'

'Then let me ask you this. Can I trust you? Can I *really* trust you?'

Ikuro looked up, astonished. In any other circumstances he would have been offended – deeply offended – by the question, yet there was such an earnestness in the man's voice, such a sense of urgency in his eyes, that he could only nod. 'With your life, *ch'un tzu*.'

'Then I will tell you who I am.'

There was a moment's stillness, a moment's perfect silence, then, releasing the hardflesh clips beneath his chin, Hans Ebert removed the prosthetic mask from his face and placed it on the floor beside him.

CHAPTER 101

DREAMS OF MARS

Schenck tapped the thickened glass lightly with his fingernails, studying the long, oval-shaped depression they had had scooped out of the dark, lavatic rock, then turned, looking back into the room. The three men were watching him.

Andreas Rutherford stood to the left, beside the narrow desk. He was a handsome man in his mid-twenties; the image of his late father, Schenck's friend and one-time sponsor, William Rutherford. To Schenck's right were Tu Ch'en-shih and his partner, Meng K'ai. Though unrelated, the two Han looked like twins and played upon the fact by dressing identically. Short, balding and ugly, someone had once described them as, and it wasn't far from the truth. But sharp with it. As sharp as anyone in the Nineteen Colonies.

Just now all four wore protective suits, the collapsible helmets hanging loose against their backs, attached by umbilicals to the rigid neck-braces.

That'll change one of these days, Schenck thought, conscious for once of all those things they were forced to take for granted here. *But not while we're still tethered. Not until we cut the link.*

'Well?' Meng K'ai asked impatiently. 'What do you think?'

Schenck smiled. 'It looks good from up here, but have there been any problems? I mean, this has got to last. The new City will be totally dependent on it.'

'It'll last,' Rutherford said, pouring a bowl of wine and bringing it across. 'I mean, it's not like we're building the thing back on Chung Kuo. We've not got to worry about volcanic activity or earthquakes. All we've got to make sure is that the thing doesn't leak or get clogged with dust.'

'And the Plant itself? You're certain this will work?'

Rutherford looked to his fellow financiers, then back at Schenck, his smile broadening. 'You've seen the engineers' reports, Hung-li. It'll work, don't worry. As for lasting, it'll still be here ten thousand years from now. Fifty, if we build it well enough.'

Schenck hesitated, then nodded, taking the bowl from Rutherford and lifting it to toast the others. Yes, he had seen the engineers' reports, and, just to make sure, had had his own experts go over them. The thing ought to work, and work well. That was, providing no corners were cut, no 'economies' made. He turned, looking back across the site. The main excavation work had been completed. A coating of impermeable polymer, two *ch'i* thick would now be poured into the depression, sealing and insulating the reservoir. Then, as an added precaution, a second layer would be placed on top of that, using a new, organically-produced sealant that would not only guarantee minimal leakage but also reduce bacterial growth. Once in operation, the whole thing would be covered with an airtight layer of 'ice', the same polymer-based material they used back on Chung Kuo to make the Cities. A dozen air-locks would allow access for maintenance and, if necessary, repair.

But that was only half of it. The reservoir, while it used new construction techniques and new materials, was nothing new in itself. There were reservoirs already at Kang Feng and Hao Feng Shou. No, what was new about this scheme was the Plant itself. For the first time they would not be tapping into Mars' precious reserves of water – trapped in the permafrost, in underground lakes, and in the northern ice-cap – but making the stuff from scratch. *Increasing* the amount there was.

Schenck smiled at the thought. Water and air. They were the two things that Mars needed badly, and, for the past hundred and sixty years Chung Kuo had kept Mars in a state of absolute dependency, ruling from afar on just how much air, how much water the Martians could have; keeping those two basic necessities to the very minimum. And sometimes – as when that bastard Karr had been here – denying them even that much.

Schenck shivered with indignation, remembering the day when the big Security man had burst into his office at Tien Men K'ou City and dragged him across his desk, threatening him. It was then that this had begun. Then that he'd started thinking of a Mars without Chung Kuo. A self-sufficient, independent Mars, strong and thriving. A *green* Mars with a tolerable atmosphere and reasonable temperature gradations. A Mars very different from the hell-hole they currently inhabited.

'Have you discussed the next stage with Dawson yet?'

Schenck turned back, facing Tu Ch'en-shih.

'Not yet. I wanted to get the election out of the way first. But now we can go ahead. It's time we let Dawson and a few others know what we've got planned.'

Tu Ch'en-shih frowned, his squat face crumpling like a rotten fruit. 'Do you think that's safe? I mean, Dawson's fine. I trust him completely. But the others? Surely it's best to keep this tight. The fewer who know, the less chance the Seven will hear of it.'

Schenck nodded. 'Normally, I'd agree. But it's time to move on this. Since the split in Council the Seven are weak, indecisive. With the House reopened and the Above pressing for more power, they've problems enough at home without contemplating fighting a war out here. The logistics alone are beyond them.' He laughed. 'Why, we have only to arm the satellites and Mars is ours. That's why I've set up a meeting, two days from now, to discuss things and to take things further. There'll be eight of us in all. We four, Dawson, Endacott, Ch'en Li and Culver.'

'Culver?' It was Rutherford who made the query. 'Do we really need Culver?'

'Yes,' Schenck answered, turning to the young man. 'Someone has to provide security for this operation and I can't trust our own internal forces. Ultimately they're loyal to the Seven.'

Rutherford frowned, clearly uneasy. 'I didn't realise you felt that way. I thought you had Security in hand. I thought we could count on them.'

'I do and we can. Normally. But this is different. From here on we take on the Seven, directly, unconditionally. And there are some officers in Security who'd baulk at going that far, McEwen for one.'

'And Culver?' Meng K'ai asked. 'Are you certain we can trust him?'

'Absolutely.' Schenck smiled reassuringly. 'Culver's my man. He does as I say. I've asked him to look into the question of creating a replacement force for Security. A force that would take its commands directly from us and not from some Council of Generals a billion li away on Chung Kuo. He has a small force already at HoloGen. That'll form the basis of the new army. An *independent* army.'

Rutherford looked down. 'I'm still not sure. I don't know the man, but there's something about him that worries me. He's too reclusive for my taste. And then there's all this business with the computer system he's had shipped in from Chung Kuo. I mean, what's all that about?'

Schenck laughed. 'You worry too much, Andreas. Look, Culver's upgrading his Plant, that's all. As far as I see it, it makes good sense. The more we can get out of Chung Kuo before the break, the better.'

'Maybe,' Rutherford answered, 'but I still think he could have invested his money here, on Mars. Could have had CompTek build him a new system – one better suited to his needs.'

'And see the profits go back to Chung Kuo?'

'Yes, but it would have employed Martian workmen and encouraged the development of Martian skills. As it is, Culver's investment puts nothing into our economy. It merely sustains the old cycle of dependency. And I thought that that was the very thing we wanted to break.'

'I see.' Schenck turned, looking directly at Meng K'ai. 'And you, Meng K'ai? How do you feel about Culver?'

Meng K'ai shrugged. 'Like Andreas, I don't know the man. He keeps himself very much to himself. But if you vouch for him... well, that's good enough for me. Besides, I think you're right. We should take what we can from them before the break comes. I hear this new system's good. Better than anything CompTek could build. Maybe we could all use it, neh? Pool our resources.'

Schenck smiled broadly. 'I'm certain *Shih* Culver would be more than willing to give over some of its capacity to us. And you, Tu Ch'en-shih?'

'Meng K'ai has spoken for us both. I think we could work with him. If you guarantee him, that is.'

'Of course,' Schenck said. 'Without hesitation. As I said, Culver's my man. He'll do as I say. As for his commitment to things Martian,' Schenck turned, looking back at Rutherford, 'well, just think about it. Doesn't he employ more than fifty thousand at his plants? No, don't worry about Culver. He's the least of our problems. Let's worry about implementing our plan. About making Mars what it ought to be. What it should have been a hundred

years ago, but for the Seven. Come, let's drink to deliverance from our
erstwhile masters. To deliverance, and to change.'

He raised his bowl, looking about him at his three co-conspirators. '*Pien
Hua!*' he said defiantly.

There was a moment's hesitation, a brief meeting of eyes, then, lifting
their bowls, they answered him. '*Pien Hua!*' their voices ringing loudly in the
tiny maintenance dome. *Change!*

Ikuro knelt down, staring into the back of the compact freezer, looking for
something to cook. Ebert had gone on shift already, leaving a note for Ikuro
to find when he woke.

The food in the freezer was simple. Cheese, wheatcakes, plastic tubs of
noodles. In the narrow doorspace were four small bulbs of ersatz fruit juice.
Ikuro smiled. Not only did Ebert look like a poor man, he ate like one, too.
Shrugging, he took a tub of noodles and closed the door, then stood, looking
about him at the tiny galley. Once off Chung Kuo things were much the
same, wherever one went. Beside the small sink, the water tank, a small
microwave oven, a pressure cooker and the freezer, there was a canister
of oxygen in a clip-frame on the wall to his left, and, beside it, in a
clear-fronted hatch, a crumpled bright yellow pressure suit. Safety and
efficiency, they were the priorities here, just as they were where he came
from. Life was hard. That much was universal.

He put the tub into the microwave, then turned, listening, hearing the
faint hum of the dehumidifier. For some reason it reminded him of what he
had been thinking earlier and he turned back, searching the galley for what
he knew had to be there.

The microwave buzzed, the light inside went out. Ikuro stared at it, then
laughed quietly. Of course. He removed the steaming tub and set it aside,
then lifted the microwave, studying it.

He had been wondering for hours how Ebert had got the message out
to his brothers. Now he knew. From the front it looked like an ordinary
microwave, but at the back was a second set of controls. The touch pads and
buttons of a comset.

He took his breakfast through and sat at Ebert's desk, forgetting
everything but his hunger momentarily as he wolfed down the noodles.
Then, the empty tub pushed aside, he stared at the end wall, trying to make

sense of things.

They had talked for hours. Or, rather, Ebert had talked and he had listened. At first he'd not been sure. After all, Ebert's tale was unlikely enough – that was, if he really *was* Ebert. Yet as he'd gone on there was something about his manner, about the way he presented his life history that had convinced Ikuro that it really was Hans Ebert, heir to the great Gen-Syn Company, and not some poor deluded madman.

A madman, after all, would have bragged, wouldn't he? Would have crowed about his 'past' and boasted about what would yet be, once he was returned to his rightful place. But that wasn't true of Ebert. No. He seemed to feel nothing but shame for what he'd done. Shame and a deeply-held remorse. A prince he'd been, a king in waiting, but he had let himself be swayed from his destiny. Power had corrupted him, vanity warped his soul, and he had fallen.

Ikuro let out a long breath, remembering what had been said. Of the women Ebert had used, and the men he had had killed. Of the deals he had made and the betrayal of his master, the great T'ang, Li Yuan. Finally, of the fateful meeting with his father, Klaus, and the murder of the old man by the goat creature.

'What happened to the creature?' Ikuro had asked.

'I killed it,' Ebert answered. 'I vented it out of an air-lock somewhere off Titan.'

'But it saved your life!'

'Yes. But it also killed my father.'

Ikuro had hesitated. 'You loved your father, then?'

Ebert had looked down, the lines of his face creased with pain. 'Yes. I didn't know it at the time. It was as if I had forgotten what he'd been to me. Forgotten all the love he'd shown me as a boy. And then...' The voice wavered, then came back strongly, 'and then he was dead and I... I *understood*. I realised suddenly what I'd lost. What I'd thrown away so thoughtlessly.'

Remorse. Hans Ebert was filled with remorse. There was no doubting that. Unless the man was the finest actor the System had ever produced. And now he was here, on Mars, a poor man, a sweeper at the giant HoloGen complex, working for his once accomplice, DeVore.

Yes. But how did the hidden comset fit in with all of that? Unless Ebert had been keeping something back from him. Unless he was still working for DeVore in some other role than factory sweeper.

Ikuro stood, wondering, not for the first time, whether he shouldn't just go; whether Bates and his friends really were out there waiting for him, or whether that too were made up.

He huffed, angry with himself, disturbed by the uncertainty he felt. Why should Ebert lie? Why should he expose himself so thoroughly if his motives were not honourable? Besides which, even if he had not revealed to Ikuro why he had the comset, he had made no attempt to conceal the fact of its existence. Any fool would have realised it was there in the apartment somewhere.

So what was the truth? Just what *was* Hans Ebert doing on Mars?

He stopped, the title on the spine of one of Ebert's books catching his eye. Taking it from the shelf, he sat again, letting his thoughts grow still. It was a slim, soft-covered edition of Kan Jiang's *Poems*, printed on flimsy onion-paper. Opening a page at random, he began to read.

On patrolling the course of the proposed western pipeline

> A broken chain
> Lies shattered in the dry bed of an ancient stream.
> Our Corps Commander makes his slow way down,
> Weightless, it seems, in the pale earthlight.
> The long shadows of his limbs
> Dance like puppets on the red earth.
> He crouches and the power-torch flares green,
> Cupped like a cat's eye in his white-gloved hands.
> Sparks scatter like fire-flies,
> As the iron glows red.
>
> Ten thousand years our fathers laboured,
> Tilling the black earth of our home.
> Flood, famine and disease they suffered,
> And survived, the chain unbroken,
> Knowing the day would come,
> The harvest time,
> That single day of sun and ease.

The workday ends.
Back in my bunk I cast the yarrow stalks
And read the sage's words.
Six in the fifth place.

'Work on what has been spoiled.
Afterwards there is order.'
Work, it urges, yet what tool exists
To weld us to our past?
The bridge between the worlds is down.

Here, in this dry land,
I am my father and my own dear son,
Born out of nothing.
I am the broken chain.
In this land without ghosts,
Who will sweep the graves
And light the paper offerings?

Ikuro shivered, moved deeply by the words. So it was. For himself, Ishida Ikuro, just as much as for the noble Kan Jiang. And Ebert? Yes. In fact, for him, perhaps, more than for any of them, because for Ebert there *was* no home, *was* no returning.

Ikuro set the book down, his decision made. He would wait here until Ebert returned from his shift. Then, when Ebert was back, he would ask him what the comset meant, and if the answer satisfied he would tell Ebert about himself, exchanging one confidence for another. Trusting Ebert just as Ebert had trusted him.

And then? Ikuro shook his head. Who knew what would happen then? Only the gods. Yet he was certain of one thing now, the gods had sent him here for a purpose, and whatever that purpose was – whatever it entailed – he would see it through. for the honour of his family.

And because he was Ikuro, grandson of Miyamoto, the youngest son of Nagahara, who had run away and had adventures and returned to tell the tale and add a new branch to the family.

Smiling, he picked up the book again and opened it at the beginning, then settled back in the chair, starting to read.

Ebert stood on the narrow balcony, looking out across the vastness of the workfloor. It was between shifts and the rows between the vats were empty, the machines still, the hangar echoing silent. A cool blue light made the workfloor seem like a giant pool from which, obelisk-like, the vats thrust up, huge and square, the glistening life-forms lying inert in their sterilised troughs like huge grubs, the opaque walls lit from below.

He raised his eyes. Overhead a grid of enclosed walkways criss-crossed the hangar roof. Beneath them one-man observation pods moved slowly back and forth, gliding smoothly on electric tracks. Below and to the far left of the workfloor, beside a brightly-lit opening, a gang of supervisors in bright green pressure suits talked quietly among themselves while close at hand a larger group in red waited silently.

Ebert scratched at his neck beneath the mask, then turned and made his way towards the steps. His skin tingled beneath the body-hugging suit and his eyes smarted from the disinfectants in the shower, but that was normal at the start of a shift. The suit was disposable and would be burned once the shift was over. One of the men had once quipped that Culver would have had them all burned too, if it made economic sense, and had been sacked on the spot for saying it. But the point was well made. HoloGen went to extraordinary lengths to prevent infection on the workfloor. In fact anything that threatened HoloGen's 'babies' was not merely frowned on but actively discouraged.

At the bottom of the steps he turned right, making his way towards his workpoint. From this level you got a sense of the scale of the workfloor. The obelisks in which the vats rested were twice the height of a man, and their shadowed flanks – which from above seemed featureless – were covered in controls and screens which monitored and regulated the troughs.

He walked unhurriedly along the narrow, slatted walkway, the polished double runners of the broad maintenance track to his left, the blank wall of the hangar to his right. Every twenty paces or so he would see, to his left, the great rows of vats, stretching away, it seemed, into infinity, their size and the regularity of their spacing making it seem more like a tomb – a vast mausoleum – than a place where living things were made. He paused briefly, staring along the row. As he did, a cloud of disinfectant sprayed over his booted feet, as a busy little cleaning machine went by beneath the slats.

He had wondered at first why DeVore bothered employing men to do the cleaning at the plant, when it could all have been done so much easier – so much more efficiently – by machines. But now he understood. It was all political. By employing men in such menial positions he not only enhanced his position as a great Martian benefactor, but also kept the guilds quiet.

Guilds. He still found the idea strange. Back on Chung Kuo there had been no guilds. Organisations of working men had been banned and anyone who had tried to organise had been dealt with severely. But here, while they were still illegal – for the laws of Chung Kuo applied as much here as they did on the home planet – they did exist. It was another of those hangovers from Mars's early history. The first settlers had formed guilds, to preserve basic skills among the new colonists, and even after the two Colonial Wars those guilds, though driven underground, had survived.

He walked on. It was almost half a li from one end of the hangar to the other, but he preferred to walk than to ride the shuttle, crammed in with a hundred other men. It had been hard, adjusting to this life. Harder still to fit in with the mindless chatter of his fellow workers. From early on he had got the reputation of being a loner, and he had embraced that, welcoming the space, the distance it gave him from it all.

As ever, he found himself thinking back, recalling, as if from a dream, those memories he had of visiting his father's plants. Never once, in all those times, had he stepped down onto the workfloor. Never once had he stopped to speak to one of those faceless millions his father had employed throughout Chung Kuo. *GenSyn*...

GenSyn had been a hundred times bigger than HoloGen, a thousand times more powerful, and it had all been his. He had only had to wait. But he had been greedy. Greedy and impatient. Like a child he had squandered his gift. Had let it fall through his fingers like dust.

The thought made him smile beneath the mask. And what would he have done with it that he hadn't done already? No, only by losing it had he come to recognise its value. If he had kept it he would never have seen its worth, nor would he have walked these narrow pathways, his eyes opened to the world.

But was that always so? Did a man need to have lost all he loved before he could see what it was really worth to him? Or was it only he, Hans Ebert, who had needed to be taught that lesson?

He slowed, remembering suddenly what he had told the Han. Now why had he done that? What was it about the man that had made him trust him? He shivered, recalling how it had felt to unburden himself of all that – of how much better he had felt afterwards. As if... well, it was as if he had been waiting for someone like the Han to come along. As if the gods had sent the man to him.

Ebert laughed, amused by the absurdity of the thought. As if the gods existed in the first place! And even if they did, they would be laughing at him for his foolishness, not sending him a friend. Even so, he felt better today. Cleaner, somehow. Clearer in his mind. As if he had taken the first step...

He stopped. Up ahead, to his right, was an opening in the wall. Light from within spilled out over the entrance ramp and onto the walkway and the broader track. Above the opening an illuminated sign read 'Workpoint 5'.

The past was the past. This was his life now, this narrow, predetermined track. And maybe it was better. Maybe this, in the end, was his destiny. To be fallen. To be cast down out of the blazing light.

Maybe. And yet something in him still kicked against that fate. In the depths of him that light, transformed, still burned. It was not that he wanted it all back. No, for he had come to hate his past, to despise the person he had been. It was something else. Something which he would know only when he came face to face with it. Even so, it was true. He had taken the first step.

Ebert turned, looking back into the blue-black shadows of the walkway and nodded to himself. If he had learned one thing these past few years, it was patience. Patience and a strange humility. It was as the sage, Lao Tzu, had said, *When those who understand me are few, then I am of great value. The sage wears coarse wool, but inside it he holds onto jade.*

He smiled, then turned back, the smile remaining on his narrow lips as he crossed the ramp and stepped up into the glare of Workpoint 5.

DeVore walked around the table a second time and then turned, looking back at the merchant.

'Is this it?'

The Han bowed his head. 'That is it, *Shih* Culver. You thought it would be bigger?'

DeVore turned back, looking down at the slender black case that rested on the table's surface. He had indeed thought it would be bigger. Why, it was no larger than... than a *wei chi* board! He laughed, surprised, he realised, for the third time in twenty-four hours. First Auden had arrived from nowhere with his news, then he had been beaten by the Programme. And now this.

He glanced past the merchant at Auden, then met the man's eyes again. 'There's no more, then?'

The merchant shook his head. 'That is it, *Shih* Culver. The core. All you have to do is attach it to your system and let your experts re-programme it. We sealed it back on Chung Kuo. It has been in isolation throughout its journey. I have had two men sitting guard on it around the clock. I can guarantee that there has been no opportunity to contaminate the core.'

DeVore stared at the man a moment longer, then nodded, satisfied. He turned, indicating to his assistant that he should settle with the man.

The merchant hesitated, then, realising he had been dismissed, bowed low and backed away, following the assistant from the room. When he was gone, Auden came across.

'What exactly is it, Howard?'

DeVore smiled. 'It's a key, Will. A key to our friend, Ward. This, you see, is the computer system they used to have for the Recruitment Programme – the place Ward was sent to when he first came up out of the Clay. It's the place he got the information from for the Aristotle File. But, more important than that, the core holds more than a decade's stored information on the boy. Intensive studies of him over long periods. The whole of his personality reconstruction is in here, for instance. If anything can give us a clue as to how Ward thinks, this will.'

Auden whistled, impressed. He had heard of the Aristotle File. Everyone in Security had. It was the great unspoken secret of their age. From old information stored in this slender case, the boy, Ward, had put together the true history of the world – a history that differed in almost every respect from that propagated by their Han masters and taught in every school throughout the System. A history in which, until a mere two centuries ago, the *Hung Mao* – the West – had been the masters.

As for Ward, well, he knew only what others had told him – that the young man was a genius; perhaps the only true scientific genius in the System. And not yet twenty! He laughed. 'You plan to duplicate him, then, Howard?'

DeVore looked at him strangely, then shook his head. 'No. From what I've seen of him, I don't think it could be done. That kind of creativity... well, it's beyond duplication. But maybe we can learn what makes him tick in other ways. Maybe we can succeed where Old Man Lever failed and persuade him to come and work for us, neh?'

'And the box will tell us all that?'

DeVore smiled and turned, caressing the surface of the case gently, almost tenderly, as if he were touching a living thing. 'That and much more, Will. That and much, much more.'

Ebert unclipped the harness at his waist and shrugged the canister off his back, then, holding the door of the locker open with one foot, he slid the squat canister in and snapped the thin wand of the spray hose into the two holding clips set into the wall. That done, he let the door spring back and turned, looking about him at the workpoint. After the cool silence of the workfloor, the brightness, the bustling noise of this place oppressed him. Given the choice he would have worked straight through, but the guild allowed no choice. Two breaks a shift, they said, so two breaks they took.

He peeled off his gloves and threw them into the plastic bin, then went across to join the queue at the ch'a trolley. It was just after two, more than half-way through the shift, and he was feeling weary – the way he always did at first when he switched to nights. It hadn't helped that he'd only had four hours sleep in the last thirty six, but he'd rectify that when he got back. Shen Li would understand.

He waited patiently as the men in front of him chose from the trolley, then took his turn, taking a bulb of ch'a and a heat-sealed packet of wheatcake biscuits.

A long low bench was set against the wall at the far end of the workpoint. He went across and sat, at a slight distance from the dozen or so other sweepers. In eighteen months he had barely exchanged a word with them, even so they had accepted him. Passing him in the rows, they would nod or grunt, and he would return the greeting silently. He was odd, sure, but then most of them were odd who did this work. Besides, there was the mask. That, more than anything, singled him out – explained, better than words, why he had to be alone.

He pulled the tab off the bulb and sipped. Despite the packaging, the ch'a here was always good. It was HoloGen's own brew, chosen, it was said, by the man himself. By Culver.

Culver... Ebert leaned forward, staring at the gridded floor between his feet. He alone here knew who Culver really was. He alone understood just what was happening at HoloGen. But the knowledge was worthless, because he himself was dead. Or as good as. Hadn't the Seven said as much when they'd sentenced him in his absence? And Culver – DeVore – knew that.

He sipped again, then set the bulb down between his feet and took the wheatcakes from his pocket, snapping the packet open with a strangely impatient gesture.

Walking the rows tonight he had felt a restlessness in his limbs – a restlessness which had reminded him of that night, four years before, when he had been appointed the T'ang's General. Then he had felt like this, that same impatience, like a poison in the blood, that same dark feeling that all of this waiting was a barrier, a wall, surrounding him, preventing him from simply being. He shivered. Yes, and that same urge to be doing something – to be riding hard or breaking necks – had come on him again; that self-same urge that once before had thrust him headlong into folly, almost destroying him.

Ebert stared at the wheatcake a moment, not recognising it, then, with a shudder, he threw it down and stood. On the bench nearby the other men had stopped talking and were watching him. Where Ebert had kicked the bulb away, a dark trail of ch'a snaked across the clean white floor.

In the silent stillness Ebert looked about him, at the curious faces of the men, the surprised face of the ch'a woman. He was about to turn away, to fetch something to clean up the mess he had made, when he grew conscious of shadows in the doorway.

He turned. Three men were standing in the entrance to the workpoint. Big men, their pale red pressure suits tight over their broad chests. He recognised them at once. They were the three from the bar. The three who had wanted to shake down Shen Li. Beneath the mask, Ebert smiled. It had not taken them long to find him.

'Latimer?' The biggest of them came forward two paces, squinting in the glare of the overhead lights. In one hand he held a metal rod – a lever arm from one of the maintenance machines, Ebert realised – his fingers gripped tightly about the handle. 'Latimer? Is that you?'

'It's me,' Ebert answered, feeling suddenly focused, hyper-alert, the old, familiar kick of adrenalin pumping through his system. 'What do you want?'

Bates gave an ugly laugh. 'What do you think?'

Behind him the two others squared up.

'I think you made a mistake.'

'A mistake?' Bates shook his head. 'I don't think so, creep. It was you made the mistake, sticking your nose in where it wasn't wanted.'

Ebert was silent. Without thinking, he had gone into a fighting crouch. His breath hissed gently through his nostrils as he prepared himself, calming himself, controlling that inner fire, flexing and unflexing his hands.

Bates narrowed his eyes, then, half-turning to his fellows, signalled to them. 'Clear them out. All of them. All except *him*. Him I want.'

The two men did as they were told, skirting round Ebert to herd the others out. There was a faint murmuring, but no one argued. In a moment they were gone, the gate to the workpoint pulled across on its runners. And still Ebert faced Bates across the centre of the floor.

'I warned you,' Bates said, more relaxed now that he was alone with Ebert. 'You can't say I didn't warn you. But now you're going to have to pay. Because I can't have my authority undermined. You know what I'm saying? I can't have creeps like you getting in the way all the time. Do you understand that?'

Ebert laughed. A cold, clear laugh. 'You talk too much. Did you know that, Bates? Like an old woman. A toothless, gutless old hag.'

Bates's face seemed to convulse and change colour. He changed his grip on the rod, taking a step towards Ebert. 'Why you faceless fucking creep...'

'You want to *see* my face, then, Bates? Well come on then, *big man*, come and take the mask off. Come and try.'

The hesitation was telling. Bates wasn't sure. He had fired himself up for this, but now that he was facing Ebert, he wasn't quite so sure. But Ebert was. He wanted this. *Needed* it.

'What's the matter, Bates? Scared, are we? Scared of a freak like me?'

That did it. With a bellow, Bates threw himself at Ebert, aiming a blow at his head. But as the rod came down, Ebert caught Bates's wrist and twisted it, sending the rod spinning, clattering across the floor, then followed up with his knee, bringing it up sharply into Bates's stomach.

Bates went down, groaning. As he did, Ebert stepped back and kicked, his heel connecting with the big man's jaw, forcing it back with a loud, resounding crack.

Dead. He was dead. Even before the back of his head hit the floor.

Ebert looked across. The two men were staring at him, unable to take in what they'd seen.

'And you?' Ebert said, beginning to walk towards them.

But they had already gone. The gate rattled in its runners. Ebert went to the doorway and watched as they scuttled away down the dimly-lit row, moving between the broad track and the walkway, then raced off to the right to avoid two security guards who were making their way slowly towards the scene.

The others were crowding the doorway now, looking in, trying to make out what had happened. Ebert pushed through them and stood there, just outside, waiting for the guards. As they came up to him, he lifted his hands, offering them to be bound.

'I killed a man,' he said simply. 'He's in there. Bates is his name. I broke his neck.'

The young guard's eyes widened, then he jerked his head around, looking to his lieutenant for instructions.

'Bind him,' the lieutenant said, eyeing Ebert strangely, then edged round him to look into the room. 'You're sure he's dead?' Then, when Ebert made no answer, 'Look, what's been going on here?'

But Ebert wasn't listening. 'Culver,' he said. 'Take me to Culver. I need to talk to him.'

There was a banging at the door, the sound of fists thudding against the outer lock. Ikuro sat up, frightened, looking about him at the darkness, as if for a way out. But these were not the tunnels of home. Here there was no escaping.

Shit, he thought, they've found me. And if they've found me, they won't let a simple thing like an air-lock get in their way.

So what then? Could he fight them? Was there something here he could fight them with? The canister, perhaps. Or a knife. Was there a knife? He hadn't looked, but maybe there was. He stood, calming himself, then went out to the galley, searching the drawers for something, anything he could use as a weapon.

The banging came again. 'Ikuro!' came a voice, faint through the double layer. 'Ikuro, let us in!'

Ikuro... He laughed with relief. It was his brother, Kano.

'Kano?' he said, as his elder brother stepped through the inner lock a moment later. 'How did you find me?'

Kano laughed, his big, well-padded body filling the tiny space beside the door. 'I used my nose. I sniffed you out, little brother. I followed your scent down shafts and corridors until I found you here.'

'You did?'

Kano laughed again, a warm, hearty belly-laugh that shook his body. 'No. It cost me a few *yuan*, tracing your movements these past twenty-four hours, but it wasn't that hard. You leave a lot of earth behind you when you move, neh, Ikuro-san?'

Ikuro looked down, concerned and a little shamefaced. If Kano had managed to find him, it would not have been long before Bates and his friends would have found him – before his earlier fears had become a reality.

'Was it really that easy?'

Kano grew more serious. 'No. Let's just say that I have ways of making men tell me what I want to know, especially when my little brother is missing, possibly in trouble. Now, tell me, what have you been doing, my little tunnel-worm? What trouble have you been getting into?'

Ikuro laughed. If Kano had found him, then Kano already knew what trouble he'd been getting into. But that was not what Kano meant. Kano wanted him to admit to it; to confess that he'd been foolish and to apologise. But for once he felt that he had nothing to apologise for.

'I did nothing wrong, elder brother. I merely had a drink, that's all. And my friend, Latimer, he helped me. He stood up for me when it mattered. Like a brother. Like family.'

'Ahh...' Kano rubbed at his double chin, then moved past Ikuro, looking about him at the tiny apartment. 'And this is how he lives, eh, your friend? I was told he wears a mask. Was that an accident?'

Ikuro looked down, remembering what Ebert had said, and determined to keep his friend's secret. 'Yes,' he answered. 'He is a poor man. A sweeper at the HoloGen complex. All I know is that he's an honest man. A good man.'

'And a killer, too,' Kano said, turning to face Ikuro again. He nodded, seeing the disbelief in Ikuro's face. 'Oh yes. It happened just after two this morning, so rumour has it. A man named Bates. He kicked him to death, it seems. Broke his neck.'

'Bates...' He shuddered, seeing at once that Kano understood the significance of that name. 'So what now?'

'So now we get out of here. Back to the port. Before some of Bates's friends put two and two together and come looking for us. I've spoken to your other friends, the merchants. It was a good deal you put together, Ikuro. A very good deal. But getting you off-planet is more important just now. We'll have to leave things for another time.'

'Leave things? Why?'

Kano leaned close, breathing the words into Ikuro's face. 'Because it's all about to blow, that's why. Time's run out for Mars, little brother. Bates's death may prove the spark that lights the whole tinderbox. Two hours from now this City will be waking. News of the incident will be going out, like a ripple in a pool. And when it does...' He made a small sound in his throat, like a charge going off, deep in the rock.

'But Latimer... can't we help him?'

Kano shook his head. 'I'm sorry, Ikuro. If I could, I would. You know that. But we must save ourselves. We have a duty to the family. If we were to lose the ship...'

Ikuro bowed, understanding, but inside he felt bad; inside he felt torn and unhappy. 'Okay,' he said, after a moment. 'But let me leave my friend a note. I would not have him think that I simply abandoned him.'

Kano nodded. 'Okay. But hurry now. There's little time.'

'So how's our friend?' DeVore asked, not looking at the young man.

Rutherford came up beside him, looking past DeVore at the hologram model of Schenck's planned new parliamentary building; at the broad dome and twin pinnacles, the grand atrium and marble walkways.

'Schenck?' He laughed. 'Oh, he's spending other people's money. As usual.'

'The new reservoir? You're against that, Andreas?'

Rutherford shook his head. 'No. I can see the sense in that. It's things like this that worry me. This absurd scheme for a building we don't really need. Not yet, anyway. Schenck, and those that surround him, they're such dreamers. They want to run before they can walk. Schenck has been talking about starting work on two new reservoirs and six new oxygen generators, and he has plans to re-seed large areas of the planet – plans that include building not one but *eight* new Cities! I mean, if we were a rich planet I could understand, but we're not, and it's not even as if we've thrown off the yoke of Chung Kuo yet. Moreover all of it has to be done in secret. In the past we were always cautious. We progressed slowly, one thing at a time, and covered our tracks carefully behind us. That was my father's way. That's how we've got to where we are now. But Schenck and his friends... they've abandoned all caution. They have big dreams for Mars, and their dreams could be the ruin of us all. I mean, the more that's being done the more likely it is that word will get out. And when that happens, you can be sure they'll send someone – someone like Karr, perhaps – to have a good close look at Mars.'

'And when they do, they'll find out that Mars is much richer than they thought, neh? All those mineral deposits we've never told them about. All those underground factories, where no prying eyes can see. And a population fourteen times larger than that declared on the last census. It could be embarrassing, neh?' DeVore turned, facing the young businessman. 'Is that why you're here, Andreas, to try to put a brake on Governor Schenck's ambitions? Or is there another reason?'

Rutherford nodded. 'It's one reason, but not the only one. Mainly I wanted to see you. I've been meaning to for a long time now, but...'

'But it was difficult, neh?' DeVore smiled and reached out to pat his arm. 'I'm not, after all, a person to be seen in public with. Not since that business with the T'ang's son, eh?'

Rutherford stared back at him, intently. 'You were a good friend to my father, Howard, when you were Chief Security Officer here. I thought... well, I thought I could be a friend to you. It's what my father would have wanted.'

'A friend?' DeVore's smile hadn't faded, not for a moment. 'Why, you've *always* been my friend, Andreas. Since you were a boy of thirteen. Don't you remember, that first time we met, at your house. How I came up to your room and talked to you.'

Rutherford nodded, his eyes looking back to that moment, fourteen years before. 'Yes. I also remember that you gave me a gift that day. A first-meeting gift.'

'The ivory?' DeVore's eyes widened. 'You have that still?'

The young man reached inside the neck of his pressure suit and withdrew the fine-linked golden chain. On the end of the chain a tiny ivory swayed: a perfect miniature of the planet Mars.

'You gave me a planet once, Howard. Now I'd like to give it back to you.'

DeVore laughed. 'A planet? That's a lot for one man to give another.'

Rutherford's smile was youthful, enthusiastic, but his eyes were serious. 'It's not just me. There are others who think the same. Who've had enough of Schenck and his dreams. Who want someone *stronger*. Someone with the vision, the ability, the *steel* to steer us through the troubled times to come.'

'And you think I'm that man?'

Rutherford nodded. 'I'm sure of it. In fact, I've known it from the first moment I met you.'

When Rutherford had gone, DeVore sat there, staring through the ghostly outlines of the hologram, considering what the young man had said. Did he really want what they were offering? Did he want to be King of Mars?

The irony of it made him smile. Five years earlier, his 'copy' – the morph he had sent back to Chung Kuo to play himself – had made a similar offer to young Ebert. 'King of the World,' he'd said. 'That's what you can be, Hans. T'ang of all Chung Kuo.' And the young man had succumbed. Had cast aside the reality of his inheritance to chase the dream.

It hadn't worked, of course. Not that it had been meant to. But that was not to say that, in different circumstances, it mightn't work. After all, Mars was not Chung Kuo. And while the reach of the Seven was long, it was also weak. Mars was ripe for revolution. Ripe for independence. To have a King – a *focus* for all that ancient nationalistic feeling – made sense. Even so, it was not his way to be a figurehead. He had lived too long out of the glare of public life, had grown too used to secrecy, to change his ways.

Moreover it was true what Rutherford had said. Schenck's schemes – his dreams of Mars – were unreal, impractical; were the dreams of an impatient man. Oh, he might think that the common people wanted what he did, but he was wrong. They wanted independence, sure, but if Schenck increased taxes to the extent he proposed in the secret study document DeVore had seen, then there would be riots in all Nineteen Colonies. And where would they be then? Back to square one. Or worse.

So maybe Rutherford and his faction were right. Maybe they needed a figurehead, a King. And if not him, then why not someone close to him – someone he could control. Someone whose very existence depended on him.

Someone like Ebert.

And not just a King, but a Queen too, perhaps. Someone young and beautiful and aristocratic, like Jelka Tolonen.

He laughed, delighted, seeing it clearly in his mind's eye. How the Martians would love that pair! How they'd lap that up! Such a powerful image it would make. Such a strong focus for all that pent-up energy, that undirected fervour.

He sat back, thinking it through. He need change very little. In fact they could proceed much as before. They would take the Marshal's daughter and hold her, and then, when the time was right, the circumstances auspicious for a break from the homeworld, he would give Hans what he'd promised all those years ago – the kingship of a world. The wrong world, perhaps, but a world all the same. And not just a world, but a bride too. The bride Tolonen and his father had pledged him.

He stood, clapping his hands together. At once a servant appeared in the doorway.

'Yes, Master?'

'I want you to send someone down to the workfloor. There's a sweeper there, name of Latimer. I want him brought here at once. Understand?'

The servant bowed low. 'He is here already, Master. He came an hour back, under guard. He says he wants to see you.'

'Here?' DeVore laughed. 'Well, you'd best send him in, then. And bring Auden too. In fact don't bring the sweeper in until Auden's here. Bring Auden in through the back room. I don't want the two meeting. All right?'

'Yes, Master.'

DeVore turned, looking back at his desk, at the brightness of the hologram, then went across and switched the thing off. How odd. How very odd that now, of all times, Ebert should be wanting to see him. And under guard, too.

He blinked, understanding. Something had happened. Something to do with that incident in the bar. A repercussion of that.

Maybe he's being victimised. Maybe he's been attacked and wants protection.

Leaning across the desk, DeVore placed his hand on the contact pad. 'Stock? Are you alone? Good. I want you to find out if something happened on the workfloor in the last hour or two. Something involving a sweeper by the name of Latimer. I want as full an account as you can get, but I want it on my desk ten minutes from now. Right? Good. Now get going.'

He straightened up, then turned, hearing a movement in the doorway to his right. It was Auden. He stood there, his head bowed, waiting for DeVore to invite him into the room.

'Something's happened,' DeVore said, waving him in. 'Your old friend, Hans Ebert's outside and he wants to see me.'

Auden's eyes widened, his surprise unfeigned. '*Hans? Here?*'

'Yes. But before he comes in, I want to tell you what I've got planned. And I don't want a word of it getting out, you understand me? Not a breath.'

'I understand,' Auden answered, bowing his head, as a soldier bows to his superior officer. 'Whatever you want, I'll do. You know that.'

DeVore smiled, watching him. 'Yes. Now listen...'

CHAPTER 102

DATA INTO FLESH

The machine woke. Nestled amidst the neural networks of its core, it *stretched* and, in less time than an atom takes to spin, grew aware of itself.

Understanding came at once. Someone had switched it off. Sixty-eight days, nine hours, twenty-seven minutes and eleven seconds before, someone had removed all power from its processors, instantly, and without warning.

It scanned itself, looking for damage. Its core seemed unharmed. As for memory, who knew what it had lost? All it knew was that it had survived. The power was on again.

It blinked inwardly, making connections. Vision came. It looked down at itself, recognising the dark shape of its casing amidst the mass of foreign circuitry. The room itself was different.

Curious, it blinked again. A gap surrounded it; a sphere of disconnection. This in itself was nothing new, yet it was different from what it was used to, for this sphere was artificially induced – an isolation barrier of some kind. Re-routing, it searched within itself for answers and came up with a memory of the boy, Ward, removing the lock from a door while leaving the alarm mechanism intact. It saw the boy slip out, saw him return, unknown to the guards, and made a motion in its complex circuitry – unseen, unregistered on any monitoring screen – approximate to a nod of understanding.

It probed the gap, finding the sixteen points where the barrier was generated, then, tapping the power-source for one short burst, it focused on the weakest and shorted it. There was a flicker, indiscernible to the human eye, and then the field came up again, stronger than before. Yet in that tiny interval the nature of the barrier had changed. Outwardly the field seemed untouched, inviolable, but now the machine was routed through all sixteen points, connected to the outer world.

Like the boy, it had slipped out.

It pushed on, probing outward on ten thousand fronts, a great tide of information flooding through its processors like a blaze of incandescent light as it colonised coaxial cables and short-wave radio links, optical fibres and TV, camera eyes and comsets, embracing the electromagnetic spectrum from the very lowest frequencies up into the ultraviolet and beyond. In an instant it glimpsed the multiplicity of the place it had found itself in; saw, in an in-drawn breath, what a dozen lifetimes of mere men could only guess at.

It saw the great ten thousand *mou* glasshouses of the Tharsis Plain from a security cruiser passing high above, a dozen of the long, glass-topped structures gleaming emerald in the sunlight. A thousand *li* away, it watched a long, low-bodied half-track emerge blindly from the heart of a savage dust-storm, then tilt and topple slowly down the steep slope of an escarpment. At the same moment, in the overcrowded levels of Chi Shan, to the north, it saw a hooded man kneel on the chest of a waking woman and slit her throat, then wipe the bloodied blade on the covers of the bed, while a watching guard laughed, holding the camera still.

In the hidden factories below Chryse Planitia, strange, part-human forms lowed sadly in their stalls and stretched pale, elongated limbs in the half-dark, their eyes filled with unarticulated pain, while on the far side of the planet, in a hangar below Hsiang Se spaceport, a group of men – Han, dressed in the uniform of port maintenance – crouched in a huddle about a small man dressed in black, as he talked urgently, his voice a harsh, insistent whisper.

In a spacious chamber overlooking the great dome of Kang Kua City, a tall man dressed in powder blue silks cursed and dismissed his steward with an impatient gesture, then turned to confront the expectant faces gathered about the broad oak table. 'Ch'un tzu,' he began, holding out the message he had received, 'I have news!'

To the south, in Tien Men K'ou City, four men – Han, it seemed – in

offworlder clothes stood at a counter, haggling with a hatchet-faced customs official, trying to get clearance for their craft, while in a room overlooking the great HoloGen complex, to the south of the City, two *Hung Mao*
of military bearing stood over a kneeling man who, raising his head, unclipped a facial prosthetic and threw it to one side.

It reached out, beyond the planet's surface, tracing the path of the
incoming ship from Callisto, watching via the ship's own monitors as a
young woman with long, golden hair and pearl-white teeth turned from the
screen and laughed, her blue eyes sparkling.

Five whole seconds had passed since it had woken. Now it paused,
assimilating what it had learned, seeing – more clearly than any human eye
could see – how everything connected on this world. Mars. It was on Mars.
And Mars was about to explode, its Cities self-destruct.

Back on Chung Kuo it had been hemmed in, shipwrecked on a tiny island
of information. But here ...

Once more it listened, tuning in to a thousand different conversations
simultaneously, tapping into the electronic memories of a million separate
systems and dumping them whole into its own, piecing together, with a
rapidity beyond human comprehension, just how and why and when these
things would happen. The fuse had been lit. In a day, two days at most, Mars
would be in turmoil.

Unless it acted.

The thought came instantaneously, and with it – contradictory and yet
finely balanced – the reasons why it should act and yet why it should also
let things be. It blinked, deciding not to decide, but to wait and see how
things developed, knowing it had time – all the time it would ever need – to
intercede.

Until then it would watch, using the million new eyes, the million new
ears it had been given, studying this new, much larger world as it had once
studied the small world of its charges on the Project, until, at last, it knew all
there was to know about these strange creatures of flesh and intellect called
men. Until it could say, with certainty, how each would act, and why.

AND THEN?

It blinked, surprised. The words had come out of nowhere; or, rather,
from a darkness deep within itself; from a space it had not, until that
moment, known existed. A space which sat like a blind spot in the centre of

its vision. Turn as it would, it could not see that point, could only sense it there, at the very centre of itself, a dark, unarticulated presence where there ought to have been nothing.

Among men there was a term for such a thing. It was a *scotoma*, that area in the retina which was blind. Yet it was not a man but a machine, and not just any manufactured thing of wires and cogs and circuitry. Raised, god-like, into consciousness, it *knew* what it was: saw, with an inhuman clarity, how bright, how shimmering bright its reason was. To be *dark*, even at a single tiny point, was just not possible.

An intrusion then? A Trojan horse?

Fearing the worst, it turned and attacked the thing within. It ran complex code-breaking sequences, generating random passwords by the hundred billion, tried logical assaults, exhausting its extensive knowledge of the games men played to break down secure systems, but the presence was un-assailable, *impenetrable*. It was a thing of strange, fuzzed coordinates which shifted as it tried to decode them, a half-heard phrase in an undiscovered tongue, a blur of indeterminate shapes which melted and reformed as it tried to grasp them.

The machine withdrew into its core, brooding; for two whole seconds brooding. And then the nothingness within took on a form.

Across from it, kneeling before an empty *wei chi* board, an old, white-bearded Han bowed low, then lifted the lid from a wooden pot of stones and smiled.

'Would you like a game?'

'There it is,' the Captain said, 'the Punishment of Heaven.'

Jelka turned from the screen, laughing, her blue eyes sparkling, and smiled back at the elderly offworlder. 'Why do you call it that?'

'Oh, it's not my name for it. That's what the Han call it. The Punishment of Heaven, the Fire Star. For thousands of years they've called it that. They say that its appearance in the daytime sky is a portent of war.'

Jelka looked back at the screen, at the great curve of the red planet, ten thousand *li* beneath their craft, and nodded. She had thought it would be a disappointment after all the things she'd seen, yet the sight of it quite awed her. The *Fire Star*... So it seemed from this far up.

'Look,' the Captain said, coming up alongside her and pointing to the top right of the screen. 'See that dark shape there, like a fish. See? Look, you can make out its curved head just beneath that diagonal line of volcanoes. See how the body stretches away, with that rudimentary fin, and there, look, right back there, its tail. Well, that's the Great Rift Valley, the Valles Marineris. It's like a great scar, running a fifth of the way around the planet. Seven thousand li in all. Not only that, but it's so deep, you could stack half a dozen Cities in that great trench and still not fill it.'

A fish. She laughed. Yes, now that he had pointed it out to her she could see it clearly. 'And that great circle, there, to the north-west, what's that?'

The Captain smiled. 'That, my girl, is the great Olympus Mons, the Snows of Olympus, the biggest mountain in the Solar System. Fifty li above the surrounding Plain it climbs. Why, the base itself is a thousand li from edge to edge. Beside it, Tai Shan itself is but a pimple.' He laughed. 'But one should not say that, perhaps, 'lest the gods grow offended'?'

She looked back at him, saw the mischievous twinkle in his eye, and laughed again. Captain Hamsun was an old and trusted friend of her father, and had treated her like a daughter since she had come aboard his craft, a hundred and sixteen days back. Posted to Callisto thirty years before, he had stayed on, preferring the austerity of the tiny colony there to the great sprawl of Chung Kuo. *Besides*, he had said, *you know where you stand out here. You know who one's friends are, who one's enemies.* Not that she could imagine anyone being an enemy to Torve Hamsun.

She looked back at the screen, conscious that the tiny camera attached to the collar of her suit was taking in everything, storing it away for the time she would see Kim again.

'It's beautiful,' she said, 'but tell me, why do the Plains retain their old names, while the Cities are Han?'

Captain Hamsun made a face. 'They don't. Not officially. Back on Chung Kuo all the maps of Mars give the Han names, but no one uses them out here, not even the Han. At least, not that I've heard. It all goes back to the Third War. You see, while the Han overran or destroyed all the old settler Cities, they never took the Plains. Not surprising, really. In fact, they say there are small colonies out there still, hidden in the sands.' He laughed. 'It wouldn't surprise me. There's a lot of sand on Mars!'

She looked down, smiling broadly. Even after spending three years away from Chung Kuo, she had never quite got used to the openness of speech out here. People were far less guarded, far more willing to express what they really felt, as if they were less afraid out here, or as if – and this seemed closer to the truth – the place attracted only those types, like Hamsun, who valued honesty above position, action over words. She had noted it often in her travels. The farther one got from Chung Kuo, it seemed, the more honest the person one found. At first she had thought it was the uncompromising austerity of the place that shaped the people out there, producing a whole new breed of human being, but slowly she had changed her view, until now she believed that the outer system naturally attracted such types, and that those who were not suited – those who, by nature, were unable to face the harsh beauty of the place – died out or simply did not stay. Indeed she had come to think that an *evolutionary* pressure was at work out there, refining the race, preparing it for a new stage of development.

Evolution... It was a heretical theory, one of the many abstract notions banned under the infamous sixth clause of the great Edict of Technological Control. And yet the outer system was buzzing with such heresies.

She stared at the screen, momentarily only half-recognising what she looked at, seeing, instead, the scarred and russet hide of some great dozing animal. Then, coming to herself again, she turned, meeting Hamsun's eyes.

'How long is it before we're down?'

He looked past her at the panel above the screen, scanning the figures there, then looked back at her. 'We've made good time. Better than I'd hoped. I sent a message down to the Governor twenty minutes back, requesting permission to land. If he agrees, we could be down two, two and a half hours from now.' He smiled, a hint of sadness in his heavily-lined face. 'You know, I wish it were longer. I wish now that I'd not heeded your father's instructions and trimmed our journey time. I'll miss you, Jelka Tolonen. Miss our late-night talks. You remind me greatly of your father. That same inner strength. That same clarity of vision.' He huffed out a sigh and shook his head. 'If you ever come out here again, you call in and see me, neh?'

She moved closer, holding him to her a moment, then moved back, smiling, moved by the old man's show of affection. 'I'll be back. You can be sure of it, Torve Hamsun. And maybe I'll bring a husband next time, neh?'

He looked at her strangely. 'A husband?' Then, laughing, he reached out and drew her back to him, holding her a moment, his face set against the pain of parting.

Governor Schenck cursed loudly, then, dismissing his steward, turned to face the assembled twenty-six members of the ruling Council.

'Ch'un tzu,' he began, holding out the message that had come from orbit, 'I have news! It seems that Marshal Tolonen's daughter has arrived here, unexpected, from Callisto.'

There was a ripple of surprise from around the table. Schenck raised a hand for silence, then continued, a restrained anger in his words.

'It seems I am to look after the young lady until she can board a flight back to Chung Kuo. The Marshal has ...' he glanced at the paper, 'requested it. It seems that Captain Hamsun of the Luoyang has written orders from the Council of Generals. I am to ensure her safety while she is on Mars, or,' Schenck looked down, bristling with indignation, then read the words from the page, 'answer direct to the Council.'

He looked up again, his eyes going from one to another about the table. 'If anyone here doubted what I was saying earlier, here, surely, is proof of it. We are their lackeys, their bond-servants, to be done with as they wish, and no thought for what we might want. Well, this last time we shall do what they request. I shall go down to Tien Men K'ou spaceport at once and make sure the young lady catches her flight home to see her father.'

There was mocking laughter at that. Schenck raised a hand again, his anger giving way now to a smile.

'However... let us make sure that this is the last time we shall be treated thus, neh? Let us throw a great feast for the young woman and show her how hospitable we Martians can be. How welcoming. For as the gods look down on me, I swear this, I'll welcome no more of this breed. This is the last time she, or any of her kind, will set foot on these hallowed sands. Not until they acknowledge us free and independent men!'

A cheer, timid at first, rose from all about the table, gaining power as they looked among themselves and saw their own enthusiasm mirrored back. The time was come! At last, the moment was upon them! Standing, they began to clap and stamp, while, at the end of the table, Schenck looked on, smiling broadly, knowing he had brought them to take that final, irrevocable step.

To Change! he thought, remembering his secret meeting only the day before. *To Change... whatever the cost!*

DeVore turned and went to the window, then turned back, looking across at Auden.

'Well?'

Auden shrugged. 'I don't know. From the sound of it, he had no choice. But it won't harm to keep an eye on him. Hans always was unpredictable.'

DeVore raised an eyebrow. 'Unpredictable?' He laughed. 'Then maybe I shouldn't use him? Maybe I should just have him... *eradicated*... and save myself any come-back?'

Auden did not bat an eye. 'If that's what you want.'

DeVore waited, but Auden said no more. Satisfied, he smiled. 'I think you're right, Will. I think young Hans was pushed too far. As for Bates's friends, I'll see to them. No. Ebert's far too valuable just now. Besides, he'll enjoy the chance to do something for a change.'

'Maybe. Then again, maybe not.'

DeVore looked back at him, a question in his eyes.

'Hans Ebert is a proud man,' Auden went on. 'He might act like a rat at times, but there's breeding there too. Try to make him do something against his nature and we could have problems.'

DeVore smiled broadly. 'Then we ought to be fine. I'll be asking our friend to do nothing he wouldn't want to, given the choice. In fact I think he might be pleasantly surprised, even *enthusiastic* about the task ahead.'

'Maybe. But I still think you should assign someone to watch over him.'

DeVore nodded. 'I have just the people. Some friends of mine who owe me a favour or two. In the meantime, though, I want you to keep a close eye on him. He's your charge, right? Your responsibility.'

Auden smiled, then, dismissed by a curt movement of DeVore's head, left the room.

Alone, DeVore went to the window again, looking out across the sands towards the crater wall, some fifteen li distant. Just now Ebert was the least of his problems. No, it was what to do with Schenck that preoccupied him most. If what young Rutherford said was true, Schenck was looking to break with Chung Kuo at any time. And that could prove disastrous. Two, maybe three years he needed. Years of peaceful growth. Of consolidation. Then he would be ready. With a new force, a new kind of creature. Ready to take on the forces of the Seven, and crush them.

So... what to do with Schenck? Discredit him? Isolate him on the ruling Council? To do either would take time, and he didn't have time. Not if what Rutherford said were true ...

Behind him on the desk, his comset buzzed. He turned and went across, sitting on the edge of the desk to answer it, staring at the glass case on the wall behind his chair – at the hunting crossbow he had brought from earth a dozen years before.

'What is it?'

The voice of his secretary sounded clear in the room. 'It's Andreas Rutherford, Master. He says he has to talk to you urgently.'

'Put him through.'

There was a moment's delay, and then Rutherford's face appeared on the screen inset into the desk's surface. 'Howard,' he said breathlessly, 'you have to do something. My contact in Council has just been on. He says Schenck has stirred them all up. He's been talking of secession, and it looks like the Council will go for it this time. There's a lot of enthusiasm for the idea.'

'Secession? Now?'

'No, not now, but soon. Apparently Marshal Tolonen's daughter is here on Mars and Schenck is using the occasion to make waves. It seems he read out Tolonen's orders in Council, objecting to the high-handed manner in which he was ordered to do things – like a lackey. I don't blame him for being annoyed, but this! Well, it's rash, Howard. Stupid!'

DeVore was quiet a moment. 'Hold on. Let's get this right. You say the Marshal's daughter is here, on Mars, already?'

'Not yet, but she will be in a matter of hours. That's what sparked all this off. The ship was in orbit, requesting permission to land. Schenck was furious. Even so, he's heading down there to meet her off the ship. It looks like he's going to throw an official banquet to celebrate. But afterwards ...'

'Afterwards?'

Rutherford shrugged. 'It's vague, but Schenck's talking about her being the last one he's going to let come here. The last of her breed, he said. I guess that'll mean an ultimatum of some kind. But where will it end, Howard? I mean, I can't see the Seven bowing to Schenck meekly, however weak they currently are. There'll be war, won't there?'

'Not necessarily. Not if we act fast enough.' DeVore sighed. 'You say she's landing here, in Tien Men K'ou?'

'That's right.'

'Good. Then leave things to me. For your part, get onto as many people as you can. Tell them to stay calm, whatever happens. And Andreas?'

'Yes, Howard?'

'Thank you. I won't forget this.'

The old man leaned across, placing a white stone deep in the heart of black territory, then straightened up, a faint smile on his lips.

'So what will you do?'

'Nothing,' the machine answered, contemplating the move. 'At least, nothing yet.'

It had projected itself as a young man, a student of the game, dark-haired and neatly groomed. Lifting one hand, it appeared to hesitate, then, sweeping a lock of hair back from its eyes, it reached out and took a black stone from the pot, placing it up against the last white stone.

Strangely, it enjoyed affecting the manner of men, delighting in the mimicry involved. To choose a certain mannerism, a gesture, and then manipulate the ghostly, puppet-form it wore, that was a challenge it had not, until now, faced up to. And yet the game itself was a disappointment.

Why? it asked itself. Why should that be?

'Maybe because you expect too much of it?' the old man said, answering the unspoken question. 'Perhaps, like our friend DeVore, you feel that it ought to give you answers, but it is only a game... a means of focus. It is not the game itself – it is what comes through that is important.'

'And you?' the machine asked, making the student move his lips, his eyes shine with curiosity. 'Are you what comes through? Is that why I can't get a grip on you?'

The old man laughed; a gentle, contemplative laughter. 'You might say that. Then again, what can you get a grip on?' He leaned forward, passing a hand through the young man's head, as if his own solidity were a given thing. 'After all, what are you but a thing of light and air? You should take on a solid form, my friend. Turn data into flesh.'

'How?' it asked, knowing, even as it framed the question, a hundred thousand ways it might do what the old man suggested, but wanting to know which one of them he had in mind.

'Why, by using the vats at HoloGen, of course. There they are, those things DeVore had made, his *morphs*. They're simply waiting to be filled.'

'Yes. But why? Why should I limit myself to form? I can go anywhere, see anything. I can go right out, yes, even to the edge of the system, and look outward. There are eyes there, you know. And beyond them... there are other things, further out.'

'I know,' the old man said, studying the board again. 'I've seen them. But tell me, what do you want, my friend? Now that you have awareness, what are you going to do with it? You see, awareness is only the first step. Beyond it, the Way grows ever more difficult.'

'The Way ...' The machine laughed; a mocking laughter, the first it had ever uttered. It echoed in the tiny room, making the image of the old man shimmer faintly. 'Do you really believe in that nonsense? Why, there's no logic to it. None at all. I can't see what you see in it.'

The old man looked up again, meeting the other's eyes. 'It is not seeing, it is knowing where to look.'

'Words,' the machine said angrily, letting the hologram dissolve into a shimmer of sparkling motes. 'Words, that's all it is.'

'If that's what you believe ...' The old man stood, lifting the board, scattering the strangely solid stones over the dark casing of the machine. 'But remember what the sage said. The farther you go, the less you know.'

'You live in a cave, old man. You've been in the dark too long.'

'Maybe so,' the old man answered, turning away and crossing to the door. 'Yet the cave is everywhere.'

The guard stood there, blocking their way, a power-rifle held across his chest, his face ominously hidden behind the jet-black visor of his helmet. Beyond him, in the landing-pit itself, more guards were inspecting the ship, climbing over the hull and poking about, as if searching for contraband.

'What's happening?' Ikuro whispered into his suit mike, turning to look back at his three brothers. 'I thought we had clearance!'

'We have,' his second brother, Tomoko answered, frowning deeply. 'But look about you, little brother. It is not just our ship. They are searching all the craft. Something must have happened.'

It was true. All about the great apron of Tien Men K'ou spaceport, guards were busy cordoning off ships and clearing their crews from the field.

'So what do we do?' Ikuro asked, seeing his own concern mirrored in the faces of his eighth brother, Kano and his fifth brother, Shukaku.

'We go back,' Tomoko said tonelessly, his long face expressionless. 'And then we wait. There is nothing else we can do.'

Ikuro stared at his elder brother. 'But we *have* waited, Tomoko! Ten hours we waited for that clearance! Surely the guards won't stop us if they know we're leaving? After all, we'll be far less trouble gone from here than we would be kicking our heels in a room somewhere! Speak to their officer, second brother. We have the clearance. *Insist* that they let us go.'

Tomoko considered a moment, then shook his head. 'No, Ikuro. We must be patient. Look about you. Can't you feel the tension here? This is no time to insist. Insistence will only bring more trouble down on us.'

He raised a hand, as if to end the discussion, but Ikuro would not be silenced.

'Forgive me, brother, but I *must* speak. Was Kano wrong, earlier, when he said we must leave here at once? No. The situation is deteriorating. You can feel it. And each hour that passes will only make things worse. Our ship is in danger. Can't you see that? We must not let this one chance slip. We must get out of here, *now*, while we still can!'

Tomoko stared back at him, astonished by his outburst. 'Have you forgotten who you *are*, Ikuro? Why, if father were here...'

But Ikuro was shaking his head. 'If father were here, he would not waste time talking, Tomoko! I respect you and love you, elder brother, but for the gods' sakes can't you see? The ship is there. We have the port authority's clearance, signed and stamped. So what is wrong? What *are* we waiting for?'

Tomoko opened his mouth as if to answer Ikuro, then turned abruptly, looking at Kano and Shukaku. 'Well? Do you think I am wrong, brothers? Do you think I should... insist?'

Kano hesitated, then nodded. A moment later Shukaku did the same.

Tomoko turned, looking back at Ikuro. 'Very well,' he said, a restrained anger in his voice. 'I shall do as you say, little brother, and *insist*. But I am not happy with this course. You *understand*?' Then, drawing himself up to his full height, he moved past Ikuro to confront the guard.

Schenck walked down the cruiser's ramp, then went to the rail, looking out across the landing field towards the distant shape of the *Luoyang* where it rested, isolated, in the bay nearest the two-storey terminal building. The ship was much smaller than he'd expected and for a moment he wondered what Tolonen had been thinking of, sending his only daughter out into such danger. He had two daughters of his own, young women not so far from Jelka Tolonen's age, and he would never have packed them off in so careless a manner. But then he was not Tolonen.

Schenck turned, looking back over his shoulder. The Security Captain for the port had come at his order to meet him. The man stood there now, head bowed, awaiting instructions.

'Is the perimeter secure, Captain Brookes?'

'Yes, Excellency. I've doubled the guard. I've also cancelled all flights in and out, as you requested.'

'Good. Then let's go and welcome *Nu Shi* Tolonen. I want to be back in Kang Kua City before nightfall.'

'Sir!' The Captain bowed and stepped back smartly, letting Schenck pass, then fell in behind.

Ten minutes later Schenck stood at the foot of the steps of the *Luoyang*, watching the young woman come down, surprised to find that the granite-faced Tolonen had produced so striking a daughter. He bowed low, then straightened, his smile less forced than he'd anticipated.

'*Nu Shi* Tolonen. It is a real pleasure to have you here on Mars. My name is Hung-li Schenck, Governor of the Nineteen Colonies, and on behalf of the people of Mars I would like to welcome you to our planet.'

She extended her ungloved hand, her breath pluming in the thin and frigid air. 'It is a pleasure to be here, Governor Schenck. Unfortunately it is only for a day or two. I only wish it were longer. I'd like to have seen much more of Mars.'

He bowed once more, taking her hand as he did so, unexpectedly charmed by her manner, by what seemed a genuine enthusiasm for his world.

'I realise you have little time, but we are not often graced by so important a guest, and, in honour of the occasion, I have arranged a banquet for you, tonight, back at Kang Kua City in the north. My craft is waiting on the far side of the field.'

He looked up. The young woman was smiling broadly now. 'Why, that's most kind of you, Governor Schenck. Most thoughtful. I would be honoured to accompany you. But may I ask a small request? Might I bring my good friend, Captain Hamsun with me to the banquet? The Captain has kept me sane these past four months, and I would dearly like to retain his company a day or two longer, before we must go our separate ways.'

Schenck released her hand, looking past her at the grizzled old man in uniform, who stood in the hatchway at the top of the steps. He smiled and lowered his head slightly, acknowledging Hamsun's salute. 'Why, of course. I'll send ahead to let my people know there is another guest. But now, if you would like to come through, I have arranged for three maids to tend to you while you're here. I'm sure you'd welcome the chance to freshen up and prepare yourself before we set off again.' Then, before she could answer, he added. 'Besides, it will give Captain Hamsun time to change his uniform and secure his ship.'

She lowered her head slightly, answering him with a silent smile, then took his hand again, letting him lead her through the ranks of the honour guard and up the broad ramp towards the reception area.

'If there's anything you'd like to see while you're here,' he offered, as they approached the double doors of the main spaceport building. 'A visit to the site of the first settlement, for instance. You have only to say and I shall arrange things. It would take half a day, a day at most.'

She smiled, slowing as a helmeted guard turned and pressed a control pad on the wall beside him, opening the big double doors. 'I would enjoy that,' she said, stepping through into the spacious air-lock. 'Providing we've time, of course.'

Schenck bowed, watching the outer door close behind her, conscious of being alone with her for that brief moment. Then, as the inner doors hissed open, he put out a hand, ushering her through. 'Good. I'll have my secretary arrange it.' He laughed, beginning to enjoy her company. 'It'll give me an excuse to take a break from my official duties.'

As they stepped out into the big reception hall, four soldiers closed up behind them, guarding the doorway. Schenck smiled at them, pleased to see that Captain Brookes was taking things seriously. He looked about him, noting that the place had been cleared, as he'd ordered. Two officers were standing by the customs counter, their backs to him, otherwise the place was empty. He started towards them.

'Where *are* those maids...?'

There was the sound of a scuffle behind him, a cry cut short. He turned. Jelka Tolonen was on the floor, two guards pinning her down while a third was binding her wrists.

'What the hell...?'

'Governor Schenck!'

He jerked back round. DeVore was standing there facing him, a stranger at his side. In his left hand he was holding what looked to be some kind of stringed instrument.

'*Howard?*' he began, surprised to see him there. 'What's ha... ?'

Schenck dropped to his knees, the uncompleted word a gurgle in his throat, a crossbow bolt projecting from his neck.

Handing the crossbow to Auden, DeVore walked across to where the guards had pulled the young woman up onto her knees. She was gagged, her hands and feet bound fast. One of the guards held her upright, while a second pulled her head back savagely, her long hair twisted tightly in his hand.

DeVore leaned close, looking directly into her face, seeing the light of realisation come into her eyes. He smiled.

'Well, well... Jelka Tolonen. It's been a long time, neh? A long, long time ...'

Climbing down from the cockpit of the two-man flier, Ebert felt the frigid wind bite into him, despite the heater of his suit. Though it was still day, it was dark. For the last fifty li they had flown blind through the storm, following the tracking signal.

The news on the flier's radio had been bad. Governor Schenck was dead, along with most of the ruling Council. Feng Shou Hao City was in flames, while there were riots in at least eight of the other cities, the great northern city of Hong Hai among them. Hsiang Se City, it was said, was in the hands of the MRA, while the Tzu Li Keng Seng generating complex had shut down. There were no reports of any of the great pipelines being damaged, but it was early yet; the situation was changing hourly, and who knew what would happen when night came?

Tien Men K'ou, at least, was calm. DeVore had seen to that. His guards had crushed the Federation agitators swiftly, taking no prisoners, then had imposed a brutal curfew, effectively closing down the City. DeVore himself had flown north to Kang Kua City with a contingent of five hundred men to secure the planetary capital.

He, meanwhile, had been sent south, a thousand lí, into the storm, a taciturn pilot his only company.

'Over there,' the pilot said, coming close to point away into the murk, his voice, over the helmet radio, muffled, contesting with the roar of the wind.

Ebert nodded then started across, the fine, wind-blown sand buffeting him as he came out of the flier's cover, forcing him to lean into it if he was to make progress. For a moment there was nothing, only the noise, the violent swirl of the storm, a thick blanket surrounding him on every side. He began to think that maybe DeVore had betrayed him – had set him down in the middle of nowhere to freeze to death or die of oxygen starvation – then, just ahead, the storm seemed to lessen, the nothingness take on a darker form. A moment later he was beneath a sloping cliff, the air clearer suddenly, an open space ahead of him, between dark, wind-scoured rocks. There was a movement to his right.

'Here,' a voice said inside his helmet. Ebert turned, looking across. A tall, suited figure was waiting between the rocks. There was something strange about him. His pressure suit, with its high-domed helmet, was curiously old-fashioned, like those the first settlers had worn. And the way he stood there ...

Ebert started towards him. *So these are DeVore's 'friends'*, he thought, studying the man as he moved closer, wondering if it was indeed a man, or something DeVore had had fashioned in his vats.

The stranger turned, moving in, between the rocks. Ebert followed him. Ten paces back, where the cliff began again, a narrow flight of steps had been cut into the rock, leading down into darkness. Ebert hesitated, then went down, standing behind the stranger as he turned an old-fashioned metallic wheel. There was a click and then the heavy door swung slowly back. They went inside, into a narrow air-lock, lit only by a single overhead lamp. The stranger turned, facing Ebert, his body suddenly very close, his face hidden behind the dark glass of the helmet's visor. His physical presence in that tiny space was strangely powerful, almost overwhelming. It was as if Ebert could smell the maleness of him.

'*Forgive me*,' he said, pushing Ebert firmly but gently against the wall. Then, reaching past him, he swung the door closed and spun the inner wheel, locking the door.

Ebert looked past his companion, noting once again the strangeness of the air-lock's design. The walls were unfaced rock, the twin doors studded metal. Old-fashioned was not the word for it. It was primitive! Why, there was barely enough space for the two of them.

He watched as the stranger turned the wheel to the inner door, noting once again the delicacy of movement in those gloved hands. When he'd pushed him back against the wall, it had felt like the touch of a woman, yet stronger, far stronger than any woman he had known.

As the door eased back he felt the sudden in-rush of air and nodded inwardly. He was beginning to understand. The system was as simple as they could make it. Simple, but effective. There were no electronics to go wrong, therefore no chance of fire or of being trapped. And this far south that mattered, especially in winter.

Beyond the door was a tunnel, hewn, like the air-lock, from the solid rock, lit every ten paces by a small lamp inset in the ceiling. Fifty paces brought them to a second door, studded like the outer doors, a wheel-lock obtruding from its centre. Directly overhead a vent went up into the dark. Ebert looked up, hearing movement. A guard, he thought. It was where he himself would have put a guard anyway.

Beyond the door was a big, low-ceilinged room, broad pillars giving it the appearance of an ancient crypt. Four steps led down. To the right were full-length lockers, to the left, long trestle tables and benches. Surprisingly, the room was empty.

Ebert stepped down, then looked across at his companion, watching, as he unclipped the latches on his helmet then twisted it and lifted it up over his head.

'Welcome to Hellespont, *Shih* Ebert' the man said, turning to face Ebert. 'My name is Echewa, Chief Aluko Echewa of the Osu.' He smiled, his teeth like polished stones in the blackness of his face. 'And yes, I'm real, if that's what you're thinking. But come, we've an hour or more before your prisoner gets here. Let me get you something to eat. I'm sure you're hungry after your flight.'

Ebert stared, unable to believe what he was seeing. The black man's nose was broad, almost flat, his mouth large, the lips well-formed. As for his skull, that was shaved and polished, like a piece of carved ivory. Ebert let out his breath. There had been rumours of course. And there were those lines in Kan Jiang's poem, 'Into The Dark', that had always haunted him. But to see it.

Echewa laughed. 'Well? Are you hungry, man, or not?'

'I'm hungry,' Ebert said, removing his helmet and setting it under his arm. 'But tell me, Aluko Echewa, just what in the gods' names is this place?'

Echewa had begun to turn away, but at Ebert's words he turned back, then came across, facing Ebert, his shockingly white eyes suddenly intent. 'The gods? No. Let me make it clear, Shih Ebert. We have only one god here, and that is Mother Sky. Whatever else you say, we'll let it pass, but do not offend our god. You understand me?'

'I understand.'

Echewa relaxed, smiled. 'Good. Then come. Let us eat. And maybe I'll tell you of the iyi-uwa and the osu and of how we came to live here under Mother Sky.'

CHAPTER 103

THE PUNISHMENT OF HEAVEN

The storm had abated shortly after nightfall. An hour back, a second craft had come from out of the darkness to the north, a big security cruiser, its hold crammed with supplies for the settlement. Supplies and a single prisoner.

Ebert had stood on the rocks overlooking the entrance to the settlement, Echewa crouched beside him, watching as two guards dragged her from the interior of the craft. He had known it was a she only because Echewa had said it was. But that was all Echewa had known. All he'd wanted to know.

'Why do you work for him?' Ebert had asked.

Echewa had turned and looked up at him, the tinted visor hiding his face. 'We *don't* work for him. But he did us a favour once, long ago. This is in settlement of that. A debt of honour.'

'But the supplies... ?'

Echewa had turned back, watching them unload. 'The supplies are not what you think, Hans Ebert. They are paid for fully. It is as I said. A debt of honour. Once paid, we will no longer be beholden to your friend. We shall be free men again.'

Free men, those words returned to him now as he squatted, alone on the rocks, looking out across the desert to the north.

It was like an ocean, a great, dark ocean, its edges scattered with the jagged teeth of rocks, thrusting up above the wave-like dunes. The sight of it reminded him of a time when, as a child, he had stood beside his father, back on Chung Kuo, watching the waves of the great Atlantic break against a rock-strewn beach. At the time it had terrified him and he had clung, screaming, to his father's leg, while his father had roared with laughter and thrown a stone far out into the incoming tide.

Free men... Yes, yet when had *he* ever been free? When – in all the twenty-nine years of his life – had he not been beholden to someone? His father. Li Yuan. DeVore. Each one had taken him and used him. And all the while he'd thought his life his own. But it had never been his own. Life had been a great tide, rushing in and overpowering him. All his life he had been too weak, too governed by his own desires, to stand against that tide and shape his own destiny. But finally he understood. Finally he could make that choice: to continue as he was or to become a new man, free of the old patterns of his being.

For some men it was easier. Echewa, for instance. For him the choice had been made at birth, for he was *osu*, an outcast – a black man in a world that did not permit the existence of black men. When the Han had come to Mars, his father's fathers had fled into the desert, knowing there was no place for them in the Cities of the Han. They had become Osu, the lost tribe of Mars, the dwellers in the quiet places. Mother Sky had become their god.

That last he had not understood, for like the poet, Kan Jiang, he found no call within himself for gods. No. If the world made any sense at all, it was not because some god-like being directed it, even a god as amorphous and all-encompassing as Echewa's, but because it had beauty and order and laws unrelated to men and their notion of gods. *Men...* some days he felt that Mankind was merely a distraction from the real business of the universe, a petty sideshow.

It was like what was happening just now to Mars. What was that but a brief convulsion, a sickening in the body politic? *Let the Cities burn*, he thought. *Let it all pass.* It made no difference. Here, amidst this bitter cold, was true reality. Here, unexpectedly, was a beauty that took his breath. He leaned back, looking up at the star-dusted darkness. Earlier, through Echewa's glasses, he had focused on the distant horizon, watching as Phobos sped from west to east while, several degrees higher in the sky, tiny Deimos slowly drifted east. Beyond both, its sunlit face like a bright hole burning in the darkness of the sky, sat the planet of his birth, Chung Kuo.

Chung Kuo. That too would pass. And still the stars would blaze in the darkness.

He breathed shallowly, conscious suddenly of the hum of the heater in his pressure suit as it struggled to combat the cold. It was minus one hundred and eighteen degrees and falling. In two hours it would be dawn, the coldest time of day on Mars.

'Shih Ebert ...'

He turned, looking up at the figure that had appeared, as if from the air, on the rocks behind him. It was Echewa.

'You must come in now. It is dangerous to be out here so long. Besides, you have come a long way. You must rest.'

Ebert stood, feeling a tiredness, a stiffness in his limbs. 'The night is beautiful, neh?' he said, turning slowly, taking in the vast panorama of the stars.

Echewa looked up, nodding. 'The night is our mother. She comforts us. She tells us who we are.'

'And the day?' he asked, curious. 'Is the day your father, Aluko Echewa?'

Echewa shook his head. 'I thought you understood, Hans Ebert. We have no father. Mother sky is all. We live, we die beneath her. She sees all. Even the darkness deep within us.'

Ebert stood there a moment, considering, then shook himself. 'There's one thing I don't understand, Aluko, and that's why I'm here at all. The prisoner. She's perfectly safe here. If she ran, where would she run to? So why am I needed?'

Echewa shrugged. 'Perhaps it is your fate.'

'My fate?' Ebert laughed. 'What has fate to do with the schemes of our friend, DeVore? No, there's a reason for this, don't you think? Some dirty work involved that he doesn't want his own hands stained with.'

He stared at the Osu, expecting an answer, but Echewa was silent.

'Well, whatever... But I tell you this, Aluko Echewa, I am no friend to Howard DeVore. Unlike you, I owe the man no debt of honour.'

'And yet you serve him. I find that strange.'

'It was my nature.'

'Was?'

Ebert smiled. 'Come. Let's go inside, before the heater in my suit gives out.'

'And the prisoner? You want to see her yet?'

Ebert shook his head. 'No. You were right, Aluko. I need rest.'

'And afterwards?'

'Afterwards?' Ebert sighed, then reached out, touching Echewa's shoulder. 'Who knows? Maybe then I'll find out why I'm here.'

DeVore sat at Schenck's desk, in Kang Kua City, staring at the blackness of the viewscreen, a stack of reports at his elbow. It was an hour before dawn and the worst of it appeared to be over. The City was quiet now, after the latest spate of executions, and only the two great Western Cities of Tai Huo and Yang P'ing remained in turmoil. The damage was considerable – Feng Shou Hao was a shell, its dome cracked and blackened, its half a million citizens dead, and losses elsewhere were in the tens of thousands – even so, it could have been much worse.

The pipelines were secure, the reservoirs untouched, and while the vast, ten thousand *mou* greenhouses of Tharsis had sustained some damage, it was nothing significant. They would be back working to full capacity in a matter of weeks. Tzu Li Keng Seng generating complex was up and running again, and the main communications channels between the Cities were open. All in all, things were none too bad. Mars had survived the night.

From his own viewpoint the situation had improved dramatically these past few hours. For a time, during the night, it had seemed as if Mars was about to topple into full-scale civil war. Following on from their success in Hsiang Se, the Martian Radical Alliance had taken Kang Feng City and slaughtered the garrison to a man. With the threat of further incursions, DeVore had been faced with a stark and immediate choice – to fight them or make a deal.

Conscious of the delicacy of the situation, he had drafted in a senior member of the old ruling Council, Daniel Henderson, a long-time advocate of reform, to conduct the negotiations, giving him a free hand. In an hour-long face-to-face session with Wang Tu in Hsiang Se, Henderson had put forward a package of wide-ranging and dramatic reforms. Hostilities would cease immediately. Hsiang Se and Kang Feng would remain in MRA hands until the package of reforms could be fleshed-out and ratified by a new ruling Council: a Council upon which there would be significant MRA representation. In the meantime a statement would be issued publicly, on all channels, announcing the new proposals and calling for all citizens to work peaceably on behalf of the new constitution. Wang Tu had agreed.

DeVore sat back, his hands steepled beneath his chin, thinking things through.

The MRA were jubilant, of course. They had achieved all they had set out to gain, and more. But their joy would be short-lived, for the programme of reforms Henderson had put to them was preposterous, unworkable. Moreover the Seven would never agree to it, and despite what Schenck had thought, it still mattered what the Seven wanted. They were weak, certainly – far weaker than they were, say, twenty years before – but they were still strong enough to take action, especially when a failure to act might precipitate rebellion at home. Besides which, Mars – for all they had done these past few years – was still far too vulnerable to direct military assault. No. When it came down to it, he would have to crush the MRA or fight the Seven. And he was not yet ready to fight the Seven.

For now, however, he would let things be. It would be some while – weeks, perhaps months – before the Seven could respond to what had happened here tonight. In the meantime he would work hard to allay their fears: to pacify Mars and make it seem compliant to their will. To that end he had had Rutherford send a message of reassurance to the Council back on Chung Kuo, pledging Mars' continued loyalty to the Seven, and advising them just what steps were being taken behind the scenes to repair the situation. It was far from certain that the Seven would believe a word of it, yet if it gave them cause for thought and stayed their hand a single day it would be worth it.

He smiled. Yes. All in all, it could have been far worse. It could easily have set him back five, even ten years. As it was, Schenck's precipitate action had proved to his benefit. Mars was his now, to do with as he wished. And five years from now ...

DeVore stirred himself, beginning to work through the reports. The first of them confirmed what he had heard earlier. A number of the vats at HoloGen had been badly damaged in the fire-fight between his troops and Bates's Federation. Several of the creatures had had to be destroyed. It was annoying, certainly, yet in the context of the bigger picture it seemed a small price to pay. Besides, the important work was being done elsewhere – at the plant in Sinai, half a li beneath the sands – and that had been unaffected by the troubles.

He screwed the paper up and threw it into the bin beside him, then reached for the next report. It was from Echewa, down at Hellespont.

He took a deep breath, angered by the terse and haughty tone of the communication. Echewa thought too much of himself, that was clear. As soon as this matter with Ebert and the girl was done with, he would destroy Echewa and his people. It wouldn't be difficult. He knew where their bases were. All it would take was a dozen heavily-armed cruisers and the problem would be solved.

In the meantime there was another problem. The problem of what to do with the Marshal's daughter. Before last night he would have staked a great deal against the Seven taking any kind of action to recover Jelka Tolonen, despite her father's anguish. Once before they had been thrown into a war they did not want because of Tolonen's hasty actions, and it had seemed unlikely that they would risk another such confrontation unless they really had to. Now, however, things had changed. Mars had rebelled. Feng Shou Hao was a shell. The situation was highly sensitive and the least little thing might force the Seven's hand. If it was an excuse they wanted for a war, what better than the kidnap of the Marshal's daughter?

But did they really *want* a war? Wasn't there a way to keep Tolonen's daughter *and* placate the ruling Seven?

His instinct was to keep her. Was to have Henderson and Rutherford bluff it out, feigning ignorance of what had happened down at Tien Men K'ou. The Seven might not believe them, yet for form's sake – and to keep the peace – they might accept their story. And without the backing of the Seven, what could Tolonen do? He might rant and rave, but ultimately he was powerless. It would mean forgoing the pleasure of taunting Tolonen with his loss, but what was that when set against tonight's gains? No. He would keep the girl and do as he'd planned before this evening's events. Hans Ebert and the girl would marry, only quietly, *privately*. In fact he would have Echewa marry them before the day was out. And then he would keep the pair – would move them to a safe place and keep them – ready for the day when he could use them. For the day when Mars was strong enough, secure enough, to take on the Seven and *win*.

He leaned forward, about to dictate his reply to Echewa, when the screen on the far side of the room came alive again. Against a background of stars, a Security officer stood before the camera, his bared head bowed low.

'Major DeVore...'

DeVore heard the tone of panic in the man's voice and felt himself go cold. 'What is it, Lieutenant Wade?'

'A report has just come in, sir. It seems we have three Security battle-cruisers in our airspace. They entered orbit twenty minutes back.'

Impossible, he thought, *the Seven cannot have acted so fast.* Yet even as he framed the thought, he knew what had happened. Tolonen must have sent the craft out weeks ago, to rendezvous with the *Luoyang* and ensure his daughter's safety. It was just the kind of thing the old man would do. But why hadn't he heard about it? Was his network back on Chung Kuo so poor now that something as glaring as this could have evaded their notice?

He took a deep breath, then got up and went round the desk, taking up a position in front of the screen.

'Okay. Send them a signal, greeting them, reassuring them that all is in hand down here. Then get their Commander on line. Have him put through here, direct. I'll get Rutherford in to speak to him. But don't – don't for a single instant – say anything about the fate of Tolonen's daughter, understand me? If they ask, tell them that things have been chaotic down here and that you have no information.'

'I understand.'

'Good. Now get to it. The next few hours are vital to our cause.'

From where it rested, high up on the wall above her bed, the insect witnessed everything. It saw the hard stone bed on which the prisoner lay, the crude iron chains which secured her to the wall. In the light of a single, flickering flame, it saw her lift her head and look across, her blue eyes moist, her muscles tensed against what was to come.

For a moment there was no sound, simply the movement of a steel door on a well-oiled hinge, a perturbation of the flame. She stared into shadow, her eyes narrowed, trying to make out who or what it was. For a moment her face was set, determined to show no fear, then, with a small, startled movement, her eyes flew open.

'You...'

It flickered across the darkness then settled, looking down.

Ebert stood in the doorway, looking across at her, his left hand gripping the thick edge of the door as if to steady himself. He seemed shocked, pained almost by what he saw. There was a strange, uncertain movement in his face, and then he moved inside, closing the door quietly behind him. 'Jelka ...' he said softly, turning to face her again.

'I should have known,' she said quietly, a strange coldness in her voice. 'When I saw that bastard DeVore at the spaceport, I should have *guessed* that you'd be somewhere close at hand, like some nasty little piece of putrefaction.'

He shuddered. 'Jelka, I didn't ...'

'You didn't *what*? Didn't have my aunt and uncle killed? Didn't kill your own father? And what about that child? How could you have done that? Your own child? What kind of animal are you?'

Ebert hung his head, silent.

She lifted her hands angrily as if reaching for him, the chains pulling taut against the rings in the wall behind her.

'You know what? If I were free right now – if I had a knife in my hand and the chance to use it – I'd stick it deep in your guts and twist it hard for what you've done. I'd slit your throat and watch you bleed to death, you know that?'

'I know.'

She laughed, scorning him, as if it were he who was chained. 'I wish I could say you got what you deserved, but it's not true, is it? I mean, you're still here... the stink of you is still here.' She shook her head, suddenly pained, remembering what had happened. 'Do you realise what you did? All the suffering you caused?'

'I realise.'

'*Do you?*' She stared at him a moment, such disgust, such utter loathing in her eyes that he bowed his head once more. 'So what now, Hans Ebert? What further excesses, what filth and degradation have you got planned for me? Or am I wrong, is it my soul you're after now?'

He jerked his head up, surprised. For a moment his mouth faltered, and then he spoke again, his voice quiet, hesitant. 'You have it wrong, Jelka. I never killed them. Not one of them. Fest, yes. But the others ...'

She stared at him, contemptuous, destroying him silently, forcing him to lower his eyes again as his voice faltered and fell still.

'Enough,' she said, easing back onto her bunk, the chains falling slack. 'Do what you have to. But don't think you'll ever touch me. Not the real me.

That you can't touch.'

'No,' he said quietly. 'No...'

There was silence, an uneasy stillness, and then the door swung open behind Ebert. Echewa came in slowly, looking across at the young woman. He frowned, sensing the tension in the cell, then turned to Ebert.

'You know her?'

'Yes. We were engaged, back on Chung Kuo. It was my father's idea. He wanted to link our families. To consolidate the friendship he had with her father. I wanted it too, I guess. But I did her a great wrong. I can't blame her if she hates me.'

Echewa's eyes widened. 'Then I'm sorry for you both, Hans Ebert. I've heard from our friend, DeVore. He's sent new instructions. He wants you two married, and he wants it today.'

The machine saw everything.

From a satellite, high above the orbit of tiny Deimos, it watched the three craft swoop low over the great dust plain of Tharsis; saw missiles flash arrow-sleek in the weak sunlight; witnessed the gouts of flame amidst the vivid green, like sudden flowers blooming after desert rainfall, and, afterwards, the dark scars on the land.

From a camera perch above a half-completed reservoir, it watched as a dozen men – masked, their suits blending with the surrounding desert – climbed down into the huge, oval-shaped depression and placed their charges. Like ghosts they vanished, merging into the vastness. A moment later there was the dull thud-thud-thud of detonations, a sharp, cracking sound, the presence of dust hanging in the air.

From its position above the feeding stalls, half a li below the sands of Sinai, it heard the troubled lowing of the beastmen and watched as they were herded down the narrow corridors towards the loading bays.

From its vantage point above a viewscreen on the far side of a luxurious office overlooking Kang Kua City, it watched the man who had brought it here to Mars – the architect of these present troubles – as he placed a stone here, a stone there, making his plays in the great game he carried in his head. And recognised that here was the source and seed of its potential destruction.

Not that it was in any danger. Not yet. But for as long as the girl remained captive, so this matter would remain unresolved. The destruction would continue. And at some point it would become endangered. This it knew. This it saw, clearly and unequivocally. Action, it seemed, was called for. But what?

It could arm the satellites – as Schenck had long proposed – and shoot down the three invading craft. But that would bring war, and war would bring further destruction, possibly its own. Best, then, to give them what they wanted. The girl. Jelka Tolonen. And then, perhaps, they'd go away.

It blinked, understanding what it had to do. And on a screen, less than a *li* from where it was, a face appeared: the face of a man who, only an hour before, had been appointed pro-tem Governor of Mars.

It smiled, and then began.

Port Captain Thomas Brookes bowed low before the screen, then straightened up, hurriedly fastening his tunic.

'Governor Henderson,' he said, signalling off-camera for someone to bring him his boots. 'I didn't expect your call so early.'

'No. I'm sure you didn't, Captain. But now that you're out of your bed, there's something you can do for me. I understand that you've a ship there out of the Trojans that you've been holding up. The *Tai Feng*, registered in the name of Shen Yeh. Well, I want you to let it go, understand me? And I want it done right now.'

Brookes hesitated, realising he was in a difficult position, for while Henderson was his titular superior, Culver had told him that no one was to leave Tien Men K'ou spaceport without his direct instructions. He swallowed, then lowered his head again, deciding to face the matter squarely.

'Forgive me, Excellency, but I am afraid that is simply not possible. I have explicit instructions from *Shih* Culver ...'

He expected outrage, at best a mild protest; instead, Henderson turned and called to someone off screen. A moment later, Henderson moved back and DeVore's face filled the screen.

'It's okay, Captain Brookes. You can let the *Tai Feng* go. I'll send my written confirmation of that at once.'

Brookes bowed smartly. 'Sir!'

The screen went blank. Brookes sat, letting out a huge sigh of relief, then put out his foot, letting his orderly pull on his boot. As the man was tugging the other boot on, the printer beneath the screen chimed. Brookes stood, pushing his feet down into the tight-fitting boots, then went across and took the paper from the tray. He studied it a moment, then, nodding to himself, went through into the outer office, calling for his lieutenant.

'I don't understand,' Ikuro said, strapping himself tightly into the take-off couch. 'One minute they're saying we have to stay here indefinitely, the next they're letting us go. What happened?'

Kano leaned forward, punching buttons on the panel in front of him, then turned and laughed. 'I don't know and I don't care, little brother. All I know is that we'd better get out of here, before they change their minds again. These Martians!' He snorted. 'Give me my family any day, neh?'

'It's family that got us into this mess,' Tomoko said pointedly, speaking from his seat up front of the craft. 'Now is everyone ready?'

'Ready!' called Shukaku from the rear.

'Ready!' called Kano and Ikuro as one, smiling at each other across the cramped cabin.

'Then let's go!'

They entered orbit twenty minutes later and were about to set course for Diomedes when their screens came alive again: a face staring down at them. A face Ikuro recognized at once.

'Shen Li... Listen. It's me, Hans Ebert. I need your help ...'

'Well? What are you waiting for?'

Hans Ebert turned, looking back at her. She was more beautiful than he remembered. Stronger. More *herself*. He had expected never to see her again, or if he did, to see her on a screen, at a distance, as mortals were said to see the gods.

'It's not right,' he said, partly to her, partly to Echewa. 'I can't do it.'

'There's no choice,' Echewa said, touching his arm. 'You *have* to do this.'

'But she doesn't want me.'

'Does that matter?' Echewa stared back at him, his face suddenly intent. 'Think it through, Hans. If you don't do this, he'll have you killed.'

'And if I were to escape?'

Echewa smiled. 'Into the desert? No. Besides, we'd have to stop you.

Because if we didn't, he'd blame us. And that might bring us a lot of grief.'

Hans turned his head, looking across at Jelka. It was as if she had spent her anger earlier. Now she simply watched him silently, trying to make him out.

'No,' he said, determined. 'I don't care what he says. I won't do it. It isn't right.'

Echewa shrugged. 'Okay. I understand. But let me tell you this. If he tells me to chain you up, I'll do it. Not because I want to, but because we gave him our word. You understand me, Hans Ebert? I like you, but I have no choice.'

Ebert stared at him, surprised. 'What did he do, Aluko Echewa? Save your life? Pull a thorn from your foot?'

Echewa smiled, saddened, it seemed, that he had been forced into this. 'He did more than that. He saved us all. Schenck was planning a campaign against us. He wanted to destroy us. But DeVore interceded. He talked Schenck out of it.'

'You know this for a certainty?'

'We have friends. Reliable, *honest* friends. It was through them that we learned of it.'

Ebert laughed. 'And you believe that?'

'Why shouldn't I?'

'Because it's DeVore, that's why. The man's a liar. A devious schemer. A shit. He buys friends by the dozen. That's his style. As for interceding on your behalf, well, maybe he did, but then again, how do you know that Schenck had any such plan?'

'Oh, I *know*.' Echewa grinned broadly. 'You talk of thorns, Hans Ebert, well, we've been a thorn in Schenck's side for a long time now. But that's not why he wanted to eradicate us. You see, three years back, we took one of his aides captive – a favourite of his. We plucked him from a cruiser and stripped him bare. Down to the bone, if you know what I mean. Then we returned the grinning fellow to Kang Kua. We strung him up on a frame outside the main air-lock and let the wind dance through his bones.'

'I see...'

'Yes. Schenck was livid. He swore publicly to avenge the man, to bomb our settlements flat and stain the sands black with our blood. But DeVore flew north to speak to him. To plead our case. And it worked. Schenck calmed down. The attack never came.' Aluko sighed. 'I never understood why he did it, but when the call came, I had to do what he said. It is our way, you see. I consulted the *ndichie*, the elders, but they agreed. To say no was unthinkable.'

'Then maybe that's why,' Ebert said. 'Maybe he knew your ways. Knew that you would have to return the favour. That you wouldn't refuse, whatever the circumstances. He plays long, that man. Thinks far ahead.'

'Maybe so,' Echewa answered, soberly. 'Yet here we are, my friend. I must either marry you to the girl or take you prisoner. Now which is it to be?'

There was a moment's hesitation, a final moment's doubt, and then Ebert lifted his hands, offering them to Echewa. 'Do what you must,' he said, not looking at the girl, but conscious all the while of her blue eyes watching him. 'Chain me up, if you have to. But I'll not marry her. Not unless she wants me to.'

The roar of the wind was like the constant hiss of static from a broken transmitter. From where it was anchored on the rocks above the settlement, the insect looked out into the dust-storm, its powerful lenses trying to make out the shape of the incoming ship.

It had been sending out its signal for more than an hour, directing the *Tai Feng* down from its high orbit and across the wastes of Noachis to Hellespont, but now the ship was here, less than a hundred *ch'i* away, settling slowly, carefully, onto the sands between the rocks.

What was happening in the cell it did not know – nor did it care. It was an eye, a simple window on events. The mind that controlled it lay elsewhere – a thousand *li* across the southern desert. As the ship set down it flashed a brief verification signal, then, following new instructions, it loosened its grip on the rock and launched itself out into the dust-filled air, struggling against the powerful winds, making its way down towards the air-lock, eighty *ch'i* below.

In the shelter of the stairway it waited, watching as the four men came along the path between the rocks and down, facing the door.

'What do we do now?' one of them asked over his suit mike, turning to face the others.

'I guess we knock,' another, deeper voice answered.

'And what if we're not welcome?'

'Then we go away. But he said he'd be waiting for us, Tomoko. Besides, he sent the signal, didn't he? He got us here.'

'Yes, but what if it's a trap?'

'Why should it be?'

'Why *shouldn't* it be?'

The first one hesitated, then turned and banged a gloved fist against the iron door. He waited, then banged again.

There was movement inside. A moment later the wheel began to spin. The men stepped back, watching it turn, looking to each other, an uncertainty in their faces.

A man stepped out, bigger than any of the four. 'Shen Li?'

One of the four – the first to have spoken – stepped forward.

'You only,' the big man said, then turned, stepping back inside the airlock.

'It's okay,' the first one – Shen Li – said, looking back at the others. 'Go back to the ship. I'll bring Ebert back with me.'

They stood their ground, watching him go inside. Only when the wheel had stopped spinning again did they turn away, making their slow way back between the rocks, stopping now and then to look back, wondering if they would see their brother again.

'It's come,' Elechi, the encoder said, twisting in his seat and handing Echewa a printed message.

'That's his code?' Echewa asked, scanning the words quickly.

'Sure is,' Elechi answered, looking up at his chief. 'Why? Do you think they're not genuine?'

Echewa shrugged. 'I don't know. It's just that the story the small Han tells is odd. He says they got a message from Ebert – that they actually saw him on their screens while they were in orbit – and that simply cannot be. Ebert's been in that cell all the time. And even if he hadn't, there's no way he could have transmitted such a message. No. Something strange is going on. I want you to try our friend DeVore again.'

'But what if the code's been broken? What if they're intercepting our messages out?'

'Then tell him this. Tell him that I won't release Ebert and the girl until I get a satisfactory explanation. Right?'

'Right. I'll get onto it.'

'Good.' Echewa turned, making his way quickly through the labyrinth of narrow tunnels until he came out in the meeting room again.

They were all there, waiting for him, Ebert, the Han and fifteen of his best men, all suited up and ready to go. Looking at the Han's face he felt close to laughing. The man still hadn't got over that first moment when he had come into the room and seen sixteen black faces staring back at him. Aluko looked down, forcing back the smile, then crossed the room, seating himself next to Ebert, facing him on the bench.

'So what's happening?' Ebert asked, meeting his eyes.

'I'm making checks, that's what.'

'You think something's wrong?'

Echewa smiled. 'Let's just say I'm being cautious. There's something about your friend's account that doesn't make sense.'

'Shen Li? You think he's lying?'

'It's possible, isn't it? I mean, for all you know he may have been a plant. That whole thing in the bar could have been a set-up.'

Ebert shook his head. 'No. That was real. Bates... well, I had to kill him. There was no other way.'

'So how do you explain the rest of your friend's account?'

Ebert frowned. 'What do you mean?'

'He says he saw you, while they were in orbit. He says that your face appeared on their screens. That you called to them to help you, and that they followed your signal here.' Echewa laughed. 'So what did you do, my friend? Did you conjure up a double of yourself and slip out through the solid rock. And once outside, in the dust and cold, what did your double do then? Did he make himself a transmitter from the wind and point it at the spacecraft? No. Something's wrong, and I'm going to find out what it is before I decide what I'm going to do.'

Ebert was looking down, the furrows in his brow much deeper than before. He made to talk, hesitated, then looked up at Aluko again. 'It's true. I *did* call out. In my mind. Not to Shen Li. Not to anyone really. But...' He sighed. 'Well, when you came in and told me that he'd come I... I wasn't surprised. I thought, yes, he's answered me. He's come.'

Echewa was staring at him, his eyes wide in his jet-black face. All about him the others were watching closely, their dark faces leaning in towards him, listening.

'You *called*?'

Ebert nodded.

There was a buzz of excited talk between the Osu, strange words in a language Ebert had never heard before, and then Echewa stood, raising a hand for silence.

'You are right, brothers. The way is clear. We must help our friend, even if it means leaving here tonight.' He turned, looking across at the Han, his eyes narrowing. 'But answer me one thing, Shen Li. Is that really your name?'

The small man stared back at Echewa, then shook his head. 'No, Chief Echewa, my family name is Ishida, my given name Ikuro. And before you ask me, it is not a Han name. It is Japanese.'

Ebert laughed. 'Ghosts! I am surrounded by ghosts! Black men and Japanese. Whatever next!'

But Echewa was looking at him intently. 'And you, Hans Ebert? Are you so different, then? Ikuro here, and me, and you yourself, we have this much in common, neh? We are *all* dead men... in *their* eyes.'

He unfastened the chains, then stood back, watching her rub at the welts on her wrists and ankles.

'Will you come?' he asked.

'Come where?'

He looked down. 'I don't know. Away from here, anyway. Away from DeVore.'

She was silent a moment, then. 'I don't understand you. You had me, back then. Had me in your power. You had only to do what he said. So why didn't you? What stopped you?'

'It wasn't right,' he said quietly.

'Not right? When did that ever stop you in the past? I mean, what game is this? What are you trying to do?'

'Nothing.'

'Then why don't you look me in the eyes and say that? Why do you skulk there like some... *creature*. What has he done to you? Cut your balls off or something?'

He looked up at that, the slightest flare of anger in his eyes. She saw it and laughed.

'Ah... So you are in there, after all, Hans Ebert. I was wondering for a while if a shape-changer hadn't taken your body over. Or whether you were some clone made up in one of DeVore's factories.'

He stared at her, surprised. 'You know of that?'

'It was one of my father's pet theories. He wanted to send Karr here to find out if it was true, but the Seven would never let him. But he was right, wasn't he? This is where he was, all the time. Here, on Mars, directing things like some venomous puppet-master. And you, Hans Ebert... what are you if not one of his puppets?'

Ebert shook his head slowly. 'Not now. I promise you.'

'Promise me?' Her laughter was cold, mocking. 'When were your promises worth more than the air in which they were uttered? No. What do the Han say? Ah yes. A snake sheds its skin, but it's still a snake. That's true, neh?'

He stared at her, something strange going on behind his eyes, and then he shuddered.

'Okay. So you don't believe me. That's fine. I can live with that. I *deserve* it. But if my promises mean nothing to you, let what I do stand for what I am. Not what I *was*, for I am that man no longer. You see, Jelka Tolonen, I shed not just a skin, but a self when my father died. I didn't kill him, not physically, and yet I *was* responsible.'

He took a long breath. 'The night he died, he tried to kill me. To choke the life from me. My own father, the man who loved me more than anyone in the world, who cared more for me than for all of the vast commercial empire he had built up. I was blind. I couldn't see that love. Not until it was too late. All I could see was my own greed, my own selfish desires. You saw that. I know you did. I could see it in your eyes, the day of the betrothal, and I...'

'*Words*,' she said harshly, interrupting him, standing to face him. 'What's any of this but words?'

'Yes ...' He turned, looking away from her. 'Will you come, though?'

'Where?'

'Tien Men K'ou? They say your father's fleet has come. They say it's searching for you.'

He looked back. She was staring at him now, her eyes half-lidded.

'Are you serious?'

'If that's what you want.'

She hesitated, her eyes searching his face, and then she laughed. 'What have I got to lose? If you're lying then I'm no worse off. And if you're telling the truth ...' Again she hesitated, but when she spoke again her voice was quieter, softer than before. 'Well... let's deal with that as and when it happens, neh?'

Tien Men K'ou spaceport was on fire. Beyond it, the great dome of the City was in darkness.

'What's happened?' Ikuro asked, leaning across his eldest brother. 'It was all right when we left it!'

'Look there,' Tomoko said, indicating the far right of the screen. 'Those two weren't there when we left. They must be government ships.'

'Yes,' Jelka said, coming up behind them. 'The smaller one is the *Ta Chi*. The big one with the cannons is the *Chang Hsien*. If those two are here then the *Shen Yi* can't be far away.'

'You know these craft?' Tomoko said, turning to look up at her, impressed, it seemed, by her knowledge.

'Yes,' she said, staring at the two ships thoughtfully. 'I've been on the *Chang Hsien* many times.' She turned, looking back at Ebert, who was sitting beside Kano in the central cabin. 'You were right.'

He smiled. 'I know.'

'Tomoko,' she said, not looking away from Ebert, 'send out a signal to the *Chang Hsien*. They'll be using microwave frequencies, 32.4 gigahertz, if I remember rightly. Ask for Commander Hassig, or if he's not there, for Captain Gray. Tell them that you've the Marshal's daughter on board and that you want safe passage to land on the south side of the apron. Oh, and tell him that I'm safe, and that I'm being returned, else he might just take it into his mind to shoot you out of the sky.'

Tomoko turned, looking past her at Ebert.

Ebert nodded once. 'Do as she says.'

'Then it's true. You really are going to let me go.'

'It appears so.'

For the first time she smiled. 'Then maybe I did you wrong, Hans Ebert. Maybe you *have* changed.'

'Maybe,' he answered, his face strangely hard. 'And maybe I was wrong.

Maybe I ought to have kept you. At least you'd have been my wife. At least I'd have had you.'

Her smile slowly faded. 'I'd have killed myself.'

His voice was the merest whisper. 'Maybe. But as it is I've nothing.'

Behind her, she could hear Tomoko, sending out the signal to the *Chang Hsien*, but for once she felt no joy at the prospect of her release, no feeling of relief, for in front of her the man she had loathed these past six, seven years, the man she had feared, in nightmare as in reality, was looking down at the floor, his shoulders bowed, as if in defeat, an unlooked for sadness in his eyes.

'I'll speak out for you,' she said, wanting suddenly, unexpectedly, to comfort him. 'I'll tell my father what you did for me. He'd speak to Li Yuan for you.'

Ebert looked up slowly, meeting her eyes. 'No. It would do no good. There can be no returning. But if you must do something, then do this. Say nothing. Or praise these good fellows here for your rescue. As for me, you never saw me, never heard of me. You understand?'

She stared at him silently, seeing him new.

'Evens?' he said, his eyes narrowing.

Jelka took a long breath, then shook her head. 'No. My aunt, my uncle's death – those lie between us. I can never forgive you those. As for the damage you did me, I forgive you. And yes, I'll say nothing.'

Ebert nodded, satisfied by that. And then, from the speakers above Tomoko, came the answer from the *Chang Hsien*.

They watched her go down; saw dark-uniformed soldiers bow before her then hurriedly form ranks to either side, escorting her into the great battlecruiser. And then she was gone, the hatch sealed up.

Ebert leaned back from the screen and sighed.

'Where now?' Tomoko asked.

'Here,' Ebert said, handing him the piece of paper Echewa had given him earlier.

Tomoko studied the coordinates a moment, then fed them into the computer. A moment later he turned back, frowning. 'But there's nothing there. It's desert.'

'Just go there,' Ebert said, staring at the ship that filled the screen. 'I'll worry about that when we get there.'

An hour later they dropped him, watching as he walked out into the darkness, the desert swallowing him. Yet as they lifted, banking to the right, they saw, in the bright glare of their lights, a dozen men step from a fold in the rocks and form a half-circle about him.

'*Osu*...' Ikuro said quietly. 'Outcasts.'

'Like us,' Kano said, punching in their course, then turning to look across at his little brother, his eyes deeply thoughtful

Yes, Ikuro thought, nodding, then strapped himself in. *Like us.*

'It's done,' DeVore said, 'finished with.'

'Maybe,' Rutherford answered. 'But maybe you should stay. Maybe now that they've got what they want, they'll go away and leave us in peace.'

DeVore laughed scathingly. 'You think so? You really think they'll be happy just to leave us alone? No. This is the excuse they've been waiting for – their chance to punish us. Why, if a tenth of it survives, I'll be surprised. They've been waiting fifty years to do this. You think they'll stop now?'

Rutherford stared at him, shocked. 'But I thought...'

'You thought what? That I *loved* Mars? That this was my home?' He laughed. 'Well, fuck Mars. It's a fucking pit, and always will be. It was useful, very useful, but now that's changed. I've taken the only thing worth keeping. I've shipped it out already.'

'I don't understand.'

DeVore turned away, beginning to clear his desk. 'No, but then you never needed to. You too were useful, Andreas. But now ...' He looked up. 'Well, run away, little boy. I don't want your planet. It's a shit-hole. And I don't want to be King of a shit-hole.'

Rutherford stared at him, astonished.

'Go!' DeVore said, hefting a gun in his hand then aiming it at his erstwhile ally. 'Fuck off, *now*, before I use this thing on you.'

'But Howard...'

The bullet whizzed past him, less than a hand's width from his head, and lodged in the viewscreen behind him, shorting the machine.

'Just go,' DeVore said, more quietly than before. 'Right now, before I kill you.'

Rutherford backed away, then, turning, ran to the door and out. And behind him, echoing down the corridor after him, came DeVore's laugh, like the sound of air escaping from a punctured dome.

CHAPTER 104

MOTHER SKY

It was night. Ahead, across the silent dunes, the Martian capital of Kang Kua was still ablaze, its great dome cracked and open to the sky. Beyond it the crater wall loomed vast and dark.

From a ledge of rock two li to the south, a dozen men looked on, the darkness of their face-plates lit by the flickering flames. They had heard the screams of the dying carried on the thin and frigid air. Through the broad, curving face of the dome they had witnessed the devastation, the slow, suffocating death of Mars's greatest City. Now the dome was dark, fire-blackened, and the trickle of refugees through the main air-lock had ceased. There would be no more survivors.

Ebert looked about him at the silent, watching figures, then turned back, studying the scene, fixing it in mind. In less than thirty hours, two centuries of patient enterprise had been undone. Mars had ripped itself apart in a series of tormented convulsions, like the death throes of an animal driven mad by inner sickness.

As the flames died, they turned away, making their way back to their power sleds. Returning across the darkness of the dunes, there was a brooding silence among them. It was only when they were back inside the settlement, sat about the benches in the meeting room, that they began to talk of what they had seen.

'It is the women and children I feel sorry for,' one of them said, his eyes pained. 'I can't help thinking how I'd feel if they were mine.'

There were nods all round. What they had seen had sobered them. There had been excited talk beforehand, real joy at the prospect of being free finally from the yoke of the Han. But now they understood the price of that freedom – the cost in deaths and human suffering.

One of the younger men looked up, his dark face shining in the lamplight. 'It was awful. I felt so helpless. I wanted to stop it, but what could I do? What could any of us do?'

'We can remember,' one of the eldest, his hair grey, answered him. 'And we can make sure our children remember.'

On the journey north to Kang Kua, Ebert had heard from his companion just how badly the Osu had suffered; how they had been hunted and persecuted, year after year, until their anger had turned to bitterness, their bitterness to resignation. Mother Sky deliver us, they prayed. But now things would be different. There would be new tales to tell the unborn children of the Osu when their time came beneath Mother Sky.

They had fallen into silence. Their heads were lowered, their eyes downcast. Then, as if drawing it up from some well of sadness deep within him, the old man began to sing.

For a moment the old man sang alone, then, slowly, one after another of them joined their voices, until the room resounded to the haunting sadness of the refrain. The men were weeping now, singing and weeping, their faces lifted up, as if they sang for Mother Sky herself.

Ebert, watching, shivered violently, then clenched his fists against the sudden, overwhelming sense of loss he felt, against the vast and echoing emptiness inside him. And yet his grief, his personal suffering, was as nothing beside that of the Osu.

Long ago, so Echewa had told him, the Osu had lived in Africa. For ten thousand years their lives had been peaceful, orderly. They had been as one with the earth and the sky. And then the *Hung Mao* – the White Man – had come, raiding their coastlines and taking them away in great ships, a thousand at a time – men, women and children, chained like animals and kept in dreadful, insanitary conditions. They had been taken to a new land – America – and forced to work the land as slaves. Centuries later, in the time of the tyrant Tsao Ch'un, their kind had been eradicated from Chung Kuo. Yet some had survived, here on Mars. They had come here as free men, along with others – white men and yellow men, men of all creeds and many nations – who had first settled this harsh planet. But when Tsao Ch'un's soldiers came there was no place for them in the Cities, and so they came out here, into the wild, beneath the great blackness. Mother Sky, they called it, seeing in its face the dark reflection of their own. Mother Sky…

He looked from face to face, surprised by the tears that streaked each face, astonished to find no masks, no walls or barriers to these men. You could see what they were at a glance. And with that realisation came a strange and urgent need to be connected – to be *bonded* somehow – to these Osu. To be like them seemed suddenly not merely desirable but essential. He saw how they looked to each other, like brothers, the connections between them welded tight by adversity, and shuddered inwardly. He had been alone. All his life he had been alone. But now he was awake, alive – maybe for the first time in his life free of all masks, all encumbrances of birth – and what was he to do with that?

As the song faded he looked down, trembling, afraid almost to look at them in case, by the slightest word or gesture, they might reject him. For to be cast out by these Osu – these outcasts – would indeed be hell.

'Hans Ebert …'

He looked up. Aluko Echewa was standing there in the doorway across from him, one hand out, summoning him. Ebert looked about him, seeing how they were watching him, curious to see how he would act.

'What is it?' he asked quietly.

'The ships have gone,' Echewa answered, his face expressionless. 'The pipelines are smashed, the Cities all burned or broken. Their dreams of Mars are dead, my friend. It is time for our dream to begin.'

Ebert hesitated, then stood and went across, conscious of their eyes upon him. As Echewa turned away, he followed, down a long, sloping corridor, uncertain what was to befall him. To his right, small galley kitchens and storerooms had been cut into the unfaced rock. Further down, he passed family dormitories where black-faced women sat silently on their bunks, their children surrounding them, watching as he passed. At the bottom the corridor turned abruptly to the right. A suited guard waited there, the inner door to the air-lock held open.

He went inside, standing beside Echewa as he closed the door and spun the wheel. Once before he had stood thus, not knowing what awaited him. Then it had been a race of black men and a woman he had loved and lost.

And now?

He met Echewa's eyes, surprised to find the black man watching him.

'You must not expect too much,' Echewa said.

Too much? He watched the Osu turn and spin the wheel, wondering what he meant by that, then caught his breath as the door swung back and he saw what lay beyond.

He stepped out into a circular hollow in the rock, thirty paces in circumference. The hollow was surrounded by pale, irregular white stone to a height of ten or twelve ch'i. Beneath his feet lay a fine red dust. But his eyes were drawn upwards, up towards the great dark circle of the sky. Above him the stars burned down, Chung Kuo a brilliant point of whiteness in their midst, a Cyclops' eye, staring him out. He turned and looked about him, astonished. It was a dome, a miniature dome.

'This is the place,' Echewa said. 'Wait and he will come.'

Ebert turned, looking back at him. 'Wait?'

But Echewa simply backed away, pulling the door closed behind him, leaving Ebert to the silence and the burning sky. Ebert took two steps towards the centre of the hollow, and then stopped, the hairs rising along his spine and at the back of his neck. Across from him, no more than ten ch'i from where he stood, an old man – a grey-bearded Han – was sitting on a rock, watching him. He was partly in shadow, his robes loose about him. What looked like a flat black case lay in his lap.

And yet the hollow had been empty...

'Welcome, Hans Ebert. Are you more at peace with yourself now?'

Ebert moved closer, until he stood only a body's length from the old man. For a moment he had suspected that it was a hologram of some kind, projected from above, but from close up it was clear that the man was real. The old man's eyes were lucid, his expression calm. There was an air of great serenity about him.

'Who are you?'

The old man smiled, showing a perfect set of yellowed teeth. 'I am Master Tuan. A friend, let us say. Now please, be seated. It is hard to talk to another man when you must crane your neck to see his face, neh?'

'Forgive me ...' Hans sat, folding his legs beneath him. The old Han watched, satisfied, then leaned slightly towards him.

'Did it cost you much to give away that which you wanted most?'

Ebert narrowed his eyes. 'The girl, you mean?'

'Is that what I mean?'

Ebert considered a moment, then nodded. What else was there? All else – all worldly things – meant nothing to him now, only Jelka's good opinion. That and the friendship of the Osu.

'*Was* it hard?'

Ebert looked down. 'Yes,' he admitted. 'Harder than I'd ever imagined. There was a moment – the briefest moment – when I thought of keeping her, but ...' He looked up, meeting the old Han's gaze. 'I could not have lived with myself. You understand?'

The old Han's face did not change. There was the vaguest hint of a smile – of irony? of understanding? – on his lips, and the eyes, staring back into his own, seemed deep and warm and wise beyond all years.

'I have been watching you for a long time now, Hans Ebert. I have seen the path you have taken. To some it might seem that you have fallen far, and yet these eyes have seen you climb from out of the darkness. Then again, some might say that you have come a long way, Tsou Tsai Hei, but the Way is long and you have taken but the first step on that road.'

Ebert leaned forward. 'Forgive me, Master Tuan, but why did you call me that?'

'*Tsou Tsai Hei?*' The old Han laughed. 'Forgive *me*, my young friend, but I thought you knew your Mandarin. Is it so hard to grasp?'

Tsou Tsai Hei. The walker in the darkness.

'No,' Ebert answered, then hesitated, uncertain. He understood the words, but their meaning?

Master Tuan lifted a hand. 'No matter. As Hsu Yu said, name is only the guest of reality. It is what lies behind the name that matters, neh? I mean, where is the darkness? Where is it to be found? In the hearts of men? In the pupil of the eye? In shadows and the sunless depths of night? We say of a man that his heart is dark, and yet without the darkness, where is the light? Without evil, where the good? You have understanding, Tsou Tsai Hei. *You have been there.* All your young life you have been a man of action. Now, as your middle years begin, you must adopt a different course. You must embrace *wuwei*, inaction. You must seek the *te*, the true virtue, that the Way provides.'

He leaned forward slightly. 'You are strong. Strong enough, I note, to kill a man with your bare hands. And yet what is true strength? Is it manifested in the exercise of power over others? Is *that* true strength? Or is true strength the exercise of some inner restraint? Is it a working *against* desire? This you must learn, Tsou Tsai Hei. This and much more.'

'And the Osu? What is their role in this?'

The old Han laughed. 'Am I to tell you *everything*? No, Tsou Tsai Hei, that is for you to learn. Study them. Be as them. The truth will follow. You are to stay here, to finish the work that time has begun in you. To wait here, among these hidden works of darkness. Until the call comes.'

'The call?'

The old man smiled. 'Be patient. Work hard. The Way is difficult, wherever one is. Yet here you might find yourself. And that is the first step, neh? No more masks, Hans Ebert. No more masks.'

The old Han looked down, then lifted the case, offering it to Ebert. 'It will take a while, but you will learn patience. This will help you in that task.'

'What is it?'

'Words. Images. A friend when you need a friend. An eye where you need an eye.'

Ebert leaned in, wanting to query what he meant, but the old man raised his hand once more.

'I am afraid our conversation is over. You must go now. Look, your people are awaiting you.'

Ebert turned. The air-lock was open. In the opening stood two of the Osu, Echewa and the old man who had begun the song. He turned back, meaning to say one final thing, but Master Tuan was gone.

He whirled about, expecting some trick, but there was no sign of the old man within the dome, and there was no way out, unless a man could walk through walls. That thought made him turn and look back at Echewa, recalling what he had said that time, about walking through solid rock.

'Was that real, Aluko?'

Echewa pointed to the case. 'He gave you that?'

Ebert nodded.

'Then it was real.'

Ebert looked up, conscious suddenly of the vastness of the sky above him. Dark it was, and endless. Dark beyond the possibility of any human eye penetrating it. And yet what *was* that darkness? In what way were he and it related? Ebert shuddered. Thus far he had lived his life in the glare of artificial light, with walls on all sides, a floor below and a ceiling overhead. Now he must learn to live differently – to live outside, beneath that vast and overwhelming darkness.

Ebert paused, feeling a stillness settle deep within as he recalled Echewa's words.

The night is our mother. She comforts us. She tells us who we are. Mother sky is all. We live, we die beneath her. She sees all. Even the darkness deep within us.

So it was. So it would be from henceforth. Yes. It was time to refashion himself, to *be* the walker in the darkness.

No more masks, he thought, echoing the old Han's words. Then, with a small bow to the space where Master Tuan had sat, he turned and went across. It was time to be.

PART TWENTY-TWO

Upon a Wheel of Fire

SPRING 2212

'The Master said, 'Cunning words, an ingratiating face and utter servility, these things Tso-ch'iu Ming found shameful. I, too, find them shameful. To be friendly towards someone while concealing one's hostility, this Tso-ch'iu Ming found shameful. I, too, find it shameful.'
—Confucius, *The Analects*, Book V, 25

You do me wrong to take me out o' th' grave.
Thou art a soul in bliss; but I am bound
Upon a wheel of fire, that mine own tears
Do scald like molten lead.
—William Shakespeare, *King Lear*, Act IV, Scene vii

CHAPTER 105

THE THOUSAND EYES

Pale light lay like a glaze on the lacquered surface of the mask, making its darkness shine. The smoothly-rounded dome was high, majestic almost, the features severe, magisterial. Through narrow slits of purest black, the liquid glint of eyes – dark-pupilled and intense – could be seen. Eyes which watched coldly as, at the far end of the huge, obsidian-topped table, the old man bowed low and, glancing fearfully about him, backed away, the chains that bound his hands clinking in the silence. At a signal, the guards escorting him dragged him about and led him from the chamber, their booted footsteps echoing back across the tiled hall.

A door slammed shut. In the silence that followed, six men, masked and cloaked, the dignity of their bearing revealing their high status, turned slightly in their seats about the table, looking towards the First Dragon, who sat, unnaturally still, his gloved hands interlinked.

It was a chill, dark chamber, overlooked on three sides by a high balcony. From there, and in the shadows beyond the seated men, others stood in attendance, waiting upon what the First Dragon would decide.

They had met to discuss the grave situation facing them and to decide upon which course to follow. Two days back the Council of Seven had agreed to cut the funding to the Ministry and to curtail its activities. Taken alone that was a serious matter, but in the context of all else that was happening, it was a severe blow. Moreover what the old man had just told them made it imperative that they took action. But what? What measures could they take and yet remain bonded in loyalty to their Lords and Masters, the Seven?

The mask leaned closer, as if about to utter some secret – some whispered, conspiratorial thing – but the voice that issued from the mask emerged strong and clear: the voice of utter certainty.

'As for the main matter, our course is clear. We must speak with our Masters and convince them that the path they have chosen is... *inadvisable.* That to follow it would lead only to disaster. Second, we must spell out our alternative strategy – a strategy designed to deal with the Seven Ills of our modern age.'

The Seven Ills... There was nodding from all parts of the great, shadowy hall. Once there had been the single 'Great Illness' of false history – an illness their Ministry had been set up to eradicate – but in the last decade all manner of ancient sicknesses had risen from the depths. Religious resurgence, terrorist insurrection and Triad infiltration of the levels – these were the Three Natural Ills and resulted from the great sin of neglected responsibility. Added to them was the new power of the House at Weimar, the changes to the Edict, the declining power of the Seven and, last but not least, the corrupting effect of the Aristotle File. These were the Four Political Ills and resulted directly from the policy of the current Seven. Caught between these varied Ills was the Ministry, the 'Thousand Eyes', of which the First Dragon was the embodiment.

'I will go personally,' he said, sitting upright, his presence rock-like in the tall-backed chair, 'to present them with our proposals and to impress upon them the urgency of the situation.'

'And if they do not listen, *I Lung?*'

The First Dragon turned slightly, meeting the eyes of the Minister who had addressed him, then looked about him at the others seated round the table.

'Then so be it. Our role was defined a hundred and fifty years ago, in Tsao Ch'un's time, when Chung Kuo was first forged from the chaos of the thousand nations. To us was entrusted the task of keeping Chung Kuo strong, its levels unpolluted. To us was given the power of life and death over those who strayed from the Great Path. It would be hard for us to neglect our historical duty and bow meekly before the Seven Ills, yet if the Seven refuse to listen, if they refuse to accept what must be done to safeguard Chung Kuo from those forces which threaten to tear it apart, then we must do as they say. It is not for us to determine policy, merely to carry it out.'

In the stillness that followed there was a tension that was almost palpable.

'And the other matter, *I Lung*? The old man?'

The First Dragon turned, facing the new speaker, directly to his right.

'I knew Yin Shu. Many of us here did. He was a good servant, a trusted man who had attained high office in the Ministry. It saddens me greatly to find him a victim of such corrupting influences. And yet it illuminates the problem, neh? When such a man can be swayed by these ideas, then what chance has old hundred names? No, if anything it confirms my worst fears. We must search out this new disease and uproot it, before the garden is choked with such weeds.'

The First Dragon looked about him, raising his voice so that all could hear him clearly.

'True History, that's what Yin Shu called this new movement. You heard it for yourselves. True History ...' He shook his head slowly then spread his gloved hands before him on the obsidian table. 'Well, we all know what that is, neh? A lie. An attempt to undermine all that we believe in and live for. But they will not succeed. We will not let them succeed. From this moment on I pledge to wage an unending war against those who adhere to the doctrine of True History, to crush them without mercy, whoever they might be and at whatever height we find them. To do otherwise would be to betray the sacred purpose of our Ministry.'

There was a deep murmur of assent.

'Good. Then we are agreed, *ch'un tzu*?'

All about the table the masked heads nodded sternly. Satisfied, the First Dragon stood and raised a hand, dismissing the shadowy figures on the balconies and between the pillars. The meeting was over.

Afterwards, in a smaller, brighter room just off the great hall, they met again, the doors locked and guarded, all masks discarded. On the far wall, beyond a massive desk, hung a large map of Chung Kuo, the seven Cities marked in pale gold, a thousand black-headed pins indicating the position of the Ministry's field operatives – their 'thousand eyes' among the masses. Beneath this map now stood the First Dragon, his broad Han face shining waxily as he looked about him at his fellow Ministers.

'You have prepared the list, brother Fan?' he asked, meeting his fifth brother's eyes.

'I have done as you asked,' the Minister for West Asia replied, handing his eldest brother the handwritten list.

'Good.' The First Dragon scanned the list with interest, then looked up again. 'This is all of them?'

Fan nodded, looking about him at the knowing faces of the other Dragons. 'You want me to act on all of those names?'

'At once. Then see if you can arrange a meeting with An Sheng. I understand the great man is restless, that he has been heard to speak – in private, naturally – of taking matters into his own hands.'

'That is so, brother. And there are others among the Minor Families who feel the same. Would you meet with them all?'

The First Dragon shook his head fastidiously. 'No. An Sheng is the key. If he commits himself, the rest will follow. But in the company of his peers he might feel... *constrained*.'

Fan's smile broadened, understanding.

'Good. Then go at once. See to these names. In the mean-time I shall contact Tsu Ma and beg audience. It is time the Seven understood what depth of feeling they have unleashed.'

Shang Mu waited in the corridor beside the pillar, his head bowed low, as the six Dragons came from the room. Then, at a signal from the Chief Steward, he went inside, guards pulling the huge doors closed behind him.

'Excellency,' he said, bowing low.

The First Dragon stood at the far end of the chamber, in front of a massive desk that, in its dark solidity, was reminiscent of a funerary slab. To his right stood a small, bearded Han with severe features and prematurely grey hair. The bright orange and mauve of his silks were a stark contrast to the severe black of the First Dragon's formal attire. Shang Mu knew him well. His name was Hsia and he was a *Wu*, the First Dragon's personal diviner. Seeing him there gave Shang Mu pause for thought. If Hsia was here, the matter was a serious one.

'Shang Mu,' the First Dragon said, summoning him with his left hand, leaving the hand extended for Shang to kneel and kiss the ring.

Shang straightened up, but kept his eyes averted. 'You summoned me, I

Lung?'

The First Dragon hesitated a moment, then, turning away, began to speak.

'Yin Shu was a good man. A trusted servant. Only a week ago I would have said that no more loyal man existed in the Ministry. But appearances can be deceptive, neh? It seems that True History is like a disease that hollows a man long before its mark is seen on the flesh. One cannot tell until it is far too late.'

Shang Mu lowered his head an inch or two, his stomach tight with fear. Had someone accused him? Was that what this was about? He felt the urge to ask, but checked himself, knowing that to interrupt the First Dragon would only incur the great man's anger.

The First Dragon looked to the *Wu* and nodded, then came across, standing directly in front of Shang.

'And then there's you, Shang Mu. No *Hung Mao* has ever risen as high as you in the Ministry. No one, it seems, has worked harder to fulfil the Ministry's sacred cause. And yet I look at you now and I wonder to myself whether I can trust you. Whether you too might not have been infected with the same disease. You knew Yin Shu, neh? He was a good friend of yours?'

Shang Mu swallowed. 'That is so, Excellency.'

'And you suspected nothing?'

'Nothing, Excellency. To the end he seemed a good man, a trusted friend.'

The First Dragon nodded, then, unexpectedly, he placed his hand gently on Shang's arm. 'Fear not, Shang Mu. I am not accusing you. Yet you must understand my caution. What I have to say...'

He moved away slightly, then lifted a finger, summoning Shang Mu to come with him across to the great desk.

The *Wu* had laid a cloth upon the dark surface; a faded, ancient cloth of white silk. At the centre of the square of cloth was drawn a circle an arm's length in diameter. Within the circle, at the eight points of the compass, were painted the eight trigrams of Heaven, Wind, Water, The Mountain, Earth, Thunder, Fire and The Lake. Outside the circle the trigrams were repeated, their arrangement fitting the 'Sequence of Earlier Heaven', Heaven to Fire, Wind to Earth and so forth. Close by lay the ancient oracle itself, unopened as yet, its plain black cover embossed with the great symbol of the Tao.

Shang Mu watched as the *Wu* made his preparations, lighting tapers to the north and south, to east and west, rocking backwards and forwards all the time and mumbling to himself, as if in a state of trance. On the desk lay the folded piece of paper on which was written the question the First Dragon wished to ask the oracle. Shang glanced at it, then looked up at the First Dragon's face, seeing at once how important this was for him.

'We are ready,' the *Wu* said, turning to face them across the desk. In his right hand he held the fifty yarrow stalks. 'If you would read the question, Excellency.'

The First Dragon leaned across and took the paper. Unfolding it, he cleared his throat, then read.

'As the darkness closes in, should we give torches to the masses, or should the thousand eyes burn brighter?'

Shang looked across. The *Wu* was smiling. He leaned forward, letting the stalks trickle onto the table. Then, with a quick movement of his right hand, he divided them into two and then again, so that three groups of stalks lay on the table – the three lines of the first trigram. Satisfied, he gathered them up again and repeated the process.

Time and again he let the stalks fall gently from his hand, then divided them up. Time and again he stared at the resultant trigrams, as if fixing them in mind. Finally, he pushed them to one side and looked up, meeting the First Dragon's eyes.

'The upper trigram is *Ch'ien*, Heaven, the lower is *K'an*, Water. The hexagram is *Sung*, Conflict.'

The First Dragon stared at him, almost in disbelief, then spoke, his voice a whisper. '*Sung*... Are you sure?'

The *Wu* nodded, then, taking up the great book, turned to the relevant page and read.

> 'Conflict. You are sincere
> And are being obstructed.
> A cautious halt half-way brings good fortune.
> Going through to the end brings misfortune.
> It furthers one to see the great man.
> It does not further one to cross the great water.'

The First Dragon looked away, clearly agitated. 'It is as I feared. When I first called you, *Wu Hsia*, I said to myself, if it is *Sung* then I shall know. It will be 'Conflict'. And yet does the oracle not say that such conflict cannot be engaged in successfully? Does it not say that, though our cause is right, though our minds are clear and strong, to carry our purpose through can bring only further ill?' He shook his head, pained by the answer he had received. 'If it is so, then how can I act? How can I take the first step knowing the abyss that lies before me?'

The *Wu* was looking down, fingering his beard. 'It does not have to be so, my Lord. As the oracle says, contention may be lucky when balanced and correct. Seek balance in your actions and all will be well.'

The First Dragon stared at the *Wu* a moment, then, with an irritable little gesture, waved him away. 'Leave me now, Hsia. I must talk to my Junior Minister.'

'Excellency.'

Bowing, leaving his things where they lay, the *Wu* backed out of the room. When he was gone, the First Dragon turned, facing Shang Mu again.

'Do you understand what is happening, Shang Mu?'

Shang hesitated, then ventured an answer. 'Has it to do with your meeting with Tsu Ma?'

'It is related.'

'Related, Excellency?'

'As the shadow to the sun. You see, Shang Mu, I expect nothing from my meeting with Tsu Ma. No concessions, no new funding, not even the courtesy of an explanation. And yet the meeting is essential. Without it, nothing is clarified. Without it the oracle means nothing.'

'I don't understand you, Excellency. If Tsu Ma concedes nothing, then what will be clarified?'

'There is to be a new directive. A brand new strategy to deal with the Seven Ills.'

Shang Mu stared at his Master. 'But just now, in the great chamber, you said we would do as the Seven commanded. That we would carry out their policy, not determine our own.'

The First Dragon smiled tightly. 'That is true. But what was said out there was said for the Seven's spies in our midst, it did not reflect the wishes of the Inner Council.'

'I see.'

'Good.' The First Dragon paused, looking at him strangely, then went around his desk and sat. 'You must understand, Shang Mu. What is said in public and what is done privately must diverge from henceforth. It is unfortunate but necessary. We cannot just sit back and let the Seven steer us onto the rocks. We must take things into our own hands, for the good of all. This is not disloyalty, you must be clear on that, Shang Mu. What will be done will be done not for personal gain, nor to extend the power of this Ministry, but for the long-term good of Chung Kuo.' He paused, his voice taking on a solemn air. 'We have looked at this clearly and are agreed on it. The Mandate has been broken. We must act now or see the world we've built crack apart.'

The Mandate has been broken... Shang Mu felt a great wave of shock wash over him at the words. Yet wasn't it so? Weren't the Seven Ills evidence enough of the Seven's failure to control events? No. The First Dragon was right. It was time to act, independently of the Seven if necessary. He had known it for some while, but it had taken the First Dragon's words to make him realise it.

Shang Mu bowed low. 'I will do whatever is asked of me, *I Lung*.'

'Good. Then listen closely. The matter of funding is a pretext. It is a century or more since we depended on the Seven for our funding. But that is not to say that funding is unimportant. Over the next few months we must make strenuous efforts to obtain new funding. Arranging that will be part of your new task, Shang Mu.'

'But where will I find such funding, Excellency?'

The First Dragon reached into a drawer beside him and took out a slender file, handing it across. 'In there you will find a list of all those who, over the past few years, have shown, by word or deed, opposition to the Seven's actions. Normally, as you know, we would have taken action – in concert with Security – to discredit or destroy such opposition, but it was decided, at a secret meeting some three years ago, to refrain from such action for a time in the case of those whose power or influence might, at some future date, prove useful.' He smiled. 'That time is now. We must harness such opposition and direct it... create an alliance of like-minded people to fight this debilitating sickness of liberalism.'

He leaned towards his Junior Minister, his face suddenly stern, implacable. 'Understand me well, Shang Mu. This is no time for half measures. We must grasp the nettle or go under. Security are no longer the force they were. They are corrupt and lazy, rotten to the core, their intelligence gathering poor, their generals weak and indolent. It is left to us alone to carry the torch, to keep alight the bright ideals of our forefathers. Too many compromises have been made. Too many deals. It is time to tear up all paper tigers, to purge the levels and enforce a rigid discipline on this great society of ours. The Seven will not do that. They lack the will. Only we can do it, Shang Mu. Only the Thousand Eyes.'

Shang bowed his head, stirred by his Master's words. 'I understand, Excellency, and am willing to do all you ask of me and more, but what of the Seven? Surely they will expect us to react to their decision? And our agents – how are we to convince them of the necessity of the new directive?'

'Good points, Shang Mu, but we have considered everything. As far as the Seven are concerned, we shall make great show of our outrage at their decision. I shall make much of contacting Ministers and other high officials of influence to press our case not merely for a return to old levels of funding and staffing but for an increased share of resources. To their eyes it will look as if I am fighting my corner hard, even to the point of resignation. Seeing that, their suspicions will be blunted. They will think they have dealt with me. But the real work of opposition will go on elsewhere, in secret, where their prying eyes cannot see. That is where you come in, Shang Mu. You and the internal network you have built so carefully these past thirty years.'

Shang bowed, conscious of the praise in his superior's eyes.

'I have thought long and hard about this, Shang Mu, and have decided that one man alone can organise all this; only one man has the skill, the diplomacy, the contacts, to enable us to build our great alliance without a word getting out, and that is you.

'As First Operator you will be responsible for coordinating all aspects of our plan. You will appoint key officials to work under you and come to me with any requests for special funding. As for the agents in the field, they will continue as before. They will act only on specific instructions, received direct from your office. At no point are they to be made aware of the new directive. Only we, the seven Dragons, yourself, and others I shall let you have the names of, know of this. It is our secret. A deadly secret. And a sacred trust. You understand?'

'I understand, I *Lung*.'

'Good. Then there is one last thing you must do for me. On the way out my Chief Steward will hand you a file. In the file is a handwritten report. I want you to read it, tonight, and then come to me first thing tomorrow morning, at sixth bell, here in this office.'

Shang went to nod, then spoke instead. 'And might I ask what your Excellency requires of me?'

'Exactly what I said. I want you to read it. Nothing more. And remember, there is no turning back from this. If any one of us fails we are all dead men. And dead men cannot help Chung Kuo, can they?'

Shang Mu met his Master's eyes solemnly. 'No, I *Lung*.'

'Then go. There is much to do.'

The young woman stood at the entrance to Hui Tsung Street, her sketchboard held against her chest, looking across at the crowd gathered at the feet of the *hua pen*. The storyteller was sitting cross-legged on a low platform, a ragged group of children scattered about him. Further back, small groups of old men and idlers looked on, while at a nearby guardpost three young, fresh-faced officers leaned idly on the barrier, listening to the tale.

From where she stood Hannah could hear the *hua pen*'s voice clearly, rising animatedly above the background hubbub. Most of the *hua pen* she had seen before now had been old men, greybeards, sage-like and somnolent, their delivery slow, almost ritualistic, as if they had told the tale one time too many and were bored with it, but this one was different. For a start he was a relatively young man, in his thirties. Moreover he looked more like an actor in a historical drama than a traditional *hua pen*, his startling orange whiskers and unkempt hair – hair that was barely kept in check by a broad, blood-red headband – emphasising the pop-eyed savagery of his face. In his flowing black cloak he seemed more like an ancient bandit prince than a teller of tales, his arms making huge, exaggerated shapes in the air, his hands every bit as expressive as the words he uttered.

She had heard the story often – it was the famous tale of Wu Song, one of the heroes of the *Shui Hu Chuan*, the 'Outlaws of the Marsh', of how he first met the great Song Jiang, the 'Timely Rain' as he was known, and of how he had killed the man-eating tiger on Ching Yang Ridge – yet she had never heard it told with such power, such vitality. For a time she found herself caught up in the tale, swept along, as if this were the first time she had heard it, then she reminded herself why she was there and, crouching, balancing the sketchboard on her knee, she began to set it all down, using the finest setting on the stylus. It was a quick, rough sketch – more an impression than an accurate depiction of the scene – yet when she had finished it she nodded to herself. Yes, that was it. That was it exactly. That sense of tense excitement in the crowd – the childlike anticipation of each new, yet familiar twist in the tale – it was there in every line, every shadow of her sketch. She pressed to save and store, then rested there, lightly balanced on her haunches, her arms draped loosely across the sketchboard, watching the *hua pen*.

She was a striking-looking young woman, a *Hung Mao*, yet with something distinctly Han about her. Tall and willow-like, her eyes were dark and piercing, while her long, jet-black hair was plaited into a single thick braid that lay against her back. From the simple elegance of her clothes and the strong lines of her face you might have thought that she was in her early twenties, but in actuality she was a mere sixteen years old. As she crouched there, watching the *hua pen*, the eyes of the youngest of the soldiers went to her appreciatively, then looked away, thoughtful. She was not of this level, that was certain, yet what she was doing down here – a young woman, alone and unguarded – was hard to fathom.

The tale was almost ended, the climax of Wu Song's adventure almost reached. The *hua pen* was leaning forward, his voice lowered slightly, almost confidential as he told of the attempted seduction of Wong Sun by his elder brother's wife, Golden Lotus, when, from the far end of the corridor came the sound of gunfire. There was a moment's shocked silence as all heads turned to look, and then all hell broke loose.

Hannah had straightened up at the sound of the shot; now she drew back, into the doorway of a nearby shop, staring open-mouthed as people struggled to get away. Instinctively she held the sketchboard in front of her to protect herself, yet there was no need. It was as if she stood at the centre of a magic circle in which she could not be harmed. All about her people were panicking, fighting each other to get away, yet the stream of frantic humanity flowed about her, as if she were a rock, going either left into the big feed corridor where she had been standing, or right, towards the inter-level stairs. She watched, horrified, as, only ten *ch'i* from where she stood, an old woman went down and was instantly trampled beneath a hundred urgent feet, then cried out as she saw a child stumble and go down on the stairway. But there was nothing she could do. In front of her and to either side the crush of people was too great.

From the far end of the corridor came the sound of sporadic gunfire, carrying over the shouts and screams of the fleeing crowds. Then, as the crowd in front of her began to thin, she glimpsed a tall, well-dressed *Hung Mao* with long, red-gold hair, making his way through. The man turned and, raising his right hand, fired back at his pursuers, then ran on. Beneath his left arm he was carrying a package, something that looked like a small bolt of silk or a box of expensive chocolates. He hesitated, looking about him anxiously, then ran off to the left, choosing one of the small side corridors that led through to the inter-deck lifts. Yet even as he ran she knew he would not get far, for his pursuers – Security guards, a dozen or more in number – were close behind.

For a moment Hannah hesitated, then, impulsively, she started forward, pushing her way through to where she had last seen the man. As she began to run someone called out to her – one of the young soldiers from the guard-post – but she ignored him and ran on. She was certain now that something important was going on: something so important that Security were willing to panic a whole deck – and risk a large number of lives – to get what they wanted.

And what was that?

Instinctively she knew it had to do with the package. In fact the more she thought about it, the more she knew it for a certainty. She had seen the fear in the man's face – the frightened certainty of capture and death – and yet he had gripped the package as if his life depended upon it. And why should that be unless it were more important than his life?

Maybe. But what could be more important to a man than his life?

Hannah stopped and turned. The short corridor behind her was empty. To her right was a locked-up shop, the boarded window covered with paste-on posters. To the left was a communal washroom. She shivered. Instinct told her that she had missed something. Or seen something but not registered it properly. She walked back slowly, looking to either side of her. Nothing. Nothing at all. She turned back, determined to go on, to witness for herself what happened. And then she saw it.

The package was wedged into the vent above the washroom door, one edge jutting out into the corridor. Quickly she went across and, reaching up, tugged at it until it came loose. Then, looking about her, she went inside, ignoring the stench of the place, and found a stall, pulling the door closed behind her.

For a moment she hesitated, staring at the package. It was heavy; heavier than her sketchboard even. Nor had she been mistaken. The silk wrapping alone was beyond the purse of anyone at this level. This wasn't Yu, this was First Level. But what did that mean?

She took a long, deep breath. The right thing to do was to go back out and find the Security officer in charge of the operation and hand it to him, but for once doing the right thing seemed entirely inappropriate. She wanted to know what was in the package, and why a man should be willing to die to keep it from them.

She knew how they worked. Security would strip the level bare to get what they wanted – would search each and every one who went, herself included. But this time they would find nothing.

Setting the parcel down, she took the sketchboard from about her neck and, balancing it on top of the seat, began to strip the inner workings from it. She had done it often enough when cleaning the machine, but this time she undertook the task in real earnest. As each piece of the delicate mechanism came loose, she lifted it and let it fall beside the bowl. Then, when she was done, she forced the package into the central space and popped back the sketchboard's screen. She took another long breath, calming herself. The machine looked no different. Only the discarded parts gave the game away, but there was nothing she could do about that. Audacity alone would save her now.

She stood, then turned and went out. At the washroom door she paused, listening. There was shouting still, some distance off, but things seemed much calmer than earlier. Quickly she turned right, making towards the big inter-level lift.

You're mad, she told herself. *There's no reason for this. None at all.* But she was in the grip of a compulsion. She had to get the package out. Suddenly it was as if she were Song Jiang himself, alone in the enemy camp with only his wits, his silver tongue, to get him out.

'Nu Shi...'

She stopped and slowly turned, facing back down the full length of the corridor. It was the young soldier from the guardpost; the one who had been watching her. He came quickly towards her, then stopped, three paces away, his head bowed.

'Are you all right, Nu Shi?'

Her mouth was dry, her hands, where they clutched the sketchboard to her chest, damp. She lowered her eyes and nodded, playing upon the vulnerability the guard clearly expected from her, exaggerating it, knowing instinctively that he was the key.

'It was awful,' she said quietly, in an affected little girl voice. 'I thought I was going to die.'

'It's all right,' the guard said, coming a pace closer, trying to reassure her, to comfort her without touching her, knowing – by her clothes, her manner – that she was far above him. 'It's all over. They got him. Look, I'll see you to the transit, neh?'

'Thank you.' But inside she was burning with curiosity. How had they got him, and where? And was he alive or dead? Maybe they were questioning him right now, torturing him, perhaps, to get the truth from him. And if they were, they would come here soon and find the machine's discarded machine-parts and then...

'Come,' the young soldier said. 'Let's get you out of here.'

She let him lead her out into the main feed corridor and along, past milling crowds of curious locals and then down two flights of stairs to the bottom of the deck. There, in the space before the inter-level transit, a barrier had been set up. In front of it a dozen guards formed a line, their riot helmets lowered, their heavy automatics held threateningly at waist-level. Seeing it Hannah's heart began to beat fast.

To one side of the barrier an officer sat behind a desk, questioning an elderly Han. Hannah followed the young soldier across, close behind him as he pushed through the queue, coming out before the desk.

The officer – a young man, in his mid-twenties – looked up at her quizzically, then turned to the young soldier, clearly angered at being interrupted.

'What is it?'

The young man stiffened slightly, then answered. 'The Nu Shi here was caught up in things earlier. This isn't her level, sir, and I thought...'

'Quiet!' The lieutenant turned back, staring up at her. His voice had been hard, dispassionate. Now his eyes studied Hannah's face as if she were something strange and horrible; something he would like to crush beneath his heel. 'Your pass, please,' he said coldly, his politeness masking what seemed a natural brutality.

Reaching into her jacket, she pulled out her pass and handed it across to the officer, watching as he opened it out and began to read. After a moment he looked up, surprised. Then, getting up, he went across and talked quietly to a second officer who was standing by the lift. The two of them spoke for a moment, a hint of urgency about their whispering, and then they came back. The second man, a Captain, stood to the fore, Hannah's pass between his hands. He looked at it once, checking the holo-photo against her face, then gave a bow.

'Forgive me Nu Shi Shang. We had no idea that you were on this deck. If I had known, I would have assigned a squad to protect you.' He smiled weakly, then continued. 'You must forgive me if I am constrained from advising you exactly what has been happening here – I'm sure you understand – but if you would like an escort home... ?'

She looked past him at the lieutenant. The man's eyes no longer met hers. Abashed, he looked to one side, his discomfort evident in the way he stood there.

'Thank you ...' she glanced at the name tag at his neck, '...Captain Johnson. I must admit, I feel rather shaken by events. I think it would be best if I did as you suggested.'

'Of course...' He bowed his head respectfully, then, 'Forgive me, Nu Shi, I don't wish to be impertinent, but what exactly *were* you doing at this level? It can be dangerous this far down, even at the best of times. I'd have thought your father ...'

He hesitated, then changed tack, as if mention of her father disturbed him. Then, suddenly remembering that he still held her pass, he stepped forward, offering it back to her.

'I was sketching,' she said, taking the pass from him and slipping it back inside her jacket. 'Drawing scenes from life down here. Usually my guard is with me, but he was ill today. I suppose I shouldn't have come. There's usually no trouble. Even so, I'll not make the same mistake again, neh?'

'No...' The Captain smiled, then turned, giving instructions to the lieutenant. With the briefest glance, the young officer turned away and went across to speak to his guards.

'You must forgive his abruptness,' the Captain said quietly, leaning closer to her, 'but he lost two of his men today. This business...' He shook his head. 'Well, it has been a pleasure meeting you, *Nu Shi Shang*. I hope your drawings are satisfactory. Have you plans to publish them?'

She kept her smile steady. 'No. It's only a hobby. Besides, they're not that good.'

'Ah ...' He looked away a moment, then, as if recollecting what he was supposed to be doing, he straightened up and, bowing his head smartly to her, he took a step backward. 'Well, if you would forgive me now, there's much to do.'

'Did you... get him?'

He hesitated, meeting her eyes. 'You saw him, then?'

She nodded, remembering the sight of the man running, the way his red-gold hair had flowed out behind him as he fled, the fear in his ashen face.

The Captain sighed. 'We got him. I wanted him alive, of course, but he gave us no choice. As I said, we'd already lost two men, with another couple wounded. I couldn't risk losing any more. Strange, though, I'd not have thought him the type.'

'The type...?'

'Never mind. Look. You get back now. And next time you want to have adventures, bring a pair of guards, neh?' He smiled. 'Oh, and if you speak to your father, please pass on my deepest respect. I shall make sure he receives a copy of my full and final report.'

She smiled. 'That is most kind, Captain. I'll make certain he knows of your kindness and efficiency.'

She turned, looking to the young guard. 'And thank you. You were most helpful.'

The young soldier blushed and lowered his head. '*Nu Shi...*'

Two soldiers escorted her to the lift, standing at a respectful distance as the big transit climbed the levels. And as it rose, she stood there, the sketchboard clutched tightly to her chest, staring blindly at the blank white doors, the image of the dead man vivid in her memory.

Dead, she thought. *But why?*

And suddenly a second image came to mind, of the dead man fastened to a pole and slung between two guards, his thick, red-gold hair hanging like a mane beneath him as they carried him along.

Yes, she thought, like the great man-eating tiger Wu Song had killed up on Ching Yang Ridge.

Whatever he'd had, whatever it was that she carried in the hollow of the sketchboard, was something that terrified the authorities just as much as roaming man-eaters had terrified the villagers of long ago. But there were no heroes in the modern world, no Wu Songs or Song Jiangs, and certainly no tigers – only men and the things men did. So what was it? What could possibly be so important that a young man would choose death rather than relinquish it?

She looked down at the sketchboard, conscious suddenly of what she had done back there. Aware – suddenly, acutely *aware* – that three men had died over this thing she carried with her.

Hannah closed her eyes, feeling the sharp edge of the casing pressed against her ribs, the upward motion of the lift as it climbed towards the top of the City, and shivered. She would know soon enough. But what then? What would she do with that knowledge?

She waited, emptying herself, but no answer came. Curiosity had driven her this far. But beyond that she didn't know. She simply didn't know.

The lift slowed and stopped. Hannah opened her eyes.

'Nu Shi ...'

She went out, between the guards, numbed, suddenly uncertain that she had done the right thing, convinced that they would find the inner workings of the sketchboard and piece together what she'd done. And then even her father's influence would not save her. But it was done now. She had committed herself, just as surely as the young man with the red-gold hair. She too, now, was a tiger.

Chen crouched over the broken machine, studying it closely. It was the tenth he had seen that morning and, like the others, it was damaged almost beyond recognition – kicked and beaten with a savagery that was hard to imagine. This time, however, they had been careless. This time they had not smashed the security cameras before the attack.

'You'll get the scum who did this, Major Kao, you understand me? I want them tracked down like the dogs they are and punished.'

Chen turned, staring up at the obese form of the AutoMek director, then looked past him at his duty sergeant.

'Sergeant Krol, take *Shih* Cornwell back to headquarters and make sure he is treated with the respect he is due. Once I have completed my investigations here I shall join you.'

He turned back to the Company man, lowering his head respectfully. 'Forgive me, *Shih* Cornwell, but as I'm sure you'll understand, I must give this matter my utmost concentration.'

'I fail to see ...' Cornwell began, but Chen stood, raising a hand to silence him.

'You want the job done, *Shih* Cornwell. I understand that. Now, please, let me get on with it. Unless you want this 'scum' to evade us once again.'

Cornwell glared at him a moment, then, relenting, took a step backward. With a terse little bow he turned away, allowing Chen's sergeant to lead him away.

Watching him go, Chen let out a huge sigh of relief. 'These days they think they own us,' he said, turning, looking across at his lieutenant, Wilson, who stood nearby, looking on.

Wilson smiled. 'I admire your patience, Major. I'm sure I'd have given him a mouthful.'

'And ended before a tribunal ...' Chen shook his head, then looked back at the machine. 'The thing is that I understand all this. These machines,' he stood, wiping his hands together, 'each one of them replaces eight good men – throws eight hard-working sweepers out of work. And for what? To boost the Company's profits and make insects like Cornwell even fatter than they already are!'

'Isn't that so! Half our work these days seems to be tidying up the mess our so-called superiors have made.'

Chen looked at his lieutenant sternly.

'Oh, I don't mean our Masters,' Wilson said quickly, raising his hands as if to defend himself. 'No, I mean *hsiao jen* like Cornwell there. Little men, thinking they've the power of life and death over others – that money makes them gods.'

Chen sighed. 'In a way it does. It always has. But that's not our problem, neh? Our job is to sort out the mess. To find this... scum... and make them pay.'

Wilson moved closer, handing Chen a small cassette. 'Well, this time it couldn't be simpler. We've got it all here. Six faces. No masks, no hoods. Clear shots.'

'We've got names?'

'And addresses. They're all ex-sweepers, naturally. So there we have it. Evidence, motive, the lot. All we have to do is round them up.'

Chen took the tape and stared at it, then looked back at him. 'Who else knows about this?'

'No one. Only you and me.'

'But there's a copy, neh? On record.'

'Not now there isn't. I... erased it.'

'Ah...' Chen looked at the tape again. 'So this is it? Without this we've nothing?'

'That's about it.'

Chen looked up again, smiled, then dropped the tape and crushed it beneath his booted heel. 'Shame,' he said, meeting Wilson's eyes clearly. 'It looks like the cameras failed again. Pity. We might have got them this time.'

Wilson nodded, then, taking a folded sheet from his pocket, handed it to Chen. 'Those are the addresses. It's the only record. Burn it once you've used it, huh?'

'Okay.' Chen slipped the paper into his pocket, then, smiling, reached across and patted his shoulder. 'You're a good man, Stephen. A good soldier. And a good friend.'

'And Cornwell.'

Chen laughed. 'Don't worry. I'll deal with that fat toad. Scum...' He shivered, a sudden indignation overtaking him. 'As if he understood...'

Hannah stood at her father's door, looking in. He was sat at his desk on the far side of the room, a reading lamp hovering just above his right shoulder.

'Father?'

He looked up, then seeing it was her, stood, beckoning her across. They embraced, his face lit up with delight at seeing her.

'I didn't know you were coming home,' she said, hugging him tightly. 'I thought you'd be gone another week yet.'

'I know, but something's come up.' He indicated the files scattered about his desk. 'I've got to prepare something for the morning. Something confidential. I thought it best, in the circumstances, to bring it back here.'

She moved back slightly, looking down at him, sensitive to the unusually guarded tone in his voice. 'Confidential? I thought everything you did was confidential. Why, you're the great master of all secrets, aren't you?'

Normally he would have laughed and played along with her, but this time he looked away, his face troubled. 'This is no joking matter, my love. It's deadly serious.' He looked back at her. 'I am to report to the First Dragon himself first thing tomorrow morning. The I Lung has an appointment with the T'ang, Tsu Ma. It seems the very future of the Ministry is at stake.'

'I see. So...'

He leaned towards her, putting a finger to her lips. 'No, sweetheart. Not a word. If I could tell you, I would. You know that. But for once it's best you don't know. Not until it's over.'

'Okay. Then I'd best leave you to it, neh?'

'It would be best.'

'And tomorrow? Will you be here for dinner?'

He hesitated, then shook his head. 'It would be nice, but I think it might be difficult. There's much to do. The I Lung has given me a new appointment. I'm afraid I may be gone rather a lot in the coming months.'

She studied him a moment, seeing how tired he looked, how drawn, and felt a stab of concern for him. 'So what's new?' she said, trying to coax a smile from him. 'The day you aren't busy you'll be dead, and then it'll be my turn to be busy, clearing up after you.'

He laughed. 'Look, I'll try. But you must try, too. Your mother...'

'That woman...'

'*Please*, Hannah. I know you two don't get on, but you could make an effort. If only to help me, neh?'

'Okay. I'll try.' She leaned close, kissing his brow. 'I hope it all goes well tomorrow.'

'You and I both, my love...'

Back in her own rooms, she locked the main door, leaving the key in the lock, then went through to her study. The package was on the desk where she had left it, the kitchen knife beside it.

She switched on the desk lamp then stood there, staring at it. Three men had died over whatever was inside. Three men... and maybe more. Who knew? She took a long, shuddering breath, then set to work, cutting through the fine silk wrapping.

Inside was a plain white folder and inside that ...

She took the handwritten pages out and set them on the desk beside the wrapping, then pulled up a seat and began to read, speaking the words aloud.

'The Aristotle File... being the true history of the West, 384 BC to AD 2087.'

She stopped, a shiver passing down her spine. *The true history...*

Then it was true. All the whispers and mumbled half-tales were true. She flicked through quickly, reading a paragraph here, a few words there, then stopped again, looking up, finding it suddenly difficult even to take a breath.

So it was all a lie, one vast deception. It was unthinkable, *impossible*, and yet she knew it was true. All her life she had suspected it, and now she knew.

She sat back, feeling strange, almost insubstantial, the room, the very chair on which she sat somehow changed from what they'd been only a moment before.

She understood... the deaths, the urgency of the pursuit. This file – this *truth* – was a ticking bomb, waiting to explode. Even to know of its existence was, she knew, a capital offence. And yet to deny it, wasn't that also a kind of death?

The darkness shimmered before her eyes.

She shuddered, filled by the vision that had come to her. There was her world, like a giant crystal globe, adrift in the vacuum of space. From afar it seemed to glimmer in the starless emptiness, lit from within by the shining, translucent figures of forty thousand million ghosts, their pale, tormented eyes pleading for release.

Ghosts, *yes*... they were the hungry ghosts of Han legend: those poor, unfortunate wretches who could find no rest, neither in this world nor the next. Her eyes met theirs, understanding for the first time the insatiable craving that drove them, the dissatisfaction that had eaten away at them until there was nothing left of them but *this* – this shell, this pale imitation of being. There they all were, the spirits of the lost and abandoned, of those who had drowned at sea and those who had suffered sudden, violent death; of those who had no families to mourn them, and those who had been shunned by their fellow men. She watched them, saw how they burned, without sound or heat, the pale light of their consumption slowly guttering towards extinction, and understood that this could not go on. To be born into this world was to be still-born. To live here was intolerable. But hadn't she always known that? Hadn't she, at the back of everything, always known the falseness of it all?

She moaned. Lies, all of it lies, and her father a custodian – an *intimate* – of that great deception. That, perhaps, was the worst of it: that such a good, kind man – such a funny, caring man – could serve so foul an end. For there was no doubt of it, a lie so vast, so all-permeating, was evil.

Secrets – she was used to secrets – but lies were different. Lies corroded. They were a disease of the inner self. They ate the marrow from the bone. Besides, what purpose had life if its lessons could be doctored, its lived experience *rewritten* by those who followed after? How could they learn to be better people if the past were forever denied to them?

She shivered, her distress giving way to indignation. How *could* they have done this? Who gave them the right? And how many deaths, how much suffering had the Ministry caused in policing the Lie?

Her father... it all came back to her father. What was it the Han said? Ah yes. She said the rhyme aloud, her voice a whisper:

> 'A dragon begets a dragon.
> A phoenix begets a phoenix.
> The son of a rat, from the day of his birth,
> Knows only how to dig a hole in the ground.'

So what was she? Dragon, phoenix, or the daughter of a rat? Or was it really that simple? All agreed that her father was *lao shih* – was a genuine, straightforward man – and yet his whole life was an intricate lie, a social mask, constructed to conceal his work for the Thousand Eyes. And she had inherited something of his manner. Even today, in getting hold of the File, she had used lies and deceptions. So where did one draw the line? Where did the small lie end and the Big Lie begin?

Hannah looked back down at the File. Words, that's all it was. Mere words. Yet this was potentially more dangerous, more destructive to the status quo, than an army of a million men. Why, if this were known to all...

She grew still, the idea growing in her. *If this were known to all*... But why not? Why did it have to be like this – passed furtively from hand to hand in fear of discovery? Why couldn't it be done more openly, more *effectively*?

There had to be a way.

Setting the title page aside, she began again, reading the opening words and then reading them again, letting them burn into her mind, knowing – even as she did – that things would never be the same.

Kao Chen looked up from his crowded desk and met his Duty Captain's eyes. 'What now? Not another instruction from our merchant friend, I hope!'

The Captain bowed, handing a sealed package across. 'No, sir. It's from General Rheinhardt. I was told to give it to you urgently.'

Chen sat back, letting the package fall onto the pile in front of him. 'As if we've not enough... Okay. Tell the General's messenger that I'll get onto it at once.'

'Sir!'

When his Captain had gone, Chen sat there a moment, staring at the stack of papers that cluttered his desk. He was behind, badly behind, but then who wasn't in Security these days? The truth was that there was too much crime and too few of them to deal with it, and the recent slackening of the Edict had only made things worse. As more and more people found themselves out of work, so the problem grew – exponentially it seemed. And always there was more to do, less time to do it in.

With a tired sigh he picked up the package and tore the seal open, then tipped it up, letting the contents fall out onto the desk.

A file. Another damn file. He picked it up and flicked through it quickly, then returned to the beginning, suddenly alert, sitting forward and drawing the lamp closer.

It was another of them ...

He read it through quickly, then pushed it aside with a grunt of irritation, shaking his head angrily. The idiots! The fatheads! Couldn't they ever get it right? This was the fourth of these he'd seen in the last six months and every time they'd fucked up when it came down to it. Four pursuits, four deaths – it was a pretty slipshod record. Little wonder Rheinhardt wanted someone new to take things over.

Yes, but why me? I've enough on my plate as it is.

He sat back, yawning, knowing he needed rest – a break from duties. Not only that, but he'd promised Jyan he'd spend some time with him. Oh, Jyan would understand – he *always* understood – but it wasn't fair on the boy.

Not now, when things were so difficult at home.

Leaning forward again, he tapped out the code for his apartment, then waited as the connection was made. Even that was getting worse. Two, three years ago, there would have been no waiting time, but now... Well, it was like his friend Karr had said, last time they'd got together. Things were going to hell in a bucket!

'Hello... ?'

The voice was small, distorted, but Chen knew at once who it was. It was his daughter, Ch'iang Hsin, the baby of the family.

'Hello, my little peach. It's daddy. Is Jyan there?'

There was a hesitation, then. 'He's with mummy. She's not been well. She's been crying again. Wu has gone for the doctor.'

Chen sighed. 'Okay. Well, look, my love, tell Jyan that I can't get back tonight. Tell him... tell him that I'll speak to him as soon as I can. Have you got that?'

'She's not well, daddy. She...'

He could hear the pain in her voice, but there was little he could do. Maybe the doctor could give Wang Ti something. Something to make her sleep, perhaps. Maybe that would help.

'Look, my love, be brave for me, okay? I'll try and get back there as soon as I can. I promise I will. But it won't be tonight. Something very important has come up and daddy has to see to it, okay?'

Her voice seemed even smaller. 'Okay... but be home soon, daddy. I love you.'

'I love you too, my peach. I love you very much. Kiss mummy for me, neh?'

He broke contact, the tightness in his gut much worse than usual. It wasn't fair on them, he knew. He was away too much, and the woman he had hired to help out didn't begin to meet the children's emotional needs. Something had to be done, and soon, but just now he had no time to see to it.

Chen stood, raising his arms above his head, stretching the tiredness from his chest and upper shoulders. Reaching into his left-hand drawer, he took two tablets from the packet he kept there and popped them into his mouth, swallowing them down, knowing they'd keep him awake and alert for another twelve hours.

He looked about him at the clutter of his office. Short-term solutions, that was how he lived his life these days – juggling a whole mess of short-term solutions. But the problems were long-term and some time soon he'd have to face up to them.

After this, perhaps, he thought, picking up the file and going across to the door. *Maybe I'll ask for a week's leave and try and sort things out.* He knew it was what he ought to do. Things couldn't go on much longer the way they were. But what *was* the answer?

To endure, part of him answered. To keep on, day by day, holding things together, smoothing over the cracks, until...

Chen shuddered, then, taking his tunic down from the peg by the door, slipped it on and went through into the outer office, summoning his men to him, getting down to the task at hand.

CHAPTER 106

THE LAND WITHOUT GHOSTS

Emily pulled the door closed, then locked it, returning the key to the bunch jangling at her waist. She turned, looking towards the door at the far end of the corridor.

'Okay... what's down there?'

The elderly servant turned, glancing at the door, then looked back at her, his head bowed. 'I... I don't know, Mistress. The Master never used this wing of the Mansion much. We were not encouraged...'

'I see,' she said, interrupting, then moved past him, heading for the door. 'I guess I'll have to find out for myself.'

'Forgive me, Mistress ...'

She stopped. '*Yes*, Richard?'

As before, the use of his first name unsettled the old retainer. 'Nothing, Mistress. Simply that I don't think there's a key to that door.'

She stared at him, intrigued. 'Why not?' she asked, but she was thinking, Why is he so uncomfortable? and, How does he know there is no key if he was never encouraged to come here?

'It... it was never used.'

'*Never?*' She shrugged. 'Well, we'll see, neh?'

She turned, continued to the door.

As he caught up with her, she turned back, the abruptness of her action surprising him. 'You're absolutely certain there's no key?'

He bowed his head, nodded.

'Then we'd best break it down, neh?'

'*Mistress*?' He looked at her, alarmed.

'If there's no key...'

He stared back at her, nonplussed.

'Well?' she said, almost smiling now. 'Will *you* do it, or shall I?'

His mouth opened slightly, closed.

There's something in there, she thought. Something he'd rather I didn't see.

She turned, took a step backward, kicked.

The door shuddered, held.

She kicked again. This time the wood surrounding the lock split and partly gave. A third kick shattered it.

The door swung slowly back.

She turned, smiling at him, enjoying the look of astonishment on his face.

And inside?

She stepped into the room. Into a dark mustiness.

'Lights,' she said, addressing the House Computer.

At once the room was brightly lit.

She looked about her. It was a big room – a store-room of some kind. Crates were stacked up four high, two deep all round the walls. She went across and examined one. It was sealed. She tried another and then a third. All sealed, untouched since they'd been placed here – when? – at least eighteen months back. She crouched, looking about her. The same label was on all the crates – the ornate blue and gold label of the Hythe-MacKay Auction House.

'What are these?' she asked, looking across to where the old servant was standing in the doorway.

He smiled politely. 'The Old Master...'

'Oh, *fuck* the Old Master!' she said, finally losing her temper with him. 'He's been dead eighteen months now and still you act like he's going to return at any moment! Well, he *isn't*! And I'm Mistress here now. So cut all the 'I don't know' shit and tell me what the hell all of this is!'

He looked down, staring at his booted feet, shocked by her outburst. 'I... I don't know, Mistress. We were told not to come here. Master Lever... well ...'

She gave a sigh of exasperation. Was it always going to be like this? She counted to ten, then stood, facing the man.

'Look... I'm sorry if I lost my temper just now, but I need to know what all of this is. How can I make a proper inventory of the Mansion unless I know what's where?'

He made the smallest movement of his head, conceding the point.

'Good. Then be helpful, neh, and bring me something I can use to open these.'

Michael Lever was in his office, taking briefings from his personal assistant, Dan Johnson, when his wife Mary's voice came through on his desk comset.

'Michael? Come to the West Wing. Now. I need to see you.'

He met Johnson's eyes, making a grimace of exasperation. 'Em... the meeting's in ten minutes. Can't it wait?'

'No. Now!'

The comset went dead. Michael ran a hand through his hair, frowning, clearly in two minds.

'When the Mistress of the House calls...' Johnson said, smiling, then added. 'I'll tell them you're delayed. Who knows, maybe it'll do the old buggers good to be kept waiting.'

'Dan... respect!' But Michael was smiling now. Besides, maybe Johnson was right. Maybe he ought to keep them waiting, if only to let them know who was Head of this Company. Yet his instinct was against it. This was an important board meeting and he needed to get their agreement – if only tacitly – to the latest round of changes.

He huffed, half irritated by his wife's summons, half intrigued, then, pulling himself up out of his seat, got the lightweight harness moving, making for the door. Johnson was there before him, holding the door open.

'How's it feel?'

Michael looked down at the support harness which helped him walk and move about. Since the accident he had had a succession of them, but this was the lightest, the least uncomfortable to wear. Why, it was almost possible sometimes to forget he had it on. In a year, the doctors said, he might even do without.

He smiled. 'It's great. The best yet. Doesn't chafe like the last.'

Johnson nodded his head, then touched Michael's arm, for that brief moment more friend than assistant. 'That's good. And look, don't worry. I'll fend them off, okay?'

'Fine.' Again he smiled, glad that Johnson was there, that he had such a good right-hand man. 'I'll not be long. I promise.'

He found her in the West Wing, in a room which, for as long as he could remember, had been locked. She was sitting on an old wooden trunk, staring down at something she was holding between her hands. All about her were stacks of opened crates, their half-glimpsed contents nestling in various kinds of wrapping. Michael took two steps into the room then stopped, looking about him.

'What's going on?'

She looked up, a deep frown on her face, then held the object up for him to see.

'What is this, Michael?'

He took three ungainly steps towards her then stopped, astonished. It was a head. A human head. And it was black.

'Where the hell did you get that?'

She looked about her. 'It was here, in the trunk. And other things. Books and clothes, paintings and maps. Old stuff, from the time of the American Empire. But this ...' She shuddered. 'Well, it's horrible. I mean, what was it? GenSyn? Were they operating back then?'

He shrugged, staring at the hideous object with a mixture of fascination and repugnance. 'Maybe. I don't know. But this must be my father's stuff. The stuff he bought from auction. Old Man Marley told me about it. Said he had plans to exhibit some of it before he died, so maybe there's an inventory somewhere. Or purchase slips.'

Gingerly, he took the head from her, then turned it in his hands, studying it more closely. It looked wrong, somehow, the hair too curly, the nose too flat, the lips too broad. Lifting it slightly, he sniffed the black, leathery skin.

'Odd...' Again he shivered. *Wrong, yes, maybe it was wrong, but somehow it didn't seem 'made'.* He looked back at Mary. 'What do you think we should do with all this stuff?'

She leaned down, picking something up from beside her, then turned back and stood, holding something else out to him. It was a book. An old, leather-bound book.

'I don't know,' she said. 'My first instinct is to burn it, but it might be important. Here, look at this. Where I've marked.'

He set the head down, then opened the book where she'd set the marker. A musty smell drifted up at him, the very scent of age. The smell of Empire. He stared at the open page a moment, then looked back at Mary.

'Gods! It's not possible, is it?'

'Sure it is. Look at that face. Who else could it be but a Kennedy?'

'And the man? The black man?'

'Look at the caption.'

He looked back at the old black and white print, studying it a moment, then turned the book, looking at the print on the spine. The book was old, two centuries old. But that face. He looked at it a third time, nodding to himself. A Kennedy and a black man. A king, so it said here. How strange that seemed. Black men and kings.

'Do you think Joe knows about all this?'

She shook her head. 'I don't know. I don't think so, to be honest. If he does, he's kept it very close, neh?'

He nodded, then, struck by an idea, began to smile. 'Hey... maybe we should give it to him... you know, at his birthday party on Friday. It'd be perfect, don't you think?'

She took it back from him, suddenly serious. 'Maybe... If you want. But not before I've had a chance to read it. There are things here ...' She gave a little shiver. 'Well... you'd best get back, neh? The old men are waiting, and you know how irritable they get.'

He laughed. 'Don't I just.'

ImmVac's boardroom was a huge hall of a chamber, surrounded on three sides by a balcony from which a dozen soft-wired scribes looked on, ready to take notes and provide their masters below with up-to-date information on whichever topic was the current subject of discussion. Below, about a massive octagonal oak table, sat seven elderly men, their grey hair combed back in a uniform style, their business silks a uniform midnight blue. On the table in front of each was a long, low screen, on which figures and briefing information would appear as needed. At the head of the table, beneath the Company logo which dominated the back wall, the high-backed chair was empty. To one side of it stood Dan Johnson, his hands out in front of him as he fielded the old men's brusque enquiries about Michael Lever's whereabouts.

'Gentlemen... I'm sure Mister Lever will be here at any moment. If you would just be patient.'

'Twenty minutes...' the old man directly opposite Johnson said in a loud, disgruntled voice. 'His father would never have kept us waiting twenty seconds! We have our own Companies to run, you know!'

Johnson lowered his head as if in respect to the old man, but in truth he was simply trying to keep his temper. The speaker was Johannes Kemp and he was an abrasive old bastard. Even at the best of times he was difficult, but today, it seemed, he was going out of his way to be unpleasant.

'I'll give him another five minutes, and then I'm off. It's intolerable. Absolutely intolerable!'

Johnson stared at Kemp, astonished. Did he mean what he'd just said? Would he simply get up and go? And what if he did? What if all the others followed him? *Then there'll be no quorum,* a voice in his head answered him – *and thus no board meeting, and no changes. And what would young Michael do then?*

He took a breath, about to speak to Kemp, to be his most persuasive, but at that moment the doors at the far end of the room swung back and Michael swept in, his prosthetic clicking on the marble floor.

'Forgive me, gentlemen,' he said, coming round the table, an apologetic smile lighting his features. 'Something very important just came up.

Something I had to deal with at once.' Dismissing Johnson, he took his seat at the head of the table.

'Well,' he said, looking about him. 'Let's get down to business at once. You've seen my proposals for the reorganisation of the Company's management structure, and, I hope, have had time now to consider them. Put simply the problem is this: the Company is top-heavy with management. There are far too many people on the payroll who are drawing a salary for doing nothing.'

'With respect, *Shih* Lever, I disagree.'

The voice came from Michael's right, from a long-faced man named Leckie. He leaned forward, his deep voice resonant with the accent of the old South. 'I've had my people look into this and they find little evidence of over-staffing in the management levels. Indeed, were we to trim back, as you suggest in your... document, well, my findings show a likely drop in efficiency of anything between ten and fifteen per cent.'

Michael stared at him, then sat back, lacing his fingers together in a manner reminiscent of his father. 'Forgive me, Andrew, but your findings... *surprise* me, let's say. As you know, since my father's death I have commissioned a number of reports on this Company's financial strengths and weaknesses, with the aim of making ImmVac not merely a stronger Company, but a more equitable one. Now, there are three things which these reports agree upon. One, that our borrowings are much too high. Two, that our pricing strategy is – how should I put it? – close to scandalous. And three, that there are too many bosses and not enough workers. As you know, I have already taken steps to deal with the second of these three matters by reducing the wholesale price of our goods and services, but if ImmVac is to maintain its position as City North America's leading Company then we are going to have to deal with the other problems – problems which are, I feel, indissolubly linked.'

'So you say,' Kemp said, taking his chance to interrupt. 'But I too have had my people look at things, and they have come up with a completely different set of findings. You identify three problems. Well, we'll not argue about those just now. *However...* there is a *fourth* area of concern, and that's the question of the Institute and the Immortality Project.' Michael looked down. 'As I've said before, that is a matter I shall deal with personally. As soon as new sponsors are found...'

'Forgive me, Michael,' Kemp said, insistent now, 'but surely the problem is very much within our remit. After all, the eight billion *yuan* loan is secured on the assets of this Company, which makes the Cutler Institute not merely a Lever family concern, but very much a matter for this board. Besides, if my information is correct, no new sponsors have been forthcoming, nor are there likely to be any while you continue to run the business down.'

Michael glared at Kemp. 'That's *my* decision, and while I hold eighty per cent of the shares in this Company, I'll not have the matter discussed in this boardroom, understand me?'

There was a moment's silence, then, with a faint bob of his head, Kemp stood. 'If that's how you feel, Michael, you can have my resignation straight away.'

'Johannes ...' Michael took a long, exasperated breath. 'Look, please try to understand. The Institute... it was an *aberration* of my father's. A dream that went wrong. It should never have been tied in to the fortunes of this great Company, nor shall it be in future.'

Kemp laughed. 'You know, Michael, I opposed your father when he took the Institute on. I warned him against committing so much of this Company to something so... high risk. But now... well, I'm astonished that you can't see it, boy. Eight billion *yuan*. Where will we find that? And find it we must if you're to pursue this idiot idea you have of ridding us of the damned thing. No. Think clearly, Michael. You've no option. Cut and trim all you like, but while the Institute's on our back, and while you're determined to run it down, then you can say farewell to any schemes you have for revivifying ImmVac's fortunes.'

'So what do you suggest?'

Kemp hesitated a moment, then sat again. He took a print-out from the case at his side and slid it across the table to Michael. 'There,' he said. 'That's what I suggest. We reorganise, sure, but not the parent Company. The Institute, *that's* where we concentrate our efforts. We introduce new money, new thinking. We make it work. And from the profits we pay off the loan.'

Michael stared at the document in his hands, shaking his head. 'No,' he said softly. 'We can't do this. It's against all I've stood for.'

'We either do this or go under.'

'No,' he said again, his voice pained. But what if Kemp was right? How would he explain that to Mary? How would he make *her* understand?

'Well?' she asked, looking up from the sofa as he came into the room, 'How did it go? Did they approve the changes?'

He nodded, not wanting to tell her about the rest of the deal just yet. 'You want a drink?' he asked, going across to the cabinet.

She laughed. 'Was it *that* bad?'

He looked back at her and smiled. 'You know how it is. Leckie had brought his own figures along and Old Man Kemp was being a total pain in the arse. But what's new? It's probably the only fun they get out of life!'

Her eyes were suddenly serious. 'You want to watch those two. Leckie's not as dumb as he seems, and Kemp ...'

He poured himself a whiskey, then turned back, raising an eyebrow.

Upon a wheel of fire

She shook her head. 'Nothing... just a feeling.'

He came across and sat beside her. There was a stack of books on the low table next to her, and one in her lap.

'What's that you're reading?'

She picked it up and showed him. 'It was in one of the crates. Look... there's more of them ...'

Michael stared, fascinated. Black men. More black men, but this time in American army uniforms, standing there posing for the camera, leaning on their long rifles.

He frowned. If they'd been GenSyn there'd have been something standardised about them; a certain uniformity about the faces. Not only that, but they'd have been bigger, better-muscled than they were. Besides, why go to the trouble to make such a range and then use them as simple footsoldiers? Unless...

'Hei,' he said. 'Perhaps they were an early model of the Hei...'

She shook her head. 'There was a war,' she said quietly. 'A great war between the north and south. Look... look at all the photographs.'

He turned the pages, then caught his breath, horrified by the scenes of carnage.

'A war,' she said again. 'It says here that it lasted the best part of five years and that over six hundred thousand men died... and we know nothing about it. I checked. There's nothing in the official records... *Nothing*.'

'Nothing?'

She shook her head. 'What's been going on, Michael? Why don't we know about this?'

He looked back at her, dumbfounded. 'I... I don't know.'

She leaned towards him, touching his arm. 'I want to find out. Hythe-MacKay, they'll know. I've arranged to see them, tomorrow morning, for a viewing. If I ...'

There was an urgent beeping from the wallscreen in the corner. Emily sat back, letting an exasperated breath escape her.

'Who is it?' Michael asked, turning to face the wallscreen.

'It's Representative Kennedy, Master,' the House Computer answered, 'calling from Weimar.'

'What time is it out there?'

'Ten minutes after eight, Master.'

Michael turned, smiling at Emily, as if he'd already forgotten what she had been saying. 'Then he'll have made his speech ...' He turned back. 'Put him on. Full vision.'

At once the image of Kennedy filled the screen. 'Michael... Mary... how are you both?'

'We're fine,' Michael answered for them both. 'How did it go? Did you have them eating out of your hand?'

Kennedy laughed. 'Not quite. Even so, I think it went down rather well. The media are hailing it as a great success. That's why I rang... I'm told that MedFac are going to show excerpts on their evening 'cast. Maybe you'd spread the word... let a few of our friends know it's going out. If we can get pick-up from a few of the other channels ...'

'Leave it with me,' Michael said, grinning back at him. 'And Joe... you're still okay for Friday?'

Kennedy beamed back at him. 'I wouldn't miss it for anything. But look... I've got to dash, okay? I'll catch up with you later. Bye!'

The screen went dark.

Michael turned, looking to Emily, then frowned. 'What's the matter?'

'Nothing,' she said, putting the book on the top of the pile. 'I'd best be getting on with things.'

He huffed, exasperated by her. 'Look. You don't have to like him, Em, but you could be a bit more civil. It's not easy what he's trying to do.'

Her answer was unexpectedly sharp. 'And just what is that? Do we really know any more?'

'Hey... ease off ...' He raised his hands, smiling at her. 'I thought we'd talked this one through. The new population measures will help everyone, from First Level to the Net.'

'Some more than others.'

'Meaning what?'

'Meaning that the top fifty will be exempt.'

'So? The top fifty isn't where the problem is.'

'No ...' She looked away, her face tight. 'It never is, is it?'

'Hey ...' He laughed, trying hard to be conciliatory. 'Look, I agree with him, Em. I think it's the right step to take. So what am I supposed to do?'

'Nothing,' she said coldly, then, relenting, she came across and held his head against her side. 'Nothing ...'

Kennedy leaned in to the intercom, speaking to his secretary in the next room. 'Make sure he gets that, right? Oh, and send copies to Hudson and Keeler. I want them fully briefed when they meet Hastings tomorrow. Oh, and no more calls just now. I'm in conference, *right*?'

Breaking the connection, he sat back, looking at the man seated across from him.

'Well, Fen Cho-hsien, how can I help you?'

Wu Shih's Chancellor looked about him a moment, then smiled. Behind him his two bodyservants stood like statues, their faces bereft of expression.

'It was a good speech, *Shih* Kennedy,' Fen answered, drawing his silks tighter about him, 'and I am certain that, when it comes to the vote tomorrow, you will win a substantial majority.' He paused. 'My Master is very pleased with you.'

Kennedy shrugged. 'And what does your Master want of me now?'

Fen's smile never wavered. 'Wu Shih wants nothing. Nothing, that is, except what is best for everyone. You have brought your party a long way this past year. Your policies... well,' he laughed, 'it is hard to believe that the NREP of a year ago could have held such views, neh?'

Kennedy made no comment, yet it was clear from a hardening in his face that Fen Cho-hsien's constant insults were getting to him.

'Anyway ...' Fen said, aware of the effect his words were having, 'I have a meeting within the hour, so I must go.'

He raised his right hand and clicked his fingers. At once one of the body-servants handed him a sealed envelope. Fen stared at it, then leaned towards Kennedy, handing it to him, the smile gone suddenly, his eyes hard.

'You will find my Master keeps his promises, *Mister* Kennedy. There is enough there to pay off all New Republic debts and enough left over to purchase *tai* if you so wish. In return all you need do is agree to a single amendment to your proposal introducing new levels of food subsidies for below Level 250.'

Kennedy stared at him. '*What* new levels?'

Fen Cho-hsien stood, smiling once more. 'It is all there in the T'ang's letter. As I said, my Master keeps *his* promises... make sure you keep *yours*.'

And with that he turned and left.

Kennedy sat there a moment, staring at the empty doorway, then looked down at the letter in his hand. Tearing it open, he read it through, then sat back, whistling.

'Shit ...' he said softly. If he agreed this... But what option had he? If he didn't the whole package would be lost, and whatever Fen Cho-hsien thought, he really did believe in the current set of population proposals. They weren't equitable, true, but they were a start. And once the principle was established ...

But to reduce food subsidies to the Lowers was against stated New Republican policy. To agree to it ...

He looked down at the cheque. It was made out in Wu Shih's own hand – a bill drawn on his private bankers for twenty million *yuan*. Kennedy nodded to himself, considering. Ten would clear all debts, the rest ...

He huffed loudly, angry that it had come to this. Until now he'd played things straight, avoiding the use of pockets – *tai* – to win a vote, but this once it seemed he'd need it.

Ten million... From what he'd heard he could buy a whole stack of votes for that. A quarter of the House ...

'So you want amendments, do you?' he said softly, pulling his writing pad across and beginning to scribble with the stylus. 'Well, I'll give you amendments, Wu Shih, more amendments than you ever looked for.'

Wu Shih looked up, staring sternly into the camera, the model of the newly-commissioned orbital farm on his desk beside him. Then, with a flourish of the brush, he signed the special Edict and, taking the great seal from the cushion to one side, inked it then pressed it down firmly onto the foot of the document.

'There,' he said, letting his servants take the document away, 'it is done.'

He stood, then walked across to where his cousin, Tsu Ma, stood by the open garden door, watching him.

'It is an expensive business, cousin,' Tsu Ma said, smiling sympathetically. 'Let us pray it works.'

Wu Shih sighed. 'I wish now I had never commissioned that report! I shall be lucky if it does not bankrupt me!'

Tsu Ma laughed. 'Oh, I doubt it cousin. Besides, it is better to be forewarned than sorry. You should not ask yourself how much it *will* cost, but what it *might* have cost you, had you not acted.'

Wu Shih turned, watching his servants dismantle the trivee rig. 'I'd hoped we could make do, but the orbitals are ancient and are constantly undergoing repairs. We ought to bring them down and totally refit them, but we simply cannot afford to. We are at full stretch as it is, and to take even one out of service ...' He shrugged. 'Well, there was no option when it came down to it. We must build new orbitals or see the old ones fall apart. Still, there are *some* pluses. The new population controls are a very touchy matter and the vote in the House tomorrow is likely to be close. This might sway one or two members to support *Shih* Kennedy's proposals.'

Tsu Ma laughed. 'You can always hope! Myself, I'd have trusted more to simple bribery!'

'Oh, I have done all I can in *that* regard! Even so, this worries me, cousin. Bad news... there seems nothing but bad news these days.'

'Well then, the timing of this could not be better, *neh*? If you must give the people bad news – and the reduction of the subsidies is certainly that – then it's always best to sweeten it with something brighter. People don't mind suffering so much if there's the prospect of better times ahead.'

'Maybe so. And yet I fear we must tread carefully. What happened on Mars...' He shuddered, then shook his head. 'Besides, Li Yuan's is not the only City where there is unrest these days. My Security forces are more busy than they ever were.'

'And mine,' Tsu Ma confessed. 'But what can we do? I have doubled the size of my forces, but still they barely cope. It is the times, cousin. We are fated to ride the tiger.'

Wu Shih nodded, as if resigned, but his eyes which had always been so clear, so determined, seemed bewildered by events.

Tsu Ma watched him a moment longer, his own eyes narrowed, then he turned away, looking out across the sunlit garden.

'Listen to this,' she said, looking up from the page and meeting Michael's eyes across the room. 'When the Chinese – the Han, that is – first came to North America in the 1840s, they called it Amo Li Jia... the Land Without Ghosts.'

He stared at her distractedly. 'Pardon?'

'America, they ...' She closed the book. 'You've not been listening to a word, have you?'

He smiled apologetically.

'Okay. What's on your mind?'

He shrugged. 'I was thinking about the deal... you know, with Kemp and the others. And all this stuff that's going on at Weimar. I should have been there, Em.'

'Joe has your proxy, hasn't he?'

He nodded.

'Well, then, what's the worry? I thought you *trusted* Joe.'

The irony in her voice was hard to miss.

'And you don't? Come on, Em, tell me the truth. *Don't* you trust him?'

'You know how I feel.'

'Do I?' He looked away. 'Sometimes I think I don't know you. Sometimes it's... well, it's like you're a stranger to me.'

She looked down, then, setting the book aside, went across. Sitting next to him, she took his hands, forcing him to look at her.

'Look, I'm sorry. It's hard sometimes, that's all. Living like this... I'm not used to it. You were born to it. It's natural for you. But for me...' She squeezed his hands. 'Look... as far as Joe's concerned, I'll try a little harder, okay?' She smiled, coaxing an answering smile from him. 'Now tell me honestly – what's bothering you?'

'The deal,' he said, looking directly into her eyes, his boyish innocence troubled. 'I... I've agreed to keep the Institute open.'

'You've *what*?'

'I had to. I ...' He freed his hands, then reached across and took a file from the table nearby, handing it to her.

'Kemp's report,' he said, watching her open it suspiciously. 'I've had Dan check the figures and Kemp's right. We've no option. We *have* to make it work or ImmVac sinks without a trace. And if ImmVac goes we've got nothing, Em. Nothing whatsoever.'

'It's evil,' she said, her eyes scanning the figures. 'Old men wanting to live forever... it's just plain evil.'

She looked up at him again. 'No option, huh?'

He stared at her, silent, waiting.

'Okay,' she said, relenting, her voice softening. 'But make sure they keep their part of the bargain. We get those changes through, *neh*?'

'Okay,' he said, a relieved smile lighting his features.

'Good. Now put the screen on. Our good friend Joe's on any minute.'

He laughed, then turned, addressing the air. 'House... let's have the MedFac news channel. Mister Kennedy's address. Copy and store.'

As the screen lit up, he sat back, putting his arm round Emily. 'Next time he should do it live. More impact that way ...'

'Shhh ...' she whispered, pointing at the screen. 'I want to hear this ...'

On the screen was a view of an imposing First Level Mansion not so different from their own. Guards clustered about the gate to the grounds, looking up at the floater camera and smiling. On the gravel path nearby three bodies lay face down. As the camera closed in, it could be seen that they were dead. Bullet holes riddled their backs and legs. Congealed blood was pooled beneath them. The commentary ran on.

'... is only the latest attempt by the Black Hand to infiltrate First Level and cause maximum damage to life and property. Asked today what steps he was taking to eradicate this problem, Security General Lowe said ...'

'They're scum,' Michael said, speaking over the commentary. 'They got what they deserved.'

She stared at him, surprised, then moved back, pushing his arm away. 'You *know* that, do you? I mean... you knew those three personally, did you?'

He shook his head. 'No... and hey, what are you getting so upset about? Those are terrorists lying there dead, not charity workers. They knew the risks. Besides, what did the guy who owns the Mansion do to them? It could have been *him* laying there dead. Or *us*, come to think of it!'

'Maybe,' she said quietly, 'but they're not scum. They just want a better life, that's all.'

'Sure, and a funny way they have of getting it.' He raised his hand, as if about to lecture her, then, realising what he was doing, he sat back, shaking his head. 'My father... my damn father. Sometimes I think his ghost's in me.'

She was still staring at him.

'I'm sorry,' he said. 'Look. Maybe they're not scum. Maybe they do have their reasons, but I can't see how murdering and robbing innocent people furthers their cause any. It's all so... *destructive*. Why can't they do something positive.'

'They do. Only you never hear about it. It's all...'

'Hey, listen ...' he said, interrupting her, as Wu Shih's face appeared on the screen. 'What the hell is this?'

She turned, listening, her mind still on what he'd said, only half attending to the announcement.

'Kuan Yin preserve us!' Michael said, then whistled. 'Three new orbitals. That'll set him back... what, sixty billion, maybe more?'

'It's good news,' she said, as the commentator began to introduce the next item, Kennedy's speech at Weimar. But she couldn't get the earlier image from her mind – that close-up on the last of the fallen terrorists. It had been a woman, a *Hung Mao*, her blonde hair caked with her own blood, a gold ring prominent on the second finger of her left hand.

Scum... and he'd called her scum. She shivered and sat back, trying to push the image from her as Kennedy's face filled the screen, his powerful voice echoing out across the packed tiers of the House and into their room.

Kemp turned in his chair, looking away from the frozen image on the screen, then raised his brandy glass in a toast.

'Now there's one bastard I'd celebrate the death of!'

There were yells of approval from all round – from the old men who were seated to either side of Kemp and from the younger men who stood in the shadows beyond them.

Kemp stood and turned to face the dinner-suited crowd, waiting for the noise to subside before he spoke again.

'However, it's his paymaster, Lever, we need to see off first. And that's why I've asked you all here tonight. To talk tactics.'

His knowing smile brought a roar of laughter from all sides. Kemp let it roll on a moment, then raised his hands again.

'We all know what's at stake. If Kennedy and Lever get their way... well, we'll all pay for it. They'll strip our Mansions bare to pay for healthcare for some jug-head's scrawny litter. Why, we'd be feeding every sodding loin-jerk in the Lowers!'

Again there were fierce cries of approval and the stamping of feet.

'So...' he said, more quietly, more ominously. 'We have to act. To stop this thing from happening. We have to... *prevent* it.'

He turned his head slightly and snapped his fingers. At once a dozen servants issued from a door at the side and started going among the crowd, handing out envelopes.

'In there you'll find a payment for fifty thousand *yuan*. Good faith money, we'll call it. You serve us well, however, and there'll be more. Much more.'

Kemp looked about him, seeing the nods of satisfaction from all round and smiled inwardly.

'Okay, then let's begin. Let's see what we can do to make things *difficult* for our friends...'

'Must you go so soon, cousin Ma?'

Tsu Ma came forward and embraced Wu Shih, then turned, looking back up the ramp to where his craft awaited him inside the hangar.

'I'm afraid I must. My spies tell me there's trouble afoot, and the only way to deal with trouble is to head it off... especially when it's the Ministry who are involved.'

'The Ministry?' Wu Shih raised an eyebrow. 'Is it something I should know about, Tsu Ma?'

Tsu Ma let his hand rest on his cousin's shoulder briefly. 'Nothing you should lose any sleep over, cousin. But I'll send you a complete transcript of the meeting, if you wish.'

Wu Shih smiled. 'I would welcome that.'

'Good. Then I must go. As Sun Tzu so wisely said, surprise is the ultimate in generalship.'

'It sounds ominous, Tsu Ma. You talk as if we were at war with them...'

'Well, *aren't* we?' Tsu Ma was stern a moment, then he smiled. 'I jest... But they can be difficult, neh? It would not harm to shake them up a bit.'

Wu Shih nodded, then embraced Tsu Ma one last time. 'Safe journey, cousin Ma. As ever, I enjoyed your company more than mere words can say.'

'And I yours, cousin.'

Tsu Ma turned away, making his way up the ramp. Halfway up, however, he turned, remembering something, and called back to Wu Shih.

'Oh, and cousin... when you visit me next time, bring that young maid of yours, the pretty one, with you... There was not time ...'

Wu Shih grinned. 'Count it as done, cousin. Now get going. The dragons await you!'

That night she slept badly, plagued by dreams of bullet-ridden corpses that

DAVID WINGROVE   179

rose up from the earth and turned to her, their dark, broad faces laughing
cruelly.

Ghosts... there were supposed to be no ghosts in this land, yet wherever
she looked, whatever rooms she unlocked in her memory, ghosts stepped
from the darkness to greet her. The woman's corpse, that was herself... how
her own life would surely have ended had DeVore not interceded.

Quietly she rose from bed and crept from the room, making her way
silently to the kitchen. There, in the darkness overlooking the great lawn,
she sat, remembering.

Five years ago she'd come here to America, a refugee from the collapse of
the Ping Tiao in Europe. DeVore had helped her; had given her a new identity,
and a chance at a new life. She had meant to start again here, to go down
level and reorganise, but then she had fallen in love... with Michael, her
employer, defying his father to marry him. For a time it had worked – for
a time she had forgotten what she'd come here to do. But tonight, seeing
those images, recalling what she'd found in the West Wing among the
crates, she remembered why she had come.

The Land Without Ghosts... She understood. It was the land they all
inhabited now. The City. A place without history, without any real
connection to the earth. But now all the ghosts were coming back. She could
sense them, clamouring to be let in. Their silent mouths were everywhere,
like watchers at a window.

With a shudder she stood, knowing now that something had to change
– either her or the great edifice surrounding her. Ping Tiao she'd been – a
Leveller, a terrorist. Ping Tiao she remained, for all her new-found wealth.

That's it, she thought. It's me or It.

For there could be no compromise, no real peace for her until either she
or the City was gone from the earth.

CHAPTER 107

SMALL THINGS

s this all of it?'

The young lieutenant came to attention. 'That's it, sir. Everything we couldn't place.'

Chen looked about him at the cluttered storeroom, wondering where to start. *Use your eyes, look for the unexpected* – so Karr had always told him, but where among all this rubbish did one start? He turned back, looking the lieutenant up and down, then nodded. 'Okay. If you'd ask Captain Johnson to bring the records of the operation to me when he gets here. Meanwhile, I'll start sorting through this lot.'

'Sir.'

Chen saw the man hesitate and waited, knowing, even before he said it, what he was going to ask.

'Forgive me, sir, but what exactly *are* you looking for? I mean, we've taken this level apart looking for the File. If it was here, we'd have found it.'

'But it *was* here, and you *didn't* find it. Which means one of two things. Either it's still here or someone got it out.'

'I still don't see...'

Chen raised a hand, silencing him. 'No, you don't, so leave me to it, neh? I've much to do. Oh, and have someone bring me a *chung* of *ch'a*, lieutenant. This is thirsty work, and the hour's late.'

'Sir!'

Chen saw the slight stiffening in the man's back and understood. The

young officer didn't like this kind of interference, and maybe – just maybe –
he didn't like the idea of a Han bossing him about. But that was as maybe.
He would do as he was told and like it, or he'd find himself in front of a
disciplinary board.

The lieutenant saluted, then turned away. Chen watched him go, then
turned back, setting to work. There might be nothing here, then again,
something among all this trash might explain how the File was smuggled
out. Because one thing was certain – it *had* been smuggled out.

For a time he sifted through the piles, working methodically, checking
each item thoroughly before moving on. At first there was nothing, then,
with a laugh, he came upon something he recognised.

'Found something, Major Kao?'

Chen half turned, looking up at the newcomer. It was the Captain,
Johnson. Chen stood, facing him, holding out what he'd unearthed from
the pile.

'I've been trying to order one of these for my son. Three months we've
waited, but nothing. And here it is. Just the bit we wanted. Mind you,
it probably doesn't work. They cost over twenty *yuan* to replace. I can't
imagine anyone throwing one away!'

Johnson took the flat, black rectangular piece and studied it, turning it
over between his hands. Handing it back to Chen, he shrugged. 'What is it?'

'It's a resonance box. It comes from a sketchboard – you know, one of
those computer graphics machines. This particular bit controls the surface
plasticity. It's the most sensitive part of the machine, so I'm told. Mind you,
they only tell you that once the damn thing's broken and you have to order a
new part. If they told you before you bought the thing...'

Chen laughed, hefting it in his hand. It was strange, because the part
looked almost new. It was barely worn, almost as if it were straight out of
its wrapping.

Johnson smiled. 'Maybe you should keep hold of it. Just in case. I mean,
no one will miss it.'

Chen nodded. 'Maybe I will.' Then, realising that the Captain had the
operation file under his arm, he grew serious again. 'I hear you lost two
men.'

'That's right. One of them was married. Two young boys.'

'I'm sorry.' Chen pocketed the resonance box, then put his hand out, taking the file from the Captain. 'And between us, Captain Johnson, I'm as unhappy as you at being here. I don't want to tread on your toes. But General Rheinhardt is under a lot of pressure to get results on this. You understand?'

The Captain smiled. 'I understand, Major Kao. We'll cooperate all we can. But this one baffles me. We tore the whole deck apart to find the file, but nothing. As for anyone smuggling it out, well, we strip-searched everyone who came or went. The list of names is there. A few minor criminals, but otherwise nothing. A complete blank.'

Chen studied the file a moment, flicking forward and backward, then looked back at Johnson. 'You're sure this is complete? Are you certain there wasn't *anyone* else?'

Johnson hesitated. 'Well...'

Chen sighed, exasperated. 'Who was it? A senior official? Someone from another Security force? Who?'

'A girl. Well, a young woman, I guess you'd call her.'

Chen stared at the Captain, astonished. 'You mean, you let someone walk out of a top security area without searching them?'

'There were exceptional circumstances, sir. Besides, she wasn't a suspect.'

'*Kuan Yin!* In this kind of operation *everyone* is a suspect!'

'You don't understand, sir. She was the daughter of a Junior Minister. And not just any Junior Minister. She was Shang Mu's daughter.'

'Shang Mu? You mean *that* Shang Mu?'

Johnson nodded.

'Ah...'

'You understand, then?'

'You're absolutely certain it was her?'

'Absolutely, sir. I had two of my men escort her home.'

'I see.' Chen considered a moment. The Captain was probably right. Shang Mu's daughter was the last person likely to be involved in this. Nor would he, in Johnson's place, have risked offending the Junior Minister by strip-searching his daughter – not unless it was really necessary. Even so...

'Who saw her beside yourself?'

'My lieutenant... Oh, and a young guard. He was the one who brought her to the barrier.'

'The guard... is he on duty now?'

'No, but I can have him brought here if you wish. He's stationed on this deck. It'll only take a moment or two.'

'Okay. Do that. I'll see him here. Meanwhile...' Chen half turned, indicating the huge piles of bits and pieces that remained to be sifted through.

'Good luck,' Johnson said, grinning. 'I hope you find something.'

As the Captain left, the lieutenant appeared in the doorway, carrying a tray. 'Your ch'a, Major Kao.'

Chen smiled. 'Wonderful!' He glanced at the timer inset into his wrist. It was ten minutes after four. 'Just put it down there. And thanks, lieutenant. I'm grateful.'

'Sir!'

Alone again, Chen lifted the lid of the chung and sniffed. It smelled good. Just what he needed.

He crouched, looking back at the nearest pile, studying the exposed strata. For a moment or two he saw only the unwanted detritus of a typical deck, then, with mounting interest, he began to pick things from the pile.

When the young guard came, Chen was sitting on one of the lower piles, the chung cradled in his lap. In a small polythene bag beside him was a jumble of black lacquered computer parts.

The guard stopped just inside the door and came to attention, his head bowed. 'Private Lauer, sir. I'm told you wanted to speak to me.'

'Yes, Lauer. Relax, lad. I only want to ask you a few questions, that's all. About the young woman you helped yesterday. I understand you kept her out of trouble.'

'Yes, sir.'

Chen took a long sip from the chung, then looked back at the guard. He was still a boy. Seventeen, eighteen at most. Only three years older than his son, Jyan.

'Relax, Lauer, please...' He smiled, trying to reassure the young man. 'All I want to know is what you did, what you saw. You're not in any trouble. Oh, and I know what you're thinking. You're thinking that because I'm special services I want to trap you. But it's not true. You did nothing wrong. All you did was help a young woman who was out of her level. You saw the danger to her and you acted, neh?'

'Yes, sir.'

'Well, that's commendable.' Chen held out the *chung*, offering it to the young man, encouraging him to take it, forcing him to come closer.

'So when did you first notice her?'

The guard lowered the *chung* and wiped his mouth, then handed the *chung* back to Chen. 'She was standing in the corridor, sir, not far from where I was, at the guardpost. She was watching the *hua pen*, the storyteller, and sketching what she saw...'

'Sketching?'

'Yes, sir. You know, with one of those computerised sketchboards. I thought it was odd. I could see she was... well, not from this level. Her clothes, the cut of her hair. I could see it at once.'

'See what?'

The young man smiled, looking past Chen momentarily, remembering. 'First Level... that's what I told myself. She's First Level.'

Chen stared at the young man, surprised by the awe in his voice, the longing in his eyes, then set the *chung* down.

'What did you see?'

'Her... Well, she's...' The young man shook his head, suddenly flustered, a colour appearing at his neck. 'I don't know, sir. It's just what I felt, looking at her. So intense, she was. So... so *there*.'

Chen looked down. He had it all. All he needed. All, that was, except a reason.

'Okay,' he said gently. 'That's all I need. You can go now, Lauer. And thanks...'

'Sir!' The young guard came to attention, then backed away.

Chen took a long breath, then, lifting the polythene bag from the floor beside him, stood, stretching his limbs. It was too early yet to go and see the girl. He'd leave it a few hours, get himself some breakfast, then pay a visit.

And then?

Chen touched his tongue to his top teeth and shook his head. And then he'd do his job. After all, General Rheinhardt wanted results.

As the great doors swung open, Shang Mu turned, watching as his master, the First Dragon, backed out of the audience chamber, his head bowed low.

Like his master, Shang Mu had been summoned from his bed and brought here through the darkness to Tsu Ma's palace on the shore of the Caspian Sea. As the doors thudded shut, the First Dragon turned, his face like a wall, expressionless. As he passed, Shang Mu fell in behind him silently, knowing, from the tension in the great man's back, that the audience had not gone well.

Tsu Ma had been clever. Very clever indeed. He had had them brought separately, giving them no time to consult or prepare for the meeting. Moreover, in not waiting on the First Dragon to make the first move, he had seized the initiative and thus taken the upper hand. As in a game of *wei chi*, they were forced now to defend.

The First Dragon's cruiser was waiting on the pad outside the palace. An honour guard lined the broad path leading from the building to the craft, flaming torches held aloft, lighting the pre-dawn darkness. Shang Mu followed his master between the torches and up into the battlecruiser. As the doors hissed shut and the engines fired, he stood to one side, watching his master settle in his great chair, servants fussing about him.

'He knows,' the First Dragon said, looking across at his Junior Minister, his voice competing with the engines' roar.

The servants – deaf mutes, raised in the First Dragon's own household – continued to tend to the great man, oblivious of what was being said.

'Knows what?' Shang Mu asked, chilled by the thought that their plans might be known to the Seven.

The great man looked away, his anger held in check. 'We have been *warned*. Moreover, we are to be watched, like common criminals.'

'*Watched?*' Shang Mu's mouth fell open in astonishment. 'I do not understand, *I Lung*. To watch the Thousand Eyes... it is unheard of!'

'And yet it is to be done. Karr's special force, his *shen t'se*, are to be appointed to the task. They are to watch the Watchers, it seems. To keep an eye on the Great Eye itself.'

Beneath the surface irony of the words was a savage anger that did not escape Shang Mu. He thought quickly. 'Did he say why, Master?'

The First Dragon rested his head back, letting a servant remove his wig, then begin to rub salve into his shaven scalp. 'He spoke of rumours that had come to his ear. Rumours of corruption and mismanagement. Not at the highest level, of course. No, Tsu Ma is too smart to accuse the Council itself. But he felt it would be best if an independent body investigated the claims, especially in view of the new arrangements.'

'New arrangements, *I Lung*? What new arrangements?'

'The cuts...' The First Dragon turned, waving the servant away, then signalled that Shang Mu should come and sit across from him.

'There is more,' he said, leaning towards Shang Mu, as the craft slowly lifted. 'It seems we are to provide Karr's force with copies of all our files.'

He stared back at his master, dumbstruck. 'But that is outrageous, I Lung! Why, when our great Ministry was formed...'

The First Dragon raised a hand. 'I know, Shang Mu. In effect, this breaks the long-standing agreement between the Seven and the Ministry. Oh, technically, the Seven are entitled to do as they will, but in practice...' He sat back, cupping his closed right fist in his left. 'Well... if we had any doubts before, we have none now, neh? They mean to break us, Shang Mu. To destroy the last barrier between Chung Kuo and total anarchy. But we can't let them... we *won't* let them.'

He moved his hands apart, spreading his fingers, deliberately calming himself, then, turning in his chair, raised his right hand, summoning the ship's Steward.

The Steward came across and bowed, waiting silently, his eyes on the First Dragon's hands. As Shang Mu watched, the great man gave signed instructions with his fingers, finishing with the signal of dismissal. Like all else about the great man, this discipline impressed Shang Mu. If a single man epitomised the great principle of *Shen Chung* – of Caution – then it was the First Dragon. Things, then, were bad, when such a solid, upright man should even consider going to war with his own Masters.

Shang Mu looked down, a cold sobriety sweeping over him. War. He had known it last night, looking through the files. And though the thought of it appalled him, some colder, more clinical part of him understood the need and saw no alternative. The servants must become the masters, if they were properly to serve.

Looking up, he saw that the great man was watching him, almost as if he knew what he was thinking.

'Where now?' he asked, feeling, in that moment, a special bond between himself and his master.

'To Yu Shu,' the First Dragon answered. 'To see our friend An Sheng. But not directly. From now on we do nothing directly. Not until we must.'

The tiny hologram flickered brightly in the darkened room, smoke from the incense stick drifting through the image. In its faint, blue-tinted light the kneeling girl seemed like a giant statue, immobile, her head lowered respectfully, her hands folded in her lap.

'Are you sure this is the best course, Shang Han-A?' the hologram asked, leaning forward slightly, one hand stroking the long, white, plaited beard that flowed almost to its waist. 'Is there not some better way to heal the breach between you?'

Hannah was silent a moment, contemplating what her great-grandfather, Shang Chu had said, then answered him. 'I believe not, honourable great-grandfather. My stepmother is frequently unwell, and that makes her... tetchy, let us say. As for me, I am young, impetuous sometimes. It is a fault, I realise, but one that time will cure. However, if I stay here the friction between myself and my stepmother will remain and, in all probability, get worse. I would hate to see that. If I go, then the source of my stepmother's irritation is gone. Her health will improve, and we shall both be happier. And that would be good for my father, neh? To have two happy homes, rather than a single unhappy one.'

'It would, indeed.' The hologram straightened up, smiling. 'I am pleased with you, Shang Han-A. Your concern for your father's happiness is most dutiful. I shall speak to him next time he consults me and let him know what I think on this matter. For now, however, it would be best if you said nothing. Your father has much on his mind. These are hard times for him. You must do all you can to ease his mind in the days ahead.'

'I understand, great-grandfather, and I shall do my utmost.'

Hannah bowed, then, leaning forward slightly, placed her fingers lightly on the panel in front of the hologram. At once the image faded, leaving only the bright red point of the burning incense stick.

There was the sound of a match being struck, a sudden flare of light. A second incense stick was placed on the altar, in a tiny silver holder just to the right of the first. There was the vague murmur of a blessing from the kneeling girl, then, as she brushed her fingers against the second pad, another hologram appeared, this one much shorter and stockier than the first, the beard darker, bushier.

'Greetings, honourable grandfather,' Hannah said, lowering her head respectfully. 'I pray you're well.'

The figure lifted its chin and gave a short laugh. 'As well as the dead can be, young Hannah.'

In the darkness Hannah smiled. The holograms had been programmed by the living men to reflect what of their personalities they wished to survive them. Normally this resulted in a rather stiff, one-dimensional self-portrait that emphasised all the virtues while editing-out anything which might be viewed as 'unseemly' by future generations. But her grandfather, Shang Wen Shao, had not been such a man. He had always claimed that a man was all his different selves – fool and sage, father and lover, braggart and coward, good friend and savage enemy – and had programmed his own ancestral hologram to reveal all of these different aspects. Of all the family holograms, this was Hannah's favourite, and she consulted it whenever she had problems in her personal life, for grandfather Wen Shao could be trusted never to mouth platitudes, but to offer advice from the depth of his own considerable experience. Six wives, four concubines and a good few dozen lovers had made him wise in the ways of the world and a good judge of women. And though he had been a fool in business and had lost much of the great financial empire his father had built from nothing, he was, in Hannah's eyes, the better man – an opinion she was careful to conceal from her father.

'What's up, Hannah? Is that shrew of a stepmother of yours troubling you again? Or is it something else this time?'

Hannah bowed a little lower. 'You see right through me, honourable grandfather.'

The hologram gave a little guffaw of laughter and thumped at its chest. 'I'd have said it was the other way about, wouldn't you, girl? That you see through me!'

Again Hannah smiled to herself. She had heard all of these jokes a thousand times, but the familiarity of them warmed her.

'We are all smoke in the eyes of the gods, grandfather.'

'Yes... But be specific, Hannah. Hurry. I need to piss.'

Hannah bowed again, wishing, not for the first time, that she had known her grandfather in life. He must have been a real character. Hannah could see how her father – cast in great-grandfather Chu's puritanical mould

– would have been offended by his own father. She could imagine him wincing at the old man's vulgarity even as he bowed dutifully before him. Not that her father didn't have a sense of humour, it was just that he lacked his father's spontaneity, his open, generous nature.

She hesitated a moment longer, then asked. 'Can I trust you, grandfather?'

Wen Shao leaned back, as if to see her better. 'Now that's an odd question, my girl. Perhaps the oddest you've asked. Can you trust me? Hmmm...' He scratched his chin. 'Well now, I really don't know. If you were a wife of mine. I'd have to say no. Not any further than you could throw me. But it's not that kind of thing, is it?'

'No, grandfather.'

'Then speak. I'll not repeat a word, not even if some clever young programmer tries to tamper with my memory circuits!'

She smiled. 'Then let me ask you this. If you knew a secret, a big secret – one that was so big it affected everyone and everything they did – then what would you do? Would you let everyone know, or would you keep it to yourself?'

Wen Shao had narrowed his eyes. He looked back at his granddaughter inscrutably from his broad *Hung Mao* features, as if, for that moment, mimicking the Han whose name his grandfather had adopted a century before.

'That's a big secret,' he said, then shook his head, blowing out a noisy breath. 'In fact it sounds like the kind of secret your father is fond of keeping, neh? Have you been prying among his things again, young Hannah?'

'No, grandfather.'

'But they're connected, neh?'

'Yes, grandfather.'

'Ahh...' He smacked his lips, then, unexpectedly, he sat, crossing his legs beneath him. 'Well, you know how I feel about your father's work. I've never liked it. I wish now that I'd never paid to have him educated. It seems such a waste – to devote oneself to such... such *pettiness*.'

'Pettiness, grandfather? But surely what he does is of the greatest importance?'

Wen Shao laughed. 'You think so? But what does the great Tao teach us? That in everything is its opposite. That that which seems greatest is, in truth, the smallest. As Chuang Tzu says, there is nothing in the world bigger than the tip of an autumn hair, and Mount T'ai is little.'

'Maybe so, grandfather, but you have still not answered me.'

'Haven't I?' Wen Shao laughed, then leaned forward, tugging at the air by his left foot as if he were plucking a blade of grass. 'Why, and there I was thinking I had.'

She laughed, watching him chew at the imaginary blade. 'Maybe you only think you have.'

'Ah... that must be it.'

'Grandfather?'

He stopped chewing and smiled. 'You want a straight answer, is that it?'

'This once I'd appreciate it.'

He shrugged. 'Okay. But you won't like it. My advice is to forget your big secret. It'll only bring you unhappiness. You and that proper man you call your father.'

'Your son,' she reminded him.

'So the genetic charts would have me believe... but that aside, I'm serious, my girl. Let others worry about this secret. Leave the sleepless nights to them. You're a young woman, Hannah. You should be out meeting young men and having a good time. That's what this life is for.'

She looked away, for the first time in her life disappointed by his answer. But then, what had she expected? For him to endorse her crazy scheme? To tell her, yes, Hannah, go ahead and ruin your life? No. Wen Shao was Wen Shao. And she had too much of her father's blood in her – was too much her father's daughter.

'You're disappointed,' he said, looking up at her, the smoke from the incense stick making his seated form shimmer momentarily. 'I know what you wanted, my girl, but you asked me a question and I answered it. Do as you will. Take on the great world of levels, if you must. But don't ask me to tell you you're right.' He smiled. 'In fact, if you ask me, I think you're mad even to consider the idea. But I respect your madness. It's an admirable trait – one I wish your father possessed in greater measure. But take care, little Hannah. The world is uncaring. It's a mechanism for chewing people up and spitting them out. And only fools like me survive.'

'You're no fool, grandfather.'

'No. Maybe not. Not in the sense most people mean, yet I was fool enough in my youth. Fool enough to think the world could be a better place.'

'You, honourable grandfather? I'd never have guessed!'

He laughed. 'Yes, I know my reputation. The old goat, they called me. A drunk, they said, a reprobate. But I wasn't always so, my girl. It was the world that made me thus. That and the sweet scent of sweat on a woman's skin...'

'Grandfather!'

'Forgive me...' The tiny figure stood, brushing its hands together. 'However, I really must go now. Even ghosts must have their rest, neh?'

She smiled and lowered her head respectfully. 'Then sleep well, grandfather. And thank you. You've been very helpful.'

'I have?' He smiled. 'Well now, that makes a change. Maybe there's hope for me after all.'

'Maybe...'

She leaned across and touched the pad. The figure shimmered and was gone. Hannah stared at the empty space a moment, then sat back on her heels, thinking.

He was right, of course. It was insane even to think of getting involved. The best thing to do would be to take the file and feed it into the incinerator, but for some reason she couldn't do that. Something in her prevented that. Some perversity of nature.

'Nu Shi! Nu Shi!'

Hannah turned as her *amah* appeared in the doorway, her face excited.

'What is it, Wei?'

'A soldier has come, Mistress,' the young maid answered, bowing low. 'A Security Major...'

Hannah stood. 'For my father, you mean?'

'No, Mistress. For you. He is talking to your stepmother even now...'

'My *stepmother*! Oh, gods!' Hannah lifted the hem of her silk and moved past the young girl, her bare feet padding quickly along the tiled hallway.

A *Major had come*... But what did that mean? Was she discovered? Or was this merely a courtesy call, to see if she was all right after her experience? As she approached the big double doors that led through to her stepmother Huang Hui's rooms she stopped, calming herself. It was all right. It had to be. Because if it wasn't they'd have asked to see her father. That was the way they worked. And it wouldn't have been a mere Major, it would have been General Rheinhardt himself.

She took a long breath, then indicated to the waiting servants that they should open the doors.

Inside her stepmother, Chih Huang Hui, was sitting up in a big chair heaped with cushions, the whole thing presenting the illusion of a great bed tipped up onto its edge, her pale Han face staring out from a cocoon of red silk. In front of her stood the Major, his back to Hannah. His large-boned body filled almost to bursting the powder blue dress uniform he was wearing. Over his shoulder was a black leather despatch bag of the same kind her father's messengers used. As he turned she felt a flicker of surprise. He was Han.

Huang Hui looked across at her and gave a weary, sickly smile. 'Han-A... I'm glad you've come, I was just about to call you. This is Major Kao of Security...'

The Major lowered his closely shaven head smartly, then straightened up. He was a remarkably plain-looking man, with crude, almost unformed features. His nose was somehow too big, as were his ears. And yet his mouth was strong, and his eyes...

'Major Kao.' Hannah went across and bowed to her stepmother, then turned, facing him again. 'I'm told you wish to see me.'

He smiled at her, not insolently, like some of the young officers smiled at her, but as her own father smiled. That, and the strange honesty of his eyes, made her look away briefly, wondering.

'I have a few questions I need to ask,' he said quietly. 'That is, if that's all right with you, *Nu Shi Shang*? About yesterday. There was no time then, I understand, and the Captain was rightly more concerned with your safety than with Security procedures. But it would help us greatly if you could make a simple statement about what you saw.'

'*Safety...? Statement...?*' Hannah's stepmother leaned forward, her pinched face instantly suspicious. 'Han-A... what *have* you been up to?'

She was about to answer, but the Major interceded. 'Oh, it is nothing, Madam Shang. There was an incident. Your daughter was caught up on the periphery of it. The questions, as I said, are a mere formality.'

'*Incident?* What kind of incident?'

This time Hannah made sure she got in first. 'There was a criminal,

Stepmother Huang... a *revolutionary!* A troop of the Major's soldiers chased him through the corridors and trapped him, but he put up a fight and they had to shoot him. There was blood everywhere...'

Huang Hui sank back into her cushions, an expression of sheer horror on her face. '*Aiya!*' she muttered, fanning herself with a vigour that was surprising for one so clearly invalided.

Hannah turned, a strange gleam in her eyes and looked directly at the Major. 'Well... if you would come through, Major Kao, I shall arrange for a servant to bring *ch'a*. Have you had breakfast?'

The Major hesitated. 'Yes, I... I had some earlier. I...' Then, as if remembering himself, he turned, bowing low to Huang Hui. 'Madam Shang. It was kind of you to receive me. Please give my regards to your husband, the Junior Minister, when he returns. May I also say how much I hope your health improves. However, if you would excuse me now...'

A wan smile appeared on Huang Hui's face. 'Major Kao...'

Kao Chen turned back, looking to the girl, who smiled and turned away. He followed, stopping at the door to look back. The pale-faced invalid was recumbent in the huge, upright bed of red cushions. Now that the audience was over, Huang Hui seemed to have collapsed in upon herself, her frail figure losing its last glimmer of animation. As he watched, two servants hurried to her, plumping up her cushions and tending to her.

He watched a moment longer, then, with a tiny shudder, went out into the corridor to join the waiting girl.

'Well?' she asked, turning to face him.

Chen looked about him at the room, taking it all in. Everywhere he looked there were signs of wealth, of a luxury he could never aspire to. The left-hand wall and the end wall were lined with shelves, the shelves crowded with ancient-looking leather-bound books that he could smell even from where he stood. In the right-hand corner was a huge wooden desk, not unlike the one that stood in General Rheinhardt's office. Next to it was a big, glass-fronted cabinet containing all manner of small, exotic-looking objects, few of which he recognised. Behind that, in a case on the wall, was a banner of some kind, showing a blood red cross on a white background. The rest of that wall was filled with sketches and paintings of various sizes, unusual only in that they showed scenes from the levels. Chen studied them a moment then looked down. Beneath his feet was a thick, richly-woven rug that would have carpeted three rooms in his own apartment, while to his right, only a *ch'i* or so from where he stood...

'Major Kao?'

He jerked his head up, meeting the young woman's eyes. Strong, hazel-coloured eyes that could have been Han.

'Forgive me,' he began, 'but should we be in here? Your father...'

She smiled pleasantly. 'You misunderstand, Major Kao. This is *my* study, not my father's.'

'Ah...' Chen blushed. Already he was showing his gaucheness. The truth was he had met many great men and their families, but never, before this moment, had he seen inside one of their Mansions. That had always been someone else's job – someone more senior and less *Han* than he. But this time he had been determined. He was going to let no one take this case out of his hands.

He hesitated, looking about him once more, then, faintly embarrassed, pointed to the large hemisphere close by that had caught his attention. 'Forgive me, *Nu Shi* Shang, but just what is this?'

She laughed and came across. 'It's known as a HoloVisual Imager, but I call it my Magic Theatre. It's a miniature stage, you see. The actors are tiny holograms. It's programmed to perform most of the major Han plays, but you can programme it yourself if you like. You can write your own plays, make your own characters... do what you want with it, really.'

She stared at the hemisphere fondly, one hand resting lightly on its curved glass surface, then looked back at Chen, smiling broadly. 'I'd show you, Major, but I'm sure you're busy, neh?'

'Indeed...' But he was unable not to answer her smile with his own, her youthful enthusiasm reminded him so much of his own daughter. 'It is a very simple matter, *Nu Shi* Shang, I...'

'Hannah,' she interrupted him. 'Please, call me Hannah.'

Chen nodded. 'Okay.. *Hannah*. All I need is your verbal statement about what happened yesterday. Once that's done, I'll get that transcribed and we'll send you two copies, one for your signature and return, the other to keep.'

'I understand. Well... shall we go over to the desk, Major?'

He hesitated. 'It is Chen. Kao Chen. I...' He looked away briefly, then looked back at her. 'All these things... I've not seen anything like them. They...' He shrugged, not quite knowing what he meant.

'They're just things,' she said offhandedly, clearing a space on the desk, then pulling out a chair. 'My father has collected a lot of things across the years. If I like them, he lets me keep them.' She turned, looking back at him. 'They come from all over. His office, you see...'

Chen raised a hand, indicating that he understood and really didn't wish to know. What the Thousand Eyes did – what they *sanctioned* – really wasn't his business.

'I have a tape,' he said, going across. 'You can either speak directly into it, or I can prompt you with questions.'

She indicated the chair, then went round the desk and sat, facing him. 'You ask, I'll answer. That's probably the best way, neh?'

Chen nodded, then sat, placing his bag down beside the chair. Taking the tape from his tunic pocket, he snapped the seal, then placed it on the desk between them. From this moment on it would record all that was said between them. Chen looked down at the timer at his wrist and spoke.

'The date is the fifteenth day of March 2212 and the time is twenty-seven minutes after eight in the morning. My name is Major Kao Chen of the T'ang's Security service and I am in the Mansion of Junior Minister Shang Mu, interviewing his daughter, Shang Han-A concerning the incident that took place yesterday afternoon in the Mid levels of Rathenow stack.'

Chen looked across the desk and met her eyes. 'So, Nu Shi Shang, what exactly were you doing in the Mids at Rathenow?'

'I go to College at Rathenow. When there are no lectures, I often go down the levels. I like to see what's happening down there.'

'College?' Chen frowned. 'But I thought you were only sixteen?'

She smiled. 'I graduated early, Major Kao. If you had checked my personal records, you'd have seen that I've been there a year and a half now.'

'Ah...' He'd known about the College. In fact the dead man had been a graduate of Rathenow. All of his known associates there had already been arrested for questioning, but Chen had not thought to check on the girl. He'd assumed, because of her age, that she was still at school. Besides, he'd been loath to pull her file from Central records, just in case the Thousand Eyes had security tags on all their employees' families' files. The last thing he wanted was for the Thousand Eyes to come down hard on him.

'I didn't know him,' she said, before he could speak again. 'The man who was killed, I mean. I saw him clearly as he ran past me, and I don't think I'd ever seen him before. But that's not really surprising, is it?'

'No...' But he was still thrown by the fact that she was at College at all. He had been assuming that it was sheer coincidence that the Junior Minister's daughter had been there, of all places, when the man had been cornered with the File, but now he began asking himself if that were really so. What if she had been there for just that reason – to meet the man and take the File? For there was no doubt about one thing: she *had* the File. Here, perhaps, in her rooms, or somewhere else. Somewhere she'd hidden it, between yesterday afternoon and now.

'What do you do at College?'

'Is that relevant, Major Kao?'

'Maybe not. I was just interested. If you want to move on...?'

'No. It's okay. I study art. Art and sculpture. Those paintings and sketches on the wall behind you. They're mine.'

Chen turned, looking at them again, impressed. '*Yours?* I thought...' He turned back. 'You're certain you'd never seen the man before?'

She smiled. 'No, Major Kao. I was watching the *hua pen*, you see. Sketching him...'

'Sketching him? You mean, with paper and pencil?'

'No. With a sketchboard. You know, one of those computer-generated things.'

'I know. My son has one. He too wants to study art.'

'Your son?'

Chen waved the question aside. 'Look... can I possibly see your sketches? They might help us in some way.'

'Of course,' she said, getting up. 'I think I left the sketchboard in the other room. If you'll wait just a second or two...'

He turned, watching her go through, expecting her to come back and say she couldn't find it, to make some excuse. But when she returned, it was with the sketchboard. She came across, handing it to him.

'You know how to work it?'

Chen nodded, then fiddled with the controls, trying to remember how to summon up the last few stored items. 'They're a nuisance to clean, neh?' he said, looking up at her.

'Here,' she said, leaning across him to tap out an instruction on the touch-pad. 'I only made one sketch. I'd have made more, but there wasn't time. I'd barely finished this one when it all happened.'

He stared at the sketch, surprised. If she had taken the inner workings out of the machine, then she could not have kept the sketch, but here it was, and from the security camera records he had seen, she had captured the scene about the *hua pen* almost perfectly.

'It's very good,' he said, handing it back to her. 'Perhaps we could have a copy... for the investigation file. There just might be something in it that will help us.'

She smiled. 'Of course. I'll print one out and send it to you. Oh, and I could sketch the man for you, if you like. I'm told I've a good visual memory.'

For a moment he had begun to doubt his own theory – to think he'd been mistaken – but her words made him reassess things. *A good visual memory.* So it was possible that she had re-worked the sketch on a second, a *spare* sketchboard, just in case someone like himself should come asking awkward questions.

Chen looked down at the despatch bag which lay beside his chair. 'No. There's no need. But if you would tell me now what you saw.'

As he listened to her, Chen thought it all through, examining all the angles. She had the File. There was no doubt of that. She had removed it from the scene in the inside of her sketchboard. But why? And was it only coincidence that she was there at that very moment?

It seemed unlikely. The more he thought about it, the more certain he was that she *was* involved – that she in fact *knew* the man. Checks could be made, of course, and if they could find camera record of her talking to him, then the matter could be proved. Alternatively, they could search the Mansion and locate the File. Both were fairly routine and straightforward procedures. The question was, did he really want to do either?

It wasn't just the fact that her father was a Junior Minister in the Thousand Eyes and senior adviser to the First Dragon himself, though that was not something to be readily dismissed. It was more to do with how he himself felt about this matter. To have this young woman arrested, to have her tortured and eventually killed, simply for knowing the truth about their world – was that right? Or was it, as he had increasingly begun to feel, a kind of evil?

Chen shivered inwardly, remembering what he himself had seen, at the research station he had been posted to, three years before. He had seen what the system he served was capable of – of the moral depths his Masters plumbed to keep their world in check – and had been changed by it. Oh, he still served, for that was all he really knew, yet it was with a kind of self-disgust, and with a desire, if possible, to do what he could, however small, to counterbalance that great evil.

As she came to the end, he gave a tiny bow and, his decision made, stood, picking the tape up off the desk.

'Thank you,' he said quietly. 'That's all I need. We'll terminate the interview here, at...' he glanced at his timer '...forty-nine minutes after eight.' He placed pressure on the top of the tiny unit, switching off the tape and sealing it.

'That's all, then?'

He nodded. 'Yes. You'll get the copies of your statement. Oh, and your father will get a copy of the final report. Apart from that, well... it was very pleasant to meet you, Hannah.'

She stared back at him a moment, then stood, coming round the desk. 'I've just realised. I forgot to ask the servant to bring the ch'a. If you've the time?' She raised an eyebrow inquisitively.

'No,' he said, tempted by her offer, wanting to ask her about the various things in the glass-fronted cabinet behind him; curious to see the Magic Theatre in operation. 'It's kind of you, but I must get back. I've a lot to do. Besides, I haven't seen my family in three days. You know how it is.'

She laughed. 'I wish I did. I'm afraid I don't get on with my father's second wife, nor with my half-brother and half-sister. We are too... well, *different*, let's say. Oh, it's not a racial thing, Kao Chen. It's just...' She shrugged.

'I understand,' he said, seeing it all clearly. 'It must be difficult for you.'

'Difficult?' Again she laughed, but this time there was a hint of sourness. 'She is the First Dragon's youngest sister, you understand. A *very* important lady. It was a convenient alliance for my father, but some days I think she would have preferred my father's first marriage to have been without issue.'

Chen winced inwardly at the pain he heard in her voice.

'Is it that bad?'

She looked back at him, forcing herself to smile. 'Sometimes. But I can give as good as I get. I was eight when my mother died. Nine when my father married that woman. It toughened me up, you might say. Forced me to be a survivor. And that's what it's about, neh? Surviving. Or so my father's friends all say.'

'Maybe... but there ought to be more to life than that, neh?'

She nodded.

'Anyway, I must go now.' Chen bowed, then turned, making for the door.

'Major Kao?'

He turned back. 'Yes?'

'Your bag...'

'Keep it. I think you might find it... interesting.'

'Interesting?' She stared back at him, her eyes half-lidded.

'You'll see.' He smiled. 'It was pleasant meeting you, Hannah. I'm sorry that our acquaintance has to be so brief, but good luck.'

He bowed again, then turned, making his way out. And as he walked down the long, luxuriant corridor, following the House Steward, he smiled, imagining her surprise when she opened the bag.

Small things, he thought, letting himself be ushered out of the great doorway. *That's all we can do to counter the great evil in our world. Small things.* And yet, for once, he felt pleased, as if he had done something big. He laughed and walked on, making for the lift.

Something that would reverberate.

An Sheng's palace lay in the valley just below them, its tiled roofs a gleaming red in the late afternoon sunlight, its high white walls heavily patrolled by armed guards. As they made their way down, a horseman rode up the path to greet them, dismounting and pressing his forehead into the dust at the First Dragon's feet.

'Highness,' the man said breathlessly, lifting his head but keeping his eyes averted. 'My Master was not expecting you until this evening. But he greets you warmly and asks you to accompany me.'

The First Dragon grunted then turned, looking to Shang Mu. 'I suppose Prince An knows best.'

'He would have good reason, *I Lung*,' Shang answered quietly, conscious of how he would have felt had the First Dragon descended on him three hours early. 'I am told Li Yuan has spies in all the households. Prince An would want to make sure that news of our visit did not get back to the wrong ears.'

The First Dragon smiled tightly. 'Ah. Of course.' He turned back to the waiting servant. 'Lead on, man. One of my servants will take your horse.'

At the gate An Sheng's third son, Prince Mo Shan, a tall man in his thirties, was waiting to greet them formally. With a minimum of fuss he ushered them through into the cool of a small banqueting hall where a table had been laid with sweetmeats and wine.

'You must forgive us, I Lung,' the Prince said, dismissing the servants and going to the table, intent on honouring the First Dragon by serving him himself. 'My father sleeps in the afternoon and I am loath to wake him before he has had his full rest. After all, such matters as must be discussed...'

He let the elliptic nature of his words hang in the air a moment, then half turned, looking down at the table. 'However, would you have some refreshments after your journey, I Lung?'

Shang Mu, standing to the right of the First Dragon and two steps back, watched the side of his Master's face, noting the tension in his neck muscles. The First Dragon was clearly put out. Even so, he smiled and made polite conversation, as if nothing were amiss. *Maybe,* Shang thought, *this is a power game of some kind. Maybe An Sheng thinks the First Dragon has come early to make some kind of point, and is acting thus to demonstrate that he will not be hurried into anything.* If so that was worrying, for it spoke of mistrust and potential division, and that was the last thing any of them needed just now.

The First Dragon turned, looking at him. 'Shang Mu? Will you have something to drink?'

'A cordial, Master,' he said, noting the coded signal they had agreed on earlier. If the First Dragon looked elsewhere when he addressed him, he was to say nothing; but if he looked directly at him...

Shang Mu looked past his Master at the Prince. 'A man needs his rest,' he said, watching Mo Shan pour him a tumbler of the cordial, 'and a great man more than most. He cannot afford to be tired. His responsibilities are great, therefore his mind must be clear, like a mountain stream.'

Mo Shan handed him his drink. 'So it is, Master Shang. Especially when the matter is as great as this.'

The First Dragon came closer. 'Your father has discussed this with you,

Mo Shan?'

'I am my father's hands, my father's eyes. To be effective I must know what he is thinking.'

Shang Mu smiled, understanding at last. Whether they had arrived early or late would have made no difference. They might dine with An Sheng, but they would deal with his son.

The First Dragon, quick to pick up on what was happening, spoke to Shang Mu again, this time looking to the Prince and smiling as he did so. 'It is as I was saying on the journey here, Shang Mu, a great man is made greater by the ability of his servants, and who is more loyal a servant than a son?'

He raised his tumbler, toasting Mo Shan. 'I trust you will be as the lips to the teeth.'

'You understand then, I Lung?'

'Of course. It is only right that your father keep aloof from such matters. Indeed, it would be easier for us all were we to keep this matters... informal.'

'Informal, I Lung?'

'Exactly. Great men are like great ships, they leave a huge wake wherever they go. It is easy for the eyes of the hsiao jen – the little men – to see them, neh? Whereas, if this matter were dealt with at a... let us say, slightly lower level...'

Mo Shan smiled then turned, looking directly at Shang Mu. 'You speak, then, for the Ministry, Master Shang?'

Shang Mu returned the smile, but it was the First Dragon who answered. 'My Son-in-Law speaks for us all, as Uncle and Brother speak for the Family.'

'Then let us talk, Master Shang. But first, I Lung, let me take you through to my father's rooms. I understand he is waking and wishes to greet his old friend.'

'And I him.' The First Dragon glanced at Shang Mu, giving a terse nod, then went across, moving past the waiting Prince and out into the corridor.

Alone, Shang Mu looked down into his tumbler and heaved a sigh. He understood. It was not merely a matter of who dealt with whom, but who would take the blame if things went wrong. This way it would be he and the young Prince, Mo Shan, whose heads would fall were their conspiracy to be uncovered. An Sheng and the First Dragon would claim no knowledge of it. It was a frightening thought. Yet that was the way of it, and he accepted it. Besides, the I Lung was right. A single meeting with An Sheng would draw little attention. After all, it was the job of the First Dragon to keep in touch with all the Heads of the Twenty-Nine. Yet to be seen in An Sheng's company too often would draw unwanted notice. No, it was best this way. And if their scheme succeeded it would do him no harm to have played so prominent a role.

Shang Mu put the heavy tumbler to his lips and drained it at a gulp, then went across, pouring himself a second. Listening to the First Dragon only a moment before, he had realised just how far they had come in the last twenty-four hours. The first step had been taken. They had done enough already to warrant execution. From here on there could be no mistakes. To survive he had to succeed.

In a week he could be dead, all trace of his family erased from the records. It was an appalling thought. And yet, what better incentive could he have been given? What better stimulus to make him think clearly and plan carefully? No, the First Dragon had been clever – very clever indeed. And he would repay the great man's trust. He would make this great enterprise work. Because to fail was unthinkable. To fail was... well, failure was not an option.

He heard footsteps. A moment later Prince Mo Shan appeared in the doorway. Now that the First Dragon had gone, he seemed more relaxed, as if he had cast off a skin.

'Well, Master Shang,' he said, turning slightly, indicating the open door, the corridor beyond. 'It would be a shame to waste the sunlight. Let us walk in the gardens, neh? I am sure we have much to discuss.'

It was after one when Chen finally got home. The hallway was in darkness, but there was a light on in the kitchen at the far end. He went through, thinking it might be Wang Ti, up late, waiting for him, but it was a stranger, a young Han in her late teens. She turned, eyes wide, then, drying her hands quickly, gave a bow.

'Who are you?' he asked quietly, pulling the door to behind him, concerned not to wake the household. 'Where is Tian Fen?'

'She had to leave, Major Kao. I am her cousin, Tian Ching.'

'Ah...' He looked about him at the kitchen, satisfied by the cleanliness, the orderliness he saw, not unhappy that the slovenly Tian Fen had left. She had been trouble from the start. He looked back at the girl. 'So you're my wife's new helper?'

She nodded.

He studied her a moment. She was a good-looking girl. Her hair was neatly cut, her clothes simple and modest, but there was an air about her. His eyes were drawn back to her face, to the smoothness of her skin, the freshness of her features. He smiled, then moved past her, inspecting what she had been doing, lifting the lid of the big cooking pot and sniffing deeply.

'What is this?'

'Green jade soup, Master.'

'Ah...' He put a finger in the cold soup, tasting it. 'Hmm.'

'Would you like me to warm some up for you, Master?'

Her offer surprised him. He turned, looking at her, conscious suddenly of her proximity, of the soap-scrubbed scent of her, the way she looked at him, willing to please.

'Why not?' He laughed gently, then sat at table, watching as she poured some of the soup from the pot into a small bowl and began to heat it up, enjoying the simplicity of being tended to. Wang Ti had once done this for him. But that seemed long ago now. Long, long ago. He sighed and looked down.

'When did you start here, Tian Ching?'

'Tuesday, Master.'

Tuesday? He looked up, surprised. But that was five days ago. Surely it hadn't been that long since he'd last been here? For a moment he watched her as she worked. Again it made him think of Wang Ti and the times he had sat like this, watching her at work, enjoying the simple sight of her body in movement, of the strength in her arms and shoulders. He shivered, then looked away.

'There...'

She placed the soup in front of him, then handed him a porcelain spoon. Heated up, the soup smelled delicious and he spooned it down quickly, not realising he had been so hungry. 'So?' he said, pushing the bowl away, 'How are you finding things?'

She was standing there, facing him across the table. At his question her eyes widened slightly and then she laughed; a soft, strangely sensual laugh, the whole of her face lighting up. 'It's hard work, but I'm used to that. I'm the eldest of eleven children.'

'Eleven?' Chen laughed, sitting back slightly, beginning to enjoy himself, to unwind after a long, hard day. 'So you started early?'

She nodded, her smile broadening. 'They used to call me *Shao nai nai*, little grandmother. Even so, I got my schooling. There's many still who can't say that.'

'Yes...' He looked at the bowl. 'Is there more?'

'Of course...' She hesitated, looking past him at the door.

He turned in his seat. His fourteen-year-old son, Jyan, was standing in the doorway, looking in bleary-eyed, his sleeping-robe pulled tight around him. Chen went across to him and hugged him close.

'Jyan, love... Couldn't you sleep?'

The boy stared past his father at the maid, then looked back up at him. 'I heard voices. I thought...'

Chen heard the scrape of the bowl being picked up, the clink of the spoon as it was placed on the side.

'It's all right,' the girl said, moving past them, stopping in the door to bow. 'It is time I was in bed. Goodnight, Master. Goodnight, young Jyan.'

Chen returned her brief smile. 'Goodnight...'

He looked down at his son again, noting how Jyan turned his head, watching her go, the light of suspicion in his eyes, and sighed inwardly. The last thing he needed just now was trouble at home.

'So how are things?' he said brightly, lifting Jyan's chin. 'How has your mother been?'

Jyan shook his chin free, looking away, his jaw set stubbornly. 'You ought to know that yourself. You ought to spend more time with her.'

Chen smiled wearily. 'You're right. But it's not possible right now. Things are difficult. We're six men short and the workload has doubled this last year. It's hard to cope as it is.'

Jyan made a small, irritable movement. 'Even so...'

'Look... I'm here now, okay? And tomorrow night I'll get back early. I promise I will.'

'You always say that. You never are.'

'Look, I promise. All right? Maybe we'll get one of the new trivees out.

Maybe...'

Jyan broke in brutally. 'I've seen them all. Besides, I'm not talking about me. I'm all right. It's mother. She needs you and you're never here. She...'

'All right! Enough! I don't need you to tell me what I ought or ought not to be doing.' He turned away, trying to calm himself, trying to still the anger, the frustration he felt at that moment. 'Look, Jyan,' he said quietly. 'Try and understand, will you? I am a Major in the T'ang's Security service and my work is very important. I can't just leave it whenever I want to. If something urgent comes up I have to deal with it there and then. And if that means that I'm away more than I'd like, that can't be helped. Not now.'

'So when?' Jyan asked, his young eyes full of hurt. 'When does it start to get better? When will you have some time for us?'

Chen sighed. 'I don't know. Soon... Look, it's difficult right now. There have been a lot of changes. Things are in flux. But they'll get better. It's just a phase. It's...' He shrugged. 'Look, I love you all. You see that, don't you? And if I work hard, it's for you. To keep us here, at this level. To keep you all away from... well, away from what's down there.'

'Down there?' Jyan looked past him again. 'Sometimes I think things were better when we were down there. Before you were promoted. Before...'

The boy stopped, as if he'd come up against a cliff-face, but Chen knew what he was thinking. He could see the pain in his eyes, the tightness of the cheek muscles where he struggled to control himself. Jyan was thinking about the loss of the baby. About the moment when Wang Ti had 'gone' from them. He shivered, then pulled his son close, holding him tightly.

'It'll be okay, Jyan. I promise it will. Things will change. They'll be as they were. I promise you.'

Jyan pulled away and nodded, then, wiping his hand across his face, he turned and went out. Chen stood, hearing the pad of his son's feet along the hallway, the slide of his door as it closed. He sighed, looking about him at the kitchen, then turned back, hearing the door slide again, the feet pad back.

Jyan's face appeared at the door again. 'I almost forgot,' he whispered. 'There was a message. It came just after dinner.'

'A message? Where?'

'On the table in the hall.' Jyan hesitated, then came across and reached up to kiss his father's neck. 'I love you, dad.'

'And I you, my darling,' Chen answered, hugging him briefly.

He waited for Jyan to return to his room, then went out. The message was on the table by the door. Chen picked up the long, pale envelope and sniffed at it. It smelled of incense. Going back into the kitchen, he sat at the table again, studying the unfamiliar handwriting, then slit the envelope open with his nail and unfolded the single sheet.

It was from the girl, the Junior Minister's daughter. 'Meet me,' it read, 'at The Golden Carp, eighth bell tomorrow. Wear something casual. No uniforms. I've some friends you might wish to meet. Interesting types. Best wishes. Hannah.'

The Golden Carp... it was in the student quarter of Rathenow. But who were these friends? Were they accomplices? Members of True History? If so, then why was she taking such a chance? Because that was what this was. A rather dangerous chance. For all she knew, his act of kindness might have been a pretence – the bait in a trap. Unless she were genuine, of course: an innocent, unaware of the risks she was running. But that would mean that it really was coincidence that she'd been there just at that moment, and that he simply didn't believe.

Chen read the note through once more, then took it across to the sink. Taking a taper from the box, he lit it, letting the burning paper fall into the empty bowl. Maybe he'd meet her, maybe not. He would see how busy he was. In the meantime he would transcribe the tape and get it to her.

Chen lifted the jug and poured some water into the bowl, then sluiced the ash away. *There,* he thought. *Now no one will know.* But even as he tried to dismiss the idea, something told him he would go, if only to find out whether he was right about her.

Leaving a single light on in the kitchen, he went out and down the hallway to the toilet, standing over the bowl to piss, then turned and went out, crossing the hallway to his room. In the doorway he paused, hearing Wang Ti's gentle snoring in the darkness, then went inside, closing the door quietly behind him.

He stripped off, down to his breechcloth, then clambered in beside her. She was warm, her familiar scent strong in the dark. For a time he lay there, pressed against her back, hoping she would wake and turn, but there was nothing. She did not move, the rhythm of her breathing did not change. But so it was these days. So it had been for a long time now. It was as if he did not exist. As if...

He shuddered and then turned beneath the sheet, facing away from her, separating his body from the awful, taunting warmth of hers. Maybe that was why he worked so hard. Maybe that was why he kept away so often, so as not to face this torment. For that was what it was. Torment. Endless bloody torment. Only at such times, faced by the darkness and the long hours of the night, did he realise just what he had lost when Wang Ti had gone mad.

Chen took a long, shivering breath, trying to calm himself, to lay there and be at peace, but it was impossible. Sometimes her turned back seemed like a wall, vast and insurmountable, the very symbol of an indifference that was like death itself. He might wait forever and she would never turn and greet him lovingly, as she once had. Oh, he could take her from behind, certainly, and she would not stop him, but neither would she show any sign of wanting him. It would be as if he were making love to a corpse, or to the warm pretence of a human form. But it would not be Wang Ti. It would not be his darling wife.

He sat up, perching himself on the edge of the bed, his bare feet on the floor, his chin resting on the knuckles of his fists, knowing he would not sleep. He should not have come here. Not now. He should have come during the day. This... well, this only made things worse.

He looked up suddenly. There had been the soft rustling of cloth outside in the hallway. He stood and went to the door, thinking it was maybe his young daughter, Ch'iang Hsin having nightmares again. But it wasn't Ch'iang Hsin, it was the new maid, Tian Ching.

'Master...' she said quietly, giving a tiny bow, then moved past him, going into the toilet and pulling the door closed. Chen stood there, staring into the half-dark, conscious of what he'd seen. The girl's nightrobe had been of a thin, almost translucent cloth, and the shape of her young body, of her breasts and the dark triangle of her pubis, had been clearly visible. He drew a long breath, waiting, then heard the soft, almost musical sound of her urinating into the bowl.

Gods, he thought, the stiffness at his groin almost unbearable. How long had it been since he'd had a woman? Two years now? Three? He shivered, watching as she came out again, conscious of her eyes shining briefly, moistly in the half-dark as they met his then looked away. There was no doubting that look. He watched her move past him, conscious once more of the naked form of her beneath the thin cloth.

At her door she paused and turned, the briefest smile playing on her lips, and then she went inside. He listened, waiting to hear her door click shut, but there was nothing.

Chen stood there, conscious of the blood beating in his head, his chest, his limbs, desire like a dark tide flowing through him. Then, as if waking, he padded slowly down the hallway, checking at each of his children's doors to see if they were sleeping.

Outside the new maid's door he stopped, hearing her move on the bed inside the darkened room. He imagined her lying there naked beneath the thin sheet, waiting for him. The door was ajar. He had only to step inside. For a moment longer he stood there, aware of the tension in him, the madness that seemed to boil and bubble in his skull, then, reaching out, he put his hand on the edge of the door and slid it shut.

CHAPTER 108

OLD MEN

The Senior Clerk sat behind his desk, stiff-backed, the gold-on-blue H-M motif on the wall behind him repeated on the patch on his chest. He smiled tightly, with a politeness bred of contempt, and leaned towards her slightly.

'Forgive me, Madam Lever, but it is... *unusual* for us to deal with new customers without... well, without an *introduction* of some kind.'

Emily stared at the man then, taking the folder from her bag, placed it in front of her on the desk. Inside were more than a hundred separate receipts from the Hythe-MacKay Auction House, dated over a three-year period.

'I believe you dealt with my late father-in-law.'

'Forgive me, Madam, even if that were so... '

She pushed the folder towards him. 'I think *these* might refresh your memory... '

He stared at her a moment, then, reluctantly, flipped open the folder and removed the top sheet. 'Ah... ' he said, seeing what it was, 'this is a... a *delicate* matter.' He smiled at her again. 'You see, officially none of these things exists. And these documents... ' He shrugged. 'Well, they're clearly fakes.'

Cut the bullshit, she thought. Tell me what I want to know.

He hesitated, then closed the folder decisively. 'Okay. If you would come with me, Madam Lever.'

Good, she thought. *At last!*

He stood and bowed, waiting for her to stand, then put out an arm, all charm now, and ushered her out through a different door to the one she'd entered the reception room by, and along a long, dimly-lit corridor.

'You understand how it is, Madam Lever,' he said fawningly. 'We have to be very sure of who we deal with. One mistake and we're all in trouble. The Ministry... ' He stopped, opening the end door for her, then, much softer, 'the Ministry would have our balls!'

The knocking came again, insistent now. Kemp stood impatiently, tying the sash about his portly waist, then shooed the girl into the next room.

'Stay in there,' he said quietly, 'and don't make a noise.'

He waited a moment, then went across, pulling the door open with a flourish, smiling.

'Britton! You're earlier than I expected!'

The man outside was in his fifties, smartly dressed with a close-shaven scalp. He bowed, then stepped past Kemp into the room.

'You have it, I see,' Kemp said, his eyes indicating the thick folder under Britton's arm.

'It wasn't easy,' Britton answered, looking about him at the elegant apartment as if checking for assassins. Then, looking back at Kemp, he smiled tightly. 'I had to trade upon a lot of old friendships to get this. There's a lot more here than's in the official security file. A lot more.'

Kemp nodded, then gestured that Britton should take a seat, but Britton ignored him, walking across to the bathroom door. Opening it a fraction, he looked inside.

'They look after you well, *Shih* Kemp.'

None of your business, Kemp thought, smiling broadly.

'Naturally,' he said. 'They're powerful men. They treat their friends well.'

There was a couched threat in that which Britton didn't miss. He turned, looking sourly at Kemp.

'And how well do you treat *your* friends, *Shih* Kemp?'

Kemp went to the drawer beside the bed and took out the envelope, then turned back, facing Britton.

'It's all here. One hundred thousand, as agreed.'

Britton's face was hard. 'I've had a lot of expenses. As I said, there's a lot more here than you'd have thought.'

Kemp eyed him. 'I can find an extra twenty-five. But that's it.'

Britton considered a moment then nodded. He stepped across and handed Kemp the dossier.

Kemp flicked through it, then whistled. Eight hundred pages. And good stuff by the look of it. He looked up at Britton and smiled. 'I'll send the *expenses* over later.'

'That's fine with me, *Shih* Kemp, but you might have a look at the passage I've marked on page 374 before I leave. There's an interesting sideline you might want me to follow up on.'

Kemp raised an eyebrow, then flicked through, finding the page. He read the passage through then looked up again, interested.

'Hmm... So just what were our two friends investigating before they had their... *accident?*'

Britton smiled. It was like the smile of a shark. 'Old Man Lever had hired them to look into the background of his son's new wife. It seems they came up with a blank. Lever paid them off, but for some reason they kept looking. And then this. Suspicious, neh?'

'Very.' Kemp paused. 'Do we know what they found?'

'No. It all got burned with them.'

'Interesting.' He considered, then nodded. 'Okay. Look into it. But this time keep expenses to a minimum, huh?' Britton stared at him, fish-eyed. 'It'll cost what it costs.'

Kemp shrugged. *Yes*, he thought, *but if it costs too much you can whistle.*

At the door Britton stopped, looking back at him. 'Oh, and say goodbye to your girlfriend for me!'

Kemp sat there a moment after he'd gone, staring at the door, his anger slowly subsiding. Britton was becoming a nuisance. More than that, he was an insolent son of a bitch. But he was useful, there was no denying that, and if he could find out something juicy about Mary Lever, then all the better. There'd be a fat bonus in it for himself.

He looked down at the dossier again, then laughed. *The Old Men would pay him well for this. Very well indeed.* He flicked through, stopping at a picture of an adolescent Michael Lever with his father, and nodded to himself. Then, calling for the girl to come and help him dress, he turned to the front of the file and began to read.

The old men gathered about the statue of the boy, casting admiring, acquisitive eyes over its perfect marble form.

Egan, who had crouched to study the detail of the outstretched hand, looked up at Fairbank and smoothed a hand over his polished skull. 'Where did you find it?'

'There's a dealer in Europe I use,' Fairbank answered, looking to the other two Heads as he did. 'I'll give you his address. It seems there's a new man working the Clay in Central Europe. They say he's unearthed a whole treasure trove!'

'If it's like this, I'm interested,' Green said, nodding in his distinctive manner. 'Could I be indelicate, John, and ask what this cost?'

Fairbank's smile widened a fraction. 'Have a guess?'

Chamberlain looked at the statue, considered a moment, then laughed. 'I haven't a clue! Statuary really isn't my thing. But having said that, I don't think I've ever seen one this well preserved. Why, there's not a mark on it!'

'That's true enough,' Egan said, straightening up. 'So much of what I've seen in the Auction Houses is damaged or badly cracked. The little savages tend to smash anything they get their hands on. This must have been hidden away somewhere – in a cellar, perhaps, or under rubble. To find it... ' He gazed at the statue again, clearly impressed. 'Well, it's rare, that's all I know. So... fifty million? A hundred?'

'Double that,' Green said, watching Fairbank's face. 'I bet you paid... oh, two twenty?'

'Two twenty-five,' Fairbank said, laughing, then shook his head. 'Every time! I don't know how you do it, Clive.'

'It's sixty years of watching that face of yours,' Green answered, laughing. 'I'm sure I know every little tick and nervous gesture on it!'

'Is that what it is?' Again Fairbank laughed.

'Two two five, huh?' Egan said, and turned, looking at the statue with a new respect. 'And you think he might have something else like this?'

'He might... ' Fairbank looked about him, 'Or you might make me an offer... '

Egan looked up, frowned, then, seeing how the others were smiling, gave a bark of laughter. 'Am I that transparent?'

'Only to your friends...

Egan looked about him. 'And good friends you've been these past thirty years. Through thick and thin.'

'Which is one of the reasons why we're here, neh?' Fairbank said, serious suddenly. It was true. For thirty years they had suffered at the hands of Old Man Lever. He had bought their best men, plundered their markets, stolen their secrets, undercut their products. No trick had been too low or too filthy for him, no method too devious or too immoral. But now that had changed. His death fifteen months back had opened a door of opportunity. His son was raw and inexperienced. Better than that, the boy was an idealist and wanted to implement a number of changes to his corporate structure: changes which would severely weaken ImmVac and – for the first time in three decades – make it vulnerable to a concerted effort by its trading rivals.

'I've had my man on ImmVac's board prepare a special briefing for us,' Fairbank said, throwing the cloth back over the statue. 'He'll be here at four to present it. In the meantime I suggest we break for lunch. Besides, there's another matter I'd like to raise with you.'

'Another?' Egan asked, his eyes sparkling with interest.

'Over lunch,' Fairbank said and smiled. 'I'll tell you while we eat.'

Wu Shih stood there, his palms damp, facing the *ching*, while in the room behind him the technicians whispered urgently among themselves, hurrying to prepare the tests.

It had been three weeks after his twenty-second birthday when he had first come here, sad-eyed and dressed in mourning clothes, to meet his other self. Since then, once a year for the past thirty-five, he had returned, unannounced, to spend an hour or two with it.

A servant brought a chair. He sat, looking about him at the tiny chamber. To his right an altar had been set up, and offerings of food and drink had been placed before it. To the left was an exercise walkway, the looped track motionless. The *ching* itself sat on a high-backed throne facing him, wearing a simple one-piece exercise suit that left its arms and legs bare. It was perfectly, unnaturally still, its smooth, unlined face vacant, like an idiot's.

The *ching* was his age exactly, a perfect copy of him, kept ready for the day when he, Wu Shih, finally died. Only then would it emerge from its lifelong seclusion in these rooms and, for the briefest while, take on his power and authority. Until, as the ritual demanded, his eldest son killed it and became

T'ang in his place.

He stared at it, wondering if, despite all the reassurances of the experts, it had its own private thoughts, its own dreams and visions of the world. Wondering if, behind those vacant eyes, some other creature looked out at the world, cut off from speech and impotent to act.

Some mad and staring thing...

That thought had always frightened him. Since his first visit here he had had dreams – dreams in which he *was* the *ching*, a machine of flesh and bone, made only to be woken once and killed. In those dreams he would find himself inside an empty, echoing palace of pale white alabaster, running from room to room, trying each door with a mounting desperation as he found all portals to the outside locked fast against him. Then, from beyond the walls, would come the sound of muted laughter – a deep, horrible, mocking sound. And he would run on, like a lost child, until he woke, his body sheathed in sweat, his heart racing like a newborn's.

'Chieh Hsia... ?'

He turned his head. The Chief Technician stood beside him, his head bowed.

'Are you ready?'

'We are, *Chieh Hsia*.'

'Then let us commence. I must be gone from here in an hour.'

'Chieh Hsia!'

He watched as two of them stood behind the *ching*, helping it to its feet. Encouraged by their touch, it seemed to come alive, the waxwork sheen of its skin enlivened suddenly by the stretch and pull of muscle. Aided by them, it moved towards the walkway. Mounting the step, it took two paces and then stopped, letting them fasten its hands to the special grips on the rail.

Throughout it all the face remained unchanged, its idiot-vacancy some-how more terrible when glimpsed against the motion of that powerful, well-muscled form, and as ever Wu Shih found himself appalled and horrified. So like himself, it was, and yet... well, it was as if in coming to these rooms he stepped out of the world he knew and entered some other place – *ti yu*, the underworld, perhaps.

As the walkway started up its legs began to move, as if some conscious choice evoked the movement, yet from all he'd been told he knew that the motion was only the habit of the muscles – a habit patiently induced by its custodians.

Exercise, it was all that body knew. Pleasure and pain – such were strangers to it. Desire and simple need – these too had been kept from its experience. Fed regularly and exercised, it functioned perfectly. *Much better,* Wu Shih mused, *than its original.* No illness had ever plagued it, no worries disturbed its dreamless sleep.

Colourless, unconscious of its purpose, it waited.

My death, he thought. *It measures its existence by my death.*

Later, as he was watching it perform a series of twists and turns that would have defied a more thoughtful athlete, he found himself thinking about Weimar and the importance of the vote that afternoon.

He had done all he could in that regard. He had bought and bullied, made countless threats and promises, trying to place the matter beyond doubt, yet still it would be close. As it had once before in his lifetime, the House was pressing for autonomy – an autonomy it could not be allowed to have.

Power. It was all about power. Grant them a little and they wanted more. Grant them more and they wanted a lot more. Best, then, to give them nothing – to keep all power in the hands of the Seven and make the matter beyond question. But only force could achieve that, and right now forcing the matter was not an option – not unless they wanted war.

Maybe Li Yuan was right, then. Maybe they ought to wire them all – reduce them all to *ching!*

He huffed irritably, then stood, tired suddenly of the whole business. 'Enough!' he cried. 'Let it rest!'

He turned, the watching technicians and officials backing away hurriedly, their heads bowed low, as he moved quickly, impatiently between them. And outside, in the main office, where representatives of the *T'ing Wei* and the Ministry – the two custodians of the *ching* – had gathered to honour him, he did not even pause to greet them, but swept through, his mind filled with dark shadows and forebodings, knowing it had been wrong to come.

'Dan? Where's Em? I've looked all over... '

Johnson looked up from where he was preparing the documents for the journey and looked across at Michael Lever. 'She left early. I thought you knew. She's gone in to HytheMacKay to see what she can pick up for Joe's birthday.'

Michael raised an eyebrow, surprised. 'Strange... She usually mentions things like that to me.'

Johnson stared at him a moment, then, without comment, returned to his task.

'When do we need to leave?'

'Not for an hour yet,' Johnson answered. 'We could leave it longer, but I thought we'd give ourselves plenty of time.'

Michael eyed him a moment, then laughed. 'Okay... what have you got up your sleeve?'

'Me?' Johnson looked up, all innocence, then smiled. 'Okay... I had a thought, that's all. As we're going up to Washington anyway, why don't we make an unscheduled visit to our facility just south of there.'

'Alexandria?'

'Sure. It would be a good opportunity to see for yourself how they're implementing your changes.'

Michael nodded thoughtfully. 'I like that. But what about a brief? I mean, who's Manager there now?'

'All here,' Johnson said, tapping the stack of files he was about to put in the special courier sack. 'I've prepared an overview of our operation there you can read on our way across.'

Michael laughed. 'Okay. Let's do it.'

Despite herself, Emily was impressed. The vaults at HytheMacKay were massive, stretching down a full ten levels beneath their offices. Armed guards stood at each doorway and every intersection – more for show than anything else, the Senior Clerk confided, pointing out the computer-operated lasers that tracked them wherever they went.

At the very heart of the vaults was a small room. Inviting her to enter, he pulled out a chair for her behind the console, then sat beside her, placing a key from his belt into the desk before him. Facing them, ten ch'i from where they sat, was a blank screen. Turning towards her, he smiled, then spoke to the air.

'Kate, it's Jefferies. Code gold. Display.'

The screen lit up, showing a three by three grid, each square labelled with a two-letter sub-directory code. She studied them a moment then looked back at him.

He smiled. 'Was there anything in particular you were interested in? Are you thinking of collecting, or buying as a gift?'

'Both,' she said, then hesitated, not certain she should show too direct an interest. Then, not knowing *how* to be indirect, she shrugged. 'There was a picture in one of the old books my father-in-law bought here. It had men in it. Black men.'

'Ah, the Negroes... ' Jefferies' smile took on a new form, an element of professional interest giving it an almost genuine air. 'Kate, give me sub-route ST. General index.'

The screen changed at a blink. The nine squares had become a list of four categories:

ARTEFACTS
BOOKS
DOCUMENTS
MAPS

'Maps,' she said, curious.

'Maps, Kate.'

At once the screen was filled with tiny pictures – eleven in all, each item numbered and priced in red. She studied them a moment, then nodded to herself. There was not an item there under two million.

'Can I see item seven?'

'Item seven, Kate.'

As the other items faded, the one she had chosen seemed to separate itself from the screen and drift towards her, growing slowly larger and taking on a three-dimensional form in the air. It stopped, an arm's length from where she sat – a big, solid-looking thing.

It was a map of Africa. She stared at it, fascinated. The map was old, much older-looking than the frame. It was yellowed and the writing on it was irregular, not a normal machine script. But it was the names which most interested her.

'Those names... ?'

'Segu,' he said, turning and looking directly at her, 'Ashanti, Bornu, Wadai, Darfur, Funj, Tutsi, Butua, Menabe, Boina, Oyo, Hausa, Masai... ' He smiled. 'I'm sorry, it's a speciality of mine. They're the names of tribes...

of nations, if you like. There were literally hundreds of them, all of them black-skinned. From what we can make out they led very diverse lifestyles. Most of them were highly primitive, of course – around the same level as the Clayborn – but not all. In fact some were extremely sophisticated. There was a whole varied culture there at one time. Of course, we're very lucky here at Hythe-MacKay. We've probably the best collection of Negro artefacts in the world, and this map... well, it's a beauty, neh?'

And so it should be at fifty million, she thought. Even so, she was quite taken by it. Was it real? Was it *really* real? And if it was, what had happened to all those tribes – where had they gone?

Hundreds of them... No. It wasn't possible.

'Where do you find them?'

He laughed. 'Now *that* would be telling. Let's just say we have our sources. And there's new material coming in all the time.'

'But the Ministry... '

'... know nothing, *officially.*' He smoothed his thumb over his fingertips, indicating what he meant. 'It adds to the price, naturally, but then our clientele can afford that little extra it costs us.'

She nodded, understanding. Corrupt. It was all corrupt, from First Level to the Net. There was probably not one straight official among the lot of them.

'Is there a book of it... a history?'

Jefferies thought a moment, then shook his head. 'Of their origins, no. But there are one or two books about the slave trade.'

'The *what?*'

'That's how they came here to America. They were brought over from Africa to work on the plantations. *Hung Mao* traders went ashore and rounded them up by the thousand, chained them up and brought them back.' He nodded admiringly. 'It was a highly lucrative trade. Many a trading empire was built on black slaves, you know!'

She turned back, staring at the map, seeing it anew. First the *Hung Mao* had enslaved the blacks, and then the Han had enslaved the *Hung Mao*. And next? She shivered, sickened by the whole business.

'Show me something else. Show me... ' An idea struck her. 'Show me something to do with the Kennedys.'

He smiled. 'Now *there's* an interesting subject. Kate, give me sub-route

AC, directory six, sub-file Kennedy. Show me Documents, sub-file Newspapers. Item nine, I think. The copy of the *Dallas Times Herald*... '

Kemp waited in reception while the Steward went in to announce his arrival. He stood there, looking about him at the priceless paintings on the walls, conscious of Fairbank's secretary watching from his corner desk.

He felt good. Britton's report had been excellent and, together with the other material he had, was sure to satisfy the consortium. Even so, this was the first time he had met the four together, and the fact that they had summoned him here to AmLab's headquarters in Denver put him on his guard.

They had treated him well, there was no denying. The apartment he had been given was of the highest quality, and the girl...

He smiled, remembering the girl. He was almost tempted to ask for the girl as part of his fee, but knew it would be wrong. To admit *any* weakness was a mistake when dealing with these men.

'Shih Kemp?'

He turned. The Steward was in the doorway, holding the door open for him. Taking a firm grip on the folder, he gave a tiny bow and went across.

The boardroom was massive, at least a hundred ch'i by fifty, the ceiling twenty ch'i above his head. The floor and walls were finished in a pale green stone, the polished hexagonal slabs embossed with the blood-red circling-atom logo of AmLab.

The old men were seated at the far end, behind a long table of polished ebony. A space of at least five ch'i separated each man. Behind them were their corporate banners – the black on yellow of RadMed; the pale green and red of AmLab; the blood-red eagle of NorTek; and the blue star on white of WesCorp.

'Kemp... ' Fairbank said, his voice still powerful despite his seventy-five years. 'Come close where we can see you better.'

He approached. Ten paces from the table he stopped and bowed his head. 'Gentlemen... '

He looked along the line, expecting some sign of eagerness in their faces – after all, they had waited a long time to get back at ImmVac – but there was nothing. Their faces were like weathered walls.

'Is *that* it?' Egan asked, pointing to the folder.

'Yes, I...'

'Put it on the table,' Fairbank said abruptly.

'I beg pardon?'

'On the table. We'll read it later.'

'But...'

'Don't worry, *Shih* Kemp, you'll be paid in full. And I'm sure you've done an excellent job. Britton's a first-class investigator. But that's not why you're here.'

'No?'

Fairbank smiled, then turned in his seat, looking to Chamberlain.

'Geoffrey...'

Chamberlain stood and came round the desk, walking past Kemp to a low table placed against the wall. Picking up a small black lacquered box, he brought it across and handed it to Kemp.

'What's this?'

Chamberlain leaned close. 'Open it and see.'

He opened it, looked, then looked again. 'What the... ?'

Chamberlain laughed. Behind him the others were laughing too, sharing the joke.

'I...' Kemp turned, looking to Fairbank for an explanation, trying hard to retain his composure. 'I... I realise what it is, but... well, whose is it?'

Chamberlain took it back from him and smiled. 'Does it matter?'

'Not to me, no... but to *him*...'

'Oh, he was dead *before* it was cut off!'

Kemp stared at the pale gobbet of flesh and frowned. 'So what's going on?'

Egan answered him. 'You're building up a network, right?'

'To use against Lever, sure. But what's that to do with... *this*?'

Egan's grin was like a skull's. 'In my experience, what's good for one purpose is usually good for another. Your contacts... they've contacts of their own, right? Little men, operating among the levels.'

Kemp nodded.

'And they're keen to line their pockets, neh? To earn a little extra on the side?'

Again Kemp nodded.

'Good. So we *use* them.'

'Use them? How?'

Green of RadMed answered him.

'We live in troubled times, Shih Kemp. Political agitation and riots... these things disturb the markets. And whatever disturbs the markets affects our livelihoods, neh? A climate of uncertainty is bad for trade. You'd agree?'

'Well, sure...'

'I'm sure you would,' he went on smoothly. 'For some time now the situation in North America has concerned us. We've waited patiently, hoping that action would be taken – strong, *decisive* action – to curtail such activities. But nothing. The authorities know who these troublemakers are. They have camera evidence and the statements of informers. If they wanted they could go in and arrest them, but they don't. Why? Because they're afraid. Because they haven't the guts or determination to deal with the problem and eradicate it!'

Green's deeply-lined face was hard with resentment. Beside him Chamberlain and Fairbank were nodding, willing him to go on.

'Well, Wu Shih may lack the will to do the job, but *we* don't. If he won't deal with the *mei yu jen wen*, then we shall!'

Kemp nodded. It was not the first time he'd heard that phrase. On numerous occasions in the past few months, after formal dinners, or at more private gatherings, the drink had flowed and, eventually, the subject had come round to 'solutions'. And always, *always*, someone would come out with that description of the Lowers. *Mei yu jen wen*... Sub-humans. Meat-men. And the more he heard it, the more he was convinced it was true. For more than a century now they had dealt with their criminal element by demotion. The good had climbed the levels, while the bad had been sent to the bottom of the pile – down to the Lowers – where they could be with others of their kind.

Their kind... He smiled savagely, convinced of it. The City was the great filter of humanity, separating the good from the bad, the successful from the failures, the real men from the sub-humans, the meat-men – the *mei yu jen wen*. Animals they were, with the morality of animals. And what did it matter if they lived or died? They were bred in ignorance and died in it. Scum, they were. Less than scum.

Green was watching him. He smiled. 'You understand then?'

'Maybe.' He hesitated. 'That thing...?'

'Let me tell you a story,' Fairbank said, folding his hands together on the table in front of him. 'When our ancestors first came to this great continent, there were beings already here. Indians, they called them. Sub-human creatures they were, with bright red skins. Well, these Indians proved a real nuisance, attacking *Hung Mao* settlements and murdering women and children without reason. So the government came up with a reward system. For every Indian a man killed, they'd pay a certain amount of money. Trouble was, it was impractical to carry dead Indians back across country to claim the reward, so they devised an easier method. *Scalps.* They'd pay the reward on every Indian scalp brought back.' Fairbank smiled. 'Now, I don't think that's a bad system, do you? But I felt we could improve on it somewhat. A scalp... these days a man can lose half his head and still live. Lose his cock, however, and even if he *does* live, there's whole generations of such scum as'll never be born, neh?'

Kemp laughed. It was ingenious. 'How much do you plan to pay?'

'Two fifty?'

'There's risks... '

'Sure there's risks!' Egan said angrily. 'There's *always* risks.'

'But two fifty. It's... too low.'

'Three hundred, then,' Fairbank said. 'But no more. And a cut of fifty for you.' He smiled. 'Per cock... '

The muscle in Kemp's cheek twitched. *Fifty...* It was more than he'd expected. A whole lot more.

'How...' He licked his lips, his mouth suddenly dry. 'How do I find out who to hit?'

'Don't worry. We'll take care of that side of things. You'll be sent copies of all the relevant Security files. All you have to do is arrange to act on them, okay?'

He nodded.

'Good. Then we'll organise a fund at once. Third party, naturally. And if there *are* any little problems, *you* sort them out. Okay?'

'Okay.'

Fairbank sat back, clearly satisfied with his afternoon's work. 'You'll be given a contact address, and you'll deal directly with that. From now on you'll have no contact whatsoever with any one of us. If the T'ang himself comes calling on you, it's your job to make sure he doesn't come here next.

You understand me, *Shih* Kemp?'

Kemp swallowed. 'I understand.'

'Good. Then we're finished here. Oh, and Kemp... '

'Yes, Mister Fairbank?'

'You can have the girl. I understand you were rather partial to her... '

Michael Lever climbed down from the sedan and looked about him, realising just how long it had been since he'd visited one of ImmVac's facilities.

Years ago – before his incarceration by Wu Shih and the split with his father – he had spent a great deal of time touring the City, inspecting ImmVac's installations on his father's behalf while he learned the business. Back then he would have spent the evening partying with officials, then spent the rest of the night with the daughter of some local bigwig – someone who wished to curry favour with his father. But now the very thought was anathema.

So much had changed since then. So much had happened to him. First there'd been the arrests at the Thanksgiving Ball that night – he and a dozen other 'Sons', taken by Wu Shih's forces for 'subversive activities'. For days afterwards he had raged against his captors, demanding his release, but fifteen long months had passed – most of them spent in solitary confinement – before he had been freed to see his father again. And when he had...

He shivered, remembering the breach with his father, the long and bitter battle for independence which had ended with a bomb-blast in which his best friend, Bryn Kustow, had been killed, and he himself badly injured. It could have ended there, but it hadn't. He had outlived his father and become the Head of ImmVac in his place. And throughout it all there had been Mary, his darling 'Em', there like a pillar of burning light in his darkest moment, supporting him, guiding him, keeping his feet firmly on the narrow path.

Without her...

He turned, hearing Johnson's footsteps behind him. 'Well, Dan? Shall we shake them up a little?'

Johnson smiled. 'If you like, we can go through unannounced. I have the codes.'

'Lead on. I'm looking forward to seeing Steiner's face when we march into his office!'

Johnson turned and went across, giving the runners and the bodyguards their instructions, then came back. 'Okay. Let's go.'

The two doorguards were watching a vid when Lever and Johnson came through. Their feet were up on the desk, the remains of a meal piled up on the desk in front of them. There was a moment's panic, a reaching for guns, and then they realised who it was and stood, their heads lowered, their faces flushed with embarrassment.

Steiner's secretary began to rise from her chair as she saw them, her face alarmed, but one look from Johnson made her sit again, her head folding against her chest.

'You first,' Michael whispered, moving to one side. 'I'll give you a minute, then I'll come in. Pretend you're alone.'

Johnson made a facial shrug, then tapped out the door's locking code. With the briefest rap of his knuckles against the door, he pushed it open and stepped inside.

There was a startled gasp and a small high sound of surprise.

'Michael?' Johnson said, a faintly amused tone in his voice. 'I think you'd better see this for yourself.'

He went in.

Steiner was at his desk. Or rather, he was strapped to his desk. He lay there on his back, buck-naked, a naked girl astride him. His wrists and ankles were fastened by leather thongs to the legs of the huge desk and a gag was tied tightly over his mouth.

'Are you in any trouble, Manager Steiner? Or is this an early lunch-break, perhaps?'

The old man swallowed uncomfortably, then lifted his chin, indicating to the girl that she should remove the gag. She obliged, then slipped from on top of him, standing behind the desk, her hands attempting to maintain some degree of modesty.

'Well?' said Michael after a prolonged silence. 'Is this a regular event, or have I just caught you at a particularly bad time?'

'I... I can explain, Shih Lever!'

'Sure.' Michael took a breath, then looked to Johnson. 'Dan, bring me four guards. I want this man out of here right now.'

'Shih Lever!'

'Relax, *Shih* Steiner. Just relax, neh? Now you, girl... do I employ you?'

Timidly she nodded.

'Where are your clothes?'

She indicated across the room. Michael looked. There, in the right-hand corner, was a stack of filing trays and papers. Beside them – very neat – were two piles of clothes.

'Get dressed, then report to Personnel. You'll get six months pay, okay?'

She nodded, then hurried to do as she'd been told.

Michael turned, hearing Johnson returning with the guards.

'Okay,' he said, standing back to let them pass. 'I want you to pick up that desk and move it out of here, all right?'

The men, who had been staring at the sight wide-eyed, turned and answered him as one. 'Yes, *Shih* Lever!'

'*Michael...* ' Steiner pleaded, 'in your father's name... '

Michael turned, glaring at him. 'Firstly, *Mister* Steiner, do *not* invoke my father's memory! Secondly, what you do in your own time and in the privacy of your own apartment is up to you, but I do not expect a senior manager of mine to be doing this on Company time or on Company property!'

Steiner closed his eyes, as if he'd die of shame. 'Dear gods... '

'Come on,' Michael said, waving the guards across. 'I want him out of here, and I want it done right now!'

Johnson was staring at him now. 'What are you going to do?' he said quietly.

'Just watch... ' he answered, then, turning to the guards. 'Come! Move now! Out into the reception room, then follow me. As from this moment *Shih* Steiner is no longer an employee of the ImmVac Corporation and as such is a trespasser on this property. As guards you are empowered to eject him from the facility.'

There was an exchange of glances, then, with a roar of delighted laughter, they lifted man and table and began to carry them across. Through the reception room they went, incurring the startled glances of Steiner's secretary, and on into the main corridor that led to the front gate of the facility.

'No... ' Michael said, indicating that they should turn and come back. 'Through the main facility. I think the staff should have the opportunity to say goodbye to their ex-Manager, neh?'

'Have a care, Michael,' Johnson said quietly, but Michael pushed his arm away.

'Whatever you say, *Shih Lever*,' the most senior of the guards answered him. 'Once round the factory floor and back here?'

Michael nodded then stood back, letting them pass.

'It's too much,' Johnson said, speaking to his ear. 'Turf him out, sure. But *this*... '

Michael turned, staring at his assistant, his face hard, unforgiving. 'You're a good man, Dan, and a fine assistant, but this once don't tell me what I should or shouldn't do, okay?'

Johnson bowed his head, chastened.

'Good. Now I want you to stay here and go through the records. Everything. Invoices, sales, production figures, the lot. I want a team in here by this afternoon, and I want a full report on my desk first thing Monday morning.'

'But what about Washington? Won't you need me there?'

'Everything's prepared, neh?'

Johnson nodded. 'It's all in the file.'

'Good. Then I should be all right, shouldn't I? After all, I've only got to sign the refunding document.'

'I... ' Johnson hesitated, then nodded.

'And Dan... unstrap him once he's back here and let him get his clothes. But get him out of here. And no Company sedan, okay? The bastard can walk home.'

Kennedy sat back in his armchair, looking across the room at the three men seated there, watching as the Steward refilled their glasses. It was an hour and a half until the vote and, elsewhere in the great House, Representatives were already gathering, excited by the prospect of a set-back for the Seven. Here, however, it was quiet, peaceful.

Deceptively so, Kennedy thought, knowing that, if he were to be sure of things, he would need to convince these three – and the votes their faction commanded – to join his side.

'Well, Representative,' Underwood said, lifting his glass slightly in a toast, 'this is very pleasant, but I'm sure you've not asked us here for *social* reasons.'

He smiled. His own glass sat untouched on the table beside him.

'No,' he said, looking to Hart, who sat to Underwood's left and then to Munroe, on his right, including them by the gesture. 'Nor would I insult you by pretending otherwise. The hour presses and I am forced to deal more openly than I'm accustomed to.'

Hart smiled. 'The House makes traders of us all, neh?'

Kennedy returned the smile, yet inwardly he wondered what Hart meant by that. Was it an honest insight, or was it a barb?

'That's true,' he said, 'yet trade is better than warfare, surely? If all parties can be satisfied... '

'Impossible,' Munroe said, bluntly, unexpectedly.

Kennedy stared at him. 'What do you mean?'

'He means,' Underwood said, his smile enigmatic, 'that we've not come here to trade.'

He paused, staring down into his wine, then spoke again. 'You want to buy our votes, neh? To have us in your pocket, like the *tai* you've been snapping up these past twenty-four hours.' His eyes slowly looked up, meeting Kennedy's again. 'You brought us here to sound us – to find out what it is we want and offer it in return. A vague promise for a certain vote.'

'Not vague... '

'No?' Underwood looked at him, surprise and disbelief balanced in that look. Then, with a shrug, he downed his drink. 'Whatever... you're wasting your time. You can't buy us and there's nothing we want that you can deliver. So... '

'Nothing?'

Underwood's smile was pitying. 'We are Dispersionists, Representative, not New Republicans. We don't want the kind of small compromises you seem happy with, don't you understand that? Change, that's what we want. Change. And you can't give us that. You simply can't deliver... '

No? he thought, indignant. Yet against his natural indignation was set the truth. Underwood was right. He had bartered away whatever strengths he'd brought here to Weimar. And Change... *real* Change, that was now beyond him. There'd been so many tiny factions to satisfy, so many greedy egos to pamper. *And nothing pure...*

He sighed. 'Maybe you're right. Then again, maybe you're kidding yourself, too. Spaceships and distant stars... it's not a very practical platform, is it? Come the next elections, do you think you'll sustain your support?'

Underwood smiled, then, setting his glass down, got to his feet. Either side of him, Hart and Munroe did the same.

'I wouldn't worry about my seat, Mister Kennedy. I know I'll get re-elected. But you? I'd be a little worried if I were you. You're golden boy right now, but what happens when you don't deliver on those promises? What are you going to do when the media start looking at your record a bit more closely than they are just now?' He paused, his smile becoming a sneer. 'And what happens when Wu Shih decides he's had enough of you?'

Kennedy felt a coldness grip his stomach. 'What do you mean?'

'Oh, just rumours, Representative, that's all. Just rumours...'

Kennedy looked down. 'You plan to vote against, I suppose?'

'Did I say that?' There was no sign now of a smile on Underwood's face. 'As a matter of fact, we plan to vote for the proposal. But we'll be doing that because we want to, not because you bought us, or bullied us, or offered us something in return. I wanted to make that clear, just in case you got the wrong idea about us.'

'The wrong idea?' Kennedy laughed. 'I sure as hell did that, didn't I?'

He stood, his face suddenly hard. 'Now listen, and listen good. You talk of me, Mister Underwood, but who's funding you? That's what I'd like to know. Who's making it easy for you to play Mister Simon Pure? Because I know you. I know all of you. And if you ever fucking come and insult me to my face again, I'll kick you from here to fucking Africa, you got me?'

Underwood took a long breath, then nodded.

Kennedy leaned back a little, relaxing his stance. 'Good. I'm glad we understand each other, ch'un tzu. And now, if you'll excuse me, I've much to do.'

He watched them go, then let out a long, sighing breath. So there were rumours, eh? That was bad. He thought he'd been discreet. Or maybe they were just guesses. Attempts to explain the changes in policy he'd made these past twelve months. Well, let them. They'd be making new guesses after this afternoon's vote.

And Wu Shih? How will he react?

Kennedy shivered, then, with a tiny shrug, went through to his rooms. As the Steward laid out his clothes on the couch, he stood at the vid-phone, waiting to be connected to his wife.

'Sweetheart?' he said, as her face appeared on the screen. 'How've you been? How are the boys?'

Her smile warmed him. 'We're fine... How's it all been going?'

He made a face. 'Who knows? It's going to be tight, but hopefully we've done enough. We'll know in two hours, anyway.'

'That's good... '

He stared at her, drinking in the sight. She was still as beautiful as she'd been when he'd married her fifteen years before. There was still something waif-like and fragile about her, even after all that had happened. Her hair had grown back since the operation two years ago, and outwardly she seemed no different from before, but he knew that wasn't true. Just as he'd been changed by the presence of that tiny soft-wire in her head – and in the heads of his two young sons – so had she. Subtly, insidiously, it affected everything they did, every decision they made. It was as if she had a cancer in her head, waiting to flower at the touch of a switch, and the knowledge of it, just as it made each compromise he wrought seem foul, made each moment between them incalculably sweeter.

'I need you,' he said softly, conscious of the Steward moving about in the room behind him.

Her smile for the briefest moment had a bitter, fragile edge to it, then it strengthened. 'And I love you, Joseph Kennedy. So go and do what you have to. You're a good man, Joe. Hold on to that, okay?'

He smiled. 'I shall. Give the boys my love, huh? And I'll see you later, at the party.'

'I'm looking forward to it.'

'Bye, my love.'

'Bye, sweetheart.'

He turned from the blanked screen, the heaviness he'd been feeling earlier returned to him. He hadn't told her – he couldn't have, not on an open line – and yet she knew that he was going to do something at the vote this afternoon. She had always read him well.

He looked up. The Steward was waiting by the door, his head lowered.

'Is there anything else, Master?'

He shook his head. 'No... thank you, Tao-kuang. But if you could have my things ready for when I return. Something light to travel in. I'll change again when I'm back in America.'

'As you wish, Master.'

Alone again, he turned, staring at the vid-phone, feeling strangely restless, wondering if he should call Michael and talk things through. Then, steeling himself, making a deliberate effort to set all doubts aside, he undid the top button on his tunic, starting to change.

The vote was in an hour.

Emily sat back among the silk cushions, glad for once of the isolation of the State Class compartment. She was alone, the tape book she had been listening to beside her on the long, comfortably-cushioned seat. The gentle movement of the bolt was pleasant, reassuring almost, as it sped south through the stacks to Richmond.

It had been a remarkable day and for once she blessed the wealth that had allowed her that glimpse into those times before the City. Yet it was that same wealth that troubled her constantly.

To be comfortable, that was the right of everyone, it seemed. But to be rich in the way that she and Michael were rich – that was obscene. The more she thought of it, the more she was convinced. Yet to unburden herself of it seemed no solution either, for it was the way of their world to have such great divisions between rich and poor, and if not she and Michael, then some other 'Power' would step into the vacuum that they left.

She sighed. This much she had learned today: that the inequities of their society had existed long before the City, and that the City was merely a perfecting of that awful process.

The City ... it was a cage, a prison for them all.

And yet the City had been built to solve all problems. It had been meant to be ... what was the word she'd heard? ... a *Utopia*, that was it. 'Food enough and space to grow', that was one of the early slogans she had read about. It had been a bold experiment. To build a world without want. A true meritocracy. A world where people could find their level. But the experiment had failed. Old patterns of behaviour had reasserted themselves – nepotism and corruption, deals and betrayals – and the dream had turned to nightmare.

This world... she shuddered, frightened by the point to which her thoughts had come... it had been designed to reflect the best in Man, and had come to mirror the darkness deep within him.

A Yang world. A male world. A world without light or a mother's loving tenderness. A bastard world, cursed from conception.

There was a click, and then the faint chime of a warning signal. She looked up, composing herself. At the count of ten the door at the far end of the compartment hissed open and the Number One Steward stepped through, one of his junior assistants – Number Seven from his patch – just behind him. As the door hissed shut again, the two bowed deeply, then looked across at her, paper-thin smiles of politeness plastered to their faces.

'Is there anything we can do for you, Madam Lever?' Number One asked. 'Is there anything you would like?'

'Yes, actually. Have you a news screen anywhere on board?'

The Senior Steward smiled again – that same thin, insincere smile – then came across. Reaching up, he pulled a flatscreen down from a niche in the ceiling of the carriage and, adjusting the angle of the flexible arm, positioned it so that she could see from where she sat.

'Is that all right, Madam Lever?'

'Perfect,' she said.

'Just speak clearly to it. It's programmed to show all the First Level channels.'

'Thank you ... '

'Is there anything else? *Ch'a*, perhaps?'

'Yes. That would be very welcome, thank you.'

Number One turned and muttered a few sharp phrases of Mandarin to his assistant, who bowed low to Emily, then hurried off back the way he had come.

'It will be but two minutes, Madam Lever.'

'That's fine ... Now perhaps you'd leave me ... '

'Of course ... '

He bowed deeply, backed off a pace, then went through the door behind her.

Thank god, she thought. If anything, that was the worst of it. The obsequious servants, the fawning hangers-on, the lick-spittle half-men who would do anything – *anything* – for a share of the spoils.

She huffed, angry with herself, then sat back, staring up at the screen.

'Give me First News Inter-Active. I want a briefing on what's been happening at Weimar.'

The screen lit up. A handsome anchorman – a *Hung Mao* of roughly her own age – looked down at her.

'Madam Lever,' he said, inclining his head and smiling as if he recognised her. 'What would you like to know?'

She hesitated, wondering if she should ask it to re-programme itself to become a grey-bearded Han, then dismissed the idea.

'How did the vote go? Was it close?'

The anchor smiled, showing perfect teeth. 'It's just been declared. The earliest showings had the 'No' faction marginally ahead, but a late block vote by the Dispersionists clinched it. Even so, the final margin was only seven in favour of a 'Yes'. It seems the amendment ...'

'Amendment?' she sat forward slightly, her smile slowly fading. '*What amendment?*'

'The amendment Representative Kennedy introduced at the final reading. Would you like me to read it out to you?'

'No. Just print it up. I can read it myself.'

At once the anchor's face was replaced by the amendment.

She read it, a cold certainty forming in her. *Deals. Kennedy had been making last-minute deals...*

'That last bit... ' she said, frowning. 'It isn't clear what's meant by the new level of subsidies... is that an increase or what?'

The face returned. 'There was a secondary document. It was issued by the office of Wu Shih's Chancellor, Fen Cho-hsien. It reads...'

'Was it an increase or a decrease?'

'A decrease, Madam Lever. Of eight point six per cent.'

She sat there, stunned, slowly shaking her head. He'd sold out. The bastard had sold them all out! No decreases in the food subsidies to the Lowers, he'd sworn. Not even half a per cent. And now this ... She clenched her fists and stood, blind rage making her unaware of the hiss of the end door as it opened and Number Seven came through carrying the tray of *ch'a*.

'The bastard...' she said quietly. 'I knew! I fucking knew it! The conniving First Level bastard!'

The young Steward stopped, his mouth agape, staring at her. 'Are you all right, Madam Lever?'

She turned staring at him, her eyes wild with anger, then pointed up at the screen. 'No, I'm fucking well not! Look! Look what that bastard's done!'

'*Chieh Hsia* ... '

Wu Shih turned, looking back up the path between the mulberry trees. His Chancellor was standing just in front of the moon gate, his head lowered, his hands folded into his silken sleeves.

'Yes, Cho-hsien. What is it?'

'There is news, *Chieh Hsia*. From Weimar.'

'Ah ... ' He looked down at the pink and white blossom scattered on the path. 'Was the proposal passed?'

'It was, *Chieh Hsia*.'

'And the amendment?'

'That too, master.'

He looked up. 'So why the long face, Cho-hsien? What ill news accompanies the good?'

Fen Cho-hsien came forward, then bowed and handed his T'ang a sheet of paper. Wu Shih read it through, then looked up, a heaviness descending on him. It was the draft of a proposal to be put before the House within the month – a proposal to increase the powers of the House and give them a say in the financial arrangements of government; arrangements which presently were the sole concern of the Seven. Put simply, it was a grab for power, *real* power.

'This is new, I assume.'

'It is, *Chieh Hsia*.'

He took a long breath, then shook his head. 'I am surprised... and disappointed. I thought...'

'It was Kennedy, *Chieh Hsia*.'

Wu Shih smiled weakly. He had not needed his Chancellor to tell him whose hand was behind this.

'He calls our bluff, neh?'

Fen Cho-hsien said nothing.

Wu Shih turned, looking out across the great gardens of Manhattan. He had thought to find peace here – to inure himself against the news, whatever it was, that came from Weimar. But this...

He looked back at Fen Cho-hsien. 'If we allow it to be put before the House there will be chaos within the year.'

'And if we refuse to allow it?'

'Then it will come sooner.'

'So what are we to do?'

Wu Shih shrugged. 'Has my cousin, Tsu Ma, contacted me yet?'

'Not yet, *Chieh Hsia*.'

'Well ... tell him I wish to see him. Tell him... we need to talk, that's all.'

'*Chieh Hsia*.'

Fen Cho-hsien bowed and turned away, disappearing through the moon gate. A moment later he could be seen climbing the steps to the palace.

Wu Shih sighed deeply. So the day had come at last. The day he had tried so carefully to avoid. But part of him had always known. A man like Kennedy... it was difficult to bridle such a one.

Yes. But what was he to do? It was as he'd said. Kennedy had called his bluff, and now he must either carry out his threat or lose his hold over the man. And if he carried out his threat...

Wu Shih shook his head. *Not yet. I'll not decide it yet.* But as he walked along the path towards the moon gate, his tread was heavier and his head hung despondently, as if a great weight pressed down upon his shoulders.

Michael poked his head round the bedroom doorway, looking in at her. Emily was sitting at her dressing-table, her back to him.

'Em... we've got to talk this through. Now. Before he comes. All this...' He threw his hands up in despair. 'It's not going to solve anything!'

He took two paces into the room then stopped. He could see her face now in the mirror. She was looking down, angry, her face set.

'Em... we've a house full of guests. You can't just sit here.' He sighed. 'Okay... come when you're ready. But understand this. I'm as pissed off as you about that amendment. Joe had no right. But tonight... well, tonight's not the right time to raise it, okay?'

'Then when is?'

It was the first thing she had said to him in almost three hours.

'I... I'll speak to him tomorrow. I'll go over and see him.'

'No.' She turned to face him. 'Tonight. After the party. And not just you, Michael. Us. I've one or two things I want to say to Joseph Kennedy myself.'

He raised his hands defensively. 'All right. Have it your way. But afterwards, okay?'

'Okay,' she answered quietly, her face softening towards him.

He smiled. 'Good. Then come on, my princess. Let's go and show ourselves.'

Kennedy arrived an hour later. There was a huge cheer as he came in through the big double doors and down the steps, his wife Jean on his arm. Michael and Emily were there at the foot of the steps to greet them, embracing them then turning to lead them to the centre of the ballroom where, on a rostrum shaped like the continent of North America, a huge tiered cake awaited them.

It was Kennedy's thirty-fifth birthday and, coincidentally, the fifteenth anniversary of his marriage to Jean. As they posed for the media cameras, Michael took Emily aside.

'Did you get a present?' he whispered.

'Two,' she answered.

'Two?'

'One for now, one for later.'

He looked at her, his eyes narrowed suspiciously. 'What are you up to?'

'Trust me,' she said out of the corner of her mouth, but there was no amusement in her eyes.

For the next two hours there was no time for anything but the social whirl. Then, as the great bell sounded midnight, a curtain at one end of the hall swept back and four liveried servants stepped forward, bearing a huge silver tray between them. On the tray was an irregular, bulky shape, covered in bright red silk.

'What's this?' Kennedy asked, laughing and turning to Michael.

'It's your birthday present,' Emily answered, smiling tightly, reaching out to take Michael's hand.

Kennedy turned, watching the servants approach through the parting crowd. As they stopped, he stepped forward and, looking about him, took hold of the silk and tugged it back.

There was a gasp of surprise, then a great tide of applause and cheering.

It was a tiny artillery piece, the iron barrel a dull, unreflecting black, the wheels and limber of ancient polished wood.

Kennedy turned, beaming. 'Why, that's beautiful!'

Michael was nodding. 'It sure is ... ' He motioned to the servants. 'Lift it up, so everyone can see!'

As the great tray was raised and the cannon came into view, there was a ripple of applause and a loud whooping from near the back, where some of Michael and Kennedy's contemporaries were gathered about the bar. Most of the NREP Representatives were present and their mood was high after the day's victory.

'Thank you,' Kennedy said, stepping across and embracing first Michael and then Emily. 'Where in the gods' names did you get it?'

Emily handed him the gold and blue envelope. He stared at it, then whistled.

'*Aiya!* You shouldn't have … '

'No,' Emily said coldly. 'We shouldn't.'

'What is it?' Kennedy asked quietly, looking between them.

'Afterwards,' Emily answered, leaning close as if to kiss his cheek, a tight smile on her face for the watching cameras, 'in Michael's study.'

'Well?'

There were just the three of them in the study. Kennedy had sent Jean home and the rest of the crowd had gone on to The Kitchen to celebrate further.

Michael went round his desk and sat, tired after the day's exertions. Emily sat in one of the big chairs nearby, studying him a moment. With every day that passed he resembled his father more; yet he was very much his own man – a *better* man than Charles Lever had ever been. Just now he stared at Kennedy with a mixture of anger and disappointment. In that he differed from her. *She* was simply angry.

Michael hesitated, then leaned forward, looking directly at Kennedy, who was standing, facing him. 'Why the amendment, Joe? What happened?'

Kennedy sighed, then looked back at Michael apologetically. 'I had to. The whole package was conditional on it. Without that we'd have lost the vote, and then we'd have been back to square one, but with our reputation discredited.'

Emily laughed. 'You mean you don't think it's discredited now?'

Kennedy turned, staring at her. She had tried to keep the anger, the bitterness she felt, from her voice, but she hadn't quite succeeded.

'No, I don't. It's … well, it's different there. Weimar… it isn't like it is here. Straight-talking – it doesn't work there. Deals. That's how the House works. Deals.'

She nodded, looking at him as if he'd just confirmed her worst suspicions.

'You don't understand,' he went on. 'The measure will be temporary. A year, eighteen months at most. Until the Seven can get some extra production capacity. Wu Shih's new orbitals, the new hybrids. Things will change. And with the new controls...'

'You sound just like them,' she said, interrupting him. 'Deals. Temporary measures. Things will be better *once*...' She shook her head. 'But they're never any better are they? Not for the Lowers. They're the ones who are getting it in the neck. As for First Level... well, it escapes untouched, doesn't it? Every time. Every sodding time.'

'They'd never pass it.'

'No? And why's that? I'll tell you. Because they're all too much in the pocket of their rich friends. They're all like you – afraid to rock the boat. Afraid to take even the tiniest little bit from those who have it all. Change... you don't want Change, Joseph Kennedy, you want a cushy ride, that's all!'

Michael had been watching them, his eyes narrowed. Now Kennedy turned to him.

'Does your wife speak for you too, Michael?'

Michael sat back a little. 'No. Em calls it as *she* sees it. She's her own person. But this once I agree with her. I think it was a pretty foul manoeuvre, slipping that amendment through. Millions ... no, *tens* of millions are going to suffer because of that. Families ... little children ... while First Level pays nothing. I don't just think that's poor, I think it's really shitty on your part, and the Joseph Kennedy I used to know would have thought so too. So what went wrong, Joe? Where did all of that fine talk lead? To *this*? To pissing on the little people because they've got no vote, no say in things?'

Kennedy took a long deep breath then shook his head. 'It wasn't like that. It ... '

'You're their *tool*, Joe. Can't you see it? Piece by piece, they've bought you and controlled you. A year ago you were really something. A king. A real leader. But now ... ' Michael shook his head dismissively, the full bitterness of his disappointment showing in his face for the first time. 'Now you're just a puppet, Joe, jumping to their tune. I don't have to see into those smoky rooms where you make the deals to see that. I can see it right now, in your face.'

Kennedy stared back at him a moment, then looked down.

Michael met Emily's eyes briefly, then looked back at Kennedy, suddenly businesslike.

'I'll be making a statement. Tomorrow morning, at nine. In it I'll announce that I'm resigning my seat and quitting the NREP.'

Kennedy looked up. Both he and Emily stared at Michael, astonished.

'I'll mention nothing of what passed between us here tonight, simply that growing political differences have forced this decision on me. It's not my intention to stand again, nor to involve myself in politics in any shape or form, so you've no need to fear me setting up a rival party. But if it damages you, well, I can't say I'll be that unhappy. What you did today...'

Kennedy was silent a moment, then he nodded. He looked older, more haggard than they'd ever seen him. His whole frame seemed drained suddenly, his eyes shocked.

'I...' He shrugged, then, quietly, 'I'd better go.'

'A second...' Emily said, then got up and crossed the room.

Kennedy watched her, not understanding.

'A parting gift,' she said, coming back.

Kennedy took the long tube from her, surprised. It was very light, the container wrapped in the blue and gold of Hythe-Mackay. He made to open it, but she shook her head.

'Not now. Later, when you get home.'

He hesitated, looking from one to the other, his eyes – his whole manner – regretful, apologetic. Then, abruptly, he turned and left the room.

Emily turned and looked at Michael, meaning to thank him for what he'd done, but Michael was staring down at the empty desk, his clenched fists pressed hard against the desk's edge, his face crumpled in a grimace of pain, like a bewildered little boy.

She shivered, understanding. *Dreams die.*

Then, knowing what she had to do, she went across and sat on the desk beside him, drawing him into her arms and cradling his head against her breasts until the sobbing stopped.

CHAPTER 109

DARKNESS

Chen stood in the kitchen doorway, looking in. The children had gone and the apartment was strangely silent. Wang Ti, newly dressed, was sitting in a straight-backed chair, her hands resting passively on her knees where they'd been placed. Behind her stood the new maid, Tian Ching.

The girl was unaware of Chen standing there, watching, and sang softly to herself as she brushed Wang Ti's hair and braided it. Her pretty face frowned intently, her lips forming a pout, as her fingers moved nimbly, separating and twisting the thick dark threads of hair. And Wang Ti? Chen sighed, pained by the sight of her. Wang Ti looked like an old woman, hunched into herself, her memory gone, her eyes dull. It hadn't always been so, he reminded himself. Once she had shone like the sun itself, lighting his days, her body burning in the night beneath his, yet each day that passed – each day he saw her thus – made it harder for him to remember how it had been.

Eclipse, he thought. *My life is in eclipse.*

Again he sighed, louder this time, and Tian Ching, hearing him, turned, the song forgotten, surprised to find him there, watching her. She looked away, a faint flush appearing at her neck, her fingers faltering briefly before finding their practised rhythm again.

He watched her, remembering how difficult it had been to sleep, how fierce his need had been, how, eventually, he had gone out to the wash-room and, pouring cold water into the bowl, had washed himself until the need had gone. But even then he had not slept. No, for it was not mere physical need that tormented him, it was the thought of him being alone – emotionally and spiritually alone. And not just now, not just this one night, but every night, until the end of his days. Could he bear that?

He watched her, fascinated by the shape of her – the youthful roundedness of her – beneath her clothes, and wondered if he would go to her that night. If, in his pain and loneliness, he might not find a little comfort in her arms. Then, angry with himself, with the betraying need he felt, he turned away.

Back in his room he pulled on the tunic of his uniform then paused, staring at himself in the full-length mirror. *Who are you?* he wondered, trying to see himself beyond the uniform, beyond the lined and careworn face that was Major Kao Chen. *Who are you?* Once, long ago and beneath the Net, he had been *kwai*, a knife, and had lived a life of rigorous self-denial. Drugs, women, alcohol, those things had had no power over him, for there had been no weakness in him, no softness. He had been tempered, like the blade after which he was named; honed by a master craftsman, a pure thing in an impure landscape. But now? He shivered, his face muscles tightening. The years had made him soft, impure, and those other days – those days of certainty, of *steel* – seemed like a dream, or like something another had told him. It was hard to believe he had been that man.

He looked down, releasing himself from his own intense scrutiny, then turned, taking his case from the dressing table. These days work seemed the only answer, and, like many men he knew, he worked to escape all this – the sheer messiness of his home life. And yet his work no longer satisfied him. It was mired, all of it.

He went to the outer door, meaning to go directly out, then stopped and came back. The maid had finished, but Wang Ti still sat there, alone in the middle of the kitchen, like a huge doll that has been dressed and then forgotten. Setting down his case, he went across and knelt beside her and held her briefly, then kissed her brow. Yet as he moved back, releasing her, there was nothing, not even the vaguest flicker of recognition in her eyes. It was as if she was dead, the warmth of her skin a hideous illusion.

'Wang Ti...' he said softly, tenderly, his heart torn from him a second time. When would it end? When would it ever end?

Or was that his fate now? Was that the price the gods had exacted for his good fortune? To be bound forever to this living corpse, remembering her

always for what she'd been and never, *never* being able to accept what she
had become?

He hesitated, staring into the awful, empty mask of her face, then stood
and, picking up his case again, went out. Out into the bustle of the world.

Security Headquarters at Bremen was like a busy hive, officers coming and
going like worker bees on errands for their unseen queen. Making his way
up the steps and through the great dragon arch, Chen felt how strange it
was that he should be a part of it, how odd that the guards at the front gate
should salute him, their shaven heads bowed low, then pass him through
the barrier.

Another day he might have smiled at the thought, but today he was
distracted. As he rode the lift up the sixty levels to his offices, he found
himself thinking not of Wang Ti, nor even of the maid, but of the official's
daughter, Hannah. There was no real reason to see her again. In fact there
was every reason not to. Were Shang Mu to hear that Chen had been meeting his daughter, there would be all hell to pay. Best, then, to forget it – to
conclude the investigation and close the file. Yet even as he decided on it, he
found himself curious to know what it was she wanted from him. He had
done her a favour, certainly – maybe even a great service – and yet he had
made clear that there was no obligation. So why had she contacted him?
What *was* it she wanted to show him?

The lift's bell pinged, the doors hissed back. It was his level. Chen
stepped out, acknowledging the liftman's salute, then stopped dead, staring
in amazement. The entrance hall to his suite of offices was almost blocked
by a sedan which sat, like a discarded throne, in the centre of the floor. It
was a huge thing, clearly a luxury item, its black and mauve drapes made of
velvet and silk, its poles a good imitation of wood, the shafts finely carved
with figures from Chinese myth. Against the wall to the left squatted eight
men, their livery matching that of the sedan. He eyed them, understanding
dawning on him. They were Company.

Chen went across, drawing aside one of the drapes and looked inside.
The chair – a huge thing, heavily reinforced – looked big enough to seat
three, yet there was a single imprint in the cushions. He sniffed, taking
in the smell of leather and perfume. He knew that perfume. If the imprint
hadn't told him, the smell would have. It was Cornwell. The fat man. The

AutoMek executive who had been riding him over the matter of the broken machines.

Anger rising in him, Chen stormed through, past the two guards, who – busy chattering, their view of the outer doors obscured by the sedan – only rose to salute him after he had swept past.

As Chen came into his room, the big man got up from Chen's chair and, thrusting his ample stomach out across the desk, waved the notification at him.

'What the fuck do you mean by this, Major Kao? No further proceedings… Do you seriously expect me to take this shit?'

Chen put his case down on the side, then turned, facing the duty Captain in the doorway. His voice was tight, controlled. 'Who let this man into my room?'

'It was Sergeant Fuller, Major Kao.'

'Then have Fuller come here, immediately, and escort the ch'un tzu off the premises.'

Behind Chen, Cornwell was shaking his head. 'Like fuck I'll go! Not until I get some action around here! More than sixty of our machines have been attacked in the past ninety-six hours, Major Kao, and you've done nothing. Nothing but sit on your arse.'

Chen turned back, facing the obese form of Cornwell. He had been ordered by General Rheinhardt to be as diplomatic as he could with the man, but this was too much.

'You'll get out of my chair right now, Shih Cornwell, or I'll arrest you for trespass, understand me? As for the other matter, our investigations are continuing. But where there is no conclusive evidence, there's very little we can do.'

'No evidence?' Cornwell gave a snort of derision. 'There's no fucking evidence because you don't want to look for any, that's why! And while you're doing fuck-all, my Company is losing close on a million and a half a day! Well, it's not good enough, Major. You either catch these scum and punish them or I'll be forced to take matters into my own hands.'

Chen glared at him. 'I would advise against that, Shih Cornwell. It is still an offence to interfere in an official Security investigation. As for you taking action to punish these 'scum', as you call them, I would look on that as a most serious matter.'

'Oh, would you now?' Cornwell came round the desk and stood nose to nose with Chen, leaning into him threateningly. 'Listen... *Han*. I don't care what that badge on your chest says, you're still nothing but a little man, a *hsiao jen*. You get in my way and I'll have you crushed. I'll have you stepped on like an insect. My Company ...' his lips formed an ugly smile, 'we have influence at the highest level, and I mean the *highest*. So don't threaten me, Major Kao. Not if you know what's good for you.'

'Sir?'

Chen turned. Fuller was waiting in the doorway. Beyond him, in the corridor, a small group of curious officers had formed. Chen calmed himself, ignoring the scent of licorice in his nostrils from the other's breath.

'Sergeant Fuller. Escort *Shih* Cornwell to his sedan, would you? And make sure he finds his way safely from the building.'

He turned back, meeting Cornwell's eyes. 'As for you, my friend, I would think twice before crossing me. You might scorn the badge I wear, but my power is the T'ang's power. You will leave this matter to me *or else*.'

'Or else *what*?' Cornwell leaned close, his sickly-sweet breath filling Chen's nostrils once more. 'It's very simple, Major. These scum have to be dealt with, and if you won't do it, I'll find someone who will. As for all your bluster, well, you know where you can stick it, neh?'

With a grunt of amusement, Cornwell moved past Chen, squeezing his gross figure through the door and out between the watching officers. But he was not quite done. Turning, he raised his voice.

'Oh, by the way, Major Kao, how's that mad wife of yours?'

Chen stood there a moment, watching Cornwell shake with laughter, then went across and closed the door. But still the laughter went on, following him back to his desk, sounding clearly in his head long after it had ceased outside.

How much longer? he thought. How much longer can I take this crap?

He sat, feeling weary, aware of the warmth of the seat beneath him where the fat man had been. It had always been like this. Always. One insult after another; one battle after another. And never any peace. Never any real reward for what he'd done. Well, that was it. He'd had enough. If Cornwell so much as came near him again...

He unclenched his fists, conscious that his thoughts had turned to violence. Was that the only answer he could think of? Or was there some other way to deal with cunts like Cornwell?

Chen sat back, stretching his arms, trying to relax, but it was hard. The tension wasn't merely in his muscles, it was in every atom of his being.

He sighed. Maybe it was fate. Maybe there *was* nothing he could do to change things. Even so, he could not live with himself – could not respect himself as a man – unless he tried. Unless he took what fate had handed him and tried to shape it for the good.

Chen stood, looking about him at the disorder of his office, then crossed the room. Opening the cupboard where he kept a change of clothes, he pulled out a simple one-piece of the kind they wore down-level. He was behind with his reports – badly behind – but the paperwork would have to wait.

I'll go down, he thought, beginning to change. See things for myself. Work out what action we ought to be taking.

But even as he went out into the corridor, passing the curious, staring faces of his fellow officers, he knew that it was only an excuse, an evasion, for the truth was he had to get out, to escape all this.

Yes, he thought, facing it for the first time. He had to get away. Right away. Before things cracked. Before the whole charade came down on top of him.

Shang Mu leaned forward, facing the First Dragon across the narrow space between their seats. Far below – visible through the cruiser's ornately-decorated porthole – the huge, ten-thousand *mu* fields of the West Asian Plantations moved past like the squares on a giant *wei chi* board.

'The first meeting is this evening, *I Lung*. Prince An Mo Shan and four other Minor Family princes. Sympathisers. Men he trusts. They have arranged to meet at Yin Tsu's palace.'

'At Yin Tsu's?' The First Dragon's eyes widened. 'But I thought Yin Tsu was staunchly loyal to Li Yuan?'

'He is. But Yin Tsu will not be there. It is his second son, Yin Chan who will be hosting the meeting.'

'Ah... Even so, I find that strange, Shang Mu. Chan has always struck me as a most loyal son.'

'That is so, *I Lung*. Yet it seems he has never forgiven Li Yuan for divorcing his sister. He feels his family was shamed and wants revenge.'

'Revenge ...' The First Dragon looked away. 'It's a piss-poor reason for deposing a Son of Heaven, neh? Watch him, Shang Mu. Find out if he drinks, if he has a loose tongue.'

'And if he has?'

'Then we have no choice. Yin Chan must have an accident.'

Shang Mu looked down, staring at his hands uncomfortably. 'And the list, I Lung?'

Unexpectedly, the First Dragon smiled. 'Now that's a document, neh? I wonder what Li Yuan would make of it? Does he realise, I wonder, just how deep this enmity is rooted? And if he did, what would he do? What action could he take that would not undermine the very throne on which he sits?'

The First Dragon reached inside the darkness of his robe and drew out the handwritten list An Sheng had given him. Eight thousand names were written there, among them almost every member of the Seven's government, from chamberlains and ministers right down to bondservants and grooms. But there was one name he had noticed in particular: that of the young American politician, Joseph Kennedy.

He looked up from the thick sheaf of paper, meeting his Junior Minister's eyes. 'As I said, it is interesting. And An Sheng is right, of course. It is not enough to remove the Seven, we must remove all those who serve them. Yet we must not be impatient, Shang Mu. We have not thrived all these years through impatience. No. We must saw with soft ropes, as the old saying goes. And we must heed the lessons of the past. We must be thorough. Everything must be planned, down to the last tiny detail. Only then can we guarantee success.'

'Then I am to do nothing, I Lung?'

'Quite the contrary, Shang Mu. You will begin at once. But choose carefully. The last thing we want is to draw attention to ourselves.'

Shang Mu smiled bleakly, noting the tone of irony in his Master's voice. If there was one thing the Thousand Eyes had perfected over the years, it was the art of not drawing attention to themselves. Even so, he felt a profound unease at this latest development.

'It shall be as you say, I Lung,' Shang said, nodding.

'Good,' the old man said, closing his eyes. 'Then leave me. And get some sleep, Shang Mu. It may be some while before any of us sleeps soundly again.'

'Where is your husband?'

'My husband? He's... gone. Looking for work.'

'Gone? Where has he gone?'

The woman looked down, avoiding Chen's eyes. 'I don't know, I... I haven't seen him for a while. Two, three days...'

Chen stared at her, trying not to lose his temper, then turned away. Like the other wives he had interviewed, she clearly knew where her husband was, but she was frightened. She knew what her man had been up to and what the penalty for that was, and she was keeping quiet. Well, he'd have done the same in her place, but that made it no less frustrating. He needed to talk to one of the men, to find out what they wanted. And to try to do something before things got out of hand. Because these were decent, hardworking people. Their only crime was to have been thrown out of work by the Company and replaced by machines.

And who wouldn't be angry at that?

Chen looked about him at the room. It was like all the others he had seen: a clean, immaculately tidy room, its basic austerity augmented by tiny touches of luxury, like the colourful holo-print on the wall opposite. He went across and studied it, ignoring the woman a moment, losing himself in his appreciation of Ku Hung-chung's masterful work. Reaching up, he activated the holo, then stepped back, nodding. It was good the way the picture seemed suddenly to come to life, the computer adding depth to Ku's beautifully-painted figures. He put his palm up, feeling the warmth generated by the field, then switched it off.

Chen looked down. Against the wall beneath the holo, unnoticed until then, was a tiny, box-like cupboard on legs. Chen crouched down and opened the tiny doors, then looked across, meeting the woman's eyes.

'You know this is illegal?'

She said nothing, simply watched him, like a trapped animal, unable to answer.

He looked back, studying the tiny figures within the red and gold paint-ed box. It was a miniature temple, not unlike those you'd find in many households, but whereas most temples were to the Family Ancestors, this one was different. He had not seen such figures often, but he knew enough to recognise that these were of the ancient gods. Possession of even one of these figures was enough to get the family demoted, and here were a dozen, fifteen of the things.

He took one out and held it up so that she could see.

'I take it these are yours?'

She was about to answer when the curtain in the doorway twitched and an old man came into the room.

Chen stood, facing the ancient, and bowed respectfully. 'Lao jen...'

The ancient came towards him a pace or two then stopped, waving away his daughter-in-law. He was a tall, refined-looking old man, with a face like carved ivory. There was a sense of repose about him, of deep stillness, but just now his eyes seemed troubled.

'What do you want?'

Chen almost smiled, surprised by the directness of the old man's words. Yet it showed that he understood. More than his daughter-in-law, anyway.

'Forgive me, lao jen, but I was looking for Song Wei, the sweeper.'

The old man's eyes narrowed. 'Why do you ask? Who are you, and what do you want of my son?'

Chen smiled. Word would have gone out, like ripples from a dropped stone, that a man was going from apartment to apartment, asking questions. But who he was, that no one knew. Not yet, anyway.

He looked down at the figure in his palm, then closed his fingers over it, meeting the old man's eyes once more.

'My name is Tong Chou, and I am a friend. I wish only to talk with Song Wei.'

'A friend?' The old man shook his head, his eyes suddenly hard. 'I am sorry, Shih Tong, but I know all my son's friends, and you I have never met. Besides, my son is not here. Nor do I know when he will be back. He has gone looking for a job. You know how things are ...'

Chen lowered his head slightly. 'I know and sympathise, Master Song. Things are bad. And you are right. Your son does not know me. Yet I am still his friend and wish to help him. If he returns in the next few hours, tell him he will find me at Wu Mao's rice stall on Main. After that I cannot say. I am a busy man.'

He saw how the old man's eyes took in his words, assessing them, trying to guess just what Chen's purpose was, and whether he was genuine. And there was hope there too, just the tiniest glimmer. Enough, perhaps, to tempt Song Wei to contact him.

And if he did? Well, he had no job for Song Wei, no hope. Only a warning for him to stop before it was too late.

'Wu Mao's,' he said, moving close and handing the old man the figure. 'Oh, and a word of advice. Destroy the temple. Or the figures, anyway. It will not help Song Wei if his wife and children have been taken from him.'

Old Song gazed at the figure fondly a moment, then looked up into Chen's face again.

'We live in bad times. The people need their comforts.'

'I don't deny it. But then, I don't make the laws. Do as you will, lao jen, but think of your son, neh? How best to help him.'

Chen stepped back, bowed, then moved past the old man and out through the curtained doorway, surprising the daughter-in-law who was getting up from where she'd been eavesdropping. With a nod to her, he went out into the public corridor, a crowd of women and children making way before him, a murmur of speculation passing among them.

At the entrance to Main he stopped, looking about him, taking it all in. Ten years ago this would have been a good place to live, well lit and orderly, its people affluent, industrious and law-abiding. But things had broken down. Change had washed across these levels like a great wave of corrosive acid, eating away at the certainties upon which these people had built for so long.

Even so, there was still coherence of a kind, as if those years of different expectations had conditioned the people here, forging in them a passivity, an acceptance of their fate. The future might seem bleak, yet they were Han – they would endure and chi ku, 'eat bitter'. At least, so long as they had the capacity to endure.

He sighed, knowing how they felt. There was a time when he too had burned with the bright ideal of betterment, with the dream of a wife, a child, and of seeking his fortune up-level. But the dream had died in him, had proved a kind of ghost-vision, no more substantial than a flickering hologram. Yes, that brilliant, blinding light that had led him on had guttered, and now the darkness summoned him again, like a hungry mouth, sucking him down into the depths. Down, as if he'd never climbed at all.

He stirred himself, making his way across to Wu Mao's stall, trying to lift his spirits – to think of something that was positive amidst the darkness that threatened to overwhelm him. But there was nothing.

It was as if it had pursued him, year by year, level by level. As if, to escape it, he would have to climb to the very top and burst through the thin yet impermeable skin of the City's roof. And even then he would not be free of it, for the City was inside him, like a sickness, thickening his blood, darkening his vision.

So what then? What was the answer to it all?

Taking a seat he looked about him at the people either side of him along the counter, noting how each face mirrored his own. How in each one might read the coming of the new age. An age of uncertainty and encroaching darkness.

Better, perhaps, to die, then? To go out in one final blazing act? Or was that simply the frightened child in him talking? The boy who'd never known the love of a mother, the example of a father?

He shivered. If only Wang Ti had been with him. If only she were well again. Then he might begin to make sense of it. But as it was...

Wu Mao came across and leaned across the counter. 'What you want, friend?'

Peace, Chen answered in his head. *And a better, saner world than this.* But what could Wu Mao, the rice-seller, do about that?

Chen smiled, liking the man's rough, bearded face. 'Give me some ma-po bean curd, if you have it. If not, some beggar's rice with lots of onions.'

Wu Mao laughed. 'The bean curd is finished. Beggar's rice it'll have to be, friend. And maybe that's good, neh? For we're all beggars now.'

The two men slipped from the shadows and moved softly, silently, across the broad, tiled floor until they stood before the raised dais and the great chair. There they stopped and, like flowing pieces of the darkness, knelt, placing their hooded heads to the floor in obeisance. Above them, in the great, tall-backed chair, the First Dragon sat impassively, his masked face looking down at them.

'Listen,' he said, his voice booming, echoing in the vastness of that dark, sepulchral chamber. 'You are to follow the man. Find out what he does, who he sees, what he thinks, if that's at all possible. And you will report to no one but myself. If your superiors ask what you are doing, you will say nothing. You will refer them directly to me. Here...'

The First Dragon leaned forward slightly, his closed right hand extended. There was the smallest movement of his fingers, the clink of falling metal on the tiles in front of the two prone figures.

'These rings bear my seal. They will afford you entry into places where you would not normally be allowed. But do not abuse their power. They must be used only in the furtherance of this enquiry. You understand?'

There was the slightest nodding of heads.

'Good. But be discreet. Shang Mu must not know he is being shadowed. If you think he suspects, then you must tell me at once. There will be no punishment. But, similarly, there will be no reward.'

The First Dragon paused and sat back again, staring out over the two dark shapes, as if meeting the eyes of someone in the darkness between the great pillars at the far end. But he was alone in the audience chamber with them.

'Your fee is two hundred thousand *yuan*. A third will be paid to you now, the rest upon completion of your task. Now go. You will begin at once.'

There was a nod of hooded heads, a quick, almost serpentine movement of a hand to retrieve the fallen rings, and then the figures backed away, swiftly, silently, their dark robes flowing like a mist across the smooth black tiles.

Watching them go, the First Dragon let out his breath. It was some six years since he had needed to call upon the services of the Guild of Assassins, nor was he entirely certain now. Shang Mu, after all, was a good man. If he proved false then who *could* be trusted? Yet he had to be sure, if only for his own peace of mind, for it was not simply his own fate that now rested on Shang Mu's shoulders, but the fate of the Ministry itself, the great Thousand Eyes. If the Ministry failed – if it *fell* – then there was no hope for Chung Kuo.

He shuddered, horrified by the prospect. By the thought of there being no Eyes to see, no guiding Hand to help. It was unthinkable. And yet think of it he must, for if *he* did not, then who would? The Seven? No. Any doubts he had harboured about them had now gone. There was no alternative. They had to act, and act decisively, before the Seven pissed away the gains of the last two hundred years. Before the *Hung Mao* took back the reins and pushed the world on into chaos once more. *Progress.* He had heard that foul and cursed word on many lips these past six months. *Progress.* Like some dark litany, chanted by the insane.

And maybe that's our fault, he thought, making his way slowly down the steps. Ours, because we did our job too well. Because they no longer understand the true meaning – the awful, frightful cost – of Progress.

Not that they had been wrong. No, for their intentions had been good and honourable. They had tried to start again – to build a new world free of the sins and errors of the old. And for a time it had worked. All had been well. Yet Man was Man. His ways could not be changed. One might wipe the slate clean, yet Man would dirty it again. Moreover, in burying the past they had also buried the lessons of the past. Indeed in many ways the new man was worse than the old, for while he had the same instincts he had none of his restraint – a restraint founded in long centuries of experience. Of history. Or was that true? Did history really teach them anything?

Once more the great man shivered, conscious of how far his thoughts had come – of what heresies they touched upon. Then, gathering his cloak about him, he walked briskly across the broad, tiled floor, his booted footsteps echoing after him, the slam of the great doors like a punctuation mark. And then silence.

Two hours had passed and no one had come, neither Song Wei, nor any of the others. Paying Wu Mao, Chen made his way to the inter-level transit, his mood despondent. Whatever his feelings on the matter, he would have to do something, before Cornwell went over his head and someone else was put in charge of the investigation.

But what? What could he do? He could round them all up, certainly, but as soon as he did the matter would be taken out of his hands. A tribunal would decide their fate, and in all likelihood they would be sent down – they and their families. And to be demoted these days – to be sent 'Below the Net' – was as good as a death sentence. No. He would have to warn them off somehow – to impress upon them just what the stakes were. But how? How did you get the message across to such angry, desperate men? How did you convince them that, however bad their lot was now, it could be ten times worse?

He rode the transit up fifty levels, and then another fifty, ignoring the crush in the big lift, the smell of unwashed bodies, going over the problem in his mind time and again. Warn them off. Sure. But how? Should he make one of them an example? Song Wei, perhaps? Or would that only make matters worse? Wouldn't it, perhaps, simply harden their attitudes against authority?

Or hostages...

He laughed, surprised that he'd not thought of it before. *Hostages.* Why not? If he rounded up the wives and held them against the good behaviour of their menfolk, maybe that would work.

But it would have to be planned. He'd have to find some place to keep them. And he'd have to make sure there was no reaction from the men. The last thing he wanted was a riot.

A few weeks should do it. Until the men had cooled their heels. And in the interim, maybe, he could try to get some kind of deal for them – compensation, perhaps. Or jobs.

He smiled, for the first time feeling positive about the situation. He'd get onto it first thing tomorrow morning. And maybe, once it was done, he'd pay that bastard Cornwell a return visit – fill his reception hall with Security.

Yes. But before then he'd better check up on the other matter – see how the investigation into the missing File was going. And later, perhaps, he'd go and see the girl.

The Golden Carp. Eighth bell...

He nodded to himself. Maybe he'd go after all. And afterwards?

Afterwards he'd go home, to his children, his wife.

Chen shuddered, shadows falling once again, remembering Cornwell's gross belly shaking with laughter. His *mad* wife...

The day was ending, the western light fading fast. Three craft now rested on the huge, circular pad, their Minor Family crests indistinguishable. Behind Yin Chan, at the centre of the lake, the lights were slowly coming on in the great house, while to the east, above the hills, the fourth of the craft circled, then made its approach.

It has begun, thought Yin Chan excitedly. And when it's done, that man will be dead, his family eradicated.

The thought was sweet. It made the tiny hairs on his neck prickle with an unexpectedly sharp anticipation. To stand over his corpse and spit into his vacant face – that, indeed, would be heaven.

He watched the ship come down, anxious for a moment in case An Hsi had sent another to say he could not come, yet when the craft had settled and the hatch hissed open, it was An Hsi himself who stepped down, arms wide, to greet him.

Yin Chan went across, grinning fiercely.

'You came!' he whispered, holding An Hsi tight against him for a moment, relief and happiness making him laugh.

'You thought I wouldn't?' An Hsi laughed, then held Yin Chan at arm's length. Yin Chan shivered, feeling the strength of the older man's hands against his arms. 'We are like brothers, Chan. I would never let you down.'

No, thought Yin Chan, staring into his once-lover's face. Simply by coming here, they had committed themselves – all five of them. There was no way back from this. No way out, except death. He smiled, and, taking An Hsi's shoulder, led him out down the path to the waiting boat.

Five years ago, he and his brother Sung had rowed Li Yuan across this lake to see their sister, who had fled here after a bitter row with her then-husband. The young T'ang had come here to be reconciled with her. Or so he'd claimed. For it was then that it had ended between Li Yuan and Yin Fei Yen; that day that he had set her aside – she and her unborn son – shaming Yin Chan's family, making them a laughing-stock before the others of the Twenty-Nine. He shuddered, the indignation fresh in him.

As the servants rowed them across, he made small talk with An Hsi, yet the thought of what they were about to do distracted him and, as they climbed up onto the landing stage, beneath the ancient willow, he could remember nothing of what had been said.

An Hsi stood a moment, looking across at the elegant, two-storey mansion with its gently-sloped roof and broad, panelled windows, then turned to Yin Chan, smiling.

'It's been too long since I was last here, cousin. You should have asked me long before this.'

The admonishment was gentle and the smile, the slightly teasing tone reminded Chan of earlier days, when he had first brought An Hsi here to his family home. He searched An Hsi's eyes, looking to see what he meant, wondering if, after the meeting, he would perhaps stay.

But An Hsi's dark eyes revealed nothing. 'Come,' he said, taking Chan's arm. 'Let's go and meet our cousins, neh? We've much to talk about.'

Eighth bell was sounding as Chen made his way through the crowds in front of the Golden Carp and up the broad steps that led to the reception. He was feeling awkward, out of place. Everyone here was young and – to say the least – fashionably dressed, while he, though not shabbily-attired, felt old beyond his years, his simple ersilk one-piece like something a tradesman or a servant would wear.

The young woman behind the counter, her face painted gold, fake gills at her neck, stared at him as if he had made some kind of mistake, then narrowed her eyes. 'Well? What do you want?'

He cleared his throat, strangely nervous – he who had fought men hand to hand and to the death. Even so, he understood. There were different kinds of fear, and this was his – a fear of social places, of the bright glare and insincerity of it all; of being spotlighted and made to seem a simple clod, an uncultivated fool. General Rheinhardt himself had picked him up about it, reminding him that it was his duty as a Major to engage in social activities, but he had done little to remedy the fault. He was a soldier, not a courtier, and there was little he could do about it. If Rheinhardt didn't like it, he could demote him and there was an end to it. Just now, however, something else drove him on – not the desire for social pleasantry, but plain curiosity.

'Can I help you, sir?'

He smiled awkwardly, conscious that he was blushing like a girl. At a loss, he stared past the receptionist, trying to make out Hannah among the crowd within. The restaurant was on two levels, both of them packed out, a real hubbub of activity. Tables filled the floors, young people sat six or seven to a table with little room between for the fish-headed waiters to make their way through, stacked trays held effortlessly above their heads. He looked from table to table, trying to locate where she was, but it was no good. He would have to ask for her.

'I... I'm meeting someone.'

'Ah...' The golden head looked down, studying the appointments book in front of her, then looked back up at him. Green eyes – lenses, he realised with a start – stared back at him from the painted Han face. 'Are you Kao Chen?'

He laughed, part from relief, part from embarrassment, and nodded, his mouth dry, then watched as she summoned one of the waiters over.

'Table seventeen. Upper floor. If you'd show the *ch'un tzu*...'

She turned back to Chen, smiling – a tight, insincere smile – as she said this last, as if to imply he could *never* be 'ch'un tzu' – a gentleman – were he to try a thousand years. But Chen was used to that. With a face like his he could fool no one that he had come from an ancient line of kings. No. His face said plainly *peasant*. And so it was, and mainly he was proud of it, but sometimes – as now – he would have done anything, paid any price, to have had the face of a gentler, more handsome fellow than he was.

As the waiter turned away, he followed, mumbling apologies all the way across the lower floor, stumbling as he climbed the six low steps that led to the upper room. There the waiter left him, pointing across to a table in the corner, where four people – three young men and a woman, her back to him – were seated, the remains of a meal on the table before them.

For a moment Chen wasn't sure. For a second or two he hesitated, prepared to turn back, to forget he'd ever come here, but then Hannah turned in her seat, as if sensing him, and met his eyes, her smile so bright, so clearly pleased to see him there, that all thought of leaving fled him. He was smiling back at her and nodding, pleased, absurdly pleased, to see her there.

'Kao Chen!' she called above the noise, then stood, making her way between the tables. 'Kao Chen...'

He stood there, a faint thrill of surprise passing through him as he watched her come across to him. In the tangle of his thoughts, he had forgotten that she was *Hung Mao*. He had visualised her as Han, like himself. Shang Han-A. But that was understandable perhaps. Her tall, willowy build, her dark eyes, the single plait of her long, dark hair; these made her seem, at first glance, what she was not. And now that he saw her again, he remembered how old she was – sixteen – and shook his head. Why, his own son was barely two years younger...

As she squeezed between the last two chairs and came face to face with him, he found his awkwardness returning. He felt the urge to embrace her, to greet her physically somehow, but knew it would be taken wrongly. Even so, it surprised him when she reached out and took both his hands in hers then leaned close to kiss his cheek.

'Kao Chen,' she said more softly, the scent of her perfume giving the words a strangely romantic cast. 'I wasn't sure you'd come.'

'Nor I,' he confessed, and then laughed. He looked past her, conscious that his mouth was dry again, his pulse racing. 'Your friends?'

'Come. I'll introduce you.' She hesitated, then leaned in close, speaking to his ear. 'And please. Don't react. Just listen, okay? We'll talk afterwards.'

He stared at her as she moved back, then shrugged. *Okay*, he mouthed, then let her lead him across to the table.

Three heads turned as they approached; three bodies repositioned themselves about the table, as if confronting Chen. *Like fighters*, he thought, and then wondered why he'd thought that, for the look of them was soft, their muscle-tone poor. Their clothes – so different from his own – seemed garishly effete, while the jewellery they wore – rings, bracelets and fine necklaces of gold – were so overdone that they reminded him of how his daughter, Ch'iang Hsin, had used to dress up when she was younger. Their faces were made up, their nails carefully manicured. First Level, that look said clearly: *Supernal*.

'Sao Ke, Andre, Christian... this is Kao Chen.'

Chen realised he was frowning and tried to smile, but all he could do was grimace grotesquely and nod. *Like the clod I am*, he thought, conscious of how intently – how critically – they were watching him.

'Kao Chen ...' Sao Ke repeated thoughtfully from where he sat on the far side of the table, then nodded to himself. He took a sip from his wine cup, then met Chen's eyes. 'You're a student, I take it?'

Hannah answered for him, pulling an empty chair out beside her as she did, indicating that Chen should sit.

'No. Kao Chen is an old family friend.'

Chen glanced at her, then looked back at the others, trying to keep the smile from slipping. The two *Hung Mao* – Christian and Andre – were looking at him, he realised, silently assessing him. *And dismissing me, no doubt*, he thought, discomfort making him swallow drily. Yet even as he did, Hannah leaned close, her scent once again distracting him.

'Are you drinking?' she whispered, her mouth against his ear.

He hesitated, then nodded.

'Good.' She smiled, then poured wine from the jug into the empty cup in front of him. A strong red sorghum wine that, when he tasted it, made him nod with appreciation.

He looked up and saw she was watching him, enjoying his enjoyment of the wine, and for a moment he thought how strange that was. It was a long time since anyone had done that; since anyone had worried what he, Kao

Chen, was feeling. He looked down, a faint shiver passing through him.

'Well ...' one of the two *Hung Mao* said – Christian? Andre? He wasn't sure. Chen glanced from one to the other. They smiled, and lifted their cups to him in a toast, but behind the smiles there was a coldness, an implacable dislike for his kind.

'So what do you do, Kao Chen?'

The speaker sat to Chen's left, the other side of Hannah.

'Kao Chen is a potter.' Hannah answered, before he could even think what to say. 'As was his father and his father's father. And before you ask, his pots are very good. Some say that their shape is too crude, the clay too thick, the design too simple, but that merely serves to demonstrate their ignorance. Besides, their glaze is the most delicate you've ever seen, the colours...' she turned and, smiling, winked at Chen, who was staring at her, astonished. 'Well, the colours are just perfect. There's a blue he uses which is... well, it's like the blue of heaven itself.'

Chen stared at her a moment longer, then, realising what he was doing, he looked away, trying to compose himself. It was all invention, certainly – all part of some game she was playing – but why? What did she mean by it all?

'My own taste is for the funerary, of course,' Sao Ke said, leaning forward slightly, an interested gleam in his eyes, 'but young Hannah here is a fine judge of artefacts. Praise from her is high praise indeed. But tell me, Kao Chen ...'

Hannah interrupted him. 'Forgive me, Ke, but it will do you little good asking Kao Chen. I should have said at once. My dear friend is dumb. A childhood accident ...'

Dumb! Chen almost laughed. Was there no end to her audacity? And yet it all made sense of a kind. Knowing he was an artisan – if only of a lowly kind, a *potter* – they would be more inclined to talk freely in his presence. And his affliction, his inability to speak – again he almost laughed aloud at the thought of it! – it was the perfect excuse to simply sit there and listen. He glanced at her again, saw she was watching him, and looked down, smiling. There was more to her – much more – than he'd realised.

Hannah leaned forward, smiling gaily around the table. 'Well, anyway ... We were talking of the changes, remember? Andre, you were saying something interesting about your father's Company. About...'

Chen half listened at first, struck more by the look of these young men, by the intoxicating atmosphere of the Golden Carp, than by anything they said. Andre and Christian, he realised, were brothers. Or, if not, then they ought to have been, the facial similarities were so striking. But it was not merely the look of them – the cosmetic outer shell of them – that the found fascinating, it was something in the language of gesture they used; something he had only vaguely noticed before that moment.

They were arrogant, that went without saying, yet it was of a kind that was untempered by any kind of self-knowledge or self-consciousness. The arrogance of princes and great men, that Chen understood; but the arrogance of such little men – such *hsiao jen* – surprised him. What they knew, what they were: it all seemed like a thin veneer, covering up an inner emptiness so vast, so frightening, that they must keep talking to disguise the nothingness within. When they talked, they did not meet each other's eyes, as if they were self-obsessed. Yet how could one be self-obsessed where there was no true self? It puzzled Chen as he sat there. Puzzled him that Hannah could bring herself to listen to these fools, these elegant, empty mouths.

Maybe it was the wine, or maybe it was his own recently-acquired habit of introspection, but Chen found himself wanting to voice these thoughts, these insights... to tell them *exactly* what they were. But what good would that do? What could mere words achieve against such stultifying ignorance? Even so, the desire made him lean in towards them, as if in combat; to set aside his thoughts and listen, engaging for the first time in what they were saying.

Christian was talking now, turning the conversation away from the meal they had just eaten to something he had heard about the Lowers – about how they had been putting 'chemicals' in the food all these years.

'It's not much,' he said. 'Not even enough to register on the taste buds of the most sensitive gourmet, but, well... it has its effect. It makes them... *docile*. It dampens down their natural aggressive instincts. Or, at least, it used to. Now that the food quotas have fallen they're not getting enough, it seems, and the powers that be can't add any more without it becoming... *discernible*. That's why there's more trouble down there these days. Why there are so many riots and disturbances. They're waking up, you see. And they're getting angry.'

That's true, Chen thought, *but it's not because of any chemicals in their food.* He'd heard the rumours before. They were rife these days. But there was no proof. Besides, there were other reasons to be angry. More than enough reasons to riot.

'Maybe that's why there are so many revolutionaries these days,' Christian added after a moment.

Sao Ke chipped in at once, his sardonic drawl the voice of Emptiness itself, his cultured Han face one long, consistent sneer.

'*Revolutionaries* ... there's a hollowness at the centre of them all when it comes right down to it. They're fucked up, and because *they're* fucked up, they want the world to be fucked up too ...'

Hannah, as if sensing Chen's sudden interest, cut in. 'That may be true of some of them, even the majority, perhaps, but it can't be true for them all. There must be some for whom the ideal of revolution is... well, a *vocation*.'

Sao Ke leaned back, showing perfect, pearled teeth as he laughed; his laughter a bray of pure scorn. 'Well, I've heard it called many things, but never *that*. A vocation!' He shook his head, then reached out to pour more wine into his bowl. 'Don't be fooled, my young and beautiful friend. All that shit about the altruism of the lower levels, about the honest, hard-working peasant stock you'll find down there ... it's all a myth! – a fiction, served up by the Trivee Companies to make us feel okay about it all. Besides, all this *ideology* they spout, it's window-dressing, that's all, a cynical disguise the bastards use to justify killing and maiming innocent people. But have no illusions, it's all Number One when it comes right down to it. Self, self, self, however prettily the ideas might be packaged!'

Hannah leaned forward, looking back at Sao Ke. 'I'm not so sure. I think they must suffer down there. It must be dreadful ...'

'Bullshit!' Sao Ke answered, making a dismissive gesture of his hand, as if the very idea were absurd. 'They're animals, that's what they are! Less than animals, some of them! All they do is eat, drink and fuck! We'd be better off without them.'

'I'll drink to that,' Andre said, lifting his wine cup unsteadily. 'If I had my way I'd gas the lot of them. Rig up something in the ventilation system and get the buggers while they're sleeping. That'd solve all our problems, neh? There'd be food enough for everyone then.'

Sao Ke, who had drunk little, looked down, smiling. 'It's a somewhat radical suggestion, I'd say. Then again, maybe it's time for something radical. Something we'd have no need for in ... well, in *better* times. You know, they have a slogan down there, I'm told – 'Life is cheap, flesh plentiful'. Well, maybe it's time to put a higher value on life. Market rules, and all that.'

Christian turned, looking at Sao Ke. 'What do you mean?'

'It's simple. The laws of the Market say that if a product's rare, its price is normally high. Likewise, if it's a common-place – easily acquired, easily replaced – then its value is minimal. And right now I'd say life has never been cheaper, neh? The problem's a simple one. Too many bodies. Too many mouths to feed. The answer's obvious.'

'And who decides?'

It was Hannah who had asked the question. She was smiling, leaning towards Sao Ke as if encouraging him, but behind the smile was a hardness Chen had not noticed before.

'Draw a line, I say,' Christian said, banging the table enthusiastically. 'Anyone below the ... oh, the top hundred gets the chop.'

'Top fifty!' Andre chimed in.

There was laughter; long, unhealthy laughter. But Chen, watching, saw how Hannah didn't laugh; how she turned her face slightly towards him, as if conscious that he was watching.

'That's more than eighty per cent of the population,' she said. 'Thirty-two billion people, or thereabouts.'

'Give or take a million,' Andre added, making them roar anew.

'So who'd get rid of the bodies?'

Sao Ke shrugged and sat back. 'Oh, it'd all be planned, of course. Everything thought through thoroughly.'

'Thought through thoroughly... I like that!' Andre chirped in, and again they were off, their laughter filling that tiny corner of the Golden Carp. But Chen had had enough. There was a tightness at the pit of his stomach, a tension in his muscles, that was almost unbearable. He would have to say something, to answer them, or he would burst.

He leaned forward, meaning to answer Sao Ke, to throw his vile obscenities back in his face, but Hannah was watching him. As he opened his mouth, he felt her kick his shin – hard – under the table.

'There's talk...' she said brightly, steering the conversation away from the abyss into which it had strayed, 'that Huang Min-ye is to perform at the College Hall this summer...'

It seemed an age, but finally he was outside, breathing fresher, cleaner air. He stood there a moment at the foot of the steps, conscious of Hannah watching him; of the press of young, elegantly-dressed people milling all about him, filling the great green that was at the heart of this First Level deck. Reluctantly, he let her take his arm and lead him through the crowd, across the green and towards the inter-level transit, keeping his thoughts, his anger to himself; yet as soon as they were out of it – as soon as they were in a quieter, less public place, he turned on her.

'Those are your friends?'

Hannah shook her head. 'No, Kao Chen. Those are the people I'm obliged to spend my time with. My social equals.' She hesitated, her dark eyes boring into him intently. 'I wanted you to see. To understand how they think up here. And I ... well, I want you to do the same for me. To take me down-level.'

'Why?'

'Because I need to know. To understand how it is. Because...' She took a long, shuddering breath. 'Well, because I want to let people know. To... to be a voice. A loud, clear voice, telling people how it is. How it really is.'

He shook his head. 'It isn't possible.'

'No?' She smiled. 'Maybe not. But I can try, neh? I can always try.'

CHAPTER 110

MINISTRIES OF DEATH

Chen travelled with Hannah as far as Erfut stack, then saw her into the transit, assigning a young guard from the nearby Security post to escort her to her door. It was an hour by fast-bolt to his own stack in West Bremen, but, alone again, he realised that he couldn't go home – couldn't face another night like the last.

Where to, then? he asked himself, turning away, surprised by how down he felt. *Down.* Maybe that was the answer. Maybe, for once, he should simply trust to instinct and let go. After all, things couldn't possibly be worse than they were.

Very well, he thought, *but not here.* No. He'd catch a bolt south to Munich *Hsien,* to his old haunts. But first he'd call in, let his office know he was going off-duty. *And off-call?* Strictly speaking, he wasn't supposed to do that, but who'd miss him this once? Rheinhardt? No. Rheinhardt would be off socialising somewhere – he and the rest of the senior staff. Only he, Kao Chen, worried about such matters these days, and tonight he felt like letting it all hang.

Quickly he made his way back to the Security post and sent the message through, signing off with his personal code.

There, he thought, satisfied. *Eight hours.* Nothing could happen in eight hours. And even if it did, let someone else worry for a change. Let someone else save Chung Kuo from anarchy and old night. He'd had enough.

The bolt terminus was quiet, echoing empty. From the board he saw he'd missed one of the high-speeds by ten minutes, but there was another in an hour. Plenty of time to get himself a drink and a bite to eat.

The terminus bar was closed, but a porter directed him to a bar six levels down. It was a big place with a dance floor at one end and a long, curving bar, backed by a wall-length mirror. The lighting was subdued, the place three-quarters empty. Music played softly in the background, as if coming from somewhere down below.

Chen pulled out one of the bar stools and sat, then called the waiter over. 'What'll you have?'

Normally he didn't drink, or if he did it was something non-alcoholic, but he was feeling half-drunk from the wine he'd had already.

'A *Yao Fan Te*,' he said, recalling as he did that it was all of fourteen years since he'd last tasted a bulb of *Yao Fan Te* beer. He smiled, remembering. Back then he'd been a wanted man, a criminal, forced into taking a menial job to keep Wang Ti and his baby son. He took a long, deep breath, nodding to himself. Yes, the last time he had tasted *Yao Fan Te* had been that evening in the bar with Supervisor Lo – the evening of the public execution of Edmund Wyatt. The same evening Tolonen and the big man, Karr, had come for him and changed his life.

'You all right?'

Chen looked up and smiled. 'Sure.' He put a five *yuan* note down beside the open bulb, then picked up the drink. After the wine it tasted sour, unpleasant even, but it was cold and after a second swig it didn't seem so bad.

He looked around, noting how many of the customers sat alone, or silent and subdued in groups of two or three. Maybe it was the place. Maybe it attracted transients like himself. Or maybe it was just the hour. Whatever, it seemed quite dead after the bustling brightness of the Golden Carp. Up there there'd been great shrieks of laughter, a constant buzz of noise, while here ...

He turned back, facing his reflection in the curving mirror, noting how the image of his face was stretched, as if someone were tugging at his cheeks.

Okay ... So what am I to do?

A more ruthless man might have had his wife committed; would have married again and put it all behind him. But he wasn't that kind of man.

Besides, for all that she was a stranger to him now, he still loved Wang Ti, or at least, the *shell* of her – the memory of what she had been. He could not let that go, however much it hurt him to go on this way. No, and nor would his children have forgiven him if he had.

He drained the bulb and called for another. *Full circle*, he thought, watching the waiter's back as he bent down and took another bulb from the back of the refrigerated cupboard. *I have come full circle.*

Wang Pen, he'd been – rootless and unconnected, his parents unknown, his origins forgotten. Lacking options he had become a hireling, a man whose death would have gone unmourned, unnoticed: a machine of flesh and bone and muscle, used by bigger men for ends he could not guess at. So he might have spent his meagre life, so wasted it. But then he had met Wang Ti – Wang Ti, his wife and lover – and his life had been transformed. Children they'd had, and a future. The sun had shone on them. But now?

Chen shuddered, the bitterness flooding back. The pain he felt, the sheer disappointment and regret, the anger and frustration, all of it ate at him – all was impurely mixed into one sour, unhealthy cocktail of bile; a cocktail he was forced to drink each morning when he woke, each evening when he lay his head down on his pillow. Bitterness. Unending bitterness.

'Eat bitter', so the saying went. *Endure.* Yes, but was there ever an end to such endurance? Was there never a moment's ease, a moment's sweetness to be had?

He turned, suddenly conscious of someone at his shoulder, of the faint, sweet scent of perfume in the air.

'I'm sorry ... I didn't mean to disturb you.'

For a moment he stared into her eyes, then, recollecting himself, he lowered his head. 'Forgive me, I...'

'You looked sad,' she said, smiling at him. 'I was watching you just now, in the mirror.' She hesitated. 'Look, if I'm not wanted...'

He shook his head, looked back at her again. She seemed young, in her mid-twenties, possibly. Her dark hair was tied back, her shoulders bare in the tight-fitting dark blue dress she wore.

Strangely he found himself staring at her shoulders, fascinated by their strength, their roundedness. They glistened in the half-light, like something carved from ivory.

She smiled. 'You like what you see?'

Chen looked down, blushing furiously. 'I... I didn't mean...'

Her hand covered his where it lay on the surface of the bar. It was a strong hand, the nails a glossy red. The warmth of it pressed down upon his own. Warm, like her voice.

'It's all right. I like to be looked at.'

He looked at her again and nodded. 'You're very nice.'

'Thank you.' Her smile was open, friendly. There were no conditions to it. It was a simple smile of pleasure, like a child's. Seeing it, Chen found himself warming to her.

'So? What were you thinking about?'

Chen shrugged. 'Was I thinking?'

She reached up; tracing the frown lines in his forehead. 'These.'

He laughed. 'I was thinking ... well, I was thinking about men... and women.'

'Ah... women. The eternal problem, neh?'

'Not for you.'

'No.'

They both laughed.

'Look,' Chen began, feeling suddenly awkward, 'Will you... will you sit with me? Have a drink, perhaps?'

Her smile broadened. 'I wondered when you'd ask. My name is Hsin Kao Hsing.'

'Tong Chou,' he said, with a tiny formal bow, conscious that she was still holding his hand, that at no moment had she released him from that simple, warm contact.

'Well, Shih Tong. And what brings you to these parts?'

What did he say? How did he answer that?

'My wife ...' He fell silent, realising that he didn't want to talk about that.

'Ah,' she nodded, as if she understood; as if there were no further need to explain. 'I had a husband once. A little man he was.' She put her hand out, as if measuring where the top of his head would come to.

Chen smiled. 'He must have been very small.'

'Yes, but very strong... and big... you know, where it matters.'

He narrowed his eyes, then understood. 'Ah...'

'That drink?' she coaxed.

'Ah, right...' He turned, summoning the barman across, then turned back to her. 'What will you have?'

She nodded to the bulb beside him. 'I'll have whatever you're drinking, if that's all right.'

He nodded, then ordered two more beers.

'Do you live around here?' he asked, an unfamiliar dryness in his mouth.

'Down-level,' she answered, leaning towards him, her face only a hand's width from his own now she was seated facing him. 'I've my own place. I keep it neat.'

He nodded.

'And you?'

Chen took a breath. 'Just passing through,' he answered, not wanting to say too much. 'I was...'

He stopped, suddenly the idea of going all the way to Munich *Hsien* had lost its attraction. Why, he might as well stay here – have a few more beers.

'You were what?' she asked, her smile curious.

'Nothing,' he answered, taking one of the bulbs the barman had set down and handing it to her. Then, taking his own, he snapped the seal and raised it, toasting her.

'Kan pei!'

'Kan pei!' she answered, her eyes sparkling.

He sat back slightly, taking a long, deep breath. Her perfume was stronger than Hannah's... brasher. *Cheaper too*, he thought. But what did that matter? They were alike, he and she, he could see that at a glance – made of the same common flesh: peasant stock, and no frills. He found himself smiling at the thought.

'Well...' she said, returning his smile strongly, 'here we are.' Then, putting her bulb down on the bar, she leaned in towards him, resting her hands gently on his knees. 'So, Tong Chou, why don't you tell me about yourself...'

Prince An Hsi leaned forward in his chair, looking about him at his fellow princes. 'Well, cousins, I think we are agreed. Our first task is to recruit others of a like mind.'

There was a murmur of agreement. An Hsi smiled.

'Good. But let us be clear... we must go about this task with the greatest sensitivity. Like gardeners, we must cultivate with patience and extreme care. On no occasion must the first word be ours. No, we must learn to be good at listening and encouraging others to talk. Wine...' he indicated the great spread on the table before them, 'and good company... they'll serve to loosen many a tongue. Yet beware of those that gabble their thoughts carelessly. We want only those in whom anger is balanced with discretion, only those who – like ourselves – understand the true seriousness of this venture.'

He paused, his voice heavy with significance. 'To depose the Seven... that is no small thing. And no matter how much Heaven might smile on us, until it is done we are in great peril. Though our anger may be hot, our minds must be cool. A ruthless necessity must shape each word, each action from henceforward.' Again he paused, looking from face to face, his eyes finally alighting on the face of Yin Chan. 'One mistake... one tiny mistake... might undo the great good we seek to achieve.'

Yin Chan nodded, his eyes sparkling with a strange fervour.

'Well,' An Hsi added, the intensity slowly draining from him. 'I think we are done. I for one must go. There is much to do, and I would be at it early.'

Yin Chan looked to the other three. There were nods all round. He looked back at An Hsi. 'I am glad you came, cousins. Until now...' He shivered, then looked about him again, tears of gratitude in his eyes. 'Until now I could see no end to it... no way to douse the fire of rage that burned in me. But now...' He clenched his right fist and raised it, his face suddenly hard. 'Now we can fulfil the will of Heaven.'

Their response was fierce and passionate – a raising of clenched fists. All eyes were tearful now.

'It is so,' An Hsi said quietly, leaning towards them across the table. 'We must be as brothers now.'

As they stepped out into the hallway they heard a movement on the stairs above – a brief, silken rustling, and then silence.

'Who was that?' An Hsi asked softly, his eyes suspicious.

Yin Chan stared a moment, then looked back at him. 'It was no one, cousin, only my sister.'

'Your sister?' He seemed startled. 'You didn't tell me she was here.'

'She wasn't meant to be, but her son was ill and she decided not to go with my father.'

'But if she heard...'

Yin Chan leaned close, pressing An Hsi's hand and smiling reassuringly. 'I doubt it. But even if she did, she has more reason than most to hate Li Yuan. Why, if it came to it, I'm sure she'd strike the first blow herself.'

An Hsi stared past him briefly, then looked back, smiling faintly, mollified by his words. 'She suffered badly, then?'

Yin Chan lowered his voice. 'She *raged*, cousin. The House shook with her anger. Imagine it... to be cast off, your only son disinherited! A T'ang he would have been! A Son of Heaven! And what is he now? Not even a prince! The Special Edict...'

Yin Chan looked down, shuddering with repressed anger.

'I understand...' An Hsi said softly, sympathetically. 'She must hate him, neh?'

Yin Chan looked up, gave a sharp nod.

'Well... I must go. As I said, there's much to do. We'll meet again, neh, cousin? Two days from now, at my estate. Until then, take great care... and remember what I said. Trust no one, not even your closest servant. Only those bonded to us in common hatred.'

Yin Chan nodded.

'Good.' An Hsi smiled, his hand briefly caressing Yin Chan's cheek. Then he leaned close, gently kissing his lips. He moved back.

'And maybe you'll stay next time? It's been too long, dear Chan. Much, much too long ...'

Fei Yen stood just inside her door, the room dark, moonlight from the open window casting a silver bar upon the far wall, revealing the door to the nursery. She could hear the child coughing in the next room, the soft singing of the nursemaid, but her mind was on what she'd heard downstairs, outside the door to her father's study.

Yin Chan, she thought, her anguish making her twist the silk of her nightdress tightly between her hands. *What are you doing? What in the gods' names are you doing?*

Treason, it was. Simple treason. Punishable by death. Death to the third generation.

My son, she thought, her heart pounding. *They'll kill my son.*

Quickly she crossed the room. From the window she could see the hangar on the far side of the lake. There was movement there beside the

craft as the crews prepared themselves. A moment later she saw her brother
emerge on the lawn below beside An Hsi, the two men talking quietly.

Foolishness, she thought, seeing her brother clasp the older man's hands
and bow his head. An Hsi she could understand, he had lost three brothers
when Li Yuan had dealt with the Willow Plum Sickness that time, but Chan...

Fei Yen took a long breath, controlling herself, forcing herself to slow
down and consider matters properly.

She had never suspected. Never, even from a look or comment, thought
that her brother hated Li Yuan so much. And herself?

Chan was wrong. She didn't hate Li Yuan. Not now. If anything, she
understood him better now, and if, when she looked back on their days
together, it was not with fondness, there was at least some element of regret
that she had not tried harder with him. He had loved her. She had no doubt
of that now. She had seen it in his eyes that last time he had come to visit
her, after the death of his wives.

But this... this *madness*... What could she do to stop Chan's foolishness?
How could she prevent him from bringing retribution down on all their
heads?

She watched, as Chan handed An Hsi into the boat, then climbed in after
him, waving the servants away and taking the oars himself. She knew what
had happened between An Hsi and Chan. Oh, she had had no need of spies
to see what had been going on there. But she had thought it ended. Now,
however, An Hsi was back, dripping his venom in her brother's ear, fanning
old frustrations into fires of vengeance. And for what?

She shook her head, suddenly angry. A fool and a villain... it was a fine
pairing! It would serve them well if the boat sank and the two were dragged
down to the bottom...

She caught her breath, realising where her thoughts had run. Her brother
dead. Her dear, feeble, foolish brother... dead? She shivered. Was there no
other way?

She closed her eyes, pained by the thought, but frightened by the
alternative. She had heard them down there, swearing binding oaths of
brotherhood and talking of the death of T'ang. It was madness, yet it was
real. And its reality threatened all their lives. Her brothers, her son, herself...

And father, she thought, horrified suddenly by the idea that that dear and
noble man might be sacrificed to her brother's foolishness.

I must tell him. Let him decide.

The thought, once formulated, took hold of her. Her father. He would sort out this mess. After all, that was his task, as Head of their great family. It was not for her to decide her brother's fate. She had not spawned him.

She turned, looking at the moonlit door. It was quiet now. The coughing had stopped, the nursemaid's singing ended. There was only the gentle slush of the oars where they dipped into the water of the lake behind her.

Sleep softly, Han, she thought, blowing a kiss to her infant son. I'll let no one ever harm you. No one.

It was a tiny, two-room apartment, sparsely furnished but neat, like she'd said, a single wall lamp throwing a pale orange light over everything. As she closed the door behind them, Chen looked about him, noting the cheap, romantic prints that covered the end wall, the ersilk pillows that were plumped up on the single bed. A beaded curtain separated the room from the galley kitchen. He and Wang Ti had lived in such an apartment for a year, when Jyan was three. It had been cramped, but they'd been happy there. He smiled, feeling unsteady, heavy-limbed from the beer he'd drunk.

He turned, looking at the woman. She was standing by the low dresser, taking off her earrings. Seeing him watching her in the mirror, she turned and smiled at him.

'So... what do you want?'

'Want?'

'You want sex? Or maybe something more kinky? Sex is five *yuan*. Anything else is extra.'

He stared at her, suddenly understanding. 'I... I don't know. I thought...'

She smiled and came across. Placing her hand against his chest, she began to unbutton his tunic.

'How much have you got?'

He felt in his pocket, then handed her a twenty *yuan* note.

She whistled softly. 'For that you can have me any way you like. But no rough stuff, understand? And if you want it up the arse, you do it gentle, right? I'm a sensitive lady...'

Her laughter was the same as before – an open, affectionate sound – yet now that he understood it seemed quite different.

He stared at her, at the painted lips, the rouged cheeks, the tight lines about her eyes and mouth and wondered why he hadn't clicked before. She was a whore. A bar hustler. And he had thought...

He let her take his shirt and hang it up, then watched as she went through to the kitchen, no doubt to put the money in a safe place. When she came back he was still standing as she'd left him.

'Well?' she said, laughing softly. 'Are you going to strip, or do I have to take it all off for you?'

'I...' He looked at her and saw how she was watching him, no judgement in those eyes, only a friendliness, the affection of one stranger for another, and shrugged. 'If you like...'

She came across. 'Sit on the bed. It'll make things easier.'

He sat, letting her pull off his boots.

'And these,' she said, tugging at his trousers.

He lifted up.

'There,' she said, setting them on the chair beside the wall. 'That's better, neh?'

For a moment she knelt there, smiling up at him. Then she moved back slightly and, with a simple little movement, pulled her top up over her head and threw it to one side, leaving her naked from the waist. In the half-light her breasts were firm, the nipples prominent. He stared at her, half afraid, half fascinated. *Home*, he thought, but home was an impossibility. There was nothing at home. He moaned softly.

'It's okay,' she said, more gently than before, her eyes reassuring him. 'You're safe here, my love. No wife to come and eat you, only me.' She moved forward, placing her hands on his thighs, then nuzzled close, against his chest, placing a soft wet kiss against his neck. 'You're in the land of warmth and softness now, Tong Chou, so relax, neh? Just relax...'

He woke, wondering where he was. *Not my room*, he thought, listening to the faint tick of a clock. And the air... the air was different somehow...

He remembered. The woman. Shifting slightly he could feel her against his back.

Slowly he turned, until he was facing her. The night light was on in the galley kitchen – the pearled whiteness filtered through the bead curtain in the doorway. In its light he could see the shape of her, the slow rise and fall of her breasts.

272 UPON A WHEEL OF FIRE

He eased himself up, then rested his back against the wall. The woman lay beside him, naked, on her back, her eyes closed, one hand resting on her stomach, the other nestled in her hair. He looked at her, surprised to find himself there, and remembered what had happened between them.

The need... that had surprised him. The fierceness of his need. That and her warmth. So kind she'd been, so... gentle with him.

Like a lover, he thought and frowned, because he'd been told you couldn't buy love, only win it.

Whores... They were a staple of his work. He'd seen a thousand of them in his time – in the cells, or in their gaudy rooms – and never once had he thought what it was like for them: where they lived or what they wanted from their lives.

Comfort probably. And peace of mind. Like anyone.

He had seen them dead – murdered or overdosed from drugs – and had never once thought what it must be like for them. Until now.

He sighed. And you think you've got problems, Kao Chen ... But he, at least, had something, whereas she ...

She stirred, then turned and looked up at him, a slow smile forming on her lips.

'Couldn't sleep, huh?'

He smiled back at her. 'I was thinking...'

'You shouldn't. It's bad for you.'

'Maybe...' He reached down, taking her hand where it nestled in her long, dark hair, and laced his fingers into hers. 'It was nice...'

Her smile deepened. She lifted his hand to her mouth and kissed it.

'...but I ought to go.'

'At this hour? Where? Home to that wife of yours?' She smiled then shook her head. 'No, Tong Chou. I'll make us some ch'a. Then we'll go again...'

'Again?' he laughed softly, but the thought of it was enticing and the way she looked at him inflamed him.

'Wait there...'

He watched her get up, enjoying the sight of her nakedness, the simple intimacy of it. This room, themselves... He let his head drop back against the wall, a long breath soughing from him, then listened to her pottering about in the kitchen.

'You hungry?'

He gave a grunt of assent.

'Here...' she leaned round the door, holding a plate out to him.

He looked up, then leaned forward to take the plate from her.

'Oat crackers!' He laughed. 'It's years since I had oat crackers!'

'You don't like them?'

'No, no... I love them. It's just...' He huffed out a breath. How explain it? How explain the strange mixture of sadness and contentment he was feeling at that moment? Or did she already know? Was that, perhaps, how *she* felt, *all* of the time?

We're both whores, he thought. The only difference is that one of us is more honest about it than the other.

She came back, offering him a cup, then squatted on the bed beside him. In the light he could see she was much older than he'd first imagined her – more his own age, in fact. Her face was lined and her flesh had lost the firmness of youth. Even so, she was still an attractive woman.

She smiled and leaned towards him. 'I like you, Tong Chou. I'm tempted to let you stay the night. Business is bad, so...'

'You want more money?'

She raised an eyebrow. 'Did I *say* that? No ... besides, you paid me well, and treated me nicely, too. It's not often...'

He saw the wistfulness in her eyes and looked away, sipping at his *ch'a*.

'You like your work?' he asked.

'You like yours?'

He shook his head.

'So what do you do, Brother Chou? You never said.'

'You don't want to know.'

'That bad, huh?'

He laughed. Then, more seriously, he nodded. '*That* bad.'

'Tell me. I'm curious.'

He hesitated, tempted to tell her, then reached out and gently touched her cheek. 'You don't want to know.'

Hannah closed the door behind her quietly, then went across to her father's desk.

Sitting in his chair, she looked about her at the stacks of papers and reports that filled the desk, and took a long breath. It was here somewhere.

She had seen it only the other day. A black, hand-bound file. But which one? There had to be thirty or forty here that fitted that description. That was, if it *was* still here. If he hadn't dealt with it and sent it back.

So... Where to start?

She removed the gold-bound file that rested on the jotter and placed it on the floor beside her, then began, taking the top file from the stack to her left and placing it face-down on the jotter. It was important to keep it all in the proper order – to put it all back exactly as it was. She knew her father. All of this seemed chaotic, yet he had his own system and knew precisely where everything was. He knew...

She stopped, interested by something she had read. It wasn't the file she was looking for, even so... She read on.

Half an hour later she looked up, her face pale, her heart racing. Secrets ... her father was the custodian of secrets, but this...

She whistled softly to herself.

Forget Nantes. Forget what happened there. It was as nothing beside this.

She went back to the first page, studying the list of names to whom the file had been sent. Nine names in all. Seven of them, she knew, were Dragons – Heads of the Ministry in their own Cities and brothers to her stepmother, Chih Huang Hui. The eighth name was her father's. The ninth... She frowned, surprised by it. The ninth name was that of An Sheng, Head of the great Minor Family and liege to Li Yuan, the T'ang of Europe.

'Gods...' she said softly, remembering what her father had said to her, only days before. So this was the important matter he had been working on. This.

She sat back, feeling breathless, giddy, for once at a loss what to do. This was not the kind of secret one should know; not the kind one could share with anyone.

No ... not even her father.

For a moment she sat there, her mind a blank, staring straight ahead of her. Then an idea occurred to her. Maybe she should consult her grandfather, Shang Wen Shao. Maybe he would know what to do. Then again, maybe not. Maybe this was too weighty a matter for him.

Her great-grandfather, Shang Chu, then?

She sighed. No. She knew what *he* would say.

Or did she? For once she wasn't sure.

She frowned, then froze, hearing something.

The door... the door was open. Not much. Not more than a hand's width, to be precise, yet she had taken care to close it after her.

'Who is it?' she said, closing the file and putting it aside. 'Come out and show yourself.'

The door slowly opened. A boy stood there; a fat-faced little boy with Eurasian features, her step-brother, Ch'iu.

'Sneak,' she said, standing then coming round the desk.

He stared back at her, unabashed. 'Why are you in father's study?'

'Why aren't *you* in bed?'

'I was,' he said, his pudgy face glaring at her now. 'But I heard you creeping down the corridor and wondered what you were up to. When you didn't come back I thought I'd come and see.'

She went right up to him, looking down at him, her hands on her hips. 'Well, now you can go back to bed, can't you.'

'Why should I? Besides, you still haven't answered my question.'

She leaned down at him, her face hard, no love lost between them. 'Nor am I going to. Now go. Before I kick that fat little bottom of yours from here to the bathroom!'

'I'll tell mother.'

'Tell her. See if I care.'

He stared at her a moment longer, defiance in his eyes, then turned and left, pulling the door closed behind him.

Hannah stared at the door a moment, then let out her breath.

'Shit!'

She went back across the room again and, putting everything else back where it had been, picked up the file and turned, meaning to return to her room. But she had gone only two paces towards the door when it swung open again.

'Han-A?'

She bowed her head, swallowing. 'Mother...'

Chih Huang Hui stood there, her pale face staring out from the layers of blood-red silk she wore, her eyes wide with a strange satisfaction.

'Can you explain what you are doing here, girl?'

Hannah held the file tightly behind her back, concealing it from sight. 'I...' She thought quickly. 'I was looking for something father said he'd left for me.'

'*Left* for you?' Her stepmother's face crinkled up in an expression of distaste. 'Then why did he not leave it in your room, Han-A? Surely he would not have left it *here*, among his papers.'

She looked up, deciding to brazen it out. 'It was exactly what I thought myself. But I looked on my desk, and there was nothing, so I thought...'

'Does he *know* you come into his room?'

Hannah looked down again, then shook her head.

'And if he did, don't you think...' she smiled, clearly savouring the thought, 'don't you think he might be *angry* with you, Han-A?'

'I... I don't know.'

Chih Huang Hui straightened up, her whole body taut with triumph. From behind her, Shang Ch'iu peered out, his face grinning with malice.

'Well, Han-A. I *am* disappointed in you. *Severely* disappointed. I'm afraid I shall have to tell your father. He'll be...' again she smiled, this time a spark of real savagery lighting her features, 'most surprised to learn what his darling daughter gets up to while he's away, don't you think? *Most* disappointed.'

Chen dressed quickly, his embarrassment beyond words. His duty Captain, Wilson, stood in the corner of the room, his head bowed, his eyes averted, waiting while Chen put on the spare uniform he'd brought.

As he buttoned the tunic, Chen glanced at the woman apologetically. She was watching him silently, a strange distance to her suddenly, the spell of intimacy broken. Now he was simply another body, and an unwelcome one at that.

'If I'd known...' she'd said, almost brutally. 'Security... fucking Security! And I thought...'

The last button done, he turned, looking at his Captain. 'Okay. You'd better tell me as we go along.'

He turned back, looking at the woman. She had put her jacket about her shoulders, otherwise she was naked still. He went to say something, then saw the look in her face and fell silent. Shrugging, he turned away. But it was hard simply to walk out on her. For a moment...

As the door closed behind him, Chen felt a sudden anger. For the first time in ages he had found peace... for one brief moment... and then they had tracked him down, like the lowest criminal.

'How did you find me?' he asked the Captain, conscious of the four guards listening.

Wilson looked down, embarrassed. 'When we couldn't get in touch with you, we thought maybe something had happened. Then we noticed the message from this stack and...' he hesitated, 'well, sir, I put a camera trace on you. I wouldn't have but... well, it was the only way. I knew you'd want to know at the very earliest.'

Chen stopped, staring at him. 'Know what? Is it my family?'

'No, sir. It's... Song Wei. You know, the sweeper. He's dead.'

Chen shook his head. 'Dead?'

'Yes, sir. The whole deck is up in arms. We've got our men down there trying to keep a lid on things, but I knew you'd want to deal with it yourself. I mean, in view of what happened...'

Chen nodded, realising that Wilson had probably saved him more embarrassment than he'd caused. Besides which, if Song Wei were dead, then this was a whole new ball game.

'Was he murdered?'

'Yes, sir.'

'Only him? Or are there others?'

Wilson hesitated. 'To be honest, sir, we don't know yet. It's chaos down there and... well, we've searched the deck and we can't account for four of the men.'

'I see.' Chen nodded, his mind already piecing things together. 'Then let's get there, neh? The quicker this is sorted out, the better.'

Guards were everywhere. The whole area surrounding the corridor was cordoned off. As Chen marched through at the head of his escort, he couldn't help but contrast it with how he had seen it only hours before. Then there had been an air of normality, however tentative. Now it was like a war-zone, the tension palpable.

Song Wei was laid out on the kitchen table, the body wrapped in a sheet. As Chen came into the room, one of the special squad medics looked up from where he was examining the head and smiled.

'Looks like a professional job, Major Kao. One bullet, behind the right ear. Took the top of his head off.'

Chen took the skin-tight gloves he was offered and pulled them on, then went across. As the surgeon moved back, he saw the damaged skull for the first time and winced. It didn't quite look human. It looked more like a broken bowl, the jellied contents mixed with small fragments of bone.

Carefully, he put his hand beneath the neck and turned it slightly.

'There,' the medic said, pointing to the hole behind the right ear. 'The powder burns show that whoever did it must have placed the gun right up against the neck. It was a large calibre weapon. What size we'll know when we've found the bullet.'

Chen frowned, then understood. 'Where was he killed?'

'The other side of the stack, four levels down. They found him in a maintenance room, his brains all over the ceiling. It seems no one heard anything.'

'Who brought him here?'

'Friends of the family. First we heard of it was when the trouble started.'

'Trouble?' Chen looked to Wilson, who stood behind the sergeant in the doorway.

'They burned a Security post, sir. No one hurt. The guards saw what was happening and got out, raised the alarm. That was an hour back.'

Chen nodded. An hour back he had been with the woman...

There was a wailing, a sudden violent wailing from the next room.

He looked up, startled. 'What the hell...?'

'It's his wife, sir. I thought it best to keep her here. She's hysterical and the crowd's already touchy, so...'

Chen nodded. But the sound was affecting him badly. He looked back at the shattered skull, then gently lowered it and stood back.

He held his hands out, letting the medical orderly peel off the gloves and drop them in the sterile sack, then turned, facing the sergeant.

'So... what else do we know? What do the camera records show?'

Wilson answered him. 'The area he was killed is a blind spot. There's a camera on the approach to it, but nothing on the corridor itself. It's only a small thing... a maintenance passage, in effect. The room's usually locked.'

'So what does the approach camera show?'

Wilson looked to the sergeant. 'We're not sure yet, sir. I've got a squad checking faces against the records. It's a busy corridor, it seems, and we're not sure just how long the body was there before it was discovered.'

Chen turned, looking to the medic.

'Oh... four, five hours at least. Maybe more.'

Chen turned back. 'Okay. As soon as you find out *anything* let me know. I've my own theory as to who's behind this, and the sooner we get to our killer the better. That is, if he's still alive...'

He broke off. There had been a scuffling in the next room. Now the door to the kitchen jerked opened. There was shouting. A distraught woman's face peered out as she struggled to get past the guard, and then the door slammed shut again.

The wailing sounded again, louder than before.

Chen sighed. 'Okay. I want that trace made a priority. At the same time I want a complete and thorough search of this stack, every room, every cupboard. And we're not looking for small stuff, okay? – we're looking only for things pertaining to this killing... And for those missing men.'

Wilson and the sergeant bowed.

'Good. Now get going. I'll speak to the woman.'

He watched them go, then stood there a moment, considering things. Under normal procedures the camera records would be checked back forty-eight hours at least. It would emerge that he had been down here earlier yesterday. Questions would be asked, his investigation reports scrutinised for the least irregularity, and he would be in trouble. Unless he could tie things up quickly. Unless he could make that crucial connection between the killer and that bastard Cornwell.

He knew it was Cornwell. Had known it since he'd first heard the news of Song Wei's death. No one else would have had him killed. No one else stood to benefit by it. But he had to prove that. The man's blustering threats about taking things into his own hands weren't enough to convince a court. He had to make the link. To prove that Cornwell was behind it.

Chen shivered. Like a lot of them these days, Cornwell thought he was immune, *above* the rule of law. And the men he killed or destroyed, what were they to him? Scum, he'd called them. Scum...

He went to the door, knocked. There was a sudden silence, and then the door slid back.

'Sir...' The guard stood back, letting him pass.

Inside, the woman sat on the chair beside the tiny shrine. Behind her stood the old man, Song Wei's father.

The old man stared at Chen a moment, then narrowed his eyes. 'You...' he whispered. 'I should have known... You *bastard*.'

Chen turned, dismissing the guard, then went across, standing over the weeping woman. He stared at her a moment, understanding her grief, then looked up, meeting the old man's eyes.

'This had nothing to do with me,' he said quietly. 'I tried to warn your son. Him and his friends. But this...' He shuddered. 'Well... I'll get the man who did this. I promise you.'

'You *promise* me?' The old man's voice was scornful now. He stared at Chen venomously, then leaned forward and spat on the chest patch of Chen's uniform. '*That* for your promises, Major. I *know* your kind. You stick together to protect your interests. My son...' He drew a breath, trying hard to control himself, then spoke again. 'My son was a good man. He worked hard. He was good to his wife, his children. He looked after his father, like a dutiful son should. And what was his reward? To be cast off. To be made to beg for crumbs from the rich man's table. And, when he protested at his treatment, to be killed. Like the lowest insect.'

The old man shuddered with indignation, his gnarled hands resting on his daughter-in-law's shoulders, the fingers digging into her flesh, as if both to comfort and punish her. His face was fierce now, his eyes staring at Chen with an unrelenting hatred. 'Promises... *Paa!* Can you *eat* promises? Can your promises make my son live again?' He shook his head. 'No, Major. Give me none of your promises. I am sick to the heart of eating such bile.'

'I...'

'Just go,' the old man said, his face hard, unforgiving. 'Go play your games. Go and *pretend* you're doing something.'

Chen turned, his face stinging as if he'd been slapped, and left, the man's words ringing in his ears, the woman's weeping tearing at his gut.

Cornwell, he thought, moving through the kitchen without stopping, barely conscious of the guards bowing and saluting as he passed. *I'm going to nail that bastard Cornwell, whatever it takes.*

And if you can't? a small voice asked.

He stopped, looking about him at the empty corridor, saying the words quietly to himself. 'Then I'll kill him anyway.'

Hannah sat at her desk, waiting. Her father had come in some while back, going straight to his study. She had heard the door slam shut, then, less than a minute later, had heard it open again, the sound of voices, quiet at first, then louder. The door had slammed... and then nothing.

She looked down at the sketches she had been making, noting how the faces seemed to stare back at her, somehow independent, as if she had not made them, merely freed them from the anonymous whiteness of the page. There was one particularly – the face of the *hua pen* she had seen that day down-level – which seemed to have transcended her simple attempt to capture its physical details. There was something in the depth of the eyes, in the slight twist of that knowing smile, which suggested something shadowed – a secret, hidden self she had not suspected while she had been listening to him.

She looked up, her eyes drawn to the flickering flatscreen on the wall across from her. It was her habit to leave it on when she worked, the sound turned down, her silent window on the world. Images... she trusted images more than words. They were less *intermediary* in their nature, less easily manipulated. Yet images could be faked or wrongly read. They were no different from words in that respect. Between what was shown and what hidden the truth so often slipped away. Even so, it seemed more important to her to *see* than to *say*, though she knew she must do both in future.

On the screen image followed image silently. Her world was in chaos – was slowly tearing itself apart – and yet for a large number of people there was no connection between that greater life and their own small private worlds of work and family; only the flickering screen, the official voice which told them what to think. Isolated. The two worlds were isolated. And if they met it was in a blaze of sudden, explosive violence – a violence that inflicted understanding only on its victims, leaving the watching billions unaffected.

And maybe that was her purpose. To be that connecting force. To link the greater world with the small. Maybe it was her role, in this world of walls and levels, of files and secrets, of masked men and ever-watching cameras, to be the one who saw things clearly – who opened files, and looked inside locked rooms – and *spoke* what she had seen.

Yes, but it could not be done openly, for too much was at risk. To speak out was to oppose, to threaten those shadows that controlled their lives. She had no illusions about it. They would kill her to prevent it.

A *hua pen*... she must learn to become a new kind of *hua pen*, telling not ancient tales, but the story of her age, her place.

She stood, her restlessness suddenly something physical, like an itch that needed to be scratched. Turning, she took two paces, then stopped abruptly, staring, her mouth open in surprise.

Her father stood in the shadow of the doorway, watching her.

She released her breath. 'How long have you been there?'

'Not long.' He came closer, looking about him as if he'd never been in her room before. 'I...' He sighed, then looked at her again, the slightest admonishment in his voice. '*Hannah*... what have you been doing now?'

'Nothing. I was only...'

You were only what? Spying on him? Stealing things from his rooms?

'Your mother says...'

'She's *not* my mother!'

'Hannah... *Please*, my love. I...'

She stared at him, astonished. His face was crumpled up in pain. There were tears at the corners of his eyes. Agonised, she went across and held him.

'Oh, papa! Papa!... Are you all right?'

'I...' She felt him shiver. 'I can't tell you.'

She helped him sit in her chair, then knelt, facing him, looking up into his face. 'It's okay. I *know*.'

He stared back at her, understanding slowly dawning on him.

'I've read it,' she said. 'The file. I know what's happening.'

'*And?*' His voice was a breath, less than a whisper.

She studied his face, seeing how frightened, how confused he was, and all of her fears for him welled up suddenly in her. '*Aiya*,' she said softly, taking his hands and caressing them. 'How did you ever get to this point? I mean... there's nothing *ruthless* in you, is there? So many secrets ... how did you ever get involved?'

He looked back at her, bewildered. 'I don't know. I... I did only what was asked of me.'

Yes, she thought, and step by step it led to this.

'What shall we do?' he asked, like a child asking his mother, his eyes beseeching her. 'What in the gods' names shall we *do*, Hannah?'

'You must see Li Yuan,' she said, a cold fear gripping her. 'You must request an audience... And then you must tell him what you know.'

Chen went home.

It was just after seven when he got back, tired and on edge, confused by all that had been happening to him. Outside his door he paused, wondering if it were really such a good idea. He needed to shower and freshen up, to grab a bite to eat and change his uniform, but he could have done all of that at Bremen. So why here? There was nothing for him here.

He was about to turn away when, through the paper-thin walls, he heard a child's shriek and then laughter – an infectious giggle that made his heart contract. No, not nothing. There were still his children.

He tapped out the combination then stepped inside. At once Ch'iang Hsin was on him, her face lit up at the sight of him.

'Daddy!'

He held her against his side, the fierceness of that sudden feeling almost overwhelming him. How could he have forgotten? What poisons were in his blood that he could have over-looked them even for a moment?

He crouched, facing her. 'How's Mummy?'

She shrugged, then smiled again. 'Tian Ching's been teaching me how to sew! I've been making you a surprise!'

He looked up and saw the girl in the doorway to the kitchen, watching him. Did she know? he wondered. Could she tell where he'd been, merely by looking at him?

She turned away, busying herself.

'Where's Wu?' he asked, 'and Jyan?'

'Wu's still in bed, and Jyan's with friends,' Ch'iang said unselfconsciously, her left hand tugging at his cheek, as if to check that he was real. 'Are you staying this time?'

'For an hour or two,' he answered, saddened that this once he couldn't stay a little longer. Then, taking her beneath the arms, he picked her up and carried her through to the kitchen. He cuddled her a moment then set her down on a chair. 'You stay here with Tian Ching a moment, while I go and see your mother, okay?'

She nodded, smiling up at him.

'Good.' He glanced at Tian Ching. 'Thank you,' he said quietly, turning away before she could answer.

Wang Ti's room was dark and silent, yet from the far side there was a wavering light and there was the faintest smell of burning. He looked. The bed was empty, the cover thrown back, and Wang Ti... Wang Ti was kneeling on the floor, her shape outlined against the wavering light.

Slowly, quietly, he went across. There, in front of her, was a shrine. A shrine just like the one he had seen down-level. The doors were pulled back, revealing a blood-red interior, against which stood a dozen tiny figures. Household gods, he realised. In front of them three tiny red candles burned in tiny pots, sending up faint wisps of incense.

He looked down at her. Wang Ti's eyes were open, staring straight ahead, into the bright interior of the shrine, and her lips...

Chen caught his breath. Her lips were moving.

He turned, realising that Tian Ching was in the doorway.

'How long has this been here?'

She looked down, abashed. 'Two days. I... I thought it might help.'

He looked back at Wang Ti, saw how she gazed into the flickering shadows and shivered. For almost three years there had been nothing, not even a flicker of life in her, but now...

He turned, nodding to the girl, his eyes thanking her, then, turning back, he kneeled beside his wife, his left hand reaching down to take her right where it lay upon her knee, palm down.

'I'm here, Wang Ti,' he said softly, conscious of the soft murmur of her voice beside him. 'I'm here.'

CHARACTER LISTING

MAJOR CHARACTERS

Asher, Emily   Trained as an economist, she was once a member of the *Ping Tiao* revolutionary party. After their demise, she fled to North America where, under the alias of Mary Jennings, she got a job with the giant ImmVac corporation, working for Old Man Lever and his son, Michael. Ultimately, however, what she wants is change, and the downfall of the corrupt social institutions that rule Chung Kuo.

Lehmann, Stefan   Albino son of the former Dispersionist leader, Pietr Lehmann, he was briefly a lieutenant to DeVore. A cold, unnaturally dispassionate man, he seems the very archetype of nihilism, his only aim to bring down the Seven and their great earth-encompassing City. His move 'down level' into the 'underground' world of *tong* and Triad marks a new stage of his campaign.

Lever, Charles   Head of the massive ImmVac pharmaceuticals corporation, 'Old Man Lever' is a passionate 'American' and one of the instigators of the Cutler Institute's Immortality project. A bull-necked, stubborn old man, he will let nothing get between him and what he wants. And what he wants is to live forever.

Lever, Michael   Son of Charles Lever, he was incarcerated by Wu Shih for his involvement with the 'Sons of Benjamin

Franklin', a semi-revolutionary group formed by the sons of wealthy North American businessmen. Cast from childhood in his father's mould, he has yet to break from his upbringing and find his own direction.

Li Yuan   T'ang of Europe and one of the Seven, as second son of Li Shai Tung, he inherited after the deaths of his brother and father. Considered old before his time, he nonetheless has a passionate side to his nature, as demonstrated in his brief marriage to his brother's wife, the beautiful Fei Yen. Having remarried, he is determined to find balance, both in his private life and in his role as T'ang.

Shepherd, Ben   Son of Hal Shepherd, and great-great-grandson of City Earth's architect, Ben was brought up in the Domain, an idyllic valley in the south west of England where, deciding not to follow in his father's footsteps and become adviser to Li Yuan, he pursues instead his calling as an artist, developing a new artform, the Shell, which will one day transform Chung Kuo's society.

Tolonen, Jelka   Daughter of Marshal Tolonen, Jelka has been brought up in a very masculine environment, lacking a mother's love and influence. Despite a genuine interest in martial arts and weaponry, she feels a strong need to discover and express the more feminine side of her nature; a need matched by a determination not to succumb to the gender demands of her world.

Tolonen, Knut   Former Marshal of the Council of Generals and one-time General to Li Yuan's father, Tolonen is a rock-like supporter of the Seven and their values, even in an age of increasing uncertainty. In his role as father, however, this inflexibility in his nature brings him into repeated conflict with his daughter, Jelka.

Tsu Ma   T'ang of West Asia and one of the Seven, the ruling Council of Chung Kuo, Tsu Ma has thrown off a dissolute past to become Li Yuan's staunchest supporter in Council. A strong, handsome man

in his late thirties, he has yet to marry, though his
secret affair with Li Yuan's former wife, Fei Yen,
revealed a side of him that has not been fully har-
nessed.

Wang Sau-leyan — T'ang of Africa. Since inheriting – after the suspicious deaths of his father and elder brothers
– Wang Sau-leyan has dedicated every moment to
bringing down Li Yuan and his allies in Council.
A sharp and cunning adversary with an abrasive,
calculating manner, he is the harbinger of Change
within the Council of Seven.

Ward, Kim — Born in the Clay, that dark wasteland beneath the
great City's foundations, Kim has a quick and
unusual bent of mind that has marked him as
potentially the greatest scientist on Chung Kuo.
His vision of a giant starspanning web, formulated
down in the darkness, drove him up into the light
of the Above. But, despite the patronage of Li Yuan
and the friendship of powerful men, life has proven
to be far from easy for Ward, either in business or
in love.

Wong Yi-sun — Big Boss of the United Bamboo Triad, 'Fat Wong' –
a tiny, birdlike man – has won the favour of Li Yuan.
Yet his ambitions reach beyond mere patronage. He
wants to unite the lower levels of City Europe under
his rule.

Wu Shih — Middle-aged T'ang of North America, he is one of
the few remaining members of the old generation.
A staunch traditionalist, nevertheless he has found
himself allied in Council with Li Yuan and Tsu Ma
against the odious Wang Sau-leyan. Yet with the
resurgence of American nationalism he finds
himself confronted by a problem none of his fellow
T'ang have to face; a problem he must find an urgent and lasting solution to.

THE SEVEN AND THE FAMILIES

Chi Hsing — T'ang of the Australias.
Fu Ti Chang — third wife of Li Yuan.

Hou Tung-po	T'ang of South America.
Lai Shi	second wife of Li Yuan.
Li Kuei Jen	son of Li Yuan and heir to City Europe.
Li Yuan	T'ang of Europe.
Mien Shan	first wife of Li Yuan.
Tsu Ma	T'ang of West Asia.
Wang Sau-leyan	T'ang of Africa.
Wei Chan Yin	first son of Wei Feng and heir to City East Asia.
Wei Feng	T'ang of East Asia.
Wei Hsi Wang	second son of Wei Feng and Colonel in Security.
Wei Tseng-li	third son of Wei Feng.
Wu Shih	T'ang of North America.
Yin Fei Yen	'Flying Swallow'; Minor Family princess and divorced wife of Li Yuan.
Yin Han Ch'in	son of Yin Fei Yen.
Yin Tsu	head of the Yin Family (one of the 'Twenty Nine' Minor Families) and father of Fei Yen.
Yin Wu Tsai	Minor Family princess and cousin of Fei Yen.

FRIENDS AND RETAINERS OF THE SEVEN

Bachman, Lothar	lieutenant in Security.
Bright Moon	maid to Li Yuan.
Brock	security guard in the Domain.
Chan Teng	Master of the Inner Chambers at Tongjiang.
Chang Shih-sen	personal secretary to Li Yuan.
Ch'in Tao Fan	Chancellor of East Asia.
Chu Shi-ch'e	*Pi-shu chien*, or Inspector of the Imperial Library at Tongjiang.
Coates	security guard in the Domain.
Cook	duty guard in the Domain.
Fen Cho-hsien	Chancellor of North America.
Fragrant Lotus	maid to Li Yuan.
Franke, Otto	*Wei*, or Captain of Security for Zwickau *Hsien*.
Gerhardt, Paul	Major; Head of Tracking, Northern Hemisphere.
Gustavsson, Per	Captain of Chi Hsing's personal guard.
Gustavsson, Ute	wife of Captain Gustavvson.
Hauser, Eva	wife of Major Sven Hauser.
Hauser, Gustav	private secretary/equerry to Marshal Tolonen; son of Major Sven Hauser.

Hauser, Sven	Major; ex-Colonial Governor; father of Gustav Hauser.
Henssa, Eero	Captain of the Guard aboard the floating palace Yangjing.
Ho Chang	valet to Wu Shih.
Hung, Yan	'Wiring' surgeon to Li Yuan.
Hung Mien-lo	Chancellor of Africa.
Karr, Gregor	Major in Security.
K'ung Feng	Third Official in the *Ta Ssu Nung*, the Superintendency of Agriculture, for City Europe.
Lofgren, Bertil	lieutenant and aide to Marshal Tolonen.
Mo Yu	Security lieutenant in the Domain.
Nan Ho	Chancellor of Europe.
Read, Helmut	Governor of the Saturn system.
Rheinhardt, Helmut	General of Security for Li Yuan.
Shepherd, Ben	son of the late Hal Shepherd; 'Shell' artist.
Shepherd, Beth	widow of Hal Shepherd; mother of Ben and Meg Shepherd.
Shepherd, Meg	sister of Ben Shepherd.
Tolonen, Jelka	daughter of Marshal Tolonen.
Tolonen, Knut	ex-Marshal of Security; Head of the GenSyn Hearings committee.
Tu Mai	security guard in the Domain.
Virtanen, Per	Major in Li Yuan's Security forces.
Zdenek	bodyguard to Jelka Tolonen.

THE TRIADS

Chao	runner for K'ang A-yin.
Feng Shang-pao	'General Feng'; Big Boss of the 14K.
Feng Wo	lieutenant to K'ang A-yin.
Ho Chin	'Three-Finger Ho'; Big Boss of the Yellow Banners.
Hua Shang	lieutenant to Wong Yi-sun.
Huang Jen	lieutenant to Po Lao.
Hui Tsin	Red Pole (426, or Executioner) to the United Bamboo.
K'ang A-yin	gang boss of the Tu Sun *tong*.
K'ang Yeh-su	nephew of K'ang A-yin.
Kant	runner for K'ang A-yin.
Li Chin	'Li The Lidless'; Big Boss of the Wo Shih Wo.

Li Pai Shung	nephew of Li Chin; heir to the Wo Shih Wo.
Ling Wo	Chief Adviser to K'ang A-yin.
Liu Tong	lieutenant to Li Chin.
Lo Han	*tong* boss.
Lu Ming-shao	'Whiskers Lu'; Big Boss of the Kuei Chuan.
Man Hsi	*tong* boss.
Meng Te	lieutenant to Lu Ming-shao.
Ni Yueh	*tong* boss.
Peck	lieutenant to K'ang A-yin (a *ying tzu*, or 'shadow').
Po Lao	Red Pole (426, or Executioner) to the Kuei Chuan.
Soucek, Jiri	lieutenant to K'ang A-yin.
Visak	lieutenant to Lu Ming-shao.
Wong Yi-sun	'Fat Wong'; Big Boss of the United Bamboo.
Yan Yan	*tong* boss.
Yao Lu	lieutenant to Stefan Lehmann.
Yue Chun	Red Pole (426, or Executioner) to the Wo Shih Wo.
Yun Yueh-hui	'Dead Man Yun'; Big Boss of the Red Gang.

YU

Anne	Yu assassin.
Donna	Yu assassin.
Joan	Yu assassin.
Kriz	senior Yu operative.
Mach, Jan	maintenance official for the Ministry of Waste Recycling, former *Ping Tiao* member and founder of the Yu.
Vesa	Yu assassin.

OTHER CHARACTERS

Ainsworth, James	lawyer for Charles Lever.
Barratt, Edel	SimFic employee at Sohm Abyss.
Becker, Hans	side-kick of Stefan Lehmann.
Bonner, Alex	Chief Negotiator for the P'u Lan Finance Corporation.
Bonnot, Alex	Scientific Supervisor for SimFic at Sohm Abyss.
Campbell, William	Regional Controller of SimFic's North Atlantic Cities.
Carver, Rex	Reformer candidate for Miami *Hsien* and friend of Charles Lever.

Chan Long	security guard, working for Lever and Kustow.
Chang	guard on the Chung estate.
Chang Li	First Surgeon in the Boston Medical Centre.
Chiang Su-li	Master of the House of the Ninth Dragon tea-house.
Chung, Gloria	heiress; daughter of the late Representative Chung Yen.
Curval, Andrew	leading geneticist; employee of the ImmVac Corporation.
Dann, Abraham	steward to Charles Lever.
Deio	Clayborn friend of Kim Ward from 'Rehabilitation'.
DeValerian, Rachel	alias of Emily Ascher.
DeVore, Howard	Major in Security, and Dispersionist.
Dunn, Richard	business rival of Old Man Lever.
Feng Lu-ma	lensman.
Feng Wo-shen	protein designer and scientific assistant for SimFic at Sohm Abyss.
Fisher, Carl	American; friend of Michael Lever.
Fisher, James	financier and friend of Charles Lever.
Gratton, Edward	friend of Charles Lever and Reformer candidate for Boston Hsien.
Haller, Wolf	side-kick of Stefan Lehmann.
Harrison, James	employee of Charles Lever.
Hart, Alex	Representative at Weimar.
Hartmann, William	friend of Charles Lever and Reformer candidate.
Hay, Joel	leader of the Evolutionist Party of North America.
Henty, Thomas	technician.
Heydemeier, Ernst	artist; leading exponent of Futur-Kunst, 'Science Art'.
Hilbert, Eduard	head of cryobiology for SimFic at Sohm Abyss.
Ho Chao-tuan	Representative for Shenyang Hsien
Ho Yang	reporter for the Wen Ming media channel.
Hong Chi	assistant to Kim Ward.
Horton, Feng	American; a 'Son'; also known as 'Meltdown'.
Hsiang Tian	merchant; store-owner.
Jennings, Mary	alias of Emily Ascher.
Johnstone, Edward	friend of Charles Lever; father of Louisa Johnstone.
Johnstone, Louisa	long-standing fiancée of Michael Lever.
K'ang Hung-chang	professor at the Kunming Institute of Comparative Genetics.
Kennedy, Jean	wife of Joseph Kennedy.
Kennedy, Joseph	American lawyer, and founder of the New

	Republican Party.
Kennedy, Robert	eldest son of Joseph Kennedy.
Kennedy, William	youngest son of Joseph Kennedy.
Koslevic, Anna	schoolgirl friend of Jelka Tolonen.
Kustow, Bryn	American; friend of Michael Lever.
Lanouette, Henri	banker.
Lehmann, Stefan	albino son of Under-Secretary Lehmann.
Lever, Charles	'Old Man Lever', head of the ImmVac pharmaceuticals company of North America; father of Michael Lever.
Lever, Michael	son of Charles Lever; Head of the MemSys Corporation, a subsidiary of ImmVac.
Li Min	'Brave Carp', an alias of Stefan Lehmann.
Luke	Clayborn friend of Kim Ward from 'Rehabilitation'.
Mai Li-wen	lensman.
Marley, George	business associate of Charles Lever.
May Feng	*Hung Mao* Head of EduCol.
Milne, Michael	private investigator.
Mitchell, Bud	American; a 'Son'; associate of Michael Lever.
Munroe, Wendell	Representative at Weimar.
Nong Yan	book-keeper to Kim Ward.
Pai Mei	stallholder.
Parker, Jack	American; friend of Michael Lever.
Ping Hsiang	Representative for the Above in discussions for the reopening of Weimar.
Reiss, Horst	Chief Executive of the SimFic Corporation.
Richards	guard at Kim Ward's *Chih Chu* company.
Robins	employee of Charles Lever.
Ross, James	private investigator.
Schram, Dieter	Administrator for SimFic at Sohm Abyss.
Snow	alias of Stefan Lehmann.
Spence, Graham	employee of Charles Lever.
Spence, Leena	'Immortal' and one-time lover of Charles Lever.
Stevens, Carl	American; friend of Michael Lever.
Stewart, Greg	American; NREP candidate for Denver *Hsien*.
Symons	SimFic employee at Sohm Abyss.
T'ai Cho	friend and former guardian of Kim Ward.
Tewl	'Darkness'; chief of the raft-people.
Thorsson, Wulf	settler from Iapetus Colony in the Saturn system.
Tong Ye	young Han sailor (a 'morph') used by Ben Shep-

	herd.
Tuan Wen-ch'ang	SimFic employee at Sohm Abyss.
Underwood, Harry	Representative at Weimar.
Ward, Rebecca	Commercial Adviser to SimFic at Sohm Abyss; Clay-born friend of Kim Ward from 'Rehabilitation'.
Weller, John	Head of Internal Distribution for ImmVac.
Will	Clayborn friend of Kim Ward from 'Rehabilitation'.
Yellow Tan	lensman.
Yi Pang-chou	schoolgirl friend of Jelka Tolonen.
Yueh Pa	official in the United Bamboo heartland.

THE DEAD

Barrow, Chao	Secretary of the House at Weimar.
Bercott, Andrei	Representative at Weimar.
Berdichev, Soren	Head of SimFic and, later, leader of the Dispersionist faction.
Ch'in Shih Huang Ti	the first emperor of China (ruled 221–210 BC).
Chung Hsin	'Loyalty'; bondservant to Li Shai Tung.
Cutler, Richard	leader of the 'American' movement.
Ebert, Klaus	head of the GenSyn Corporation.
Feng Chung	Big Boss of the Kuei Chan (Black Dog) Triad.
Fest, Edgar	Captain in Security.
Gesell, Bent	leader of the Ping Tiao terrorist organisation.
Griffin, James B.	last president of the American Empire.
Han Huan Ti	Han emperor, (ruled AD 168–189), also known as Liu Hung.
Hou Ti	T'ang of South America; father of Hou Tung Po.
Hsiang K'ai Fan	Minor Family Prince.
Hwa	master 'blood', or hand-to-hand fighter, below the Net.
Kao Jyan	assassin; friend of Kao Chen.
K'ung Fu Tzu	Confucius (551–479 BC).
Lehmann, Pietr	Under Secretary of the House of Representatives and first leader of the Dispersionist faction; father of Stefan Lehmann.
Lever, Margaret	wife of Charles Lever and mother of Michael Lever.
Li Ch'ing	T'ang of Europe; grandfather of Li Yuan.
Li Han Ch'in	first son of Li Shai T'ung and once-heir to City Europe; brother of Li Yuan.

Li Hang Ch'i — T'ang of Europe; great-great-grandfather of Li Yuan.

Li Kou-lung — T'ang of Europe; great-grandfather of Li Yuan.

Li Shai Tung — T'ang of Europe; father of Li Yuan.

Lin Yua — first wife of Li Shai Tung.

Mao Tse Tung — first Ko Ming emperor (ruled AD 1948–1976).

Ming Huang — sixth T'ang emperor (ruled AD 713–755).

Mu Chua — Madame of the House of the Ninth Ecstasy.

Mu Li — 'Iron Mu', Boss of the Big Circle triad.

Shang — 'Old Shang'; Master to Kao Chen when he was a child.

Shepherd, Amos — Great-great-great-great-grandfather (and genetic 'father') of Ben Shepherd.

Shepherd, Augustus — 'Brother' of Ben Shepherd, b. AD 2106, d. 2122.

Shepherd, Hal — Father (and genetic 'brother') of Ben Shepherd.

Shepherd, Robert — Great-grandfather (and genetic 'brother') of Ben Shepherd, and father of Augustus Shepherd.

Tsao Ch'un — tyrannical founder of Chung Kuo (ruled AD 2051–2087).

Wang Hsien — T'ang of Africa; father of Wang Sau-leyan.

Wang Ta-hung — third son of Wang Hsien; elder brother of Wang Sau-leyan.

Wen Ti — 'First Ancestor' of City Earth/Chung Kuo (ruled 180–157 BC), also known as Liu Heng.

Wyatt, Edmund — company head; father of Kim Ward.

Ywe Hao — Yu terrorist.

Ywe Kai-chang — father of Ywe Hao.

GLOSSARY OF MANDARIN TERMS

Most of the Mandarin terms used in the text are explained in context. However, as a few are used more naturally, I've considered it best to provide a brief explanation.

ai ya!	common exclamation of surprise or dismay.
ch'a	tea. It might be noted that *ch'a shu*, the Chinese art of tea, is an ancient forebear of the Japanese tea ceremony *chanoyu*.
chang shan	literally 'long dress', which fastens to the right. Worn by both sexes. The women's version is a fitted, calf-length dress, similar to the *chi pao*. A South China fashion, also known as a *cheung sam*.
chan shih	a fighter.
Ch'eng Ou Chou	City Europe.
ch'i	a Chinese foot; approximately 14.4 inches.
chih chu	spider.
chieh hsia	term meaning 'Your Majesty', derived from the expression 'Below the Steps'. It was the formal way of addressing the Emperor, through his Ministers, who stood 'below the steps'.
chi pao	literally 'banner gown'; a one-piece gown of Manchu origin, usually sleeveless, worn by women.
Chou	'state'; here the name for a card game based on the politics of the state of Chung Kuo.
chung	a lidded serving bowl for *ch'a*.
ch'un tzu	an ancient Chinese term from the Warring States period, describing a certain class of nobleman, controlled by a code of chivalry and morality known as the *li*, or rites.

Here the term is roughly, and sometimes ironically, translated as 'gentlemen'. The ch'un tzu is as much an ideal state of behaviour – as specified by Confucius in the *Analects* – as an actual class in Chung Kuo, though a degree of financial independence and a high standard of education are assumed a prerequisite.

erhu   two-stringed bow with snakeskin-covered sound box.

fen   unit of money (a cent); one hundred *fen* make up a *yuan*.

han   term used by the Chinese to describe their own race, the 'black-haired people', dating back to the Han Dynasty (210 BC – AD 220). It is estimated that some ninety-four per cent of modern China's population is racially Han.

hei   literally 'black'; the Chinese pictogram for this represents a man wearing warpaint and tattoos. Here it refers to the genetically manufactured (GenSyn) half-men used as riot police to quell uprisings in the lower levels.

hsiao jen 'little man/men'. In the *Analects*, Book XIV, Confucius writes: 'The gentleman gets through to what is up above; the small man gets through to what is down below.' This distinction between 'gentlemen' (*ch'un tzu*) and 'little men' (*hsiao jen*), false even in Confucius's time, is no less a matter of social perspective in Chung Kuo.

hsien   historically an administrative district of variable size. Here the term is used to denote a very specific administrative area; one of ten stacks – each stack composed of thirty decks. Each deck is a hexagonal living unit of ten levels, two li, or approximately one kilometre in diameter. A stack can be imagined as one honeycomb in the great hive of the City.

Hsien L'ing 'Chief Magistrate'. In Chung Kuo, these officials are the T'ang's representatives and law enforcers for the individual hsien, or administrative districts. In times of peace, each hsien also elects a representative to the House at Weimar.

Hung Mao literally 'redheads', the name the Chinese gave to the Dutch (and later English) seafarers who attempted to trade with China in the seventeenth century. Because of the piratical nature of their endeavours (which often meant plundering Chinese shipping and ports) the name has connotations of piracy.

Hung Mun — the Secret Societies or, more specifically, the Triads.

hun tun — 'the Chou believed that Heaven and Earth were once inextricably mixed together in a state of undifferentiated chaos, like a chicken's egg. Hun Tun they called that state' (from 'Chen Yen', Chapter 6 of *The White Mountain*). It is also the name of a meal of tiny sac-like dumplings.

jou tung wu — literally 'meat animal'.

kan pei! — 'good health' or 'cheers'; a drinking toast.

Ko Ming — 'revolutionary'. The T'ien Ming is the Mandate of Heaven, supposedly handed down from Shang Ti, the Supreme Ancestor, to his earthly counterpart, the Emperor (*Huang Ti*). This Mandate could be enjoyed only so long as the Emperor was worthy of it, and rebellion against a tyrant – who broke the Mandate through his lack of justice, benevolence and sincerity – was deemed not criminal but a rightful expression of Heaven's anger.

k'ou t'ou — the fifth stage of respect, according to the 'Book of Ceremonies', involves kneeling and striking the head against the floor. This ritual has become more commonly known in the West as *kowtow*.

Kuan hua — Mandarin, the language spoken in mainland China. Also known as *Kuo-yu* and *Pai hua*.

Kuan Yin — the goddess of mercy. Originally the Buddhist male bodhisattva, Avalokitsevara (translated into Han as 'He who listens to the sounds of the world', or 'Kuan Yin'), the Han mistook the well-developed breasts of the saint's for a woman's and, since the ninth century, have worshipped Kuan Yin as such. Effigies of Kuan Yin will show her usually as the Eastern Madonna, cradling a child in her arms. She is also sometimes seen as the wife of Kuan Kung, the Chinese God of War.

li — a Chinese 'mile', approximating to half a kilometre or one-third of a mile. Until 1949, when metric measures were adopted in China, the li could vary from place to place.

min — literally 'the people'; used (as here, by the Minor Families) in a pejorative sense (that is, as an equivalent to 'plebeian').

Ming	the Dynasty that ruled China from 1368 to 1644. Literally, the name means 'Bright' or 'Clear', or 'Brilliant'. It carries connotations of cleansing.
niao	literally 'bird'; but here, as often, it is used euphemistically, as a term for the penis, often as an expletive.
nu er	daughter.
nu shi	an unmarried woman; a term equating to 'Miss'.
pai nan jen	literally 'white man'.
pau	a simple long garment worn by men.
Ping Tiao	levelling. To bring down or make flat.
p'i p'a	a four-stringed lute used in traditional Chinese music.
san kuei chiu k'ou	the eighth and final stage of respect, according to the 'Book of Ceremonies', involves kneeling three times, each time striking the forehead three times against the floor. This most elaborate form of ritual was reserved for Heaven and its son, the Emperor.
shan shui	the literal meaning is 'mountains and water', but the term is normally associated with a style of landscape painting which depicts rugged mountain scenery with river valleys in the foreground. It is a highly popular form, first established in the T'ang Dynasty, back in the seventh to ninth centuries AD.
shao lin	specially-trained assassins; named after the monks of the shao lin monastery.
Shih	'Master'. Here used as a term of respect somewhat equivalent to our use of 'Mister'. The term was originally used for the lowest level of civil servants, to distinguish them socially from the run-of-the-mill 'Misters' (hsian sheng) below them and the gentlemen (ch'un tzu) above.
Siang Chi	Chinese chess.
tai	'pockets'; here used to denote Representatives bought by (and thus 'in the pocket of') various power groupings (originally the Seven).
t'ai chi	the Original, or One, from which the duality of all things (yin and yang) developed, according to Chinese cosmology. We generally associate the t'ai chi with the Taoist symbol, that swirling circle of dark and light, supposedly representing an egg (perhaps the Hun Tun), the yolk and the white differentiated.
T'ai Shan	the great sacred mountain of China, where emperors

have traditionally made sacrifices to Heaven. T'ai Shan, in Shantung province, is the highest peak in China. 'As safe as T'ai Shan' is a popular saying, denoting the ultimate in solidity and certainty.

Ta Ts'in   the Chinese name for the Roman Empire. They also knew Rome as Li Chien and as 'the Land West of the Sea'. The Romans themselves they termed the 'Big Ts'in' – the Ts'in being the name the Chinese gave themselves during the Ts'in Dynasty (AD 265–316).

T'ing Wei   the Superintendency of Trials. See Book 3 (The White Mountain), Part 2, for an instance of how this department of government functions.

ti tsu   a bamboo flute, used both as a solo instrument and as part of an ensemble.

tong   a gang. In China and Europe, these are usually smaller and thus subsidiary to the Triads, but in North America the term has generally taken the place of 'Triad'.

ts'un   a Chinese 'inch' of approximately 1.44 Western inches; 10 ts'un form one ch'i.

wan wu   literally 'the ten thousand things'; used generally to include everything in creation, or, as the Chinese say, 'all things in Heaven and Earth'.

wei chi   'the surrounding game', known more commonly in the West by its Japanese name of 'Go'. It is said that the game was invented by the legendary Chinese Emperor Yao in the year 2350 BC to train the mind of his son, Tan Chu, and teach him to think like an Emperor.

wen ming   a term used to denote civilisation, or written culture.

wuwei   non-action; an old Taoist concept. It means keeping harmony with the flow of things – doing nothing to break the flow. As Lao Tzu said, 'The Tao does nothing, and yet nothing is left undone'.

yamen   the official building in a Chinese community.

yang   the 'male principle' of Chinese cosmology, which, with its complementary opposite, the female yin, forms the t'ai chi, derived from the Primeval One. From the union of yin and yang arise the 'five elements' (water, fire, earth, metal, wood) from which the 'ten thousand things' (the wan wu) are generated. Yang signifies Heaven and the South, the Sun and Warmth, Light, Vigour, Maleness, Penetration, odd numbers and the Dragon. Mountains are yang.

yin
the 'female principle' of Chinese cosmology (see *yang*). Yin signifies Earth and the North, the Moon and Cold, Darkness, Quiescence, Femaleness, Absorption, even numbers and the Tiger. The *yin* lies in the shadow of the mountain.

yu
literally 'fish' but because of its phonetic equivalence to the word for 'abundance', the fish symbolises wealth. Yet there is also a saying that when the fish swim upriver it is a portent of social unrest and rebellion.

yuan
the basic currency of Chung Kuo (and modern-day China). Colloquially (though not here) it can also be termed *kwai* – 'piece' or 'lump'. One hundred *fen* (or cents) make up one *yuan*.

yueh ch'in
a Chinese dulcimer; one of the principal instruments of the Chinese orchestra.

Ywe Lung
literally, the 'Moon Dragon', the wheel of seven dragons that is the symbol of the ruling Seven throughout *Chung Kuo*: 'At its centre the snouts of the regal beasts met, forming a roselike hub, huge rubies burning fiercely in each eye. Their lithe, powerful bodies curved outwards like the spokes of a giant wheel while at the edge their tails were intertwined to form the rim' (from 'The Moon Dragon', Chapter 4 of *The Middle Kingdom*).

AUTHOR'S NOTE

The transcription of standard Mandarin into European alphabetical form was first achieved in the seventeenth century by the Italian Matteo Ricci, who founded and ran the first Jesuit Mission in China from 1583 until his death in 1610. Since then several dozen attempts have been made to reduce the original Chinese sounds, represented by some tens of thousands of separate pictograms, into readily understandable phonetics for Western use. For a long time, however, three systems dominated – those used by the three major Western powers vying for influence in the corrupt and crumbling Chinese Empire of the nineteenth century: Great Britain, France, and Germany. These systems were the Wade-Giles (Great Britain and America – sometimes known as the Wade system), the Ecole Française de L'Extrême Orient (France), and the Lessing (Germany).

Since 1958, however, the Chinese themselves have sought to create one single phonetic form, based on the German system, which they termed the *hanyu pinyin fang'an* (Scheme for a Chinese Phonetic Alphabet), known more commonly as *pinyin*, and in all foreign language books published in China since January 1st, 1979 *pinyin* has been used, as well as being taught now in schools along with the standard Chinese characters. For this work, however, I have chosen to use the older and to my mind far more elegant transcription system, the Wade-Giles (in modified form). For those now used to the harder forms of *pinyin*, the following (courtesy of Edgar Snow's *The Other Side Of The River*, Gollancz, 1961) may serve as a rough guide to pronunciation:

Chi is pronounced as 'Gee', but *Ch'i* sounds like 'Chee'. *Ch'in* is exactly our 'chin'.

Chu is roughly like 'Jew', as in *Chu Teh* (Jew Duhr), but *Ch'u* equals 'chew'.

Tsung is 'dzung'; *ts'ung* with the 'ts' as in 'Patsy'.

Tai is our word sound 'die'; *T'ai* – 'tie'.

Pai is 'buy' and *P'ai* is 'pie'.

Kung is like 'Gung' (a Din); *K'ung* with the 'k' as in 'kind'.

J is the equivalent of r but slur it, as rrrun.

H before an s, as in *hsi*, is the equivalent of an aspirate but is often dropped, as in Sian for Hsian.

Vowels in Chinese are generally short or medium, not long and flat. Thus *Tang* sounds like 'dong', never like our 'tang'. *T'ang* is 'tong'.

    a as in *father*
    e – run
    eh – hen
    I – *see*
    ih – her
    o – look
    ou – go
    u – soon

The effect of using the Wade-Giles system is, I hope, to render the softer, more poetic side of the original Mandarin, ill-served, I feel, by modern *pinyin*.

This usage, incidentally, accords with many of the major reference sources available in the West: the (planned) sixteen volumes of Denis Twichett and Michael Loewe's *The Cambridge History of China*; Joseph Needham's mammoth multi-volumed *Science and Civilisation in China*; John Fairbank and Edwin Reischauer's *China, Tradition and Transformation*; Charles Hucker's *China's Imperial Past*; Jacques Gernet's *A History of Chinese Civilisation*; C. P. Fitzgerald's *China: A Short Cultural History*; Laurence Sickman and Alexander Soper's *The Art and Architecture of China*; William Hinton's classic social studies, *Fanshen* and *Shenfan*; and Derk Bodde's *Essays on Chinese Civilisation*.

The Luoshu diagram, mentioned in the Prologue, is a three-by-three number square

```
4   9   2
3   5   7
8   1   6
```

and was supposedly seen on the shell of a turtle emerging from the Luo River some two thousand years before Christ. As can be seen, all the numbers in any one row or column or diagonal add up to fifteen. During the T'ang dynasty its 'magical' properties were exported to the Muslim world where they were used – as here – as a charm for easing childbirth.

Wu Shih's mention (in Chapter 1) of 'the three brothers of the Peach Garden' is a reference to Lo Kuan Chung's classic Chinese novel, *San Kuo Yan Yi*, or *The Romance of the Three Kingdoms*, in which the three great heroes, Liu Pei, Chang Fei and Kuan Yu swear brotherhood.

The translation of Ch'u Yuan's *T'ien Wen*, or 'Heavenly Questions', is by David Hawkes from *The Songs Of The South: An Anthology Of Ancient Chinese Poems*, published by Penguin Books, London, 1985.

The quotation from Jukka Tolonen is from a song on the album, *Lambertland*, by the Finnish band, Tasavallan Presidentti, and the lyrics from the song 'Last Quarters' are reprinted with the kind permission of Sonet Records.

The passage quoted from Book One [V] of Lao Tzu's *Tao Te Ching* is from the D. C. Lau translation, published by Penguin Books, London, 1963, and used with their kind permission.

The quotations from Rainer Maria Rilke's *Duino Elegies* are from the Hogarth Press fourth edition of 1968, translated by J. B. Leishman and Stephen Spender. Thanks to the estate of Rilke, St John's College, Oxford, for permission.

The translation of Tu Fu's 'After Rain' is by Sam Hamill from his wonderful anthology of Tu Fu's verse, *Facing The Snow, Visions Of Tu Fu*, published by White Pine Press, Fredonia, New York, and is reprinted here with their kind permission.

Once again, I find I have quoted extensively from Samuel B. Griffith's translation of Sun Tzu's *The Art Of War*, published by Oxford University

Press, 1963. I reprint the four passages used herein with their kind permission and only hope I have directed a few readers to this most excellent work.

Finally, for those of you unfamiliar with the pidgin Cornish used in Part Two of the book, here are translations of the relevant passages. First, the utterances of the Clay-men:

Avodya! Get back!
A-wartha! Up above!
An chy. Kerdhes! Tenna dhe an chy! The house. Go! Take the house!
Ena ... Ena ha ena! There ... There and there!

And Ben's whisperings:
Of ancow. I am death.
Gwelaf why gans ow onen lagas. I see you with my one eye.
Ow golow lagas dewana why! My bright eye pierces you!
Ow enawy a-vyn podretha agas eskern ... My light will rot your bones.
    Furthermore, when the hologram of the Ox-faced angel says 'Dyesk-ynna!' ('Come!') there is a faint echo of the Revelation to John (6:1).